BOOKS BY NEAL ROBERTS

IN THE DEN OF THE ENGLISH LION

A Second Daniel
The Impress of Heaven

THE
IMPRESS
OF HEAVEN

In the Den of the English Lion
Book 2

NEAL
ROBERTS

Cover Design by Greg Simanson
Edited by Laurel Busch

This is a work of fiction. Names, characters, places, brands, media, and incidents are either the product of the author's imagination or are used fictitiously. Any resemblance to similarly named places or to persons living or deceased is unintentional.

ISBN: 978-0-9978803-3-5

A FREE DOWNLOAD

Sign up for Neal's newsletter and journey for free to England's shores in 1558 with young Menachem in the exclusive prequel scene, *Escape.*

authornealroberts.com

To all the women in my life who have treated me
better than I deserve, which (as Noah might say)
may well be all of you.

PERSONS OF THE STORY

ELIZABETH, BY THE GRACE OF GOD, QUEEN OF ENGLAND, FRANCE AND IRELAND

NOAH AMES, barrister
MARIE AMES, his wife by remarriage
JESSICA, LADY BURLINGTON, his daughter by his first marriage

JONATHAN HAWKING, barrister
ARTHUR ARDEN, barrister, his friend
ANDRES SALAZAR, barrister, his friend
DAVID "CHEERFUL" KILLIGREW, his friend, nephew to Sir Henry Neville

FRANCIS BACON, Queen's Counsel
GARDNER, Senior Yeoman of the Guard
FRANCIS, Yeoman of the Guard

THE CECIL FACTION

ROBERT CECIL, knight, Secretary of State

THE LORD ADMIRAL
THOMAS, LORD HOWARD, Rear Admiral, his cousin

CHARLES, LORD MOUNTJOY, head of Her Majesty's Forces in Ireland
WALTER RALEIGH, knight, Captain of the Yeoman Warders

THE ESSEX FACTION

ROBERT DEVEREUX, EARL OF ESSEX
GELLY MEYRICK, his principal attendant
NICHOLAS SKERES, his servant
ROBERT POLEY, his servant

CHAPTER 1

IN THE FOREMOST PEW of a hushed room packed with spectators, Serjeant Noah Ames awaits the opening of the Earl of Essex's trial on charges of high treason against the Crown. On the dais await many of the most famous officials in England. Displayed behind them is every item of colorful heraldry that can be mustered for an occasion outside a genuine throne room. An ornately woven arras bearing Queen Elizabeth's coat of arms and her motto *Semper Eadem* drapes from the thirty-foot ceiling to the back of the unoccupied throne.

From behind Noah come the overloud voices of an old man and his wife, evidently discussing him. Although spectators upon this occasion are supposedly limited to the nobility and members of the learned professions, the pair's uncultured manner of speech shows them to be no more than common merchants. Without turning around, Noah cannot be sure whether they speak so loudly because they wish to be overheard, or simply because, being hard of hearing themselves, they believe they're speaking in moderate tones.

"That's the Queen's Jew lawyer, right in front of us," croaks the old woman.

"Who, *this* one?"

"Don't point, Elias. No. *This* one, right here."

"What would *he* be doing here?" inquires the old man.

"Probably come to rejoice, if the earl's carted off to Tyburn."

"What's his grudge against the earl?"

"Why don't you *ask* him?" she says.

"*Pshaw!* Don't be ridiculous."

After a moment's silence, she intimates in a stage whisper, "They say he blames the earl for executin' that Jew doctor who tried to poison the

Queen before he could plead for clemency."

The old man replies, "Thick as thieves, eh? Should never have let that snake close enough to the Queen to sting her in the first place."

Noah looks to his right where his co-counsel, the young Arthur Arden, returns his gaze and smolders at the presumptuousness of the two know-nothings behind them. Noah pats Arthur's hand comfortingly, careful to seem unperturbed.

"Anyways," says the old woman, "he's got no love for our Essex, and *that's* the truth!"

Our Essex! This is becoming almost too much for Noah himself to bear. As he considers a riposte, however, the Lord Steward pounds his staff on the floor three times, mutely ordering the assembled to rise, which they do, with a thump and rustle.

A dark-stained oaken door behind the dais swings open, and in walks the diminutive Sir Robert Cecil, Secretary of State, who glances about quickly, and strides to his place behind the elevated podium at the center of the dais. As attested by his elaborate costume, Cecil has served the Crown as its leading minister since the death of his father Lord Burghley less than two years ago. He glances down at the small satin pillow carefully positioned before the dais where, by royal command, the accused will kneel until the conclusion of the trial. "Yeoman Warder! Kindly escort the earl into the chamber," he solemnly pronounces.

Grizzled old Yeoman Gardner, long familiar to Noah, leaves his post alongside the dais, and tramps heavily to the rear portal through which the spectators entered. He shouts a command, and the door swings open.

The downcast figure of Robert Devereux, Earl of Essex, mournfully enters the chamber escorted by two burly guards. The colorful uniforms of the Yeoman Warders contrast sharply with the dark penitential garment worn by the accused earl, a monk's robe of deepest black, devoid of any color or flourish to signify his station. His face partly concealed by a cowl, his only adornment is a large golden pendant in the shape of a cross that hangs from a heavy gold chain around his neck. The guards march him respectfully to his assigned place, as marked by the pillow. His cowled face too low to be seen, he faces the dais as his escort stamps noisily to the rear, departing through the door by which it entered. He glances along the dais, pausing a moment as his eye finds Sir Francis Bacon at one end. He kneels.

Satisfied with the earl's submissive posture, Cecil intones ceremoniously: "Who shall prosecute for the Crown?"

A voice responds promptly. "Queen's Counsel Sir Francis Bacon, for the prosecution."

Cecil nods his approval. "And who shall assist the earl in his defense?"

At first, there's no response, the only sound that of a rising wind outdoors that rattles the clerestory windows. After a few moments' silence, Cecil arches his eyebrows expectantly.

Noah, his stomach knotted, succumbs at last to the expectations of court and counsel. Girding himself, he rises to answer the call.

"Serjeant Noah Ames, for the prisoner," he says, his clear voice ringing through the chamber.

An unearthly gasp arises from the spectators behind him, followed by howls of protest against the "Jew lawyer." Evidently, the spectators have been given no foreknowledge that the barrister who'll be defending the earl is the very man most commonly believed to *despise* him. Amidst the tumult, Noah silently recites a Hebrew prayer asking God's forgiveness, and recalls the events that led him to this bizarre juncture.

<hr />

Eight Months Earlier
Westminster, England

OUTSIDE THE COURT of Queen's Bench, Noah dismounts, pats his horse's muzzle, and hands off the reins to the courthouse stableman. "This mount belongs to Sir Robert Cecil. I borrowed him last night, and promised to return him this morning."

"I *thought* he looked familiar," says the stableman. "Who're ye here to see this lovely morning, Serjeant Ames?"

Noah pats the note in his pocket. "I've been summoned by Sir Robert, John."

The stableman nods. "I'll have the boy take you inside to 'im." As ever, Noah hands him a good gratuity.

An eager-looking young page appears and leads the way through the rear entrance down a labyrinth of hallways, chambers, and jury rooms, stopping at last before a closed door of dark-stained oak. He opens it a crack, and peers inside. "Sir Francis!" says the page. "I didn't expect you to be here. I was told to bring in Serjeant Ames."

"Indeed!" says the voice of Francis Bacon. "Until a few moments ago, I did not expect to be here myself. By all means, bring in Serjeant Ames." The page lets Noah in, and bows out, leaving the door ajar.

Noah is familiar with this room. It's sometimes used by judges or members of the Privy Council to view outsized documents, such as land maps. It's sizable and well-appointed, housing a large central table that can readily accommodate twenty. At the moment, however, the room holds only Sir Francis and Noah.

Noah bows. "Sir Francis, it is ever a joy to see you."

Sir Francis rises with evident pleasure. "As it is to see you, Serjeant Ames."

Noah takes a seat one chair away from Sir Francis to make use of the abundant space. "What's this all about?" Noah asks.

"I assume you've been summoned here on the same business as I. Sir Robert evidently wishes us to join him in hearing Lord Mountjoy's plans for the upcoming campaign against the Irish rebels."

"Shall we not be joined by any *military* men?"

Sir Francis shakes his head. "Only one. But he's a *good* one. Although Her Majesty *had* wished to hear this presentation personally and to have the Lord Admiral beside her, they're both a bit under the weather." He lowers his voice. "The Lord Admiral is getting on in years, you know."

Noah nods sadly. "So, who shall it be, besides us politicians and barristers?"

Sir Francis leans back, his chest swelling with pride. "None other than the Captain of the Yeoman Warders!"

Noah's eyebrows shoot up in admiration. "Sir Walter Raleigh. We lawyers shall provide a poor second chair to a warrior of such stature."

Sir Francis waves his hand. "It's all been decided, anyway. Lord Mountjoy already has the nod. Both the Lord Admiral and Sir Walter concur that Mountjoy's the best man to replace Lord Essex as leader of Her Majesty's forces in Ireland, now that Essex has returned...*prematurely*... and been placed under house arrest."

The smile drops from Noah's face and he shakes his head.

"What is it, Noah?" asks Sir Francis. "You seem almost disappointed at Essex's well-deserved disgrace. I should have thought you'd feel vindicated at last in your low opinion of him."

Noah sighs. "As you know, Sir Francis, I believe my opinion of Lord Essex to be well-founded. I have therefore never felt a need for vindication, although I'll confess it is somewhat heartening to be joined by others at last, even if they ought to have recognized his failings long ago."

"You'll pardon if I observe that you do not *appear* to be 'heartened,' as you say."

"No, I am not *preponderantly* heartened. Like everyone else, I am sorely disappointed that Her Majesty's plan for subjugation of the Irish rebels has been turned on its head by that one willful man, that he reached a truce with the rebels as he had been expressly *forbidden* to do, that he left his post in Ireland contrary to Her Majesty's command, and then compounded it all with his personal invasion of Her Majesty's closet before she could be properly attired."

Sir Francis smirks. "I take it, then, that you are in agreement with the commission's removing him from command in Ireland and ordering him imprisoned with no date for his release?"

"As for his removal, I think that the commissioners' emergency decision was absolutely necessary and completely justified. As for his indefinite imprisonment…well, you know as well as I that no Englishman may be imprisoned indefinitely without a full trial."

"And you regard as legally insufficient the inquest conducted less than a week after his return." Sir Francis smiles. "So do I. So does Attorney General Coke." He looks at Noah appraisingly. "I have to admire your commitment to the precept that the rights of every Englishman cannot be secure unless the very *devil* is assured a full trial."

Noah snickers. "Cleverly phrased, Sir Francis."

"Page!" shouts Sir Francis. The page appears quickly in the doorway. "Has Sir Robert arrived, as yet?"

"Not yet, sir."

"Very well. In the meantime, I wish to confer privately with Serjeant Ames. Close the door behind you." The page bows and obeys.

Sir Francis leans toward Noah and speaks quietly. "I don't suppose you've heard what the Queen has in store for Lord Essex?"

"No," Noah replies hesitantly.

"His many supporters are driving her mad with their demands for his release. But he's truly exhausted her patience this time, and she'll have none of it. Instead, she's considering disposing of the whole matter *privately*."

Noah finds that prospect alarming, for when the Queen's father, Henry the Eighth, disposed of public grievances privately, the offender would never leave the Tower alive.

Sir Francis evidently perceives Noah's horror. "Oh, don't worry," he assures him. "Her Majesty merely intends that his lordship be tried in Star Chamber. Are you familiar with the procedure of that forum?"

Noah is chagrined. "I've assisted there a few times, but I must confess that, if Star Chamber has some uniform code of procedure, I've never been able to detect its workings."

"Well, Her Majesty knows you to be a quick study."

Noah squirms in his chair. "*I?*" He doesn't like the turn taken by this conversation.

"She hasn't made her mind up quite yet, but I expect that is a mere formality. In preparation for Essex's appearance at Star Chamber, the Queen intends to commission you to investigate his conduct during past military campaigns and to report your findings to her."

Noah's stomach suddenly feels queasy. He regards Sir Francis skeptically. "Surely, Her Majesty has many alternative candidates having less…personal history with his lordship."

"You mean…who don't *detest* him?" Bacon's question meets with no response. "Well, whatever your feelings, Her Majesty is well aware of them, and she evidently finds them irrelevant, which is all that matters. She trusts your judgment, Noah, and your objectivity, regardless of your personal feelings."

There comes a light knock at the door, which opens a crack to reveal Sir Robert Cecil peeking in, eyebrows arched. "We're a bit late. Are we interrupting a discussion of importance?"

"Not in the least," says Sir Francis, as he and Noah rise and bow.

"Good!" says Sir Robert. He enters and takes the seat between Noah and Sir Francis.

Lord Mountjoy enters immediately afterward and strides confidently to the opposite side of the table, followed by a page who struggles mightily to hold onto an ungainly armful of long scrolls. Mountjoy removes his gloves and begins taking the scrolls from his page, one by one, and placing them on the table. He makes a handsome appearance, with his high forehead and tightly curled black hair. Sir Francis plainly follows his movements with interest. But then, Sir Francis is well known to be especially fond of the more attractive specimens of his own sex.

Just as Mountjoy is about to begin, in rushes Sir Walter Raleigh. "I *do* hope my tardiness has not made a great hash of things!"

Instinctively, Noah and Sir Francis shoot to their feet and bow, Sir Robert rising more deliberately.

Sir Walter beams at Mountjoy and shakes his hand warmly, as they exchange a few private words. Then, to Noah's surprise, Sir Walter comes 'round the table, and takes the vacant seat next to his. He leans toward Noah and whispers, "I must ask you sometime about certain events in the early Bible."

Noah smiles and nods. "At your leisure, Sir Walter." As public disclosure of Noah's religion has transformed him, as if by magic, into the court's resident expert in Hebrew history and law, over the past few years he's spent a good deal of effort actually learning the subject.

Mountjoy begins his presentation, holding up each map as he explains it. As the little direct sunlight penetrating into the room comes from behind him, the watermark of his distinctive family crest lights up at the center of each map as he holds it up, a long-horned bull behind a shield flanked by a woman and a man. As he finishes with each map, he slides it along the table toward his page, who rolls it up again, but only after unfurling and handing him the next map. In this way, the presentation proceeds seamlessly.

As Mountjoy is primarily a man of action, it takes him only about twenty minutes to outline his plans for taking the fight to the Irish rebels. Despite Noah's lack of military experience, he finds Mountjoy's concise explanation highly satisfactory in both scope and clarity. Sir Walter and Sir Francis seem favorably impressed, as well.

Sir Robert, although also apparently well pleased, leans his elbows on the table, and rests his head upon his hands in contemplation, his brow furrowed. After a long pause, he says: "Sir Charles...pardon me, *Lord Mountjoy*...you have very ably discussed with us *your* battle plan, for which we thank you most humbly. But now I am concerned with the *enemy's* battle plan."

"Rest assured, Sir Robert, Tyrone's battle plan is foremost in *my* mind, as well." Mountjoy arches an eyebrow. "You wouldn't happen to have a *copy* of it, would you?"

Sir Walter and Sir Robert laugh aloud. Noah and Sir Francis share a smile, as they realize at the same moment that Sir Robert has unwittingly taken on his late father's demeanor, assuming the same contemplative posture, laughing in the same way at precisely the same kind of jest. And Sir Robert is immediately lost in thought again, just as his father would have been.

Noah breaks the silence. "If I know Sir Robert, m'lord, he was not thinking of Tyrone, but rather of our Sovereign's great enemy, Spain. And the possibility of Spanish intervention on Tyrone's side."

Sir Robert lets out a jovial laugh. "Serjeant Ames, I find it unnerving that you have learned to read my mind."

"At some level, Sir Robert, all good tacticians think alike," says Noah.

Mountjoy replies. "Yes, gentlemen, I had anticipated that question. Even with Spanish King Philip dead, his daughter, the Infanta, may yet march in his footsteps. And, if the genealogists are to be believed, she may eventually make a claim to the British throne in her own right. As you know, this has been a principal concern of Lord Essex." He winces, as he realizes he should have omitted any mention of that troublesome man. Sir Walter looks away, as his own well-known disputes with Essex have caused everyone to look his way.

Mountjoy urgently mutters something to his page, who searches through the remaining scrolls. Evidently, the top of each scroll has been marked with a unique identifying number. Finding the required scroll, the page unfurls it and hands it to his master, who holds it up to view.

The left side of the map shows Ireland, its size somewhat diminished to allow Cornwall, at Britain's southwestern tip, to be shown on the right. At two places in Ireland and one in Cornwall, the cartographer has drawn symbols apparently representing an array of English forces and battlements.

Sir Francis is taken aback. "Surely, you do not anticipate a Spanish invasion of *Cornwall*!"

Mountjoy sighs. "One must prepare for *all* contingencies, Sir Francis. Indeed, it was mainly because Spain's most recent attempt went *unanticipated* that its landing in Britain, if it had been successful, might have proven calamitous to the realm."

"Once again," says Sir Robert wistfully, "we were saved by sea and wind, which was none of our doing. Indeed, we would never even have *learned* of the attempt, had hundreds of drowned Spanish sailors not washed ashore."

Mountjoy resumes. "I brought this map to show you, not so much our Cornish defenses, as the preparations we're currently making against possible interference by the Spanish in Ireland itself." He points to Ireland's southern coast, and various symbols indicating English forces. "As County Cork is a likely landing point for the Spanish, we shall set up these widespread battlements, not only to assure ourselves of early warning, but also to give us the greatest ability to contain the Spanish by slowing their movements, should they successfully disembark.

"Strange as it seems, we also need be concerned about a possible landing up *here* in the far north, in Donegal. We have intelligence that the Irish rebels have nearly *begged* the Spanish to land there, and, as you can see from these diagrams, we intend to reinforce our existing strength there, as well."

Just then, Noah notices something unusual about this latest map. He glances at Sir Walter, whose eyes meet his, as he has evidently noticed the same thing. Although Mountjoy is about to slide the map to his page to be rolled up, he stops when Noah speaks. "M'lord, it is evident that you and your page take every precaution to guard these very sensitive maps from disclosure or theft. May I ask who prepared them?"

Mountjoy seems surprised by the inquiry. "You mean, my cartographer?"

"Yes, m'lord."

"His name is John Tyler. He's been with me many years."

"Does he always use the same paper for your maps?"

Now all eyes are on Noah, as questions about such details seem out of place anywhere but in the courtroom. Sir Walter seems mildly amused.

"Yes," says Mountjoy, "he uses my bespoke Italian stock."

"And it bears the distinctive watermark of your family crest that I was just admiring."

"Yes. Why?"

"Because the paper on which this last map was prepared does not bear your watermark," says Noah.

"Of what *importance* is that?" asks Sir Francis.

Mountjoy skeptically holds up the map of Ireland and Cornwall to the sun's rays, and his eyes flash in realization. "It may mean nothing," he says, then looks toward Noah with grudging admiration. "But it may mean…*a great deal.*" Mountjoy looks to his page, who shrugs in return. "No need to speculate now. We shall investigate this question, and I will personally let Sir Robert know of any explanation I find."

"Thank you, Lord Mountjoy," says Sir Robert. "Her Majesty wishes me to extend to you her undying thanks for your efforts on her behalf."

Mountjoy bows low, and says: "That is all the thanks for which the true subject might *ever* hope."

"Amen," mumble the others, every one thinking how Essex would never have entertained such a sentiment.

AS NOAH LEAVES the courthouse, he's hailed by the familiar voice of a young man. Scanning the lobby, he spots Jonathan Hawking waving an arm.

"Serjeant Ames!" shouts Jonathan again, quickly closing the distance between them.

"Jonathan! So good to see you! What have you been up to, of late?"

"Oh, workaday matters."

"How fares your practice?" asks Noah, as he and Jonathan saunter toward King Street. "I have heard that, since the conclusion of our business with Lord Essex's men, you have become the most sought-after barrister in all England."

"So *I* have heard, as well," replies Jonathan doubtfully. "And I must confess that I *have* acquired a better class of clients and earn larger fees. Yet," he sighs, "to my mind, things have not much changed. I feel as though I am…stagnating."

"Well," says Noah, adopting his favored pose as the voice of experience, "there is more to life—even to a *barrister's* life—than the law."

"I suppose," replies Jonathan. "Tell me, how goes the fair Lady Jessica?"

"My daughter is currently staying in the country, at the residence of the Earl of Somerset."

"Oh? Enjoying an autumnal holiday?"

Noah frowns. "I should expect you to know my daughter better than that, by now. Lady Jessica may *act* the ingenue, but she is never entirely uncalculating. She was invited by Lady Somerset in contemplation of marriage to the earl's son, Viscount…Something-or-Other."

"Oh," says Jonathan, suddenly serious, "I had no idea that she'd rejoined the ranks of the marriageable. She seemed to withdraw from such matters permanently after your family's…origins were publicly revealed by Lord Essex."

"She *did* withdraw for a time. In truth, I do not know what revived her interest, but I suppose it's not every day one is courted by a viscount. She has informed me that his landholdings are quite extensive."

"Naturally," observes Jonathan, his voice flagging.

Noah stops short, and Jonathan nearly bumps into him.

"What's wrong?" asks Jonathan. "You suddenly look as though you've had one of your famous epiphanies."

Noah considers a moment. "A short time ago, I left Lord Mountjoy's presentation concerning his upcoming deployment in Ireland. All his maps had been prepared on paper bearing a watermark of his family crest. Except *one.*"

"Which one?"

"I'm sure I shouldn't discuss this in any detail, but, as a general matter, it showed certain coastal positions in Ireland and Cornwall."

"Was it a particularly sensitive map?"

"For *some* purposes, I suppose," replies Noah. "Perhaps I'm losing my grip, seeing Essex's hand behind everything questionable. At first, I thought that the original map might have been stolen by a spy. But it just occurred to me that I've likely been worrying about nothing, for, if the map had been copied by an unauthorized person onto paper lacking the watermark, he would simply have restored the watermarked original to Mountjoy's papers and taken the *copy* with him."

Jonathan nods. "In which case, Lord Mountjoy, none the wiser, would have shown you the original, and the spycraft would have gone undetected."

Noah waves the thought away. "Oh, for heaven's sake! The cartographer likely ran out of his favored paper, and used whatever was at hand. Any spy who would needlessly remove an original would have to be a dunderhead indeed, to enhance the likelihood of detection."

As they reach King Street, to their left, on Thieving Lane, languish numerous beggars in all states of disrepair. Although, during times of plenty, a London beggar can usually scrounge enough to keep body and soul together, the recent famine has left many to perish of hunger or disease. Despair is evident in their eyes. On this occasion, Noah and Jonathan both look the other way.

"Care to share a carriage as far as Holborn?" asks Jonathan.

Noah taps Jonathan's boots with his walking stick. "Something wrong with *those*?"

"Not at all. I just thought perhaps you'd prefer to ride."

Noah shakes his head. "Not on a perfectly clement day, such as this. Come, walk with me." They go up King Street, and turn right on the Strand. "I enjoy walking past my old haunts at Serjeant's Inn. It reminds me that there was a time when I hoped for nothing more than an eventual position on the Bench."

"Things might have turned out simpler for you, I suppose."

Noah shrugs. "Indeed. They could not be much more complicated than they're about to become."

"How so?"

Noah lowers his voice to speak in confidence. "Although it may all come to naught, Sir Francis just informed me that Her Majesty intends to commission me to investigate Essex's past conduct of military affairs."

Jonathan's eyes go wide. "Setting the sheep to guard the ravenous wolf? That *would* be complicated for you, wouldn't it? How could she expect you to be evenhanded?"

"That's just what I asked Sir Francis. Her Majesty is thoroughly versed in my history with Lord Essex. Evidently, she has greater faith in me than I have in myself."

"That says a great deal about her confidence in you, I must say." Jonathan turns to Noah with a smile. "Will you be seeking the assistance of a more junior barrister in this investigation, by any chance?"

Noah is dismayed that the question has been raised so soon. Although he expected every young barrister to vie for a chance to assist in an investigation of such importance, he expected to have more time to consider whom to choose. It's especially unfortunate that it's Jonathan who's raised the question, for, as soon as the possibility of such a commission was mentioned, Noah immediately considered Jonathan and, just as quickly, dismissed the thought.

"Jonathan, I could not possibly ask *you* to assist in this."

"Why not?" Jonathan asks, sounding hurt. "We've worked together for years!"

"And shall *continue* for years to come! Just not in this matter." He looks at Jonathan impatiently. "For one thing, I care too much for your immortal soul."

Jonathan scowls. "Oh, please. You must be England's only Hebrew *bishop*! Why, you have an animus against Essex *yourself*, as you just acknowledged."

"But *you* blame him for Goodman Graves' death."

"Only because he had a *hand* in it."

"We don't *know* that, Jonathan."

"Doctor *Lopez* thought so," Jonathan observes hotly.

"Nonsense," replies Noah. "Lopez, may he rest in peace, admitted *in your presence* that he had no touchstone to determine whether it was poison or no." As pedestrian traffic is passing nearby, Noah draws up close to Jonathan and mutters. "Do you think I've forgotten that you swore to see Essex beheaded?"

Jonathan broods. "Oh, that was said in a fit of pique!"

Noah turns on him. "Oh? You *forswear* it, then?"

Jonathan stares at the ground. "No," he mutters.

"I thought not. Jonathan, I give you all credit for your honesty. But I cannot in good conscience place you in a position of such temptation. Besides, I promised Goodman Graves to look after you, and I feel morally obligated to do so."

"Who's it to be, then?" asks Jonathan. "One of the jesters? Arthur? Andres?"

"I haven't had an opportunity to give it a moment's thought, Jonathan. You caught me quite at unawares."

The rest of the walk takes place without conversation. They soon pass the Lord Keeper's house, where Essex is lodged against his will, and an image comes to Noah's mind of a caged predator, preening for escape. As Noah prepares to turn north toward his wife's house on High Holborn, he invites Jonathan to join them for dinner.

Jonathan seems sullen. "Not today. But thank you very much…and please extend my compliments to Mistress Ames, and, if you see her, to Lady Jessica."

"I certainly shall, Jonathan. And, as you continue on your way"—Jonathan waits attentively—"do not neglect to count your blessings. After all, you are…"

Jonathan can't help but smile. "Yes, I know: 'the most sought-after barrister in all England.' I really should have that printed on my calling card." They part ways with accustomed affection.

Noah little suspects that he'll be seeing Jonathan again before the sun sets.

And Jonathan little suspects that he'll be seeing Lady Jessica quite soon indeed.

CHAPTER 2

ARRIVING AT HOME, Noah finds the house unusually quiet. Marie is in her study, preoccupied with affairs of the shipping concern that she established with her first husband, and Noah does not wish to disturb her. Rather than to dine alone, he skips dinner and retires upstairs for a rare nap.

When he awakens in the late afternoon sunlight, he finds that he's unable to recall his dreams, though he has a vague recollection they were unpleasant. He plods downstairs to the kitchen, and scents of savory pumpkin soup and beef stew waft up, making his mouth water.

Marie is in the kitchen, preparing to serve supper, having laid out two settings of plates and utensils.

"Where's Cook?" asks Noah.

"I sent her home early," replies Marie.

Although hardly the conventional homemaker, Marie seems to find a certain joy in simple domestic tasks, and, as she bustles about the food, Noah takes a moment to admire her beautiful face and form. Unable to fathom how he has won a woman of such merit and beauty, he's come to see his life with her as the best kind of dream, one from which he hopes never to awaken.

He takes his accustomed seat, as she ladles out some pumpkin soup and favors him with a smile.

"I received a letter today from Stephen," she says. "He's safely arrived at Sir Henry's embassage in Paris."

"Oh, that's good to hear!" he says. "Was Sir Henry there to greet him?"

"No. Evidently, it is part of Sir Henry's duties as Her Majesty's ambassador to trail after the French king whenever, and wherever, he decides to move his court." She sits, draws herself up to the table, and lifts her spoon. "Does it not seem we've entered some brave new world, where Sir Henry Neville serves as Her Majesty's ambassador to France?"

Noah thinks for a moment, and nods. "Indeed, it is strange simply to hear our Henry referred to as '*Sir.*' Until quite recently, 'Sir Henry' meant his father, may he rest in peace." He sips a few spoonfuls of soup, and is pleased to find that its taste rises to the promise of its aroma.

"I heard you protesting in your sleep. Did you learn something disturbing at Westminster today?"

He sips a few more spoonfuls to give himself time to formulate a response. Although he almost never holds anything back from her on grounds of confidentiality, he occasionally omits some potentially upsetting item of information about the Earl of Essex, who both he and Marie strongly suspect of involvement in the murder of her first husband eight years earlier. Unfortunately, there is no way that mention of Essex can be entirely omitted from an account of today's events. He begins. "While awaiting Sir Robert, I met briefly with Sir Francis Bacon…"

"I still cannot understand how Bacon can be called the first 'Queen's Counsel,' when you were Her Majesty's counsel well before he was."

"Now, now, Marie. It is but a mere title, bringing with it little fee or privilege. Her Majesty thought it best to confer it upon a member of the national church, and I could not disagree with her. Besides, as you know, he has proven a far better ally than we could ever have hoped, given his long sponsorship by Lord Essex."

Marie bristles at the mention of Essex's name, and sits up rigidly. "Was Essex at today's meeting?"

Noah shakes his head and shifts uncomfortably. "Since his unauthorized return from Ireland, he is in disgrace, and under arrest at the Lord Keeper's house in the Strand. He is forbidden not only to come to Court, but to appear *anywhere* at Westminster."

"House arrest is far better than he deserves," she mutters.

"Which brings me back to today's events. As I mentioned, Sir Francis and I had been summoned to see Sir Robert Cecil. While we awaited him, Sir Francis told me something I found somewhat…surprising."

Marie rises, ostensibly to clear away the soup plates and serve the next course, but Noah knows that her true purpose is to position herself so that she can turn her face away, should she find the news upsetting.

"Sir Francis told me that Her Majesty is being hounded by Lord Essex's many supporters, who remind her that he cannot be imprisoned indefinitely without trial—"

"Not even by the Queen?" she asks, her back still toward him, her contempt for Essex palpable.

While Noah wishes to scoff, he dares not, and replies earnestly instead. "Not even by the Queen. Not since the advent of Magna Carta." He resumes his tale gingerly. "Her Majesty is quite decided that Essex shall hold no further place in her favor, or even in her service. Rather than to release him, she is therefore considering *giving* him his full trial."

Marie turns excitedly with a gravy spoon in her hand, stern vengeance in her eyes. "And she wants *you* to prosecute him!"

"No, Marie! Now, will you allow me—"

Her eyes go wide, and her nostrils flare. "She wants you to *defend* him!" In her fury, she drops the spoon, which clatters to the floor.

"*No such thing!* Now, Marie, will you allow me to tell you this, or are you too impatient to hear it?"

"I *am* impatient…but tell me, nonetheless." Pouting, she picks up the fallen spoon, places it in a washbowl, and turns back toward the food.

He gives her a moment to cool down. "Her Majesty is considering granting me a commission to investigate Lord Essex's past military affairs, to record my findings, and report back to her."

Marie calmly brings two plates of beef stew to the table, putting one at Noah's place, and the other at her own. Noah recites aloud a brief Hebrew prayer over the food, Marie placing her palms together and bowing her head in the customary Anglican posture of devotion. Although it isn't the Hebrew custom to assume such a posture, Noah knows of nothing to forbid it, and it makes her seem so angelic that he has no wish to interfere.

When the prayer is finished and she's said her "amen," she cocks her head curiously. "Tell me. If Her Majesty were to appoint you to conduct Essex's defense, would you do so?"

He replies warily. "I doubt Her Majesty would wish me to represent Essex, Marie. She knows I have a personal animus against him. It would be arguably unethical for me to represent his interests."

"Oh? Does Her Majesty feel bound by the niceties of barristers' ethics?"

"I did not *say* that barristers' ethics would be her reason for not wishing me to defend him."

Marie glares across the table at him. "Of course not," she says. "Her Majesty would not appoint you because the great Noah Ames would feel compelled to do everything in his power to obtain Essex's acquittal. Is that not right?"

He thumps his hand lightly onto the tabletop in an emphatic gesture he rarely invokes, as it never seems to put an end to any discussion. "Marie, my love. Please do not let this become an argument between us. It is a discussion that we shall almost certainly never need to have." At least, he *hopes* they'll never need to have it. But how can he be sure, when he's a mere advisor to the great ones of his time? To his great surprise, Marie seems to be assuaged for the moment.

"Have you seen Jonathan Hawking?" she asks.

"I ran into him as I left Sir Robert. When I told him of my likely appointment, he asked whether he might assist, and I told him that I could not in good conscience allow it."

"He must have been sorely disappointed."

Noah can only shrug, as he gave his word long ago never to tell anyone that Jonathan has sworn to see Essex beheaded.

"Did he ask about your daughter?" she asks.

Noah tries hard to recall. "Um…well, yes, he *did* ask about Jessica."

"And what did you tell him?"

"I told him that she's been invited to the home of an earl in contemplation of marrying his son."

Marie appears about to ask another question, when there's an urgent knock at the front door. As the sun is now setting, Noah takes one of the tapers from the kitchen and goes to answer it, a thin line of waxy black smoke billowing behind him the length of the hallway.

Outside, a young fellow in weather-beaten clothing waits with a letter in hand.

"Are you Serjeant Ames, suh?" he asks.

"I am," Noah replies.

"The father of Jessica, Lady Burlington, suh?"

"The same."

Although Noah thinks it a bit absurd that such especial care should be taken to make a positive identification, the fellow seems relieved by his answer and thrusts the letter toward him. "Letter for you from Wells—in Somerset, suh—from Lady Jessica."

Marie evidently overhears this, and comes up behind Noah, listening attentively.

Noah asks the young man: "When were you dispatched with this letter?"

"Two days ago, suh."

"*A mere two days?* To cover all that ground?"

"Aye, suh. Barely rested since I left. She told me if I didn't come straightaway, she'd draw and quarter me herself. Then, she kicked me in the bum to speed me on my way."

Noah sighs. "Well, young man," he says, reaching into his pocket, "in light of such indignities, we must be more than fair with you. What is your charge for such exceptional service?"

The messenger shakes his head. "She paid me in full, suh," then adds sheepishly, "but if you would be so kind as to tell her exactly what date and time you got this letter, I would much appreciate it." He unwittingly rubs his bum.

Noah hands the young man a generous gratuity despite vigorous refusals. He has long found that he can do no less for anyone having had the misfortune of dealing with Jessica in one of her fouler moods.

He barely has time to close the door before Marie takes the letter from his hand, slits open the envelope, and begins reading aloud by the light of the taper. The letter is mercifully brief. "'Dearest Daddy,'" she begins.

"Uh, oh," says Noah. "'Dearest' means she wants something she thinks me disinclined to give. 'Daddy' means she's in trouble."

"Yes, dear," says Marie, with mock indulgence. "Very clever. Pray, let me continue. 'As you know, I have been staying for the past week at Somerset Manor at the invitation of Lady Somerset. Although I was led to believe that I had been invited to meet their son Viscount Wellston with a view toward possible matrimony, instead, a most horrid, detestable, and ignominious proposition has been made to me, such that I must be removed from this place at the earliest *possible* moment. Although I am in no physical danger and have been extended the use of a kindly maidservant, I feel that I have been treated most disdainfully, and shall refuse to leave my rooms until I have been taken away from these premises by a gentleman of mine own choosing. I understand that you have great responsibilities to Her Majesty and all the Realm, but I do hope that you will come fetch me personally, as I know you to be the most loving and affectionate father of...Jessica, Lady Burlington.'"

"Oh, for heaven's sake!" says Noah, pacing the hallway in exasperation. "She's practically in *Wales*! I can't be running off for a week to fetch my grown daughter. Especially not *now,* when I'm to appear before Her Majesty in two days' time."

He returns to Marie by the door, gently takes the letter from her hand, and squints in the candlelight for the pertinent language. "She says she was presented with 'a most horrid, detestable, and ignominious proposition.' Do you suppose...?"

Marie looks at him as though he's a bit dimwitted. "I don't suppose he's asked her to slaughter the pigs, Noah."

"No," he says with distaste, "I suppose he's proposed some type of inappropriate relations. But knowing Jessica, she would be outraged by a suggestion of *any* relations short of immediate marriage."

Through the front door comes the sound of a fast-moving coach coming to a noisy halt. A brief commotion on the walkway is followed quickly by rapidly approaching footsteps and an excited pounding on the door. "What's this now?" says Noah in exasperation. He opens the door immediately.

There stand two of the young barristers who assisted him and Jonathan in their first hostile encounter with Essex's men several years ago. They appear quite harried, and more than a bit confused to find Noah and Marie already at the door.

"Arthur! Andres!" exclaims Noah.

"Pardon us, Mistress Ames," Arthur blurts. "Serjeant Ames, you must come with us. Jonathan is about to get into *big* trouble. We followed him to the Boar's Head in Eastcheap. He's already surly, and he's been drinking. Andres and I were about to return home but, as soon as we realized who'd just come through the door, we raced here to fetch you, instead."

"Who came in?"

"Gelly Meyrick," Arthur replies, "Essex's man."

Noah scowls and rubs his temples, for Jonathan has nearly come to mortal blows with Meyrick more than once.

Arthur grabs him by the elbow. "Sir, we have to go *right now!*"

Bewildered, Noah stuffs Jessica's letter in his pocket, shrugs apologetically to Marie, kisses her quickly on the cheek, and trots after the two young men to their open coach.

Arthur and Andres leap up to the drivers' seats. Noah flips open the side door, high-steps into the coach, shuts the door, and sits down, bracing himself for a bumpy ride through the rugged streets of Elizabethan London.

"Let's not assume the worst, gentlemen," he says hopefully. "This may yet resolve without violence."

As Andres snaps the reins, he and Arthur exchange a skeptical glance.

———————⌒∘⌒∘⌒———————

JONATHAN SPRINGS ACROSS the table and seizes Meyrick's throat with both hands, firmly shutting his airway in a death grip.

Meyrick's eyes bulge as he chokes on a swig of ale, utter shock on his porcine face, suds oozing from the sides of his mouth and dripping down his cheeks. Hurled backwards by the momentum of Jonathan's lunge, the rear of his chair slams hard onto the floor, rattling his brains.

Jonathan loosens his hold and drops knee-first onto Meyrick's ample belly, forcing the remaining ale to spout from his mouth like seawater out the blowhole of a whale.

Although Meyrick has goaded Jonathan into this onslaught and should have expected it, Jonathan made sure to give no warning that the constant jibes had at last hit a raw nerve and pitched him into a fury.

Meyrick grabs Jonathan's hands with a strength born of desperation, and tugs them firmly from his throat. Gasping for air, he shoves Jonathan off, and raises his upper body off the floor onto his elbows, where he remains for a moment, breathing in great gulps until his respiration can slow to a regular, if agitated, pace.

Jonathan stands up, his head spinning from drink, and gazes quizzically down at his victim, as though not quite sure how Meyrick ended up in such a discomfited posture. While he woozily recalls that, for a split second, he *intended* to pummel Meyrick to death, he realizes almost immediately, even through the haze of drink, that he has much to lose by doing so. While drunken brawling might result in a small fine (or the stocks) for someone else, for Jonathan it could also result in permanent disbarment from his chosen livelihood. And, if he actually *kills* Meyrick, he'll be hanged as high as the next man.

The tavern keeper Mistress Quickly rushes to Meyrick's defense and shouts in Jonathan's face. "Get out! I'll have no brawling in here. This is a *respected* house, and I am a *respected* woman!" She glances over her shoulder at Meyrick, who's making an earnest, if wobbly, attempt to stand, and turns back to Jonathan: "You should be *ashamed* of yourself, you should, *a barrister* and all, beating my valued customer! *Sir Gelly,* no less!"

Before Jonathan can begin to explain himself, a look of surprise flashes across Mistress Quickly's face as she's shoved roughly aside by Meyrick, who strikes Jonathan above the left eye with an iron right fist. Reeling from the blow, Jonathan instinctively turns away and doubles over, covering his wounded eye socket with his left hand.

"C'mon, you little bounder!" bleats Meyrick. "I'm not finished with you yet." He yanks Jonathan by the shoulder to bring him face-to-face again.

But Jonathan, having used the momentary respite to seize Meyrick's chair in his right hand, spins around and plunges its legs forcefully into

THE IMPRESS OF HEAVEN| 29

his belly. Now it's Meyrick's turn to double over. But he rights himself surprisingly quickly. Enraged, he clutches at Jonathan's neck, coming up just short of his mark, being held at bay by the chair.

Jonathan's eyes feel as though they're on fire. But he quickly flips the chair around to use it again, this time as a battering ram. He shoves the seat up against Meyrick's belly and rushes forward with all the strength his legs can muster, hurtling Meyrick up into the air off his feet, backwards and off-balance, straight toward the tavern window.

———————⇒∘⟨∅⟩∘⊂———————

AS ANDRES WHIPS the coach down Candlewick Street past London Stone, the jostling becomes intolerable. Noah's inner ears have tickled with vibration since leaving Holborn. But now, they hurt like the very devil, and his gut feels as though it's been struck with a mallet.

Relentlessly maintaining its speed, the coach veers left down Eastcheap, the setting sun now directly behind, brightly illuminating the peaceful street ahead.

Just as the Boar's Head comes into view, a sizeable piece of its front window explodes onto the street in a million crystalline shards, Gelly Meyrick flying through it backwards, followed by the disjointed spindles of a demolished chair and a sooty black puff of pulverized glazier's putty. Meyrick's motionless form comes to rest atop a hedge, emitting a dusty smoke, covered with glass shards and shredded leaden strips torn from the wooden sash that formerly held the window panes together.

Noah quickly realizes that Meyrick is completely insensate, and thinks with dread that he might well be dead.

Jonathan shambles guiltily out the front door, followed by Mistress Quickly, who ineffectually beats him in the bum with the bristled end of a broom, as though he's an oversized rat she found on her floor. Jonathan seems to take no notice.

As the coach pulls up to the tavern, Jonathan's bruised eyes briefly meet Noah's and, with an imploring look of utter despair, he collapses in a heap on the walk. Before the coach can come to a complete halt, Noah leaps down, and crouches by Jonathan's prostrate form, relieved to see that he's still moving, even if his motion consists only of writhing in pain. Jonathan opens his eyes partway, his left eye swollen nearly shut, and already black and blue. Although his other eye is developing a black ring of its own, it seems undamaged.

Noah stands up and glowers down at him, shaking his head slowly, intoning with evident disgust. "The most sought-after barrister in all England."

Jonathan covers his eyes in shame.

Noah turns to Arthur and Andres. "You two. See to Sir Gelly. *Gently.*"

Mistress Quickly's voice comes from behind him, addressing the tavern's scrub boy. "Here's a ha'penny. Go fetch the constable, quick as you can."

"Wait!" shouts Noah, turning swiftly around. The boy looks up at him, then back at his mistress, unsure what to do. Noah reaches into his pocket and pulls out a coin. "Here's tuppence. Forget the constable, and go fetch the glazier."

Mistress Quickly's mouth falls open indignantly, and she puts her hands on her hips. "Now, don't you be tellin' this boy what to do, Master High-and-Mighty. Works for *me,* he does."

Noah gives her his most ingratiating smile. "Mistress Quickly, I believe?"

"That's right," she replies staunchly. "And who might *you* be? The voice is familiar," she says, cocking her head suspiciously, "but I don't quite recall the face."

Noah is amazed by her memory, as she has indeed heard his voice before, but only *once*, and that nearly eight years earlier, when he wore a mask and held a cocked pistol to the head of another of her "valued customers." Before she can draw the connection herself, he bows respectfully and alters his voice slightly. "Serjeant Noah Ames, at your service."

She looks curiously at his doublet, which is not the dignified garment one would expect to see on a serjeant at law, and glances around at Arthur and Andres, who both wear barrister's robes.

"Oh, I get it," she says. "Come to clean up after your fellow barrister, have ye?"

"More than clean up, Mistress Quickly. We've come to make amends."

"And 'ow do ye plan to do that?" she asks. "I've got a busted chair and crockery inside, and this window's got to be repaired right quick. Gonna cost me *plenty*! And I've a right to get it from this here ruffian." She waves dismissively at Jonathan. "He'll spend a week in the stocks, too, if I can arrange it."

Although Noah wishes to avoid escalating the discussion, she's left him no alternative. "Why, madam," he says in an authoritative tone, "this man fell as you beat him with a stick! Are *you* quite blameless in this affair?"

Her mouth falls open again but, before she can retort, he gently draws her aside by the shoulder. "See here, Mistress. I'm *dreadfully* sorry for the inconvenience you've suffered as a result of this unfortunate…misunderstanding."

"Misunder—?" she begins to object.

"Certainly, it was. You would not wish to embarrass Sir Gelly, would you?"

"Sir Gelly? Why, I *saw* the whole thing! It was your *friend* what—"

"Yes," he concedes in advance. "But, madam, did you also *hear* the whole thing?" She observes him warily. "These two gentlemen have a long, long history of contention between them. Although I have not yet investigated the matter, it is certain that Master Hawking would not have raised his hand in anger without the most *profound* provocation. Think back. Is this not so?"

Although reluctant to cede the point, she seems to be slowly yielding. "Well, Sir Gelly *was* sayin' some mighty nasty things."

"And these things that he said would most certainly come under public scrutiny, that is, if these two gentlemen were to be haled before a magistrate on your information. You *do* see that, don't you?"

From the corner of his eye, Noah sees to his great relief that Meyrick is *not* dead. Arthur and Andres have gingerly taken him down from his prostrate perch on the hedgetop, seated him on the small patch of turf in front of the tavern, and now offer him weak beer from a mug, which he seems too groggy to accept. Noah also espies Mistress Quickly's boy winking at him behind her back, and slipping silently away, which Noah takes to mean that it will be the glazier, not the constable, who'll be summoned.

"Well, who's gonna pay for all the *damage*?" she demands stoutly.

"*I* am, Mistress Quickly…and right now," he assures her. "And I care not a *whit* which of these two gentlemen was at fault for any broken item," he says, quite certain that Jonathan was responsible for the lion's share of the wreckage. "To the extent that there has been some breach of honor here, why, they shall both answer to me, and they *shall* reach an accord. Come. Let us assay the damage together and determine how to put things right."

As he escorts her into her own tavern, he's surprised to see that the damage is no worse. It seems to be limited to one upended table, two broken crocks, and one chair demolished beyond recognition, small pieces of which are strewn in a jagged line running from the overturned table to the window, which now has a gaping hole in it. Mistress Quickly quotes the cost of each damaged item, excepting only the window. As her quotations seem reasonable, Noah pays her on the spot, and makes a mental note of the total.

Once she's counted out her money, and looks far more agreeable than before, Noah leans toward her and asks quietly, "When do you expect the parish constable to make his next rounds?"

"Night watch'll make its first rounds in about two hours, regular as clockwork. That's when they like their evenin' ale."

Noah nods sagely. "I see. Well…while I would never advise you to *lie* to the watch, I *would* ask you not to tell anyone more about the…incident…than you feel required to do."

She's unexpectedly amenable to the proposition. "Oh, they'll surely ask about the window, and no mistake. But there's somethin' I ask *them* when they get too nosy about my affairs." She stuffs the coins in her purse, and tugs the drawstring tightly shut. "I just point to their tankards, and ask 'em: 'You *payin'* fer those?' Shuts 'em *right* up."

A middle-aged man standing outside juts his head in through the gaping hole in the window, and whistles softly. It's the glazier, carrying his cap in one hand and a small toolbox in the other. He looks to Mistress Quickly, wide-eyed. "What 'appened 'ere?" he asks.

"Never you *mind* what 'appened," she replies. "How much to *fix* it, and when can ye have it done?"

The glazier counts up the missing and broken panes. "Twenty panes, plus muntin and putty," he smiles, "and a full day's work for me. All told, that's a crown right there, and no doubt." He folds his arms and sniffs, obviously prepared for an expression of outrage.

Although Noah can count the missing panes himself and see that the glazier has overcounted by four, he decides not to quibble. As he opens his purse and withdraws a crown, the glazier's eyes light up in anticipation, but Noah conspicuously hands the coin to Mistress Quickly, and turns to the glazier. "You shall be paid as soon as the repair is made to Mistress Quickly's *full* satisfaction. Is that clear?"

The glazier masks his momentary disappointment with a half-smile, and dons his cap. "I'll be back first thing in the mornin', meddem. Good evenin' to ye both." He bows, and wanders off.

Mistress Quickly is obviously mollified by these most recent events, though her mind is no doubt feverishly seeking for some means to keep part of the crown for herself, regardless that Noah has shown it to the glazier already.

"Well, madam," he says, "have I been true to my word?"

She smiles. "Y'have, sir." She leans toward him. "But, I'd be right worried about yer young friend there. He's got some kinda problem he ain't shared with no one." She whispers almost inaudibly. "If y'ask me…it's about a woman." She winks. "It *owways* is."

Noah nods. "You are no doubt correct, mistress. This entire exercise has been my attempt to secure an opportunity to address the issue with him…whatever it may be…so that my *young* barrister friend can eventually become my *old* barrister friend, if you see what I mean." He smiles at her again. "And I am truly relieved to find that *you* personally are unharmed. Or I would have fetched the constable *myself,* I assure you."

She curtsies coyly.

He bows low in return, and sighs. "Now, there's a gentleman I need to speak with before I can be confident that this matter shall remain among us. If you will pardon me."

He steps outside. On the ground several paces to his left, Arthur and Andres sit silently beside Jonathan, who now sits up with his legs folded, wearing a doleful expression, his blackened eyes downcast. To Noah's right stands Gelly Meyrick, a bit wobbly, precisely where Arthur and Andres seated him earlier, staring blankly across the street, as though he knows Noah wishes to speak with him.

Noah braces himself, steps beside Meyrick, and joins him in peacefully gazing at the same vacant spot across the street. There are several bloody nicks on the left side of Meyrick's face, as well as an inflamed scratch running the whole length of the back of his neck, no doubt from scraping against the ragged end of a burst lead strip. After a moment of silence, Meyrick speaks quietly without looking at him.

"I know what you're gonna ask, Master Jew."

Noah risks a small jest. "*Serjeant* Jew, Sir Gelly."

Meyrick smiles wanly. "Serjeant *Ames,*" he says. "Sorry, didn't mean nothin' by it."

"Thank you for that," says Noah.

Another silent moment passes. "You're gonna ask me to forget about what just 'appened with your Master Hawking." As Meyrick is quite right, Noah does not reply. "Well, I ain't gonna do it. I've looked him straight in the eye, and don't like what I seen there. He means to kill me…if I don't kill 'im first." He turns to Noah imploringly. "He *wants* to kill me."

Noah cannot deny it. "I expect he blames you for the death of his old master, Goodman Graves."

"What? His *investigator*?"

Noah nods.

"I ain't 'ad nothin' to do with Graves, and that's the truth! Heard he died of old age and excitement, anyhow."

"The physician was unable to say precisely what killed him."

"Well," says Meyrick emphatically, "it weren't *me!*" His gaze shifts to the orange sunset. "Whatever Hawkin's problem is, I'm not gonna make it easier for him. If the constable can take 'im off the streets for a few months, I'll sleep better for that long."

"Sir Gelly," says Noah hesitantly, "do I have your word that you said *nothing* to provoke him this evening?"

Meyrick shakes his head mournfully. "Nah, can't say that. I said a few things to 'im. Nothin' as shoulda made him *crazy,* though."

"You know, Sir Gelly, you and I have had our run-ins, yet *we* seem to have moved past them. If you wish to see your handiwork, I can show you an eight-inch-long scar across my abdomen."

"Yeah. And I got thrown from my horse *twice* that day. Got more'n a few breaks and bruises of my own on your account."

"Well, my point was…"

"I *see* yer point," protests Meyrick, with irritation. "I'm not *stupid*, whatever you all may think. The difference between you and Hawkin' is: You're not *crazy*…and he *is*. Belongs in Bedlam Asylum. *Ach!* I don't know why I spend a *second* in this sewer of a city. Now that Essex is stuck in the Lord Keeper's house, I'm not even allowed to *see* 'im. Meanwhile, my wife's got two places up in Herefordshire where I could set myself out to pasture." He seems to be softening. "Tell you what, Serjeant. I've some business out of town that'll take me about ten days. If you can work it out with Lord Essex before I get back, then I'll let things alone. If not, I'll go straight to the constable and scream bloody murder."

Noah considers his words. As they don't seem to require his assent, he says merely: "Thank you again, Sir Gelly."

Before setting off, Meyrick turns to Noah. "It's *Hawking* who should be thankin' *you,* Serjeant Ames. I wouldn't turn away from him to *piss,* if *he* asked me."

Noah watches Meyrick lumber away with a peculiar gait caused, no doubt, by recent events, then silently summons Arthur, who looks at him with dread.

"Yes, sir?" says Arthur.

"Was Jonathan upset because of something I told him today?"

Arthur hesitates, as though wondering if his answer would breach some confidence. Evidently deciding that it wouldn't, he nods.

"I thought as much," says Noah. He beckons Andres, asks him to wait with Arthur, and ambles over to speak with Jonathan privately.

Though Jonathan's eyes are still fixed on the ground, Noah can see that his mere approach has caused some apprehension. He looks down, and sees Jonathan tense at the sound of his voice. "I needn't tell you, Jonathan, that it's only the fool who places himself and his friends at the mercy of his enemies. And you have accomplished just that."

Jonathan looks up quizzically, his battered face a sorry sight.

"Sir Gelly has told me that he'll go to the constable as soon as he returns to London in ten days' time," says Noah, "*unless* I come to terms with Lord Essex before then. If word of this altercation reaches the Lord Chief Justice, you'll very likely be expelled from the Bar. Your career now hangs by a thread, Jonathan. Your failure to control your temper has placed you at Meyrick's mercy, and me at Essex's. I hope you're proud of yourself."

Jonathan cannot bring himself to speak, but covers his face with his hands once more.

Noah tamps down the pity growing inside him. "You must leave town tonight, right away, for several days. While I have purchased the tavern keeper's silence, there may be other witnesses to Sir Gelly's flight through the Boar's Head window, and we've no assurance of *their* silence."

Jonathan drops his hands, and speaks at last. "But if I leave London immediately, sir, my disappearance may be taken as an admission of guilt."

"That's only if you have no verifiable reason to leave town...but you *do* have one."

Jonathan looks up at him quizzically, his left eye open only a slit. Although Jonathan's injuries pain Noah, he is adamant not to let on. "As punishment," says Noah, pronouncing judgment, "you shall be required to perform a Herculean task. One that would cause the *wisest* man to quail with fear."

"Anything," says Jonathan with resignation.

Noah withdraws Jessica's letter from his pocket, and lets it drop at Jonathan's feet.

"Go and fetch my daughter."

CHAPTER 3

NOAH AWAKENS well before dawn, and cannot fall back asleep. Even Marie's gentle breathing beside him fails to overcome a nagging feeling that he's already bungled a major clue to some mystery about which he yet knows nothing.

An early letter slipping quietly under the front door sharpens his unease. When a second letter follows soon after, he surrenders any hope of sleep and rises in the dark.

Being careful not to disturb Marie, he quietly dons his silk serjeant's robes and creeps stealthily down the stairs, lighting a candle only when he reaches the kitchen to break a piece of bread off last night's loaf.

He snatches the two envelopes off the floor, and finds that they bear no markings other than his own name. He douses the candle between moistened fingers and shuts the front door firmly on his way out. A moment later, he leads Bucklebury out of the stable, who, once mounted, begins walking toward the Tower of London.

Noah hopes that one of the letters signifies Sir Walter's acquiescence to meet with him at the Tower this morning. As the sun peeks over the horizon ahead, he stops Bucklebury at a spot overlooking the lazily flowing Thames to read the letters. Once Bucklebury's hooves cease their familiar clop, the eerie quiet of the morning makes Noah realize how alone he is on this deserted road, and how assailable by any thief who might happen along. As he often does at such times, he pats Uncle Avram's dagger for reassurance, grateful that it was recovered after a violent incident near Oxford, years ago.

Perched warily atop Bucklebury, he slits open the first of the letters. It's from Sir Robert Cecil, who reports that he will be going to the Tower later this morning, and that Lord Mountjoy's adjutant has gone there already to discuss measures taken to secure his lordship's military maps.

The second letter is from Sir Walter, accepting "with joy" Noah's proposal to confer at the Tower this morning, though Noah, in the brief note to which Sir Walter has replied, made no mention of the topic of their proposed discussion. Noah carefully replaces each letter in its own envelope, deposits them both in his saddlebag, and canters off to the Tower, now doubly sure of his destination.

———⌖———

"GOOD MORNING, SERJEANT!" roars Raleigh, as though he's already been up for hours. "Have you yet had your morning meal?" He puffs on his long-stemmed pipe.

"Not as yet, Sir Walter," Noah replies, with a bit less energy. "I left home this morning before any of the servants arrived."

"Would you care for some eggs in the Yeoman Warders' mess? It's not much, but it's better than nothing."

"That would be *delightful*!"

Though the Warders' simple chairs and tables are so shopworn that they might have arrived centuries earlier with William the Conqueror, the mess is a tidy place. The chicken's eggs are delectable, as is the toasted bread that arrives with it. Noah can't help but notice Sir Walter finishing off everything that's left.

"Once you've been at sea for several months," says Raleigh with a faraway look, "and the last of the laid-in food has gone rancid—and you're sharing even *that* with the bilge rats—you swear never to allow another unspoiled morsel to go uneaten."

"I can barely imagine," says Noah humbly, almost in a whisper. "I don't know that I'd *ever* stop eating, once I'd got home."

Raleigh laughs heartily. "Oh, you would eventually, although it might take a few days for you to be persuaded to put down your fork." He surveys the tabletop. "Have we quite finished?"

"I believe we have."

A deep voice interrupts them. "Pardon, Sir Walter. Is this gentleman Serjeant Ames?"

Noah turns to see a tall young Yeoman Warder standing behind him with a letter.

"I am Serjeant Ames," confirms Noah.

The Warder bows. "Sir Robert Cecil has sent a letter ahead." He hands it to Noah, bows and leaves.

"Pardon me a moment, Sir Walter," says Noah, opening the envelope raggedly with his finger. He reads the first sentence, and paraphrases it for Raleigh. "It appears that Sir Robert is on his way here with Lord Mountjoy."

Before Noah can read or say anything further, Raleigh snaps to his feet, as though suddenly remembering something that slipped his mind. "Oh, my! I'd no *idea* Mountjoy was coming. I was told that his adjutant had arrived some time before you, and I'm afraid I neglected to greet him. Come along. We shall greet him together." Without another word, Sir Walter strides briskly along a chiseled stone hallway.

Noah awkwardly stuffs the letter in his pocket and follows the determined Sir Walter, who nearly gets away from him. As Noah catches up, the two of them burst out together into the bright morning sun, swiftly traversing the courtyard where, as a grocer's boy, Noah had unwittingly met the uncrowned Queen Elizabeth.

Entering a dark hallway on the ground floor, Sir Raleigh turns, smiles, and holds open the door for Noah. "Almost there! Third door on the left." Sir Walter leads him down the hall, and comes to a halt before a door of rough wood. "Here it is," he says, and opens wide the small chamber, beginning his apology even before looking inside. "I am *so* sorry—" He stops, his eyes wide, his mouth agape.

The sight is so gruesome it's beyond Noah's capacity to take in all at once. Although he's arrived at scenes of recent murder in the past, never has he seen anything comparable to this charnel house.

A young man in Mountjoy's colorful livery lies motionless, splayed across the table in a contorted position suggesting he writhed in agony immediately before dying. His eyes wide with surprise, his face bears the unmistakable expression of sheer terror.

A dagger has been plunged through his throat with sufficient force to skewer him to the table. Blood has streamed off the tabletop and flooded the floor, and the room is now redolent with its stomach-turning, coppery scent. Several shiny crimson puddles lie near the body, while, further from the corpse, the gore has already coagulated, its stagnant surface reminding Noah of the wrinkled film he once saw atop a black pudding, a gentile dish forbidden to Jews, as it contains not only pork but animal blood.

Sir Walter, a veteran of many hard-fought campaigns, freezes for only a moment. He carefully sidesteps the slippery red pools, and presses two of his fingers just below the victim's ear. He shakes his head. Placing the palm of his hand across the man's forehead, he seems perplexed. "The body's already lost a good deal of its warmth," he says.

Noah croaks, "Where is Her Majesty?"

Alarm passes fleetingly across Sir Walter's face, but he shakes his head reassuringly. "She's not here at the Tower. She's at—" Leaving his thought incomplete, he runs to the courtyard door through which they entered moments earlier, flings it open, and bellows to the ranking Yeoman Warder in view. "*Francis! Francis!* There's been a *murder*! Sound the alarum, and come down here *at once!*"

Noah steps out of the chamber to clear his head of the brutal scene and stumbles down the dark hallway into the bright daylight of the courtyard. A moment later, the Tower grounds swarm with Warders running to their appointed stations. Bells of different pitches jangle everywhere. Although it takes a moment for the big bell in the main tower to be swung into action, soon its deep, mournful voice joins in the general din.

Francis runs up to Raleigh. "Where is the victim, sir?" he asks.

Raleigh points with his chin. "In there."

Before Francis can go to see the body, Sir Walter grabs him with both hands, and demands in a stern voice: "Where are Sir Robert and Lord Mountjoy?"

"They've arrived, sir. When the alarum rang out, they'd just come through the inner portcullis. We shut it behind them, sir."

"Good," he replies, and points toward the bloody chamber. "Go look through the door briefly, if you like, but *don't go in*! And return here at once."

As Francis trots down the hall to the murder scene, Raleigh shakes his head fretfully at Noah. "What the devil shall I tell Lord Mountjoy happened to his man?"

Noah considers the question. "The worst thing is, the devil may yet be on the grounds."

Sir Walter nods slowly. "True. The portcullis may have shut him *in*, not out."

Francis returns, his face ashen and grim as he looks to Sir Walter. "Orders, sir?"

"Assemble a group of our longest-serving men to escort Sir Robert and Lord Mountjoy to the main salon in the royal quarters, and keep them there under guard. Tell those gentlemen there's been a murder on the grounds, and that I shall be with them shortly. Assure them that Her Majesty is not endangered in any way, and that we are dispatching Warders to double her guard at Nonsuch Palace."

Francis nods smartly and begins to walk away, but Raleigh grabs his shoulder. "Frank, trust *no one! Not even our own men!*" He points to the murder scene. "That poor blighter was murdered almost as soon as he arrived. Have Gardner assemble ten of his most trusted men, and report to Nonsuch to augment the Queen's personal guard. And tell *him* that no one is to be trusted." Turning to look straight at Noah, Sir Walter continues giving Francis orders. "Write down the names of the men who go with Gardner, and give a general order that no one is to enter or leave the Tower until further orders from me, personally, *on pain of death!*"

"Aye, sir!" shouts Francis. As Raleigh releases him, he sprints off toward the Tower's portcullis entrance, anxious to begin execution of this lengthy list of emergency orders.

Noah waits in silence. He would feel entirely useless, except that his single observation has been so carefully heeded.

Raleigh asks, "You don't suppose Her Majesty is in any immediate danger from this traitor, do you?"

Noah offers Sir Walter what little comfort he can. "Probably not immediately. But, he's been crafty and audacious enough to slaughter a military guest on her *doorstep.* Sir Walter, if he can gain entry and move about inside the Tower of London, Her Majesty cannot feel safe *anywhere.*"

Raleigh nods grimly. "Then, our first order of business must be to find out who he is."

"And to ascertain his motive for this bloody deed."

—————— ⋙⋘ ——————

NOAH IS STILL loitering in the dark hallway outside the bloody chamber when the alarm bells cease their clamor, leaving nothing behind but a phantom echo in his ears. Although he's been left here to ensure that no one tampers with the crime scene, he has no idea what to do if anyone tries. He's no guard, and Uncle Avram's dagger would offer scant protection against a trained assassin.

Such thoughts are soon dissipated by the jangling of a troupe of Warders marching in his direction through the courtyard. It seems to him at first that the murderer might be among them, but he decides that could not be so. As some of the victim's copious blood would surely have stained the murderer's clothing, if the Warders had seen him they would already have him under lock and key.

While Francis and the remainder of the escort mill about outside in the yard, the door swings open, and in stride Sir Walter and Sir Robert, followed by a stunned-looking Lord Mountjoy. Noah bows low, and backs away from the chamber doorway to allow their admittance.

"Has anyone come this way, Serjeant Ames?" asks Sir Walter.

"No one, sir."

Sir Robert glances briefly through the chamber door, gasps, and immediately steps out of Mountjoy's way. Mountjoy braces himself, as though expecting a savage blow, and peers into the chamber for a long time. It seems his heart will break. At last, his eyes drop from the bloody scene to the floor before his feet, and Noah imagines the sinews of his mind snapping back into their natural state of command.

"This man was of good family, Sir Walter," says Baron Mountjoy. "I shall have to write to them. What shall I say?"

Raleigh hesitates. "Other than to provide the cold comfort of praise, m'lord, we have nothing to tell them at the present time."

Mountjoy looks to Raleigh darkly. "*At the present time?* This was no foot soldier, Sir Walter. As my adjutant, he would have been nearly as secure as the general staff. Do you not think his family entitled to see him arrive with me safely, at least as far as *Ireland*?"

Sir Walter accepts the rebuke without objection, and casts his eyes down.

"M'lord," sighs Sir Robert. "Her Majesty's enemies are everywhere. The Tower is not the only *sanctum sanctorum* to be violated by their foul deeds. Nor is your adjutant (may he rest in peace) the first to perish at their hands. Every subject of this kingdom lives under the Sword of Damocles. *We* three, more than any others." He shakes his head morosely. "Those around us are ever in peril. I am returning to the royal quarters, if you need me further. Please keep me advised of your findings." He bows and departs.

Noah braves a word. "M'lord, no one has examined this chamber, except Sir Walter, and he only to ascertain whether the victim had expired. May I step inside?"

Mountjoy looks to Raleigh, who nods his reassurance.

"You may, Serjeant Ames. And may God guide you to bring the culprit to justice."

Noah bows humbly, and takes a step toward the chamber door. Before entering, he turns to Mountjoy. "M'lord, may I ask this man's name?"

"Trenowden."

It sounds vaguely familiar. "From Cornwall?"

"West Devonshire, I believe, although the name is Cornish."

"Did Master Trenowden have any duties with respect to your

lordship's maps?"

"*Lieutenant* Trenowden currently had no such duties."

"I see. Did the lieutenant have a key to your lordship's map room?"

Mountjoy is plainly exasperated by Noah's questions. "I don't know, Serjeant Ames," he says, gesturing toward the chamber, inviting Noah to enter. "*Did* he?"

As Noah enters the chamber, he's relieved to see that he's been followed in by Sir Walter, who shows not the least reluctance to touch the dead, rifling efficiently through the victim's pockets. Noah shivers to imagine the battlefield conditions under which Raleigh learned to steel himself so.

Raleigh removes a ring of keys from one of the victim's pockets, and brings it out to Mountjoy. "Do you recognize these keys, m'lord?" he asks.

As Noah listens attentively to the conversation murmuring on in the hallway, he leans uncomfortably close to the dagger protruding from the victim's throat. Its brass handle bears the stamp of a family crest so crudely impressed as to be nearly unrecognizable. A glance at the Mountjoy crest emblazoned across the victim's livery, however, confirms that the design on the handle is the same. As the victim's leather sheath holds no dagger, Noah surmises that the lieutenant was murdered with his own weapon.

"I don't recognize the keys," says Mountjoy, "but Trenowden had my trust, and the run of the manor. It would not surprise me if one of his keys fits the lock to the map room."

"Does your lordship have such a key?" asks Raleigh.

This remark is followed by a jingling of keys. "You can compare them with these," says Mountjoy, "but, even if one of my keys fits the map room, I must confess I do not know which one it is."

In a moment, Raleigh replies. "I am no locksmith, m'lord, but none of Trenowden's keys appears to match your own. We'll need to bring them to your house in Dorset to see which locks they fit...unless the page who assisted you the other day is perchance at hand, with a key of his own."

Noah spies something small and white clutched in the victim's left hand. Upon closer inspection, it appears to be a corner of paper torn from a larger sheet. He removes it carefully.

"I'm afraid my page has returned to Dorset," says Mountjoy. "You can examine his keys when you come up."

Noah, satisfied that nothing further can be learned from the body without the assistance of a physician, bends over to look under the table, where the scent of blood nearly overwhelms him. Although he feels his gorge rise, with effort he manages to hold down the eggs he so enjoyed in the Warders' mess.

Another shred of paper now catches his eye, this one larger, with torn edges. It's alighted atop a partly congealed pool of gore. Something is written on it. Although he cannot make out the letters in the dim light, he can see that the blood absorbed by the paper is gradually obliterating the writing, spoiling important evidence. He reaches down, carefully lifts the paper straight up between his thumb and forefinger, and stands up, holding it away from his person to prevent the blood from soiling his clothing.

"What have you found, Ames?" asks Raleigh.

"Two scraps of paper. One has some writing on it."

"Come, bring them to the light of the window."

As Noah does so, he fits the corner shred neatly to the inscribed strip. A perfect fit. He's disappointed nevertheless. Although it's too much to expect the paper to contain a complete message, for a frenzied moment he'd hoped the writing would impart enough information to identify the murderer. Such is not to be. In fact, it requires a few turns merely to orient the writing so that it can be read.

Raleigh and Mountjoy look over Noah's shoulder.

"What does it say?" asks Mountjoy.

Noah furrows his brow. "The inscribed paper bears three partial lines. The right-hand portions of the first two lines have been torn away. Although the last line appears to be physically intact, the writing at its center has been dissolved by blood soaked into the paper. See for yourself," he says, and holds the scraps up for all to see.

```
Porth
Kil
Ch. Lev.  31        bre
```

"I only wish it told us more," says Raleigh.

"Well," says Noah, "even without the writing, it tells us *something*. For one thing, I would surmise that obtaining this writing was *not* the murderer's object. To the contrary, it seems likely the murderer was unaware the victim was holding it."

"Why do you say that?" asks Mountjoy.

"Anyone prepared to murder someone to obtain or destroy this writing would have searched for it thoroughly after the murder was done. Yet, this killer did not do so. The victim's fist was still clamped shut when I examined it. If the murderer had searched for the paper at all, he certainly would have pried open the fist, found the shredded corner, and searched under the table for the written part of the paper, just as I did. If he *had* done so, he would have removed it, and it would not have remained there to be found by me." He scratches his head. "The location where the writing was found reinforces this conclusion."

"How's that?" asks Raleigh.

"I found the inscribed strip lying atop a pool of blood under the table. If the writing had already lain on the floor *prior to* the struggle, it would have been *under*, or at least, *in* the pool. My conjecture is that it wafted down unseen, probably as the killer departed. While this writing might well be a remnant of some important intelligence, it seems impossible to make sense of it without more information. And, it is at least *possible* that the killer knew of the writing, but believed it to be unimportant…although I do not believe that for a second."

"Nor do I," says Mountjoy.

"Nor I," concurs Sir Walter.

The door to the courtyard flings open, and in rushes Francis, breathless and sweaty. He bows to Mountjoy. "M'lord."

"What is it?" demands Raleigh.

"We've discovered how the killer got in and out of the Tower."

"We'll go see," says Raleigh, "but first padlock this chamber."

Francis locks the chamber and tests it twice, to be sure. Raleigh nods approval.

"Lead the way!" orders Mountjoy, and the three follow Francis across the main courtyard to the ominously named "Traitor's Gate," which is now guarded by four perplexed-looking Warders.

Francis escorts Mountjoy, Raleigh, and Noah to the lock and heavy chain that usually secure the gate. He holds up the lock for them to examine. "It's undamaged, as you can see."

Raleigh asks, "Then, how did the killer get in and out?"

With some effort, Francis lifts the near end of the heavy chain, and shows them a single broken link, in which two straight cuts have left a gap the width of a man's thumb. "It's been sawn through," says Francis. "The locksmith says it would have taken no less then twelve solid hours to saw through it twice like this, even with a good saw. And he says sure it would have broken more than one blade in the process."

"Twelve hours!" says Mountjoy, incredulous. "What negligence is this, to allow a man to stand outside Traitor's Gate and saw through a chain for twelve solid hours?"

As Raleigh and Francis are at a complete loss, Noah chimes in. "No negligence at all, m'lord."

"What?" says Mountjoy indignantly, nostrils flaring.

"None at all, m'lord. I expect that the murderer, or his confederate, sawed through piecemeal, over several days, or even weeks." He turns to Francis. "How often is the integrity of this chain checked?"

Obviously unsure what Noah is getting at, Francis replies. "There's always a watchman on duty in this precinct who checks the lock once each hour."

Noah points to the lock. "But, as you say, the lock is undamaged. I asked about the *chain*."

Francis' face grows bright red, and he answers after some hesitation. "Examining the chain is not a part of the watchman's duties."

"Why *not*?" asks Mountjoy pointedly.

Raleigh interjects. "Because the lock can be sawn through in only *two* hours. It makes no sense for someone to struggle with a heavy chain all night and part of the next day, when he could break through much more efficiently simply by cutting the lock."

Noah nods. "And this tells us that the murderer knew well the rhythms of the Tower. He knew when a guard would come to check the gate, and so would stop sawing until he was alone again. He must also have known that the chain would *not* be routinely examined. He might even have known he could escape during the pandemonium of the alarum."

Raleigh wipes his brow with a handkerchief. "My God, the murderer could be a Yeoman Warder."

Noah asks Francis, "How did you discover that the chain had been sawn through?"

Francis appears chagrined. "I came over here a couple of minutes ago, saw the gate was closed and the lock secure but, to be sure, I shook the gate, and the chain just...*fell off.*"

"I have my doubts that the murderer either entered or exited through Traitor's Gate," says Noah. "And I *strongly* doubt the killer is one of the Warders. If he were, he would have had no need to saw the chain, or even open the gate—except to throw us hounds off the scent, I suppose."

Mountjoy turns to Francis. "Which Warder escorted my adjutant to the chamber?"

"I did, sir."

Mountjoy regards him skeptically. "You were the last to see my adjutant alive, and the first to discover the sawn chain?" Now he's incensed.

"Aye, sir," replies Francis sheepishly.

"Sir Walter, arrest this man at once, on suspicion of murder!"

CHAPTER 4

THE NIGHT IS so dark, and Jonathan so exhausted, that he nearly falls off his horse. He rights himself in time, fortunately, as he would otherwise have tumbled into the path of the horse he's leading. To add to his miseries, the throbbing pain around his swollen left eye repeatedly urges him to rub his face with his hand. But every time he tries to do so, one of the horses tugs its reins, reminding him that he has no hands free.

After his fight with Meyrick the previous evening, Arthur and Andres spirited him out of London to Kingston-upon-Thames. Though they mercifully let him sleep through the following morning, they insisted on putting him on horseback that very afternoon, citing orders of Serjeant Ames.

Before Jonathan would agree to bring along a second horse, however, he insisted that Jessica's note be read aloud to him, and he's quite certain she'd made no mention of her transportation requirements. Nonetheless, in light of her recent social disappointment, he'd thought it better not to risk her wrath. *Two* horses. Just in case Her Pampered Ladyship desires one.

As the object of his assigned quest is the retrieval of Lady Jessica, he can't help but direct some resentment toward her, even though the blame for his current exile from London belongs solely to him. She's always been so determined to remarry "upwardly" that she's never given him a moment's thought. On those rare occasions when he's been in her presence, it's been painfully obvious how his low birth caused her to regard him as no better than one of her father's favored servants, which is ironic, given her own *Hebrew* birth which, by convention, would have to be regarded as even lower than his.

A small point of light shines in the darkness up ahead. It seems almost beyond reason to hope that he's stumbled upon the very inn Andres mentioned while helping him onto his horse to begin this lonely journey.

At first, with no moonlight, the two-story structure looms as a black vacancy cut out of the stars. As he approaches it, however, a sign above the door comes into view, swinging gently in the night breeze, intermittently illuminated by a single candle in the window. When at last he reaches it, he's pleased to make out a colorful picture of a hart's head, and the rustically lettered words: Hind of Brakenhale. This is it. Perhaps his luck has improved, at last. He ties the horses to a post, and knocks quietly on the door.

A long time passes—*so* long that he hopes the innkeeper has not already gone to bed with a full inn and a fuller belly. As he's about to knock louder, the door opens a crack, and a middle-aged woman appears.

"Can I help you?" she asks suspiciously. Her hair is bound up, and she's already in bedclothes, with a worn blue robe drawn tightly about her waist.

"I'm in need of a room for the night."

She opens the door a little wider and brings the candle to the opening. Catching sight of his bruised eyes, she's startled. "You one of them *brawlers*? Don't want no brawlers in this establishment."

"No, madam," he enunciates in his most erudite manner. "I've not been drinking, and I'm not a…brawler." He wonders vaguely whether a single drunken brawl qualifies him as a "brawler," but he's perfectly prepared to fib to an innkeeper, if it means getting a room for the night. "I was struck by a branch yesterday, and, as you can see, it has left me with a pair of blackened eyes."

She hesitates. "But you're all right, otherwise?"

"I am," he assures her, wondering both why she's interested in the general state of his health, and how much longer this colloquy will continue.

"All right," she decides. "I've a room upstairs. Sixpence a night. Out by ten. You've no animals?" She glances behind him.

"I've two horses, but no dogs or cats, or anything like that."

"You look like you could use some supper, too."

This is almost too good to be true. "Goodwife, for a cold supper, I should remain your good servant, for good and all."

She smiles. "Can't afford no servants. But I *could* use a hand with one of me other guests who drank a bit too much."

"Just so long as he's not a *brawler*."

She smiles at having her own word tossed back to her. "He's just an overnight, so I can't swear to it. He's a bit mouthy, but he won't be doin' any *brawlin'* in his present condition. That's certain. He's passed out drunk in my parlor. Just need to cart 'im off to 'is room for the night."

"Shall I stable my horses before coming in?"

"Nah. Let's tuck *him* away first. His room's on this floor. It'll only take a moment."

She steps back from the door, and lets Jonathan in. He glances around. Although the curtains are a bit faded, they have the abraded look of cloth softened by frequent laundering, which speaks well of her dedication to cleanliness, if not of her financial condition.

She leads him into the parlor, where a drunkard is hunched over in the corner behind a table, snoring softly. She holds her finger to her lips, and puts the candle down on the table, illuminating the drunkard's face. Jonathan recoils.

It's Robert Poley, commonly known as "Bobby the Drunk." Several years before, this same Poley had been passed out on the floor of the Boar's Head in Eastcheap, when Nicholas Skeres and other Essex men resolved to murder Jonathan and his investigator Graves. Although Jonathan and Graves were extracted from that predicament by the armed intervention of Noah Ames and four other masked barristers, Graves died later that night, though whether from natural causes or foul play was never determined. A short time later, Poley became notorious as one of the three men who'd shared company with the playwright Christopher Marlowe on the day he was murdered.

Jonathan considers excusing himself, forsaking the siren song of room and board and going back out on the road.

But he doesn't. Whether his decision to stay arises out of gallantry, sheer fatigue, or something else, he'll never be sure. Instead, he makes the fateful decision to help the innkeeper cart this sot to his room. Besides, Poley is so inebriated, he might not awaken as he's moved, and, even if he does, he might fail to recognize Jonathan, with his swollen and blackened eyes.

The innkeeper slings Poley's left arm over her shoulder. Jonathan does the same with his right, and together they lift him off the seat. Although Jonathan expects a whiff of urine, there is none. In fact, for a drunkard, he seems surprisingly clean. Poley never opens his eyes while being assisted to his room, though he murmurs something which must be very witty, as he snickers at it. To cooperate in his transit, he slowly pedals his legs like a man keeping lazily afloat during a pleasant swim.

Jonathan uses his free hand to turn the knob and shove open the door to the room, being careful not to fling it so roughly it will strike something hard and startle Poley. They bring him over to his bed, and plop him down, face up, placing his head somewhere in the general vicinity of the pillow.

While the innkeeper removes the drunk's shoes and places them on the floor by the bed, Jonathan glances around the room by the candlelight. In the corner lies Poley's weather-beaten old trunk. Next to it, covered with fine black glove leather, lies a long, thin cylinder that piques Jonathan's curiosity, as its unimpeachably fine quality is completely at odds with everything else in the room, especially Poley.

The innkeeper leads Jonathan quietly out into the hallway, and closes the door behind him. She leads him to the front desk.

"I'm Jane Nightwork," she says, "and who might you be?"

"I'm Jonathan Porter," he replies, "from Southwark. Pleased to make your acquaintance." He's been working on an alias since the moment he decided to spend the night, to avoid having his name bandied about in case his arrival becomes a topic of conversation among the other guests. Now that he's actually spoken his false name aloud, he's pleased that it sounds even more plausible than he imagined. Although this is now the *second* lie he's told the innkeeper, he reckons he had good reason to tell both. Regardless, he's found lying entirely too easy, and hopes it will not become a habit.

"What's your occupation down in Southwark?"

"I'm footman for Lady Burlington...a very refined lady."

Goodwife Nightwork arches her eyebrow skeptically. "She *must* be, to have such a well-spoken footman."

Although he's fairly certain she's suspicious of his story, he thinks he knows how to put her at ease. "Sixpence, you say?"

She nods.

He takes a shilling from his pocket and puts it on the counter. "And will that cover the room, and also what I'm to eat tonight?"

She smiles, obviously tolerant of men who lie about their identity, at least when they pay twice what they're asked. "Aye. And what you're to eat tomorrow morning, too."

He tilts his head toward the drunkard's room. "I wonder if your besotted guest will remain for breakfast."

She shrugs as she pockets the coins. "Those what don't stink usually still have some sense about 'em. Probably eat me out o' house and home. That one'll be here past dinnertime."

"Oh? How do you know that?"

"Says his friend is meetin' 'em here for dinner. He told me his friend's name, but I forget it. Fella with a scarred face." Jonathan nods nonchalantly, as if feigning interest, when in fact a jolt just shot through his body at the mention of the scarred man, who can only be Nicholas Skeres.

Essex's chief agent, Nicholas Skeres, will be coming to this inn by noon tomorrow to meet with Poley, who likewise attends on Essex in his own small, besotted way. But there's an enormous difference between the two men. While Poley is merely contemptible, Skeres is *ruthless.* And *crafty.* As Essex has evidently dispatched Skeres to do his bidding, the errand will surely be such as to require discretion, and that means his task is *important.*

Once the horses are properly fed and stabled, Goodwife Nightwork leads Jonathan to the kitchen, and lays before him the food remaining from supper, which includes bread, a small piece of dried roast beef, and plentiful greens. It's a better supper than he could have hoped for at this late hour, and he's truly grateful. The innkeeper seems embarrassed when he takes her hand and bows in gratitude. She leads him to his room, directly above Poley's, and bids him good night.

Jonathan removes a few items of outer clothing and lays them at the foot of the bed. As he removes his boots, and lowers his head to the pillow, he fully intends to contemplate what's inside the fancy cylinder in the room below, what carefully laid plan will form the topic of the next day's dinner conversation between Skeres and Poley, and what he can do to 'toss a spanner in the wheellock.'

But before he can contemplate any such thing, he falls sound asleep.

———————◦◦✐◦◦———————

THE DOOR BURSTS open.

"Get up, you slug!" shouts Nicholas Skeres.

Jonathan bolts upright as though he's been struck. It takes him an anguished moment to realize that Skeres has entered the room *downstairs.* It's uncanny how sound can travel up a stovepipe. His heart racing, he places his feet quietly on the floor.

"How am I to trust you with anything, when you're drunk or sleepin' every minute?" demands Skeres.

Poley replies with his customary aplomb. "*Whu—?*"

"Do you know what time it is?"

Poley splutters. "Ah, uh…it's not *noon* yet, is it?"

"It's nine, and the innkeeper says you've got to get your sorry arse outta this room within the hour, or it'll cost Jake an extra day."

Jonathan blinks to clear his vision. *Nine?* Skeres is three hours early. He begins to doubt his wisdom in staying the night. *And who the devil is Jake?*

"Innkeeper says you drank three bottles of wine last night, and had to be carried in here with the help o' some footman who happened by."

Well, thinks Jonathan, *I did one thing right, lying about my identity. The innkeeper's not much for holding back information about her guests.* Careful not to make the boards squeak, he dresses quickly, leaving aside his heavy boots. In his stockinged feet, he insinuates himself into a chair by the stove, and listens intently.

"Well," says Poley, in a pout, "I don't see what business it is of hers if a man takes a drink or two."

"Or *fifty!*" Skeres shoots back scornfully, but then continues in more temperate voice. "Do you know what you're carryin'?"

"How'd y'mean?"

"You're carryin' the privates of every high-rankin' officer in this benighted kingdom." This is followed by a moment's silence. "*Ach!* Why do I even bother explainin' to the likes o' you? Just do as yer told, and stop gettin' boozed all the time!"

"What difference does it make?" asks Poley. "I thought we had another three days to get to Bridgwater. We're not due till Tuesday night!"

"Aye," says Skeres, "but we've got to be sittin' in the Rose & Crown at eleven *with the package in good condition,* or we've 'ad it. And if you lose the package, what *then*? What if that footman 'ad been a little grabby, and decided to filch the tube? *Then* what?"

"Well, he didn't," replies Poley, in a sulk.

Jonathan smacks his forehead, regretting that he lacked the foresight to "filch the tube," quite forgetting that he *still* has no idea what's in it, and *couldn't* have snatched it with the innkeeper so near at hand.

"Nah, but that's none o' *your* doin', is it? You was two sheets in the wind, and wouldn't even 'ave *known* he'd done it 'til I got here. You dolt! I'm tired o' your drinkin'. You shape up, or I'll get somebody who can do a job without jumpin' into a vat o' spirits every blessed night." Skeres becalms himself again. "C'mon. Get up. Let's go 'ave somethin' to eat. Innkeeper says it'll be ready by now. I took the private room. And why not? *Jake's* payin'!" He chuckles smugly.

Jonathan realizes this is his chance to escape unseen, perhaps his *only* chance. He tugs his boots on, waits for Poley's door to close, and counts to fifty for good measure, then opens his own door and peers down the stairs in time to see Goodwife Nightwork disappear out the front. He pulls up his hood, just in case one of Essex's men catches sight of him from the side, and, heart pounding, saunters down the stairs and out of the door at a leisurely pace, being careful not to turn his head.

Although he wishes to bid the innkeeper farewell, he cannot see her from the front of the house. He glances about as he walks toward the stables, but still she's nowhere to be seen, so he waters the horses and clops away, lamenting his uneaten breakfast, trying to make sense of what he just heard. As he reaches the main road, the sun peeks out of its hiding place behind the clouds, and the stiffening leaves susurrate in the cool, dry autumn breeze.

An hour later, he stops at a tavern to eat, and water the horses again. Before remounting, he opens his saddlebag to examine the well-worn map of "points west" provided by Andres to aid in his penitential pilgrimage. Jonathan's destination of Wells has been marked with a finely inked circle, but he has only the vaguest idea where Skeres' destination of Bridgwater lies. As he searches the map for it, he finds it less than twenty miles southwest of Wells.

Jonathan is startled to realize that Skeres and Poley are nearly certain to be on the very road he's now traveling. He turns sharply about, peering back the way he came. Although it seems unlikely they could have caught up to him (as they were in no rush), even in the bright day, a chill runs up his spine, as though they might come into view at any moment. But why should he care? He's broken no laws, and they have no way of knowing his suspicions.

But what *is* in that cylinder by Poley's trunk? What did Skeres say it contained? "The privates of every high-ranking officer in this benighted kingdom"? He laughs as he visualizes the cylinder containing numerous private parts. Obviously, Skeres was using a figure of speech. He surely meant that, should the tube fall into the wrong hands, many men would be doomed. But why use that *particular* metaphor? While such disgusting phrases are no doubt used with abandon in the vulgar speech favored by Skeres and his ilk, it probably originates with the horrific punishment meted out at Tyburn, where a convicted traitor would be "drawn and quartered," or, more precisely, hanged nearly to death, castrated, disemboweled, and cut in four pieces. *Could the tube hold evidence of high treason?*

And *who* would be at risk if the tube were lost or stolen? "High-ranking officers," Skeres had said. But what *type* of officers? After all, *anyone* holding high office is a "high-ranking officer." Yet, "high-ranking officers" seems to denote *military* officers most precisely. Could the tube contain evidence of treason by high-ranking military officers? "*All*" of them? Or, making allowance for the imprecision of careless banter, *many* of them? Shaking his head, he returns his attention to his map.

Map! Why, *of course*! Although this shoddy little map has been folded and weather-stained countless times, an *important* map would be transported *in a leather tube,* to prevent creasing, and to protect it from the elements.

He struggles to recall Noah's recent suspicion about a missing map, but finds himself unable to conjure up more than its vaguest contours. There was something about a watermark missing from one of Mountjoy's military maps. Of that, he's certain. Although Noah dismissed his own conjecture in the course of the conversation, he's been known to revive suspicions previously dismissed as overly audacious, only to find that he was quite correct in the first instance. Jonathan remounts, intending to dredge up Noah's exact sense as he rides.

He resumes his journey at a quicker pace, for several reasons. For one thing, he's become frustrated by the degree to which leading an extra horse has slowed his progress. More important, he wishes to avoid any possibility of being overtaken (or even seen) by Skeres and Poley.

Most important of all, however, is the feeling welling up in his breast that he might not merely have an *opportunity* to frustrate one of Essex's plots, but might be *duty-bound* to do so, "for Queen and Saint George," as charging English soldiers are often heard to yell.

—∘◦⟨⟨⟩⟩◦∘—

JONATHAN PASSES INTO Somerset, where the farmland begins to level out, and becomes flatter all afternoon.

He blocks the descending sun with his hand, and peers into the distance. Although dark clouds loom at the very edge of the horizon, they're quite distant, and there seems to be no wind to carry them his way.

As he approaches a pretty stream grandiosely labeled the "River Sheppey" on his map, a tavern identified as the Bunch of Grapes comes into view. It's the simplest kind of structure, its sides fashioned of sawn wood, dotted with a few small windows. He recalls from his map that only a few miles now remain between him and the earl's residence at Wells, where Jessica will be waiting impatiently.

Wishing to avoid any misstep and the additional delay it would entail, he decides to inquire which local road would best serve for the final leg of his journey, so he ties the horses off at a watering spot near the stream, and steps inside the tavern.

Four well-fed farmers sit around a worn old table near the center of the room, while the tavern keeper serves them ale at a leisurely pace. Although at first Jonathan is surprised to see any customers at all in a countryside tavern during daylight hours, he soon realizes that they've most likely completed their autumn harvest in the past few days, and now have more time on their hands than they know what do with. They turn to look at him.

The tavern keeper seems concerned. "Highwaymen?" he asks.

Jonathan just looks at him, confused.

The tavern keeper points to his own eye. "Your eyes."

Jonathan is abashed, as he has completely forgotten about his bruises since his full vision returned the previous day. He examines his reflection in a small corroded looking glass hanging on the wall. Although the pain has receded, one of his eyes is still badly misshapen, and both are black and blue.

"No highwaymen," he replies. "I was struck by a branch." He blushes at his own recurring lie, hoping they cannot detect it in the dim light. "May I ask you gentlemen some advice?"

The most corpulent replies: "So long as it's not how to handle the wench what gave you those shiners!" They laugh aloud, and Jonathan laughs along.

With some effort, and a good deal of huffing and puffing, the fat one nudges a chair toward Jonathan with his toe. "Take a seat, young feller," he says in the strange Devon speech. He's evidently from a bit further west.

The tavern keeper places a tankard of ale in front of Jonathan, who draws lustily from it, finishing nearly half at once. When he puts it down, all eyes are on him.

"So, what brings you to these parts, m'lad?" asks the tavern keeper.

"I'm footman to a lady, and I've come to fetch her back to London."

The others exchange meaningful glances, and wait attentively for Jonathan to continue.

"I was hoping you gentlemen could tell me which road would be best."

"That all depends," says one who's remained silent until now. "Where's the lady?" Something about his expression tells Jonathan that his response might garner advice about more than just the best choice of road.

"She's staying at the earl's residence in Wells."

They suddenly look away from him, and each other. One gazes at a blank wall. Another whistles softly as he studies the ceiling. Three find interesting things on the floor. "And he seemed such a *nice* lad," sighs one wistfully, as though reminiscing about the recently deceased.

"Meanin' no disrespect, young man," says the tavern keeper, 'but is she that very proper lady with long brown hair, young, thin, and…what did my Bessie call her…very *comely*?"

"Yes, that sounds like her," says Jonathan, with concern. "Why? Has something untoward befallen her?"

"Beg pardon?" says the tavern keeper.

The fat one rolls his eyes, and blurts: "For heaven's sake, Burt, don't you speak English? This here lad wants to know if the lady's all right!"

Burt seems surprised. "Oh! Well, why didn't ye just say so? *She's* all right. Those *around* her don't seem to be smilin' much, though…includin' my Bessie."

"Is Bessie the lady's maid attending upon her ladyship?"

"She's my *daughter,*" Burt says pointedly. "She's *also* a lady's maid for the earl's wife, Lady Somerset. But ever since *your* lady flew into a rage and moved into one of the outbuildings, she's out there attendin' *your* lady."

Just to be sure, Jonathan asks: "We're talking about Jessica, Lady Burlington?"

Burt nods with dismay. "We sure are! I doubt there could be two like *'er*. What's more, if you're goin' up there, you better be ready for a tussle!"

"But, I've come to *assist*!" protests Jonathan.

The tavern keeper snickers. "Don't seem to make no difference to this one." He turns serious. "My Bessie says she musta had the hardest life there could ever be, as she's just the saddest thing that's ever been. All…closed off, like. Weeps 'erself to sleep every night, I'm sorry to say." For some reason Jonathan cannot fathom, the words strike him like a dagger to the chest.

Something must have caught the tavern keeper's eye, as he steps over to the small window and looks outside warily. "Where you spendin' the night, young man?"

"Depends upon the lady's wishes. I was hoping to spend the night at the earl's, if she permits."

"*Tonight?*"

Jonathan nods.

"The way those clouds is comin' in from the west," says Burt, "I'd strongly advise against movin' on from here tonight. If you need a place, you can stay at my farmhouse across the way. I can stable and feed yer horses, and it'll cost you a lot less than an inn." He turns to the others. "And I hope *you* lot have your places shut tight. This looks to be a real tempest." The others serenely swig their ale, evidently prepared for the worst.

Jonathan downs the last of his ale, and plunks down his coin. "I'm very grateful to you, sir, but I'm afraid I can't keep the lady waiting any longer. I really must be going. Now, if you'll be kind enough to tell me the best way?"

Burt shrugs. "Just keep goin' the way you was. There's no wall around the grounds, so, when you see the big manor house, look to your right. Your lady is stayin' in the cottage at the edge of the grounds. And so's my Bessie, so you just be kind to her. You can't miss the cottage. It's got a *huge* oak in front of it. Must be as old as the earldom."

Jonathan raises his eyebrows. "Sir, rest assured I intend to be kind to everyone I meet there." He smiles wanly. "*Especially* your Bessie, for whose anticipated kindness I heartily thank her father."

The tavern keeper nods, unimpressed with Jonathan's courtliness. He opens the door, steps outside, and beckons Jonathan to follow. He leads Jonathan away from the tavern, evidently to avoid being overheard, and places his arm around Jonathan's shoulders. Jonathan can see for himself that the storm is rapidly approaching from the west.

"You know, young man, I'm not wont to be givin' advice for no reason. But, meanin' no offense, if you'll permit me to observe. You come in here lookin' like you just got the stuffin' beat out o' yer face. You've made it yer occupation to attend on a *very* headstrong lady. And you're *leavin'* when we're about to get hit with a heavy storm, when ye *could* spend the night indoors."

Jonathan nods.

Burt continues reluctantly, as though his reasoning is so manifest it ought to be unnecessary for him to go on. "Well, if you want to live anything like a full term, you're gonna have to start makin' some better choices. Know what I mean?"

Jonathan sighs, as he's already considered everything Burt just said. "I shall, sir. I assure you. After tonight." He thanks the old man, and remounts. Taking the spare horse by the reins, he canters away and glances back.

The tavern keeper is still shaking his head in disbelief as he watches Jonathan ride straight into the storm.

CHAPTER 5

ARRESTED AT TRAITOR'S gate on suspicion of murder, Francis seems about to swoon, his brow shiny with copious sweat, his face blanched with fear, his pitiable expression that of a man drowning.

Suffering his hands and ankles to be shackled by men he commanded mere moments earlier, Francis' eyes dart desperately from Sir Walter to Noah, mutely pleading for one of them to intervene. But his arrest has been personally ordered by Lord Mountjoy, who's still here, and there's nothing they can do for the present. Noah watches him led away to confinement.

Once Francis is out of earshot, Raleigh addresses Mountjoy. "M'lord, this evidence is thin, indeed."

Mountjoy draws himself up to full height. "Sir Walter, were it not forbidden to discuss the Royal Succession, I would let you know my mind more fully."

There seems something evasive about Mountjoy's formality. "M'lord," says Noah, "I assume you refer to the Act that forbids writing anything that affirms someone's right of Royal Succession. But, certainly the Act does not render it unlawful for officers to cooperate in investigating an attempted *interference* in the Succession."

Mountjoy regards him skeptically. "Is that your legal opinion, Serjeant Ames?"

"I have read the Act several times, m'lord. It is *certainly* my view, or I would not have offered it."

"And what assurance have we that Her Majesty shares your view?"

Noah glances at Raleigh, as they share the knowledge that nothing sounds quite so insolent to a general officer as a courtier's purported reliance upon the Queen's private assurance. But there's no other way to reply. "Her Majesty has assured me of such, m'lord. Were it otherwise, she would be endangered by the very Act designed to protect her."

Mountjoy seems mollified by the response, but continues to observe Noah keenly, as though contemplating his trustworthiness.

Noah thinks that perhaps Mountjoy would speak more freely in his absence. "Shall I tend to other business while your lordship and Sir Walter confer privately?"

Mountjoy shakes his head. "You may as well stay. Sir Walter, when word of this murder gets out, as it is bound to do, the 'million' will be tempted to disregard the Act. To keep it foremost in their minds, it is vital that your investigation be seen to ferret out every lead, ruthlessly."

Raleigh nods. "Does that include arresting Yeoman Warders on the flimsiest of evidence, m'lord? For that will require me to enlist more men. And who can tell whether they shall be as loyal to Her Majesty as those I've wrongly detained?"

Now, Noah wishes he *had* been dismissed.

Mountjoy holds Raleigh in a steely gaze. "Do you object to the Act, Sir Walter?"

Raleigh returns the gaze with equal conviction. "As Her Majesty has no heir apparent, it seems only prudent to prohibit the Succession from becoming a topic of correspondence or publication. At the very best, such chatter is insulting to Her Majesty, and in unspeakably poor taste. Still, as Serjeant Ames has observed, the Act does not equate idle conversation with treason. We all know *real* treason when we hear it." He looks to the horizon. "I for one believe the Act was primarily intended to prohibit correspondence between Her Majesty's subjects and any foreign potentate who might care to *meddle* in the Succession."

Mountjoy's face turns bright red. "I'm sure we're all edified by your legal scholarship, Sir Walter. Now, if you will pardon me, I shall rejoin Sir Robert in the royal quarters."

Raleigh and Noah bow low.

Sir Walter watches Mountjoy disappear from view, then speaks as though he were still present. "Bit *thin-skinned*, are we?"

"He has a great deal on his mind," says Noah. "With the murder, it's just that much more."

Raleigh ponders a moment. "He'll do fine in Ireland. He has far more sense than Essex."

"It seems as though you've been entrusted with this murder investigation."

Raleigh sighs. "So it seems. I suppose I shall have to follow the mystery of the map-room key at least as far as his lordship's home in

Dorset."

"It's not only the key for which you'll be searching. There's also the missing portion of the note."

"How do you mean?"

Noah takes from his pocket the two recovered parts of the torn note. "Where's the *rest* of this note?"

"I suppose it could be drowned in blood on the chamber floor, in which case the writing will have been obliterated."

"We must search there first to be sure, but I expect it is *not* there, and frankly I *hope* it is not, as we do not wish the trail to go cold." This is greeted with a look of confusion. "If the murderer knew nothing of the note, as I surmise, and if the remainder of the note is not now in the chamber, then it must have been torn off *before* Trenowden arrived here."

"Do you mean to suggest that, when he arrived at the Tower this morning, he had only a *piece* of the note?"

"Quite possibly," says Noah. "And if that's true, then I expect you'll find that Lieutenant Trenowden was involved in an altercation somewhere else, shortly before he came here. It was during that *earlier* scuffle that the paper was torn."

"What would the scuffle have been about?"

Noah shrugs. "Someone was probably struggling to keep the message from the lieutenant, or to wrest it away from him, if he had it already. Perhaps it was someone who wanted it kept secret, and knew Trenowden was about to divulge it. In that case, this other person may still possess the other strip of writing. If you can find the missing piece and reassemble it with the two strips we've already recovered, you'll have the complete message."

"Unless it's encrypted," suggests Sir Walter.

"Well, yes. But then, at least you'd have the whole encrypted message."

"Of what importance is it to have a complete message, if we can't read it?"

"Having the *whole* message would make it more readily decipherable, or so say people who decipher such things," says Noah. "Sir Henry Neville comes to mind. Unfortunately, he's elsewhere for the time being."

"Neville? Where is he?"

"Paris. And Her Majesty has declined to allow him to come home for the time being. He's very busy, you see, collecting a debt."

"Ah, yes. King Henri of Navarre borrowed a tidy sum from Her Majesty, didn't he? I wouldn't have accepted that ambassadorship under *compulsion.* Bloody things cost a fortune for the poor gull who gets stuck with one."

"Why, Sir Walter," says Noah mock-earnestly, "you have been reading Sir Henry's letters!"

Raleigh chortles. "Don't tell Mountjoy. He'll have me arrested." They share a quiet laugh, which is a blessed relief from the events of this accursed morning. "You seem a useful fellow, Serjeant Ames. Would you be available to travel with me tomorrow morning to Mountjoy's place in Dorset?"

"I expect I shall be unable to do so, as I am scheduled for an interview with Her Majesty tomorrow morning…unless she remains unwell. I must check with Sir Robert."

"By all means," says Sir Walter. "I shall await you outside the royal quarters. You'll need an escort to leave the Tower, in any event."

———————◦○◦———————

SIR ROBERT AND Lord Mountjoy sit in close conversation at the direct center of the opulently appointed salon in the royal quarters. Noah, who's had to pass through three hastily assembled checkpoints, patiently awaits Sir Robert's attention. It's Mountjoy who spots him first, and silently directs Sir Robert's attention to him.

"Yes, Serjeant Ames?"

"Sir Robert, I was wondering if you had word about whether Her Majesty feels well enough to see me tomorrow morning, as planned."

Sir Robert looks genuinely confused. "Serjeant Ames, how is it possible that yesterday you could read my *mind*, but now you cannot even read my *letters*?"

Noah's eyes go wide and he bows, shamefaced. He calls himself many bad names, principal among which is "idiot."

"Please forgive me, Sir Robert. My reading of your advance letter was interrupted by Sir Walter, who asked me to accompany him to m'lord's adjutant. With all the subsequent commotion, your letter quite slipped my mind."

Sir Robert nods indulgently. "Quite understandable! I'll save you the trouble of reading it. Her Majesty has firmly decided to issue the commission…that I believe you have already discussed with Sir Francis." Sir Robert glances sidelong toward Mountjoy to indicate that this last phrase had been chosen to avoid revealing any more than necessary.

"I see," says Noah.

"But, she still wants to see you tomorrow morning at nine in her bedchamber."

Noah can feel the color drain from his face. "Is Her Majesty still bedridden?" Especially because of his religious faith, his own security depends heavily upon the Sovereign's good graces and good health. It's unlikely that Noah will be indulged by the Queen's successor, to whom Noah will be just another Hebrew.

"I didn't mean to alarm you, Serjeant. Her physicians assure us she will be up in a few days. Now, will that be all?"

"Yes, Sir Robert. M'lord. Please pardon the interruption." He bows low and leaves, feeling less worthy than a sewer rat, as this is the first time he's ever heard the Queen was ill without thinking of *her* welfare before his own. He supposes it's a result of the increasing frequency of her illnesses, or perhaps he's just been harrowed by all this talk of Succession. Whatever it is, he wishes she could live forever. More selfishly, he earnestly wishes she would outlive *him*.

As he leaves the royal quarters, Sir Walter awaits him, as promised. "What is the verdict?" asks Sir Walter. "Shall Her Majesty receive her trusted counselor tomorrow morning?"

"If you mean me, then, yes," says Noah. "I'd quite forgotten, however, that I cannot leave London before making an additional visit after my audience with the Queen. Assuming I can arrange it for tomorrow afternoon, I might be at liberty the following day. Would you be willing to wait a day before going?"

Sir Walter pauses for thought. "Yes, I could wait the additional day. In fact, it would give me all day tomorrow to turn this place upside down for more clues. I assume Lord Mountjoy would approve, as it would create the *appearance* of diligence."

Noah smiles. "It must be done, in any event. If we're unable to solve this mystery, you would be severely taken to task if your search had stopped short of upending the Tower."

"Please let me know tomorrow, as soon as possible," says Sir Walter. "Your letter will surely find me here. Come. Let me escort you out personally. Wouldn't want any confusion at the gate. There are many nervous Warders just now."

"Thank you. But, please do one thing for me, Sir Walter, before you leave the Tower."

"Certainly. What is it?"

"Have a reassuring talk with Warder Francis. Being arrested for a job well done is poor thanks, indeed. He must be suffering the terrors of the damned."

———————————⟐———————————

APPROACHING THE HOUSE that afternoon, Bucklebury chuffs excitedly to see two horses tied to the post. Evidently, both are familiar to him, as he sidles up to them sociably.

Noah recognizes one as belonging to Arthur, and the other…he's not quite sure. Marie knocks on the front window, smiling broadly and beckoning him to hurry inside. Well, perhaps this day might bring a *welcome* surprise, at last. Two robust male voices greet him as he enters.

"Serjeant Ames!" says Arthur, reaching out a hand that Noah clasps at once, greeting him warmly.

The other young fellow, also tall and blond, looks quite familiar, but he simply *can't* be the person Noah thinks he is. If so, his face is quite changed, thinner and more angular. Still, it *might* be he, as Noah hasn't laid eyes on him in years.

"David?" he ventures. "David *Killigrew*?"

The young man's handsome face lights up in a smile, revealing pronounced cheekbones and deep-set dimples. "That's *'Cheerful'* to you, sir! *Someone's* been telling tales out of school. Who told you my given name, at last? Was it Uncle Henry?"

Noah regards him skeptically. "Sir Henry? He'd rather have *died*! What's worse, he enlisted every Neville and Killigrew to join in the fun at my expense, including Lady Anne. Robert Cecil, too." He wags his finger in playful admonition. "Wicked, wicked, all of you. I am *surrounded* by iniquity!"

"So, who gave it away?"

"Promise not to hold a grudge against the telltale?" asks Noah.

"Promise."

Noah leans in close to David's ear, as though to impart a secret, but says quite loudly: "The Queen of England!"

There's an outburst of astonishment and mirth. Marie pretends to be hearing the story for the first time, though Noah told it to her months ago.

"*Really?*" asks David incredulously.

"Before leaving for Paris, Sir Henry told Her Majesty that he would send her a message by horseback the following morning. She asked: 'By young *David*?' Henry looked at me, abashed, and before he could reply to her question, Her Majesty sucked in her breath and put her hand over her mouth. That's when I *knew* I had him, at last. Evidently, Her Majesty had been in on it, too, and had spoiled it quite by accident."

Arthur says in a histrionic voice, "And so you see, young *David.* To the incisive Noah Ames, the secrets of crowned heads are as nothing!"

Noah frowns. "Oh, don't talk nonsense, Arthur. Tell me. How long have you two been here at the house?"

"About an hour," says Arthur. "We expected you around four. What kept you?"

Noah's not about to spoil the mood with talk of the horrors at the Tower. "Just some late business. But what brings *you* here? Only good things, I hope. Please, sit."

Cheerful explains that he's attending Merton College, Oxford, just as Sir Henry and Noah did many years before, but that he's taken a leave of absence for the present term. As Lady Anne has been spending much time away from her Lothbury home during Sir Henry's embassage, David thinks to sojourn there.

"Then, you have some weeks without firm commitment?" asks Noah.

"Yes," replies David, "except for the next two days, which have been filled by my dear mother with agonizing social engagements that I am *strictly* forbidden to decline."

"Have you ever met Sir Walter Raleigh?" asks Noah.

Cheerful's eyebrows shoot up. "Never had I the pleasure. Why do you ask?"

"Would you be interested in accompanying Sir Walter and me to Dorset for a few days? That is, assuming he approves."

"When are you planning to go?"

Marie interrupts. "*Yes,* Serjeant Ames," she says indignantly, "when *are* you planning to go?"

"I'm sorry, dear," replies Noah. "I'd no idea until this afternoon that he wished me to accompany him. Unless Her Majesty forbids me from doing so, I shall have to go with Sir Walter to Dorset, day after tomorrow. Would you care to come along? It will probably be a week or so."

"I can't," she replies with disappointment. "With Stephen in Paris, there would be no one left to mind the store."

"Pity," says Noah. "It might have been a welcome diversion for you. Anyway, we shall see tomorrow what Her Majesty has in mind."

"Will you be needing a young barrister or two, willing to work for food?" asks Arthur.

Noah's surprised. "Do you mean to imply that both you and Andres can escape Queen's Bench right at the start of Michaelmas Term?"

"We've both been handling so many cases," Arthur explains, "we need a respite, so we plan on escaping together for a week or so, up to my family's farm in Oxfordshire, if nothing better comes along."

"Unless I'm mistaken," says Noah, absentmindedly running his thumb over the scar on his abdomen, "Mistress Ames and I once escaped London for your family's hospitality."

Arthur grins. "If you come up there again, I'll promise you better lodgings than an old, cold barn."

"Oh, it served its purpose. Tell me, what sorts of cases have been coming your way?"

"Well, we're two of the famous 'jesters,' aren't we? So, we've become 'saviors of the common man,' at least of those prosperous enough to pay our fees. Did you think Jonathan was the only one to reap notoriety out of helping you give a black eye to the basest scoundrels of London?" He leans in to Noah. "Almost no one knows that ruckus had anything to do with Essex."

"Let's keep it that way," mutters Noah, who beams to learn that they've turned their joint exploit to professional advantage, particularly as he'd feared it might have the reverse effect.

Marie claps her hands. "Well, shall we discuss it all over supper?"

David and Arthur rise, and shuffle in place. "In light of the hour, I'm afraid I can't," says David, "although I do hope that I shan't spoil my welcome by declining."

Before Marie can express her disappointment, Arthur sheepishly chimes in. "I'm sorry to say that I also have no choice but to decline this evening."

"Ah, well," she says, "we shall have to put off our merry reunion for another time. Soon, though."

"Thank you, Mistress Ames," the boys say simultaneously.

Noah pauses a moment, looking proudly at these two strapping young fellows, trying to reassure himself that he's played at least a small role in bringing them along. Then, serious matters return to mind.

"Marie," he says, "please allow me to show these two rascals to their horses. I have something to tell them."

"Certainly," she replies. "I have a few ledgers to finish, or tomorrow I shall have to recommence a lengthy set of tabulations." She stands on tiptoe to kiss each of the boys on the cheek, and returns to her study.

Noah leads them out the side door to extend their walk together.

"Listen, you two. I don't know whether I'll be going to Dorset or not. If I go, I shall leave word with Mistress Ames whether you and Andres should follow me. *If* you come," he says, looking about to make sure he's not overheard, "I want you all to be armed…surreptitiously, of course. And, for heaven's sake, do *not* let it get out that you are following me."

David looks to Arthur. "Is this how it started last time?"

Noah cuts off such talk. "*Tsk, tsk.* This is *completely* different, so don't go conjuring up dreams of derring-do. You'll only make matters worse."

"Pistols, too?" asks Arthur.

Noah nods.

Arthur chortles, and turns to David. "This is *precisely* how it started."

Noah stares at him forbiddingly, then smiles. "Off with you both. And don't forget, as far as Mistress Ames and the rest of the world are concerned, you're off on holiday."

With newfound purpose, the young men mount, give Noah an informal salute, and head back toward Gray's Inn together.

<hr>

"OH, IT'S SUCH a *shame* they couldn't stay for supper!" says Marie, emerging from her study.

"Yes," says Noah. "They're fine young lads, aren't they?"

"So much so," she says, misting up, "they make me miss my Stephen."

Noah puts his arm around her, and kisses her cheek. "They do bring him to mind, it's true. But, you *must* take comfort that he's having the time of his life in Paris."

"I suppose so," she says, pulling herself together. "Do you know what those two told me when they arrived? They said they'd actually come to speak with *me.*"

"Truly? About what?"

She sits him down on a soft chair, and takes a wooden one for herself. "Noah Ames," she begins earnestly, "is it true that you dispatched Jonathan Hawking to fetch your daughter yesterday?"

"Yes," he replies. "I was going to tell you this morning—"

"But you skulked out of here so early, you had no opportunity."

"*Skulked?* I had no intention of avoiding the topic, I assure you."

"And why did you send *Jonathan*?" she asks.

"He was very upset, and, well, confidentially…"

"He got into a drunken brawl with Gelly Meyrick?" she ventures. "And had to depart London to avoid prosecution and disbarment?"

"I see Arthur has told you, already. Marie, why the cross-examination?"

She ignores his attempted evasion. "Why was Jonathan upset in the first instance?"

Notwithstanding his awful day, Noah prepares himself to play out the role of witness, as he can see that Marie will brook no resistance. "Because, as I told you yesterday, I'd told Jonathan he could not assist me in investigating Essex."

She nods, and smiles sagely. "Now, what makes you think *that's* what he was upset about?"

"Well," he pauses, thinking back, "*Arthur* told me."

"*Did* he now? Did he not simply nod when you asked him whether Jonathan was upset about something you'd said earlier in the day?"

"Yes," he replies warily. "See here, Marie. Where are you going with this?"

"What *else* did you tell Jonathan yesterday that might have upset him?"

"Nothing. No, wait. I told him about a map. But I haven't told—"

"It's not about a *map!*" she snaps impatiently, obviously leading somewhere definite with her questioning. "What *else* did you say that might have upset him?"

Noah just sits there, open-mouthed. Marie raises an eyebrow at him inquisitively.

Still, he just sits there at a complete loss.

She shakes her head in amazement. "For the smartest man in England, you can be completely *oblivious* when it comes to some very important matters!"

He mentally catalogues the things he understands least well, and one stands out foremost. "*Women?*" he ventures meekly.

She casts him an encouraging smile.

"But what had I told him yesterday about *women*? I'd told him nothing. I—I merely told him that Jessica was in Somerset. Could *that* be it?"

"What *else* did you tell him about Jessica?"

"That she was considering marrying—"

"That's *quite* enough, Noah. Yes! You said that she was thinking of marrying, and he got upset. Now, *why* would a young man get upset at such news?"

Noah feels a complete idiot, because in fact he is still guessing.

"Because—"

"— *he's in love with her!*" she blurts out.

"No," he gasps.

"Yes," she replies wide-eyed, as though her dimwitted student has just awakened to a difficult concept. "What's more, it's difficult to believe you could have missed the signs."

"But, how was I to know?"

Marie's face is a picture of consternation. "Don't men talk to one another about such things?"

"I suppose we don't. He certainly never mentioned anything to me. Would a girl like Jessica be *interested* in someone like Jonathan?"

"How do you mean?"

"Well, he has no title, no property," reasons Noah. "He *has* an excellent reputation within the profession, but, other than that, he has only…himself."

"The heart knows no such bounds, Noah. Men and women of different station and means fall in love with each other all the time. Why, Jessica is a case in point, is she not? You've told me that her mother, as a child, trod the mud of Southwark food market—"

"As did her *father*," says Noah wistfully.

"Well, there you are! Why should Lord Burlington have wed someone of such humble origins?"

"Well…" he offers, "Jessica is quite special."

She shakes her head fondly. "How you *dote* over that girl! But do not miss my point, Noah. He not only *fell in love* with her. He *married* her! Don't you think it's high time for *Jessica* to follow her heart, instead of some strange calculus she's dreamed up, where title and property outweigh true love? Heaven knows, Lorenzo left her a title, and money enough to last a lifetime."

He sighs. "I suppose there's no line on a ledger sheet where one may account for the value of true love."

"No, indeed," she says and sits back, pleased to have made her point, "and I've prepared enough ledger sheets to know."

"I hope I have not botched things awfully by sending Jonathan to fetch her."

Marie shrugs. "We'll know soon enough." She pats his knee. "Who knows? You *may* have done the best possible thing."

He feasts his eyes on her, and feels very fortunate, indeed.

He'll talk with her tonight about tomorrow's audience with the Queen. But he cannot bring himself to spoil her mood by speaking of the day's murder at the Tower or, worse, his upcoming visit to the Earl of Essex.

CHAPTER 6

AS LIGHTNING PULSES in the lowering clouds, a whirlwind sprouts up in Jonathan's path, spinning the fallen leaves into a tight little fury, dusting him with dirt, and pelting him with tiny pebbles that sting his face and hands like so many needles. Because it takes one hand to lead the spare horse, he has no choice but to resist the impulse to shield his eyes. All he can do is turn his face away. Though not a drop of rain has fallen, already both horses snort indignantly.

When he first began this last leg of his journey, he allowed his heart to rise as he crested each hill, in the hope that the earl's manor house would come into view. After a few miles of such ups and downs, however, his better judgment resumed control, reminding him that his destination was still miles off.

There's a bright flash in the clouds. A sharp crack of thunder rumbles overhead from right to left like a cannonball across a wooden deck. His nose twitches, and the air bristles with excitement. The horses chuff, demanding greater speed. Though Jonathan wishes very much to comply, he must be careful to choose the right pace, as even the slightest tug from an animal as powerful as a horse could wrest the reins from his grasp, and cause them to become separated.

He takes a mental inventory of what he's carrying that might be damaged by a hard rain. There's the map, of course, but that's tucked firmly into his leather saddlebag, and is hardly irreplaceable. Just in case he were to be confronted by any of the road pirates known as highwaymen, he's also brought along several knives and pistols. Although he'll have to clean and oil them all after they dry out, he decides that none is likely to be put out of commission by rain.

But he also carries a fair store of gunpowder. Thus far on his journey, he's avoided fording any streams, sometimes traveling a mile or more out of his way to find a bridge instead, as gunpowder is a tricky business. One can never be sure how much moisture it will absorb before losing its special power to ignite. Immersion would surely ruin it for good. Although rain alone is unlikely to soak the powder through, he cannot risk its failing at a crucial moment. If it gets wet, he'll simply have to replace it. How he'll do that out here in God's country, he has no idea.

He risks a little speed, and the riderless horse instinctively conforms. Soon, the sky darkens further, assuming a brackish hue, and he detects the faint smell of seawater. All around him, stray bolts of lightning dart from cloud to cloud like fiery sprites, throwing pulses of thunder that boom like cannon fire. A grassy hillock appears up ahead. This time, he feels sure he's nearing the earl's residence.

As he crests the hillock, there it is, at last. He finds himself looking down on a small, manicured valley. Directly ahead is a large, beautifully maintained manor house built in the style of the day, with its decorative cross-hatching of brown-painted wooden beams over white stucco. It's surrounded by a low hedge and elaborate gardens through which runs a small brook that appears to be running dry. Well, he thinks, that's about to change in the coming deluge.

A few furlongs to the right of the manor house, behind a massive oak, is a two-story cottage in the same style. Next to it stands a long, well-roofed paddock. Although currently unoccupied, the paddock appears to be a place where horses are assembled in preparation for a hunt or race. No walled stable is visible from the hill, but Jonathan imagines it's hidden from view by the manor house.

In a moment, the sky grows dark as midnight, and he can see rain beginning to fall in the distance, rapidly approaching. He canters down toward the paddock, tightly grasping both sets of reins. Then, just as he attains the shelter of the paddock roof, all the rivers of heaven overflow their banks at once, as water dumps from the sky behind him and pounds the roof above. The horses seem mollified to have found shelter at last from the worst of the elements.

He needs to secure his own mount first, as it carries the saddlebag holding weapons and powder. He dismounts, loosely ties off the other horse to free his hands, and ties off his own mount firmly, using a strong seaman's knot, known as a "bowline," taught to him many years earlier by old Graves, who'd spent much of his youth at sea.

As he turns to tie off the other horse with the same knot, all at once the air sizzles, and a thick bolt of lightning crashes into the trunk of the great oak, frighting both horses. While Jonathan's own mount merely tests its knot, the other horse jerks itself loose from the post, and trots out of the paddock into the torrent. He runs after it.

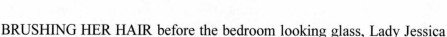

BRUSHING HER HAIR before the bedroom looking glass, Lady Jessica waits impatiently. "Bessie!" she calls. Though she hears no reply, it might have been drowned out by the rain on the roof or the persistent rumble of thunder. She goes to the head of the stairs.

"Bessie?" she calls down, a bit louder.

The lady's maid appears at the foot of the stairs, and looks up hesitantly. "Yes, m'lady?" she says, apparently distracted by something behind her.

"Have you forgotten what you went downstairs for? Or have you simply been dazzled by the tumult outdoors?"

Bessie kneads her hands anxiously. "Well, m'lady, it's pitch dark out there…but…by the lightning…I thought I saw the silhouette of something."

Jessica frowns. "What do you think you saw?"

Before replying, Bessie glances back over her shoulder. "I—I'm not sure, m'lady, but it seems to be gone now, anyways."

Jessica purses her lips impatiently. "Bessie, what did you see?"

"I thought it was a – a man," she says uncertainly. "He was—I *think* he was…chasing a *horse*."

"Tsk, tsk! Bessie, *really*! In this downpour? You must rein in your imagination. Have any letters arrived from my father?"

"No, madam. Just your afternoon note from the viscount slipped under the door, as ever."

"Bring it up to me," says Jessica. "I'm sure it's the same as yesterday's." She returns to her room, rolling her eyes. "'Your ladyship *misunderstood* my true intentions. May I not come to see you? I shall simply *die* without you.'"

Bessie climbs the stairs and hands her the envelope. She slits it open and reads silently. There's a faint knock at the door downstairs. Bessie curtsies and goes to answer it.

IT'S RAINING SO hard Jonathan can barely see, but still he tramps through the wet grass after the horse, which seems to be enjoying itself immensely, leading him a merry chase. It seemingly *wants* to be caught, but every time Jonathan approaches, it turns, clops away a short distance, and turns back to see if he'll follow yet again. After a half-dozen of these little dance steps, Jonathan gets wise, at last.

"Fine!" he says to the horse. "You want to stay out here in the rain? See if I care. If you need me, I'll be in the nice dry house. Then, I'll groom my *own* mount, and *you* can stay out here and soak all night, for all I care!"

The horse high-steps in place, and chuffs indignantly.

Jonathan turns away in a huff, and tramps back toward the paddock, where his own horse waits patiently. Crossing a mud puddle, he suddenly feels hot breath on his neck, and a meaty shove in his back. Down he goes, face first.

He flips over rapidly and wipes the muck from his eyes, preparing to face his attacker. But there's only the horse, who now waits patiently, reins dangling, tail swishing.

Jonathan mutters under his breath, cursing all horse-kind, and leads his equine assailant to the shelter of the paddock. He ties the horse off (securely, this time), and, despite his earlier threat of neglect, wipes it down with a rag he finds in a saddlebag. As he has no brushes or proper grooming equipment, that simply will have to do for now.

He senses the faint odor of charred wood, but can see that the ancient oak has taken little hurt from the lightning. He shudders to think how much damage *he* would have suffered from such a bolt, and resolves to seek the shelter of the cottage without further ado. But there's another pool of mire right by the front door, and the soles of his boots are slippery from the grass.

He falls face first again. Thoroughly exasperated, he raises his face out of the puddle, and, with a muddy knuckle, knocks feebly at the base of the front door, which promptly swings open on a warmly lit foyer. Lightning flashes, and a plump maidservant looks down, greeting him just as he might have expected.

She screams.

"What is it?" shouts Jessica from the top of the stairs.

"Ach! I'm afeard it's a *mudperson*, m'lady!"

Still prostrate, Jonathan speaks softly to avoid frightening the girl further. "*Bessie*, I presume?"

"O, Lor' bless me!" shouts Bessie, recoiling in horror. "*It knows my name!*"

It? Jonathan rises slowly to his knees. "I know your name simply because—"

"*Step out of the way, Bessie!*" commands Jessica, who has evidently flown down the stairs, and now stands only a few feet behind the lady's maid.

Bessie looks behind her, gasps, and darts aside.

There, at the base of the staircase stands the beautiful Lady Jessica, her silky brown hair flowing girlishly down her shoulders onto her lithe frame. And Jonathan would feel nothing but joy in seeing her, were it not for the two-foot-long flintlock pistol she has aimed at his chest.

"Don't shoot!" he pleads. "It is *I*! Jonathan Hawking!"

Jessica cocks her head incredulously. "You're not...Jonathan Hawking!"

"Yes," he persists. "Don't you recognize me?"

By the suspicious look on her face, she certainly does *not* recognize him. "No, you're not. What would Hawking be doing in Somerset?"

"Your father sent me."

She cocks her head again. "Why would my father send Jon Hawking here?" she asks, and then, incensed, proceeds to answer her own question, gesticulating with the gun. "Oh, of *course*! Not for a moment can the *great* Noah Ames excuse himself from the Queen's court! Not even to protect his only living daughter from a fate worse than death!"

"*I* can protect you!" protests Jonathan.

"You? *Protect* me?" she says with a short laugh, pointing the pistol at his disheveled form. "From whom? The other *mudpeople*?"

"Would you be so kind," he urges her quietly, "as to put the pistol down?"

She looks at the gun as though she's forgotten she was carrying it, uncocks it, and removes her finger from the trigger, which is a great relief. Jonathan stands up, revealing just how muddy he's become.

"Yes, of course," says Jessica. "I have quite forgotten myself." She turns to Bessie, who has reappeared now that the pistol is disarmed. "Bessie, please bring this fellow indoors, and—"

"Oh, but mum," protests Bessie, "I *can't* bring him in this way! He'll make such a mess, I'll lose my position!"

Jessica takes another look at Jonathan's muddy form, and shakes her head in exasperation. "Oh, go 'round back. Bessie will let you into the mud room, and get you cleaned up. How *ever* did you get so filthy?" Unwilling to stay for an answer, she brushes away her own question, and stomps into another room, muttering under her breath.

As Jonathan goes around to the rear entrance, he stops for a moment in the pouring rain and does his best to wash off the worst of the mud, especially from his hair. By the time he reaches the door, Bessie awaits him with rags cut from old towels and clothing. She leads him in by the elbow, and sits him on a chair next to the door.

As she begins to towel off his head, he restrains her by the wrists, smiles, and gently takes the towel from her. "Thank you very much, Bessie. But, as you can see, my eyes are tender, and one is quite swollen. Please permit me to do that part." She nods, and he dabs his eyes with the towel.

Bessie takes out a small comb and, as she combs his hair straight back off his face, seems quite pleased with what she's found. "My, my! I would never have guessed there was such a fine-looking young gentleman under all that muck!"

He scrapes the mud from under his fingernails. "Oh, it's my custom," he says. "I appear at every unfamiliar home covered in mud, just so people will remark how much better I look when I'm cleaned up."

At first, Bessie appears to credit his remark, but quickly realizes he's having her on. She lets out a pleasing laugh. There's a knock at the side door leading to the manor house.

"Uh, oh," she intones. "That would be the viscount! I'd better answer the door before m'lady does. Or hand him his head, she will." She scurries off, leaving the mudroom door wide open behind her, providing Jonathan with a view out onto a central hallway lined with doors.

Jonathan continues to clean up, as he listens in on the conversation.

"Oh, but m'lord," he hears Bessie plead, "m'lady has given *strict* instructions that I'm not to admit *anyone* under *any* circumstances."

"But this is my family's *house!*" protests a youthful baritone.

"That's all right, Bessie," Jessica pronounces from upstairs. "As I shall be leaving anon, kindly show Viscount Wellston into the parlor." She slams her door.

The next voice is the viscount's. "What was all that ruckus?" he asks Bessie. "That scream sounded like you. Are you quite well?" Overcome by curiosity, Jonathan peers through the open doorway, and finds himself looking down the hall at a young man who's looking right back at him. The man is about his own age, perhaps thirty, and impeccably dressed, as though for a stylish hunt. He has dark brown hair combed straight back, bright blue eyes, and a well-proportioned face, though to Jonathan he seems a bit foppish. "Who the devil are you?" he asks Jonathan.

Just then, Jessica appears behind the man, and walks right past him into the mudroom. "Viscount Wellston, permit me to introduce Jonathan

Hawking—"

Jonathan shoots to his feet and bows, speaking quickly. "Good evening, your lordship. As Lady Jessica has told you, I am Jonathan Hawking, her father's *footman,* and shall be assisting her ladyship on her journey home." He glances at Jessica, hoping she'll take the hint and play along.

"A common footman?" mutters the viscount dubiously and turns to Jessica. "Is this whom your father sends to escort you home? Why, I could have provided someone of equivalent station *days* ago!"

Jessica holds up her hand. "I have no further need of your assistance or your *attentions*, your lordship. Goodman Hawking is quite sufficient to protect me on my way!" She marches out of the mudroom toward the parlor.

Wellston hesitates before following her. He turns to Jonathan. "Protect her? From *whom*?"

Jonathan shrugs. "Mudpeople?" he ventures.

The viscount scowls. "*Ach!* Are they on the grounds *again*?" He walks out speaking loudly, as Jessica is now in the parlor. "See here, Jessica. This fellow's services, while I do not doubt…" His voice trails off as he leaves the hallway and enters the parlor. As soon as he does so, however, Jessica emerges the very way he went in, and crosses the hallway into a room on the opposite side, with him in tow.

Wellston pleads with her repeatedly, but every time he begins to make his case, she marches out of whatever room they're in, making it clear she has no intention of hearing him out. After a few minutes of this, she finds her way back to the mudroom, and shuts the door behind her—right in the viscount's face. She regards Jonathan curiously, and whispers. "My father's *footman*? What are you *thinking*?"

Before Jonathan can reply, Wellston opens the door sheepishly, and comes in. "But *when* are you planning to leave?" he asks. "I don't know why you must leave at all."

Jessica turns on him dramatically, her eyes wide, nostrils flaring. "Oh, but m'lord, you know *precisely* why I must leave!" Wellston's face reddens, and he avoids Jonathan's gaze. "As for *when* I shall leave? Why, *tonight*! This very instant! My trunks are all packed in the cart, and I shall leave at once!"

"But, can you even *do* that? In a thunderstorm?" He looks to Jonathan for help, but Jonathan is careful not to provide him with so much as a change in expression.

"Oh!" Jessica exclaims. "I would hazard far more than a mere tempest to escape *you,* m'lord. Now, kindly leave this house at once! You may re-enter it once I have gone. Rest assured, I shall ne'er darken your door again!"

Wellston is obviously at a loss. Then, his face lights up as though something brilliant has occurred to him. "I shall follow you to London in a few weeks. Perhaps you will have cooled down by then. I shall write to let you know I'm coming."

"And when you do," she shoots back, "I shall see that Ludgate is shut to bar your entry, m'lord. And don't think I can't do it. Do you know who my father is?"

"*Your* father?" he exclaims. "*My* father's the Earl of Somerset!"

She points her finger at his chest and stands on her toes to meet his gaze on his own level. "And my father is the Queen's own barrister! You would do well not to forget that. Her Majesty privately gave me advice some years ago, which I would have done well to heed, for then I would not have come at your dear mother's call." She puts her hands on her hips. "In fact, if you follow me to London, Her Majesty shall surely hear of it, and you shall find the way barred by more than just a *gate*, I assure you!"

Without shifting her gaze so much as an inch, she extends her hand to Bessie, who has slunk into the mudroom with a man's hat in hand.

"Bessie?" says Jessica. "The viscount's hat, please!"

Jessica's eyes never waver from Wellston's, her color high, her incensed silhouette set in stark relief against the black mudroom door, her elegant jawline tautly drawn. Bessie curtsies sheepishly and hands the hat to Jessica, who presents it to the viscount dismissively. "Good evening, m'lord!"

Wellston stands defiant at first, while the others regard him expectantly. He's incensed, but ultimately shows the good sense to accept his hat and say nothing. He grunts, glowers at each of them (in descending order of station, of course), and storms out of the cottage, slamming the door behind him.

Jessica turns to Jonathan, and sighs. "Well, I suppose I've put my foot in it. We can't stay the night now. He'll probably have the magistrate come to evict me before dark."

Jonathan shakes his head. "Are you jesting? He'd rather *give* you this house than see you leave it. He looked quite smitten to me." Bessie nods in agreement. "But you're right about having to go. To stay the night would defeat the whole purpose of your masterful performance."

"Bessie," says Jessica, "I should like to speak with Master…*Goodman*

Hawking privately, if you would be so kind."

"One moment, please," says Jonathan. "Bessie, can you tell me the next time the earl will dispatch a messenger to London?"

"You mean, to deliver letters and such?"

"Yes," says Jonathan. "I must send an urgent letter to Lady Jessica's father in Holborn."

Bessie counts days on her fingers. "You're in luck," she says. "The earl will send a courier tomorrow noon. He sends someone twice a week, like clockwork, so there's always at least two men on the road."

Jonathan nods, and takes an angel from his pocket. "Do you suppose *this* could persuade the courier to come to us, a few miles from here, before heading to London?"

Bessie looks at the coin, and her eyes open wide. "Lor' bless me, goodman. For that much, I'd go meself. Oh, but you don't have to give him such a large vail. If he gets the letter while he's still here, he'll carry it for a shilling. Why don't you give me the letter, and I'll make sure of it?"

Jonathan glances at Jessica. "Because it's not been written yet."

Jessica regards him askance. "Why not?"

He squirms. "Because I don't know what it's to say."

"Bessie," says Jessica, "please give the courier the coin, and tell him we shall send instructions where he may find us in the morning." Bessie curtsies, and closes the door behind her. Jessica turns to Jonathan. "If you don't know what the letter's to say, how can you know it's important?"

"M'lady—" he begins.

"*Please,* Jonathan," she says impatiently. "You're no footman, and we've known each other for years. Call me 'Jesse' in private."

Until now, he's actually been put at ease by the formality between them, as he's always known that the moment he thinks of her as a friend, he'll want her as a lover. As he now does. "*Jesse,* then. I must send Serjeant Ames our itinerary."

She seems puzzled. "That should be quite simple. You need simply tell him where we intend to stop along the way, and when we expect to arrive in London."

"That's just it. I don't know *when* we'll get to London, assuming we'll even travel together."

"Whatever do you mean?" she demands.

He runs his fingers through his damp hair, preparing for her tirade. "While I was traveling here," he says, "I believe I saw two of Lord Essex's attendants transporting a stolen map."

"I see," she says contemplatively, "but wouldn't that rather be the concern of the person from whom the map was *stolen*?"

"It's the concern of *every* Englishman, as I believe it to be a *military* map being smuggled out of the country to aid the enemies of England."

Her large brown eyes go even wider. "Did you see the map in the possession of these men?"

"No," he confesses.

Jessica turns to him with a quizzical expression. "Then, how do you know they even *have* it?"

"They're carrying a leather cylinder of a type I have oft seen used to transport maps."

She regards him skeptically. "But that could contain *anything*: Legal documents, land maps, and whatnot. Tell me: How do you even know the map was stolen?"

"That's just it," he says abashedly. "I don't."

She's starting to simmer again. "Let me understand. You're going to write to my father saying that, instead of escorting me to London as promised, you intend to follow two of Essex's men on the *chance* that a cylinder they're carrying contains a military map that you're unsure has even been *stolen*?"

"That's about the size of it," he says with resignation.

She stares at him incredulously. "Have you taken leave of your *senses*? I mean, even apart from your responsibility to my father and myself, you could be chasing a *phantom*! Who told you the map was stolen?"

"Your *father* did, a few days ago, although it was largely surmise on his part." He has no intention of telling her that Noah dismissed such surmise. There will be time enough later for humiliation, if he's wrong.

"But *where* do you think the map is being smuggled off to?"

"As it shows the location of military installations in Ireland and as it's being taken west, I fear it may be headed to the Irish rebels."

"Whose map is it?"

He's about to admonish her about secrecy, but decides against it, as seriousness is already etched into her expression. "It belongs to Lord Mountjoy," he says, "the new commander of Her Majesty's forces in Ireland."

She regards him thoughtfully. "Have you any powder?"

"*Gun*powder?" he ventures.

"No. *Face* powder, you sot! Of *course* gun powder!"

He smiles. "I have sufficient gunpowder...you *pip*!"

Her mouth drops open. She gasps, and tries to slap him playfully, but he restrains her wrists, and she struggles to break free as they laugh together.

"Oh!" says Bessie, who's walked in on them and gone red in the face. "I beg your pardon, madam." She curtsies, and turns away.

"What did the courier say?" asks Jessica, binding a lock of her hair that's come loose.

Bessie turns back primly and averts her eyes. "He said he needs to have the letter tonight, because he's been instructed to leave first thing in the morning. If that's inconvenient, he's offered to return the vail."

"Never mind the money," interjects Jonathan. "You may tell him he'll have the letter within the hour."

Bessie curtsies and leaves.

"What shall you write?" asks Jessica.

"That depends in part upon you," Jonathan replies. "I could leave you at Bessie's father's farm, where you'd be comfortable for a few days. But *I* must be at the Rose & Crown in Bridgwater by eleven in the evening, day after tomorrow. I overheard Essex's men saying they'd be meeting someone there at that time. If it turns out I was wrong about the map, I could come straight back and escort you home."

"And if it turns out you were *right*?"

"If so, or if I'm unable to *determine* whether I was right or wrong, I should have to follow them and could not return to you. That is not something I would wish, you understand, but I would have no choice." He sighs. "If you wish, I can ask your father to send someone else to the farm to fetch you. It would take some additional days for them to arrive, I'm afraid, for which I'm truly sorry." He looks down on his sodden boots. "If I'm proven a fool, Jesse, it would be neither the first time nor the last. But I could not live with myself if I were to learn that I'd allowed my fear of embarrassment to lead to the slaughter of hundreds, perhaps thousands, of English soldiers or, worse yet, to an invasion of England herself, and a bloody papist inquisition."

Jessica stands erect, proud and stern. "I shall come with you."

Jonathan's heart races, as he fantasizes about this angel accompanying him on what he expects to be an otherwise lonely, perilous, and losing fight. But, what is he thinking? Noah will surely *strangle* him if he brings Jessica along. What if she's captured, hurt, or killed? Noah would never forgive him, and he could never forgive himself.

He shakes his head. "I'm afraid it's quite out of the question."

"Goodman Hawking, you are a cheeky footman, indeed!"

"But you would be helpless!" he pleads. "Do you even know how to shoot?"

"Why do you suppose I asked about your supply of gunpowder?"

"And ride?"

"Mistress Ames has taught me to ride faster than you men. That's certain!"

"What if something…untoward were to happen to you? That would be my responsibility."

"No, that's where you're wrong. It would be *my* responsibility, for having volunteered. Why do you men always parcel out amongst yourselves the responsibility for a woman's choices? Does it help you to feel you're in control?"

"You shall not go!" he says resolutely.

"Yes, I shall!" she shoots back. "And if you will not bring me with you, then I shall follow you all alone, though I be taken by highwaymen and put to all manner of ill use."

Whether said in jest or not, this cuts him to the quick, and he shoots to his feet in alarm. Placing his hands firmly on her shoulders, he looks into her eyes. "No! No!"

"Why, Jonathan!" she says, taken aback. "I didn't mean to upset you."

Although he knows she'd be safest at the farm, he cannot stand the thought of her being outside the scope of his protection. He drops his hands to his side and turns away. "If you're to go with me," he says at last, "you must obey me unquestioningly, or you'll get us both killed. You have no experience with these people. I do."

"Tell me. Did you get your black eye from your 'experience' with these people?"

"Not with *them,* but with their confederate."

"When?"

"Just before coming here."

She regards him suspiciously, and places her hands on her hips once again. "Did my father send you to fetch me as punishment for fighting with Essex's men?"

"Of course not. That's ridiculous!" There slips the easy lie again.

"But he did send you here to get you out of London, didn't he?"

Jonathan nods curtly. "Well? Do I have your word that you shall obey me unquestioningly in all matters of safety?"

She considers a moment, then nods. "If that's what it takes, yes."

"Have you any writing paper?"

"Reams."

"Two sheets should do. Let's get started. The storm has passed, and daylight is wasting."

CHAPTER 7

IN THE HUSHED anteroom to the Queen's bedchamber, Noah is the only living soul waiting to be admitted to the royal presence, which is hardly what would ordinarily be expected, as news has gone out that Her Majesty has fully recovered from her illness.

Because of yesterday's murder at the Tower, however, there's no bustle of obsequious courtiers at Nonsuch Palace. Almost no one outside the royal household has been admitted to the grounds. Instead, Yeoman Warders roam the grounds in stern-faced groups of twos and threes.

The bedchamber door swings open, and three black-robed physicians file out, paying Noah no heed, their dour faces unreadable. His eyes follow them through the anteroom and out into the hallway.

"Serjeant Ames?" says a pretty young lady-in-waiting in the bedchamber doorway.

"I am Serjeant Ames," he confirms.

She curtsies. "Her Majesty will see you now."

He rises, and enters the darkened chamber. The lady-in-waiting closes the door from outside, leaving him alone with the Queen.

Of the dozens of bedchambers scattered about the castle, this is the one to which the Queen commonly escapes for undisturbed rest. But on the few occasions Noah has been here, he's never felt at ease, for, even on the sunniest of days, the chamber is a dark red he associates with death. Although it's beautifully appointed, it's even smaller than his own bedroom in Holborn, lending it a cloistered feel. The moldings, furniture, and flooring are of a dark brown so uniform they might have been stained by the same artisan on the same day, their fine woodgrains so similar they might have been cut from the same oak. Further sucking the life out of the little chamber are thick maroon drapes and wall hangings.

Queen Elizabeth lies in her four-poster bed, her back propped up against several pillows in stately fashion. To her side, a small window lets in a scant ray of sunlight that strikes her hand and seems to pierce her white papery skin, lending it a pinkish cast. Although she's still abed, her hair and face are made up as though for a meeting of the Privy Council.

He approaches the foot of the bed, where he'll be better lit than in the doorway. "It is good to see you, Majesty."

She smiles. "Is that all? Not 'it is good to see you looking so *well, Majesty*'?"

He smiles. "Truthfully, ma'am, I can barely see you in here, it is so dark. I do not doubt you look well, but whether you're looking well or no, it does my heart good to look upon you, knowing you are *feeling* better."

"Ah, my true Hebrew baron!" she says fondly, and coughs.

"As you know, Majesty, I covet no title, and would be of little use to you if I were competent to hold one. While some of your courtiers have no idea whether they can trust me, they can at least rest assured that my religion disqualifies me as their rival for royal favor."

She nods. "I know it well. Sit down, Noah. I have a favor to ask of you."

He sits on a hard-backed chair by her bedside. "I am yours to command, Majesty."

"And yet, in this matter, I choose not to command. Rather, I ask a favor you may be loath to grant, in light of your wife's strong feelings on the subject of…Lord Essex."

"I am yours in all things, madam. Please, say."

"I wish you to investigate Essex's conduct of England's military adventures and to report back only to me. I wish to know, not only what you have been told by others, but whether, in your heart of hearts, you believe his lordship can ever again be entrusted with command."

Although she almost certainly knows that Bacon has broached the subject with him, evidently she expects Noah to behave as though he's hearing fresh news. This little dance of mincing steps is not uncommon between them, in fact is more the rule than the exception.

He nods gravely. "Your Majesty is well aware of the history of…disagreement between Lord Essex and myself."

"Utterly. But it is of no import. I have it on good authority that you are the *only* courtier I may trust to give me the unvarnished truth, regardless what it may cost you."

Noah smiles. "May I ask the name of the admirer of whom you speak?"

"Why, Lord Burghley, of course! May he rest in peace. You *are* aware that I nursed him through his final illness?"

"I know it well, madam. And if there is a more exalted way to depart this earth I cannot imagine what it might be."

She smiles, and coughs again. "Burghley held you in high regard, Noah. But he had a keen eye for your flaws, as well."

"Majesty, a *blind* man could see my flaws, and Lord Burghley was far from blind."

"He said you were the proudest man in England, and that, on those occasions when the Good Lord told the Hebrews they were a stiff-necked people, He had *you* specifically in mind."

"Me?" He scratches his head. "You teach me of myself, Majesty. I would not have attributed the sin of pride more to myself than to another man. Besides, despite my appearance, I assure you I am not old enough to have been present during the times recorded in the Old Testament. Indeed, I was but a small boy when Jesus performed those deeds recorded in the New."

She purses her lips in a restrained smile. "He also told me that you could never find it in your heart to forgive him for kneeling before Lord Essex in seeking his help to be restored to my good favor."

Noah turns his face away.

"Ah," she says, "then it is true."

"It was never within me to *withhold* forgiveness from Lord Burghley, Majesty. He was my benefactor without question, and Your Majesty's most devoted servant. Yet, it is true that I have rarely been so upset with anyone in my adult life as with him upon that occasion."

"Did you tell him that you forgave him?"

Noah can feel his face redden. "As his actions demeaned only himself, Majesty, he needed no forgiveness from me. Yet, I will admit, I never told him that I forgave him for so debasing himself, which I am ashamed to admit to you now." He sighs heavily.

"No matter. Next time you pray, confess your sins, and beg his forgiveness. Heaven knows, I have done so many times with regard to my late sister of Scotland."

"Oh, madam! You cannot doubt that she left you no practical choice in the matter."

"Well," she sighs, "Mary Queen of Scots is dead. And on my writ, however badly handled."

"I shall certainly pray for Lord Burghley's forgiveness, Majesty, and I thank you for your spiritual counsel." She nods. "As I am to investigate Lord Essex's conduct, I shall need a commission providing me access to the Lord Admiral and Lord Mountjoy, also Sir Walter Raleigh, and even Lord Essex himself."

She takes a sealed paper from the tabletop beside her bed, and hands it to him. "Here is your commission. You may speak with Lord Essex whenever you wish, *if* he deigns to grant you an audience, but do not discuss with him any matter within the scope of your commission until you have spoken first with everyone else of import. I do not wish his wiles to color your perceptions."

"Yes, ma'am. Now that I have agreed wholeheartedly to accept this commission, may I ask a return favor of Your Majesty?"

She regards him curiously.

He clears his throat. "There was a murder yesterday at the Tower—"

Her eyes go wide, and she gasps. "Oh, I know it! I heard you were present when the body was found! How awful!"

He nods. "Yes, Majesty, and Sir Walter has taken charge of the investigation. He wishes me to accompany him to Lord Mountjoy's manor in Dorset tomorrow to assist him in the investigation. I was wondering…"

She nods and chuckles. "You may accompany him, Serjeant Ames, but prepare yourself to be peppered with questions about the Old Testament and Hebrew history. He wishes to write the definitive text of such matters in the English Language."

"Really?"

"Oh, yes," she assures him, and turns serious. "But I *command* you to take all precautions to defend yourself from those who wish Sir Walter's investigation to fail in its essential purpose. I find myself with few enough trusted counselors, as is the plight of many aging princes. I do not wish to have need to give out another commission, such as I have given you today. Now, if that is all, you may go, and godspeed."

He looks fondly upon her one more time, and bows out of the room.

———— ❧ ————

AS NOAH ACCEPTS Bucklebury's reins from the palace stableman, he spots Yeoman Gardner among the Warders, and tips his hat. The old man smiles and bows in return.

"Serjeant Ames!" cries Sir Francis Bacon from across the courtyard. "Permit me to ride out with you!"

Noah nods and waves. As Bacon is already on horseback, Noah mounts, and awaits his approach. The palace gate creaks open before them, surrounded by Yeoman Warders whose numbers seem to have multiplied during Noah's brief visit.

"Bound for Richmond Palace?" asks Sir Francis, drawing his horse alongside Bucklebury.

"I'm afraid not. Are *you* bound for Richmond?"

"Yes. I'm going in advance, to make sure all is in readiness for Her Majesty. Most of these beefy young Warders will be escorting her there in a day or two." They pass out through the gate, which swings closed behind them, and there are several sharp cracks of metal against metal, as bolts are drawn and locks snap shut on the opposite side. "Can't be too careful nowadays."

"No one ever regretted his own prudence," observes Noah. "Unfortunately, you and I shan't be traveling together very far today. I'm bound for London."

"Yes, I see. Well, I shall take my own road in a mile or so. But I have something to tell you...privately, and I thought this might be a fit occasion." They jog down the path through a thick wood toward the main road.

"Yes?" Noah prods, as Bacon seems to be having trouble finding the right words.

"You know, of course, that Her Majesty and Lord Essex have common ancestors?"

Noah expects that Sir Francis is about to warn him that the Earl of Essex believes himself to be descended from King Henry the Eighth, something Noah learned from Lord Burghley years before in sworn confidence. Unsure how to behave, he decides to allow Sir Francis to reveal his confidence at his own pace. Noah begins by saying what is commonly believed. "I believe Her Majesty's mother, Queen Anne Boleyn, was sister to Essex's great grandmother, Mary Boleyn. That would make all forbears of those two sisters common ancestors of the Queen and Lord Essex." When Bacon does not answer at once, Noah's face reddens. "Did I make a hash of those relations? Please forgive me. You know, it's really not—"

"No, no," says Bacon reassuringly. "You are quite correct. The family tree you have recited is accurate...as far as it goes."

"Have I missed something?"

"No," say Sir Francis. "That is...*yes,* but nothing that has not been missed by countless others before you, because it has been kept secret all these years."

Noah nods patiently. Among Jews, claims of special genealogy are regarded as supercilious, except that it seems important for each Jew to know whether he or she is a direct descendant of Aaron of the Bible, or is otherwise descended from the priestly class, known as "Levites." Not so among the high-born of England, where competing claims to the throne can turn on a single degree of kinship, and contention between warring houses can decide whether the realm will be torn to tatters.

"What have we all missed?" asks Noah.

"I must forewarn you that what I'm about to tell you is the best guarded secret in England. Do I have your word you shall never repeat it to anyone?"

"You have it."

"Not even to the lovely Mistress Ames?"

"I swear that I shall not attribute it to you, even if it's something she and I already suspect," confirms Noah.

"Fair enough. I have no way of knowing whether this is true or not, but both Her Majesty and Essex believe it. And the information evidently came down to them from separate sources." He turns to Noah. "Her Majesty's father was Lord Essex's great grandfather."

Noah tugs on the reins, bringing Bucklebury to a halt. "Mary Boleyn had an illegitimate child by Henry the Eighth?" asks Noah.

Bacon turns his mount to face Noah, and pulls to a stop. He nods. "So *they* both believe. The child's name was Catherine Carey. Her eldest daughter was Lettice Knollys, Lord Essex's mother."

Noah continues to play the student. "Is that why Her Majesty banished Lettice Knollys from court forever, when it was discovered she had secretly married the Queen's favorite, Robert Dudley?"

"Well," Bacon reasons, "Lettice married the man the Queen *wanted* to marry (but could not, for political reasons), which I suppose would be quite enough to throw *any* woman into a blind rage. *Aggravating* that offense was that Lettice had been Her Majesty's dearest friend since youth. And, it must have been especially hurtful that Dudley's thrust to marry into the Tudor line had been deflected into its *illegitimate* line."

"So, all through his youth," says Noah contemplatively repeating his response to Lord Burghley years ago, "Essex was fired with the belief that the blood of the English lion courses through his veins."

Bacon smirks. "As you can see, any further analysis could run afoul of the Act forbidding discussion of the Royal Succession. But I thought it might be important for you to know that in your future dealings with Lord Essex."

Noah bows his head respectfully. "I shall bear this important information in mind in future. Thank you so much, Sir Francis, for providing it to me."

"You're most welcome, Serjeant Ames," says Sir Francis. "It might help you to understand some of Lord Essex's...attitudes." He turns and peers the way he was heading before he stopped. "Ah, I see we have come to a parting of the ways. I bid you good day, Noah."

"And you, Sir Francis."

With that, Bacon shakes the reins, and proceeds on a path leading northwest, while Noah heads due north. As their paths diverge, Noah considers Bacon's motive in telling him something he already knew about Essex's vaunted opinion of his own birthright, and realizes that he was trying to do him a real service. Sir Francis was telling him (or unwittingly *reminding* him) that, because of the special relationship between the Queen and Essex, an accurate report highly critical of Essex might have the perverse effect of alienating the Queen and winding up in the dustbin.

Noah smiles. Surely, Bacon must assume that he's made Noah's commission seem a near-hopeless endeavor, requiring godlike discretion. Little does he know that Noah already held that view of his thankless commission. Perhaps it's only his imagination, but he thinks he can hear Bacon laughing in the distance.

<hr />

NOAH STOPS ONCE along the way to pen a note informing Sir Walter that he'll be at liberty to travel to Dorset tomorrow. He'll send it by messenger upon returning home, should he be so fortunate as to secure Essex's cooperation.

As Noah trots up to York House, he has to wend his way through a throng of Essex's supporters, who eye him warily. The nearer he approaches the door, the more his heart sinks. Although he's never before had a private encounter with Lord Essex, their few *public* encounters have gone badly, indeed.

He first met Essex outside The Rose theater, immediately after the murder of Marie's first husband, which Essex falsely claimed to have witnessed. Their next encounter took place a few months thereafter, when Essex threw a party at the Wanstead hunting lodge, at which he made an abortive attempt to publicly humiliate Noah, but wound up embarrassing himself instead.

Then, after several months during which Noah was threatened, harassed, and assaulted by Essex's attendants, Essex seized upon the occasion of a clemency hearing at Richmond Palace to challenge Noah's right to practice law, publicly disclosing his Jewish faith, and drawing a sword against him in open court. When the Queen chose that moment to make her presence known, she ordered Essex's hand chopped off, which it would have been, had not Noah begged her to exercise mercy.

The last encounter took place about six years ago. Although Noah and Essex have not spoken since, they have peaceably occupied the same room on several state occasions, where Essex's part was central, and Noah's peripheral and silent, or nearly so.

Noah cringes to find himself now in need of Essex's cooperation in saving Jonathan's legal career, and is highly uncertain how he'll be received.

As he prepares to hand off Bucklebury to the stableman, the Lord Keeper's footman emerges from the house, and bows respectfully.

"Serjeant Ames?"

"That I am," he replies. "Did the Lord Keeper Egerton receive my note this morning?"

The footman nods. "He did, sir. Lord Egerton regrets that he had no choice but to travel abroad today."

Noah is crestfallen, for if he's unable to gain access to Essex today, he will need to remain in London until he can do so, as he simply cannot allow Jonathan to be disbarred without doing everything possible to avoid it. "Has Lord Egerton left word whether I am to be admitted to m'lord of Essex during his absence?"

"He has, sir," the footman says, "and assures you that he has no objection to your seeing the earl…assuming the earl will see *you*." He smiles impishly.

This is a positive step, albeit only the first in a two-step dance. The Lord Keeper is, in a sense, Essex's jailer, so that his consent to Noah's visit is necessary. But, even though it's been obtained, the prisoner is under no obligation to receive Noah or any other visitor.

Still holding Bucklebury's reins, Noah asks: "And has Lord Essex granted me leave to visit with him this afternoon?"

"He *has*, Serjeant," says the footman agreeably, now that the dance is done. "If you will follow me." Noah releases the reins, and Bucklebury is led off to the stables.

The footman leads Noah up the steps to the main entrance, and then to a separate wing devoted exclusively to its singular high-born prisoner. Several weavings of Essex's distinctive tangerine-and-cream livery grace its entrance. Stopping before a heavy wooden door, the footman knocks discreetly.

"Enter," says a voice from inside, and the door swings open onto a large oaken study in which the Earl of Essex sits behind a massive desk. A long letter lies open on the desktop, tightly scrolled at the bottom. "Thank you, Samuel. You may go." The footman bows and leaves. Noah's eyes lock onto the earl's.

Essex's face is impassive and unreadable. His cheeks are hollow, and his slender frame has thinned to the point of gauntness. He wears his doublet unbuttoned, as his abdomen becomes famously swollen during times of severe adversity.

"Good e'en, m'lord," says Noah, bowing low, breaking the silence. "Thank you for taking time to see me."

Essex laughs quietly. "It's not as though I had to make time between my many visitors—as Her Majesty allows me none." He inks a quill pen, and signs at the foot of the letter before him. He blots his signature and sits back. "Please, take a seat. Would you care for a glass of wine?"

"No, thank you, m'lord," says Noah, taking a seat across the desk. "I have been traveling all day, and would probably fall asleep in my chair."

"Very well," says Essex, "before you say why you have come to see me, would you be kind enough to tell me how it came about that Her Majesty, yet again, has given *you* this special dispensation?"

Noah thinks for a moment before replying, as the Queen has forbidden him to discuss with Essex the subject matter of his commission. "Her Majesty often makes exception for those upon whom she relies most heavily, m'lord."

"Especially for *you*! Very well. As you have been forbidden to tell me, so be it. I am curious simply because none of my regular attendants has been granted such a boon. It gets very quiet here, especially with Egerton away."

"I suppose, m'lord, that, after leaving the battlefield, it would take time to re-accustom oneself to the quiet of the study. I trust your retirement will be merely temporary."

"What would *you* know of the battlefield, Master Barrister?" Essex inquires, sitting up, as though curious to hear Noah's reply.

"Only such as I have been told by your lordship and other warriors, m'lord."

Essex regards him with annoyance. "Well spoken, Master Hebrew," he says, as though Noah might have missed his initial barb. "At least you can distinguish warriors from sniveling courtiers. But I wonder whether you can likewise distinguish your friends from your enemies, even at court."

Noah waits quietly, as Essex seems to have a point to make. "Do you know who in the Privy Council gave the Lord Chief Justice approval to retry your former client Lopez at Queen's Bench, while his clemency petition was still pending before the Queen?"

Noah clears his throat. "No, m'lord. I never learned the truth of it."

"But you thought it was *I,* did you not?"

"I had merely surmised it, as your lordship seemed most persuaded of his guilt."

Essex snickers caustically. "Be careful of surmise, counselor. It can get you into trouble. As I think it important to know who one's friends are, I shall grant you the favor of telling you." He sits back smugly. "It was your dear *friend,* Lord Burghley."

Noah's mind races, as he tests what Essex has just told him against the sum of his knowledge. Although Burghley's allowing Lopez to be retried seems contrary to Burghley's own wishes at the time, it would account for much of the secrecy that followed Lopez's swift execution, which seemed to be forgotten at court almost as quickly as it took place. Noah resolves to think more about this, as he does not put it past Essex to lie for his own advantage.

"I thank your lordship for this confidence, and shall think on it further. To answer your lordship's question, I have come on a private matter concerning one of those very attendants to whom your lordship has alluded, those who are presently forbidden to speak with you."

"Wait, don't tell me." Essex seems to search his memory. "*Meyrick?*"

"The very *same,* m'lord. Why would you have supposed it to be he?"

Essex sighs. "He is wont to be more than a bit overzealous in what he perceives to be my interests. I have often chided him on it."

"*Over*zealous, m'lord?" Noah wishes to take full advantage of Essex's easy conversation.

"Oh, come, Serjeant Ames. Do you really believe I dispatched him to capture your party of merry men, after your escapade at Oyer and Terminer?"

"The possibility *had* crossed my mind, m'lord."

Essex laughs. "I instructed him merely to invite you to Essex House, so that you and I could discuss your arguments in the case of Doctor Lopez."

"*Invite,* m'lord?"

"*Escort,* if you prefer. No force was intended, and none was authorized."

Noah rubs his scar. "That is a great comfort to learn, m'lord. But I cannot imagine why Sir Gelly would have felt it necessary to follow me many miles out of London, and to draw his weapon against me."

"I should think it obvious," replies Essex. "He'd been humiliated by your rapid departure from London. At that time, he had twenty men-at-arms at his command…having nothing to do with *you,* of course. Notwithstanding all those men, he'd been bested on horseback by a scholar, his young assistants, and a *woman,* no less. It cut him to the quick."

"I am delighted to hear it, m'lord."

Essex laughs. "Serves him right. So, what has he done this time?"

"He goaded a young barrister friend of mine into an altercation."

"Hawking?"

The accuracy of Essex's conjecture is disturbing. "Why, *yes,* m'lord. At a tavern in Eastcheap."

"Ah, the Boar's Head, no doubt. Didn't he and his investigator have a run-in there some years ago…with Skeres?"

"You have quite the memory, m'lord. Yes, they did, and the investigator died later that night."

"I recall. Although I subsequently learned that the death was caused by fright, not poison, I was furious to hear the altercation had taken place at all, and expelled from my attendance Skeres and everyone else who'd had foreknowledge of that meeting. The potential for violence was patent."

"Was Meyrick one such attendant?"

"He *was*—although only tangentially, as I recall. So, you've come to see me about a tavern fight between Gelly (pardon me, *Sir* Gelly, after Cadiz) and Hawking."

"Yes, m'lord. As barristers are strictly forbidden to engage in violence of any kind, Hawking stands to be disbarred, if the Lord Chief Justice learns of it."

"Well, he shan't find out from *me,* I assure you."

"Thank you, m'lord, but it is Sir Gelly who has threatened to tell the Lord Chief Justice."

"*Threatened?* Seems to me that's the sort of thing one does right away, or not at all."

"So it would seem to me, as well, m'lord, but Sir Gelly was leaving town for ten days, and said—"

"Ten days? Where's he going? Herefordshire?"

It troubles Noah that he's just given Essex information he could not otherwise have obtained. "He didn't say, although he did *mention* his wife's homes in Herefordshire."

Essex looks pensive. "*Ten* days, you say?"

"Aye, m'lord. As I was saying, he promised not to report the fight if I could work things out with you before his return to London."

Essex shakes his head in consternation. "With *me*?" He sighs. "He has always failed to appreciate that, when he involves me in such trivial and distasteful matters, it diminishes my stature in the eyes of the world."

"No doubt, m'lord. But I, for one, shall tell no one that your name ever came up. And, in this instance, it might turn out for the best that he has deferred to you."

"You want me to persuade Meyrick not to report the fight?"

"Yes, m'lord, if you would be so kind."

Essex laughs to himself. "And what do you offer in exchange?"

There's a long silence.

"How do you mean, m'lord?"

"Well…what can you do for *me*?"

"I—I have nothing that would be of value to your lordship. I am a simple barrister."

Essex leans menacingly over the desk. "You're not a simple *anything*!" he says, suddenly red-faced. He takes a moment to compose himself. "Return to me in a week, and we can discuss an arrangement. In the meantime, even if your only item of value is your barrister's services, perhaps we can add that to the bargain."

Noah's head swims, as he has no idea what Essex is getting at.

"Tell me," Essex continues, "how fares Her Majesty?"

"Better, m'lord. Although she has not yet risen from her sickbed, she is on the mend and shall return to state affairs shortly."

"Good!" he says with questionable enthusiasm. "I suppose neither you nor I wish to contemplate the alternative. And we're forbidden even to *discuss* it, aren't we?" Noah notes this new mention of the Act, which seems to be on everyone's mind lately.

"M'lord, I must leave town for a few days myself, and cannot be certain to return to you in a week. May I beseech your lordship to instruct Sir Gelly to do nothing in respect of this matter until you and I speak again?"

"Certainly," says Essex. "Now, if that is all…"

It takes a moment for Noah to realize he's being dismissed. He shoots to his feet. "Thank you again for seeing me, m'lord."

"You may go." He gives Noah a forced smile. "I trust I shall see you again soon."

CHAPTER 8

RIDING ALONG in the cool autumn sunshine, Jonathan is happier than he has any right to be while engaged in pursuit of a phantom map.

His riderless horse is no longer riderless. Instead, perched on its back is the fair Lady Jessica, whose mood seems to be slowly improving after this morning's row.

When he insisted that she leave her cumbersome wardrobe behind at the farm, she was so furious that he thought her participation in this adventure would end before it began. Fortunately, Bessie succeeded where he could not, by reassuring her that her precious clothing would remain quite safe and undisturbed in a vacant corner of the barn.

"I hope you realize just how valuable that clothing is," says Jessica.

"I've no doubt," he replies, "which is why it is better off being carefully stowed away in a stationary shelter than being dragged about the English countryside, exposed to the elements. And do you not agree that our movements will be far more nimble without extra horses, a carriage, and trunks full of clothing?"

"Nimbleness is not the only virtue, Jon. A young woman of station must keep up appearances, lest she be treated as a common wench or goodwife."

"In these peculiar circumstances, it is far better you not be recognized as a woman of station."

"And why is that?"

"See where we *are*!" He sweeps his arm all around them. "In the middle of nowhere, protected by nothing but our own speed and pistols! A highwayman will be far less likely to trouble us, now that our appearance signifies we're traveling without wealth."

"And that's another thing!" she exclaims. "Is it really necessary for each of us to have a loaded pistol at the ready? Might not a horse's jostling set one off? It makes me feel as though *I'm* a highwayman! Which well-bred woman travels in this manner?"

"You know quite well that your pistol will not discharge unless it's cocked. Besides, I'd rather we be taken *for* highwaymen than *by* them."

From the corner of his eye, he can see her indulge that thought, placing herself in the role of highwayman, or rather her fanciful conception of one. She relaxes her shoulders, squints slightly, arches an eyebrow, and toughens her countenance. The juxtaposition of her refined beauty and her derring-do expression is so inapposite he nearly laughs aloud. Fortunately, he catches himself in time.

The road takes a turn through a dense wood, and they find themselves in a dark forest of ancient trees, some so thick that the road has to wend its way around them.

"How much further to Bridgwater?" she asks.

"Oh, not far, I should imagine. Perhaps another seven miles. In any event, we shall arrive in plenty of time to observe Skeres' meeting. I should dearly love to get a look at that map."

"Yes," she says, "for then we might abandon this silly quest, and return to Bessie's farm."

"I believe it's her father *Burt's* farm. And we can only abandon the quest if we confirm the map is *not* the one your father spoke of."

On a sudden breeze comes the sound of hoofbeats behind them, around the bend. From the sound, there's still enough time to get off the road undetected and allow the horsemen to pass by none the wiser.

"Follow me!" says Jonathan in an urgent whisper. Spotting a thick copse of tall green bushes a short distance off the road, he takes cover behind them, and quickly dismounts, peering through the bushes at the road they just left. Jessica comes up behind him, and follows suit.

"What is it?" she whispers.

He holds up his finger to silence her, and mouths the words "you'll see." As they wait, the birds that went silent at their approach resume their song. Jonathan relaxes slightly, as he knows that birdsong will help disguise their presence.

After a longer interval than expected, two men clop into view, one on horseback and the other driving a cart. Although their faces cannot be made out clearly at this distance, he has no doubt they're Skeres and Poley, as a long leather cylinder juts up from the cart. Jessica turns to Jonathan inquiringly. He nods to her. "'Tis they," he mouths.

But then the two travelers on the road do something he doesn't expect. They come to a halt and dismount. As they move about in quiet

THE IMPRESS OF HEAVEN| 97

conversation, Jonathan catches a glimpse of Skeres' scarred visage. The conversation becomes a bit heated, but still Jonathan cannot make out their words. Skeres flings his arms up in exasperation, and turns away from Poley. Shaking his head, Skeres hitches both horses to a low-lying branch, and treads off heavily on the opposite side of the road.

Poley merely shrugs. Heedlessly ambling toward Jonathan and Jessica's concealed position, he studies each tree carefully, as though selecting one to be uprooted and replanted in his personal garden. Apparently finding a massive oak to his liking, he steps up to it, drops his breeches, and begins relieving himself on its trunk, making a loud splashing sound. Jonathan glances at Jessica, who seems unperturbed, but shakes her head impatiently.

For Poley, however, relieving oneself can evidently be a lengthy and musical process. He whistles a jaunty tune often heard in taverns of late. The splashing continues as he completes the first verse and the refrain. As the second verse begins, Jessica looks to Jonathan, as though to inquire whether it usually takes so long for a man to relieve himself. Jonathan merely shrugs, as he cannot break the silence. And the whistling and splashing continue apace.

As Poley finishes his second refrain, the splashing abates at last, and the whistling ceases. Jonathan peeks out, expecting him to pull up his breeches. But, after a few seconds' silence, the splashing resumes at its former robust rate and, in celebration of the joyous process of voiding his bladder, Poley abandons his former whistling and begins to *sing* a third verse aloud with total abandon:

And, as she'd had so long a day, she said 'My lovely lad,
I woke anon to find I have no longer what I had...'

Jonathan turns to Jessica, amazed at this epic urination. Jessica smiles despite herself. A soft sneezing sound escapes her, and she covers her mouth to avoid laughing aloud. Unable to suppress her mirth, she kneels on the ground, and Jonathan can see her abdomen convulse in silent laughter. At last, the splashing and singing cease together. Poley hitches up his breeches and roughly adjusts them to his portly frame. Jessica looks up at Jonathan, her face still red, and joins him in peering through the copse at Poley.

Jonathan can barely believe their good fortune in the horses' unbroken silence. But now their luck seems to turn Turk, for Poley glances at a spot very near the copse and walks over to it with a curious expression. As he approaches their place of concealment, Jonathan reaches into the holster affixed to his mount and withdraws his pistol. Jessica watches in horror as he crouches next to her and places his thumb on the hammer. He shakes his head to reassure her that this is mere precaution.

"What the devil...?" mutters Poley. Then, to Jonathan's amazement, he bends over and scoops an abandoned pistol off the ground. Although it's cheaply made, by its look it has not lain there long at all, its metal showing no sign of rust, and its cheap wood no sign of weathering. Poley sniffs the chamber and arches an eyebrow. Evidently, it still smells of gunpowder, which means it's lain there no more than a few days. It dawns on Jonathan that they've inadvertently taken refuge at the site of a very recent gunfight.

"Come on, Bob! Let's get going!" shouts Skeres, who's returned to the road and unhitched their horses. Holding the reins, he shouts impatiently. "What'd ya find there?"

"It's a pistol!" shouts Poley.

"Well, bring it along," replies Skeres. "We gotta be movin' on."

But Poley does not immediately return to the road. Instead, he rustles through the brush, looking for more signs of the fight that took place here.

Jonathan wonders whether his own side of the copse was occupied by someone engaged in the fighting. Scanning the ground at their feet, he notices something glassy not six inches from Jessica's right foot. He turns his head slightly to get a better fix on it.

It's a lidless human eye, staring up at him from the undergrowth. Although he wishes to draw Jessica's attention away from it, it's already too late. She's noticed his momentary startlement, and followed his gaze down to the eye. As she realizes what she's looking at, her own eyes grow wide as saucers, and she inhales deeply, preparing to scream. Jonathan grabs her, and places his hand firmly over her mouth, so she can do no more than whimper in near silence.

Jonathan glances back through the copse, and is relieved to find that Poley has at last heeded Skeres' command to return to the road. He removes his hand from Jessica's mouth, and brings his finger to his lips. He risks a few quiet words. "I'm sorry to have done that," he says, "but we couldn't risk being discovered. They're about to leave." But Jessica appears not to hear him, as she still gapes at the eyeball in horror. "There was a gunfight here a few days ago. Evidently, that's one of the casualties."

Skeres and Poley casually resume their journey, seeming to take forever to disappear from view, at last.

Out of sheer curiosity, Jonathan feels a need to view the corpse well enough to determine what happened here. Although he considers asking Jessica to turn away, he knows she won't cooperate. Locating the eyeball again, he crouches down, and brushes aside some leaves concealing the remains from view.

It's the corpse of a man somewhat shorter than himself who wore nothing but rags. Most of the skin of his face has been shorn away by a single blast of loose shot. Judging by the pattern of the facial wounds and the absence of powder burns, Jonathan surmises that the fatal shot probably came from a musket fired at significant range, perhaps from the road itself.

"You want to see what a *real* highwayman looks like?" he asks Jessica.

She shrinks back, unable to take her eyes off the corpse. "I can see well enough from here, thank you," she replies shakily.

Jonathan rises from his crouch. "Poor sod," he mutters.

She looks at him, confused. "Why would you express pity for a highwayman, if that's what he was? Hadn't he taken to robbing innocent people at gunpoint?"

He's not sure why, but her question irritates him. All right. If she wants to know, he'll show her.

"Come here," he says impassively, no longer supplicating.

Jessica takes a few hesitant steps toward him, and the corpse.

"Don't worry," he says. "He's never going to move again." With the point of his pistol, he shoves away some woodland detritus concealing the ribcage, which is naked and undamaged. The ribs are clearly defined. "Look carefully at his chest. What does it tell us about him?"

"That he was thin?" she ventures.

"That he was *starving* to death. And look at his clothing. It's in tatters."

"Isn't that from being left out here in the woods?" she asks.

"Not for a mere few days. If his clothes had been in decent condition to begin with, they'd be no more than a bit faded by now. Not these! These were already rags when the fight broke out. Poor sod was probably starving, and chose the wrong quarry to turn highwayman. The pistol that Poley found probably belonged to this man. I got a pretty good look at it, and it was trash when it was made. He'd probably found it on another failed highwayman, and it jammed on him." Jonathan shakes his head bitterly, and returns to the horses to prepare for the remainder of their journey.

Jessica approaches him gingerly. "Are you angry with me?" she asks.

He turns to see an expression that melts his heart. He shakes his head. "No, not at you, especially."

"But me…a little bit?"

He exhales and turns to her. "Jesse, you live in a rarefied world that I cannot fathom, where rich highwaymen hoard their ill-gotten gold in secret caves, and 'mudpeople' roam the countryside for the sole purpose of frightening plump little lady's maids."

"I don't understand," she says meekly.

He points to the corpse with his pistol. "*That* is a typical highwayman! He was probably a carpenter or a farmhand until his luck ran out. In case you haven't noticed, the harvests these past few years have been inadequate to support the population of this island. The Privy Council has gone so far as to issue a decree requiring the landed nobility, such as your viscount, to care for the starving and sick. And what does he do? He dubs them *mudpeople*! And bewails their entry onto his grounds to beg for alms!" He points to the corpse again. "All right. So this man was an outlaw. Does that make him unworthy of pity? For trying to stay alive?"

Jessica has obviously never thought about such matters in any depth, and has surely never seen anything like this close up.

He relents. "Jesse, I deeply regret speaking to you so sternly. I know you are much too kind-hearted to think of people in that way. Come, let's move away from this terrible place." As she seems to be in a near-trance, he leads her by the hand to her horse. Reaching his arm around her slender waist, he can feel her trembling. He helps her to remount.

In silence, they resume their journey far from the main road, as that's the route Jonathan expects Skeres and Poley to take. In a short while, he finds a stream running due west, and they keep to its bank. He steals a glance at Jessica. She seems still to be preoccupied, which makes him profoundly sorry. All this time, he's thought of her as absolutely perfect. And now he's gone and changed her.

⤙∘⟨⟩∘⤚

A SHORT WHILE later, they crest a ridge. Up ahead, a band of minstrels and jugglers are making their way slowly in the same direction. As there are six of them, and they have only two horses among them, they can travel no faster than human legs can manage.

"I've been thinking," says Jonathan a short while later.

"About what?"

"Well, judging by how long it took Poley to empty his bladder, he must have imbibed a good bit no more than a couple of hours earlier."

"Fascinating!" she says. "Do you suppose he drinks?"

He ignores her pertness. "The only place on that road where he could have had so much ale is…"

"Burt's tavern. Yes, I see. What do you make of it?"

"I'm not sure, but while they were there I suppose they might have learned, whether through Burt or, more likely, one of his customers, that Lady Burlington and her footman were traveling this very road just ahead of them."

"And if they recognized my name," she adds, "they might have associated it with Noah Ames. Oh, but they wouldn't expect you to be with me, as you're not really my footman."

He nods. "Now you see why I identified myself in that manner."

"Still, they'd be on the lookout for me, traveling with a man."

"So, if we show up at the Rose & Crown together, dressed as we are, they might be *waiting* for us."

"But they have no reason to think we know aught of the map. Have they?"

"It's unlikely…but not impossible, now that I think on it. I *did* identify myself as your footman to the innkeeper at the Hind of Brakenhale, where I first ran into Poley."

"Had you given the innkeeper your true name?"

"No. 'Jonathan Porter.'"

"That's a little too close for comfort," she says. "I'm glad you did not allow them to overtake us on the road earlier. And it might be imprudent for us to appear at the Rose & Crown together."

Because of their superior speed, they draw nearer the band of minstrels. The jugglers wear face paint in a white-and-black diamond pattern. One of them keeps four balls in the air as he walks. One of the riders sings a familiar love-tune in which a man and woman converse in melodic rhyme. But whenever it comes time for the woman's voice to respond, a young man croaks her reply in humorous imitation of a female voice. Although there are two women in the company, evidently they cannot sing.

"Do you know this song?" Jonathan asks Jessica.

"Of course," she replies.

"Then, answer for the lady."

"Are you mad?" she asks. "You wish me to sing with a band of common minstrels?"

"You promised to obey me unquestioningly," he sniffs.

"That promise was limited to matters of *safety,* as I recall. Are we *imperiled,* lest I sing?"

"Properly viewed, this *is* a matter of safety. Oh, never mind. You probably don't sing well enough to pass for a minstrel, anyway." Jonathan snickers.

When next it comes time for the woman in the song to answer, Jessica's voice rings out loud and clear over the young man's croaking reply. Then comes a man's line again. The next time Jessica answers, the croaking voice does not reply. Instead, the whole band turns as one to hear her sing the next line.

Jonathan is stunned. Her voice is beautiful beyond compare, not an affected soprano, such as the Italians seem to cherish, but rather a warm, confident contralto in the finest Celtic and English tradition that brings to mind robust young womanhood.

The song, the horses, and all come to a halt.

"Lady," says the young man who formerly croaked the lady's lines, "you got some set of pipes there. You sound like an angel come from heaven!"

Jessica bows in the saddle, and the band erupts in applause.

∞◦◯◦∞

ALL AFTERNOON, THE Rose & Crown bustles with preparations for Bridgwater's annual late-harvest festivities. Several new servants with strange faces, and even stranger accents, have come from far afield to complement the inn's kitchen and serving staff. Supper, which will be served both indoors and outdoors this evening, promises varied and sophisticated entertainment.

While the jugglers limber up out of doors, the players and minstrels who've converged on the inn from far away now exercise their talents in closed common-rooms roped off from the public. Some of the town's youngest folk, undissuaded by Do Not Enter signs and thick cordons, press their ears against the doors, eavesdropping on a cacophony of disjointed dramatic recitations, musical scales, and copious throat clearing.

In the courtyard, more than an hour before the scheduled opening of festivities, excited townspeople begin to gather, gabbling in anticipation. The Rose & Crown's hearty ale already flows freely, fueling the noise and excitement.

A makeshift platform has been set up in the courtyard to serve as a performing stage. The foremost spectators' bench has been set aside for town fathers known to attend every year, even though one never knows whether, to the crowd's dismay, they will be moved to hold forth on some arcane question of politics or religion. Immediately behind the front row is a set of benches reserved for the inn's transient guests, as management has learned from experience that, having once stumbled upon the festival by chance, some will be so delighted as to return year after year.

The stout innkeeper emerges from the inn, wipes his hands on his ale-stained apron, and steps onto the stage to manly hoots, accompanied by a polite round of applause from the womenfolk.

A middle-aged man shouts, "Hey, Hops!"

The innkeeper scans the crowd, and locates the owner of the voice: "That's *'Goodman Cooper'* to you, m'lad!"

The crowd applauds heartily at the correction.

"Well, whatever yer name is, there'd better be no shortage of ale!"

"Goodman Smith," says the innkeeper sternly, "*no one's* got enough ale for the likes o' you!" Then he turns to the crowd with a big smile. "But we've plenty for *everyone else!*" This is greeted with laughter, and far greater applause.

The innkeeper puts his hands up, seeking quiet, and the crowd calms down well enough for him to be heard. "Now, I know we're not supposed to get started with the entertainment this early, but—"

"Bring it on!" come several shouts, followed by a loud banging on the tables.

The innkeeper hushes them again. "By mere chance, we are fortunate to have with us this afternoon Master Augustine Phillips, a *most* renowned player appearing of late with the Lord Chamberlain's Men on the stage of the new Globe Theater in London, in Master William Shakespeare's very popular play about our dear departed *King Henry the Fifth!*"

"Down the French!" shouts the rambunctious Goodman Smith, needlessly reminding one and all of King Henry's reputation as conqueror of France.

"Goodman Smith," says the innkeeper, "it's a bit early to cut you off, but I'll do it, so help me!"

"Anything but that!" cries Smith, pretending to cower in his seat. "I'll be good. I promise!"

"I expected as much outta you," replies the innkeeper sagely.

A thickly accented voice emerges from the benches reserved for transient guests. "Perhaps Goodman Smiss would care to try eez *own* hand at 'downing ze French' outside zees establishment!" It's a swarthy young Frenchman of athletic build, with a handsome, but weather-beaten countenance, and a rapier that hangs snugly in a well-worn scabbard at his side.

The innkeeper quickly tamps down the potential confrontation.

"Ah!" he shouts, clasping his hands together before his heart, "a gentleman from the sunny fields of France! You are most welcome, m'sieur!" He applauds, ostentatiously enlisting the crowd to join in, which they do, though less than wholeheartedly. "Perhaps you would be so kind as to tell us y'name, suh!"

With a smile, the Frenchman shakes his head, and tips his hat to the innkeeper.

The innkeeper nods indulgently. "Suit yourself. Anyway, suh, welcome to Britain and our fair establishment. God save King Henri of France, as well as our fair Queen Elizabeth!"

"God save the Queen!" returns the crowd noisily, raising their tankards and drinking deeply. While the Frenchman obviously notices the crowd's glaring omission of his king's name from its benediction, he merely smirks and returns to his ale.

The innkeeper resumes his announcement. "And now, appearing before you, as King Henry the Fifth of England—"

"And *Wales!*" shouts Smith.

"And *Wales,*" agrees Cooper, worn down by exasperation. "Let's have a nice round of applause for Master Augustine Phillips, as King Henry the Fifth, before the Battle of *Agincourt!*" The innkeeper steps down and turns to watch.

Phillips mounts the stage in stern regal fashion, a clean-shaven man of middle years with thick black hair grizzled at the temples, wearing king's livery, a broadsword, and a simple gold crown. The crowd gives him a rowdy welcome, but soon quiets down respectfully, as the regal illusion is quite complete.

A young man's voice shouts from offstage:

O that we now had here
But one ten thousand of those men in England
That do no work today!

Although all eyes remain riveted on the king, if anyone cared to glance over at the young fellow who just spoke, they might have remarked that his face and clothing are covered in a black-and-white diamond pattern betokening a juggler, rather than a player, which makes him an odd choice to deliver a nobleman's line. One might even have noticed the stark disparity between the young man's practiced speaking voice and a juggler's lowly station. He sounded more a barrister than a juggler, perhaps even the most sought-after barrister in all England.

With a confident smile, King Henry replies:

What's he that wishes so?
My cousin Westmoreland? No, my fair cousin:
If we are mark'd to die, we are enough
To do our country loss; and if to live,
The fewer men, the greater share of honour.

The speech's effect on the crowd is magical. Here is King Henry, come from the grave, to remind them they're descended from heroes of old, and that the fragile island kingdom handed down to them is still precious and worthy of great sacrifice. The King looks out over the crowd as he concludes, peering through each patron's eyes into his very soul.

We few, we happy few, we band of brothers;
For he today that sheds his blood with me
Shall be my brother; be he ne'er so vile,
This day shall gentle his condition:
And gentlemen in England now abed
Shall think themselves accursed they were not here,
And hold their manhoods cheap whiles any speaks
That fought with us upon Saint Crispin's day.

For a long moment, he barely moves. There is not a sound...until he bows. Then, the whole place erupts in cheers and applause. He turns to the innkeeper, who wipes away a tear, beaming with patriotic pride.

The innkeeper steps onto the platform, a bit wobbly at first, and walks to center stage, where he grasps Phillips' hand and speaks some laudatory words beneath the crowd's hearing. He turns to the audience.

"Ladies and Gentlemen, let's have another round of applause—" Before he can finish the thought, the place erupts once more. Several older men and woman burst into cheers as they applaud. "I'm sorry to say that Master Phillips will be unable to stay for the remainder of the festivities"—there are boos and raucous cries that the innkeeper frowns into silence—"but Master Phillips must be going *immediately* to points west, where he is eagerly awaited by his family."

The audience begins a chant of "stay, stay, stay," but the player shakes his head and will not relent. Without a word, he smiles, broadly waves once to the crowd, and disappears through the doors of the inn.

As the applause dies down, the well-spoken juggler watches discreetly as two men quietly enter the yard from the inn, one with a long-healed but disfiguring facial scar, the other stout, with a rubbery face that tells of too much drink. Stooping over to avoid obstructing the view of the stage, they traverse the section reserved for transients, and take seats on either side of the Frenchman, who nods in recognition.

While the revelers sup on their main course, a band of minstrels takes the stage with its musical instruments, and begins with a wistful song of times long past. As the crowd quiets down, the leader of the little band rises, and walks to the wing of the stage, where the young painted juggler converses with an elegant young woman in black minstrel's clothing.

The bandleader takes the young woman's hand and leads her to center stage. She wears a slender sequined mask that covers a small area about the eyes, but the visible portion of her face is well-formed and refined. Through the eyeholes peek a large pair of dark eyes that suggest an exotic, perhaps a gypsy or an Arab. Although she wears the same simple black form-fitting costume as the other minstrels, she fills it out in a way that makes every man immediately sit up and take notice.

As the masked Jessica smiles and curtsies gracefully to the crowd, several men climb over the benches in front to get a closer view. The Frenchman and his two companions eagerly take center seats on the front bench, roundly ignoring the sneers of contempt from the town fathers seated on either side.

While every man in the audience finds this maid very appealing, the Frenchman seems quite smitten. He waves over a serving wench, whispers something in her ear, and gives her a coin large enough to make her eyes light up. She scurries away on an errand.

As the Frenchman beams up at Jessica, she smiles reservedly in return. The minstrels begin the song of lost love that Jessica sang with them at first meeting, and the effect on the audience is palpable. The male singer seems to delight in her grace as much as the audience does, and deliberately cedes all attention to this lovely flower. The song ends lightly with an indefinite chord that lingers in the air. The applause is thunderous.

"Encore, s'il vous plaît!" the Frenchman cries.

Jessica looks questioningly toward the bandleader, who smiles and nods vigorously, waving for her to proceed. She smiles in return, and another song begins. This is a maid's song of longing for the return of her lost knight, at the climax of which the singer begs her absent love's forgiveness. When Jessica reaches that point, she falls to her knees and clasps her hands together, imploring the Frenchman in song, as though he were the only man in the audience, nay, in the *world*. As the song ends and the applause comes, the serving wench brings the Frenchman a rich silk hair-ribbon, which he immediately proffers to Jessica.

As Jessica leans over to accept the gift, the Frenchman kisses her cheek politely, but also discreetly cups her buttock in one hand. Startled, she recoils. He winks at her. "Mais, ma petite, après tout, tu n'es pas une noble," he says, suggesting that the small liberty he's taken should be regarded as a mere trifle by a woman of her low station. After all, she's not a noblewoman.

She smacks his hand away and replies. "Si je ne suis pas une noble, c'est à voir, monsieur. Mais, ceci nous savons déjà: *Vous* n'êtes pas noble!" *Whether I am noble remains to be seen, sir, but it is already plain that* you *are not!*

He smiles in astonishment, and winks at her again. She blushes.

"Vous êtes de Paris?" he asks with a bemused expression. *You're from Paris?*

While the crowd looks on, still applauding, she covers her mouth coyly and speaks a little more hesitantly, as though encountering some difficulty in translating. "O, non, monsieur, mais j'ai visité la ville dans ma jeunesse." *No, sir, but I visited the city in my youth.*

"Donc, nous nous reverrons plus tard, peut-être?" he asks. *So, we shall see each other later, perhaps?*

She smiles coyly. "Peut-être." *Perhaps.*

She curtsies shyly, and leaves the stage.

The Frenchman sits through the next song looking self-satisfied. As it ends, he says to Skeres. "Did zat girl not have a cultured singing voice? Like she was *teached*?"

Skeres looks at him askance. "*Taught*. Maybe. Why?"

"Her French was also…not bad."

"Not as miserable as your English?" retorts Skeres wryly.

The Frenchman ignores the slight, and starts on another ale, already lost in thought. The next song has reached its second verse before he begins to wonder why he no longer sees the juggler she was conversing with earlier.

———————⇒∘⊂⟋⟍⟍∘⊂———————

A frisson of combined disgust and fear rides up Jessica's spine as she returns to the practice room by the kitchen, and slams the door behind her. She'd blushed on stage, not because she was embarrassed by the Frenchman's advance, but because she'd foolishly replied to his remark in perfect French, which he was sure to realize very soon was absurdly improbable for the minstrel waif she was pretending to be.

As she removes the mask and quickly changes back into her own clothing, she glances through the window and spots the Frenchman rising from his bench with a concerned expression.

What has she done?

———————⇒∘⊂⟋⟍⟍∘⊂———————

HAVING WAITED TO reenter the inn until Jessica began singing for the crowd, Jonathan stealthily opens a guestroom door on the deserted top floor. He cringes as it creaks on its hinges.

He guesses that, for all Skeres' blustering, the leather cylinder remains in Poley's possession, and he nearly laughs aloud, as there it lies in Poley's dark room, right across his trunk. The sot was so eager to begin drinking that he neglected to lock his door.

Even from here, Jonathan can hear Jessica singing sweetly in the yard. Although he has no doubt she'll captivate the Frenchman and his companions for at least a few songs, he's unsure how much time he needs to do his prying. He enters the room, leaving the door ajar.

As he picks up the cylinder, something loose slides around inside it. His heart falls. Could it be there's no map in it at all? He unties Poley's simple knot, and flips open the cylinder's lid. As peering inside the opaque cylinder is sure to be useless in the dark, he turns it vertically, placing his hand underneath the opening to catch whatever might tumble out.

A small leather pouch slides down the tube and flops into his hand. Although it was probably flat at one time, its shape has curved in conformity with the contours of its cylindrical hiding place. As the pouch's flap is unsecured, Jonathan looks inside, being careful not to disturb its contents. It contains perhaps four or five envelopes of varied sizes and colors, all sealed with lumps of wax. To the naked eye, these appear to be personal letters, although, in the dim light, he cannot make out the writing. But none is fat enough to hold a military map. He closes the pouch, puts it aside, and returns to the cylinder.

His heart pounds. This is the moment of truth. If nothing remains in the cylinder, then he will have both delayed Jessica and placed her in serious danger for no good reason, and will be sure to look the fool in her eyes. He will also have stolen into someone else's room and examined his private papers which, even if he gets away with it, violates not only the law but his own tattered ethics, as well. And he shivers to think he might *not* get away with it.

He lifts the cylinder above his head and peers up into it. Lining the inside is some sort of written parchment or paper, but it's pressed too tightly to fall out on its own. With two fingers, he carefully draws it out but, before he can unscroll it completely, he hears someone stealing slowly up the stairs down the hall.

Glancing at the doorway, he sees that the door of the room across the hall is now wide open. He feels sure it was shut when he entered Poley's room.

He quickly rolls up the map and stands it on edge on the floor, out of sight of the door. He closes the cylinder, puts it back where he found it on Poley's trunk, and withdraws into the darkest corner of the room, his nerves on catlike edge. He draws his dagger and waits, suddenly realizing that the music outside in the yard no longer has a female voice in it. He berates himself. Jessica's performance must have finished, but he's been too preoccupied to realize.

The footsteps leave the staircase and creak stealthily toward him along the hallway. As the steps are too heavy to be those of a woman, Jonathan mentally prepares himself for a desperate struggle with the intruder. (Even in his current state of alert, he recognizes the irony of characterizing someone beside *himself* as the "intruder," especially as this might be Poley returning to his own room.) As the footsteps reach the doorway and stop, several things happen at once.

The intruder carefully pushes Poley's door, which swings fully open and stops of its own weight. The door across the hall creaks loudly. He hears a loud bong, such as iron makes striking something meaty, and the intruder collapses face first into Poley's room. At the doorway, a woman's voice mutters something that sounds like "cochon," which he knows to be French for "pig."

As Jonathan has no idea what's happened, he's still waiting, dagger in hand, when Jessica's pretty face peers around the door jamb. She steps into the room over the insensate man and regards Jonathan impatiently.

There's a frying pan in her hand.

"Well? Are you just going to *stand* there?" she whispers. "Bring him into the room, so we can close the door!"

Jonathan sheaths his dagger and drags the intruder all the way in. It's the Frenchman. "He's going to have a devil of a headache when he awakens," he mutters. Jessica shrugs, unconcerned. Before closing the door, Jonathan peers down the hall, which is still deserted.

"So, did you get a look at the map?" she whispers, as soon as the door shuts.

He nods and unrolls it before her. It's a map of Ireland and Cornwall, with little drawings apparently signifying military positions at various points along the seacoasts.

"Is that *the* map?" she asks in awe.

He nods gravely. "It certainly appears to be. But wait! There's only one way to be sure." He brings the map to the little window, and spreads it across the rays of sunlight that stream in. White light shines brilliantly through a detailed crest at the center of the paper, almost as though the watermark were about to burst into flames. Indeed, it glows so brightly they have to squint to see it. By comparison, the rest of the map seems drab and lifeless.

"This is *it*!" he confirms in a triumphant whisper.

Jessica bounces excitedly. "Oh, Jonathan, you are wonderful!" She looks at him wide-eyed. "Are we going to *steal* it?"

Although he's secretly overwhelmed by her praise, he represses his feelings, and regards her skeptically. "You'd like that, wouldn't you?"

"Isn't that why we came here?"

"No," he replies. "They'd merely track us down, kill us, and take it back. Besides, other copies of this original map may already have fallen into the wrong hands. There's at least one copy in existence, for whoever stole this replaced it with a near-perfect copy. No. It's much more important for us to find out where this original is being shipped off to. And that may tell us why it was so important for it to *be* the original."

"We're just going to put it back?" asks Jessica incredulously.

Jonathan nods, rolls it up, and replaces it in the cylinder, followed by the pouch of letters. He closes up the cylinder and carefully puts it back precisely as he found it.

"Then, where are we going now?" she asks.

"Anywhere but here!" he exclaims hoarsely. "If they find us, we're doomed!" He points to the frying pan. "Leave that downstairs somewhere, but don't go into the kitchen, or they're sure to think you filched it. Meet me at the stables…and try to look casual. If our luck holds up, we should catch up with Phillips and his man by nightfall."

"With *whom*?" she asks.

Jonathan smiles. "*Henry the Fifth.*"

"Oh, the player! But, why him?"

"Because," Jonathan says, his brow furrowed, "I suspect he knows where these devils are going!"

CHAPTER 9

AS NOAH FINISHES dressing in his room upstairs at the Winchester Inn, he parts the rough flaxen curtains and peers down at the stables. The groom who led Bucklebury out into the open air now brushes him lightly, in preparation for adornment with the Queen's livery.

Noah aches to think he still faces two, perhaps three, days on horseback before reaching Lord Mountjoy's home in Dorset. To make matters worse, the morning sky is growing darker instead of brighter, and an unsteady wind occasionally whips up the autumn leaves.

As the Queen instructed Noah to take every defensive precaution, he's felt compelled to carry a pistol. With the jostling of consecutive days on horseback, the holster has sorely chafed his old chest wound, which stung all night like a hive of bees, disturbing his sleep. He wonders whether the wound might not reopen, even after all this time.

There's a knock at the door. "Time for breakfast!" comes Sir Walter's well-rested voice.

Noah opens the door, beckons him in, and shuts it again. "Good morning," says Noah. "Tell me. Does your offer of a carriage ride still stand?"

Sir Walter responds with exaggerated surprise. "Could the constant Noah Ames be changing his mind?"

"Actually," says Noah humbly, "we left *that* Noah Ames behind in Holborn. I'm the pliable version."

"Backache?"

Noah shakes his head. "Old battle scar."

"Given you by whom?"

"Sir Gelly Meyrick, years ago."

The mention of Meyrick's name rankles Sir Walter. "*Sir* Gelly, indeed!" he mutters contemptuously.

"It's a long story," says Noah.

"I have a few myself," says Sir Walter, who then brightens up. "*Certainly,* my offer still stands. Your wound will fare much better on Lord Mountjoy's cushioned benches. I'll have Carter tie your horse to the rear."

"Before you do that, may I ask whether it would be possible for Lieutenant Carter to *ride* Bucklebury the remainder of the way, or sit up front beside the driver?" He leans in to Sir Walter and says quietly: "There is something I need to discuss with you, at length…privately."

"Oh?" says Sir Walter, arching an eyebrow. "Of course."

They amble down to breakfast and ravenously consume the humble fare, eager to resume their journey.

As their small company gathers before the inn to depart, Raleigh explains to Carter his choice of riding arrangements. The young lieutenant jumps at the chance to ride the sleek Bucklebury, at least as long as the weather holds up. Bucklebury seems to have no objection.

Before mounting, Carter pauses and looks to Noah: "Shall we first remove the Queen's livery from Bucklebury, Serjeant Ames?"

Noah waves away the question. "Of course not. He may be your mount, but he's still my *horse*! I doubt Her Majesty would be scandalized to find one of her fine young officers momentarily mistaken for one of her attendants."

Carter mounts, obviously proud he might be taken as a figure of the Queen's court. The driver takes the reins of the closed carriage, and Sir Walter and Noah step in and shut the door. Only a few minutes after the carriage begins to move, Noah already feels some relief.

"You were right, Sir Walter. These cushions relieve the jostling a great deal. I expect I shall soon forget my ancient wound. Lord Mountjoy was most kind to lend you this coach for the trip."

"I'll be sure to add your thanks to my own," says Sir Walter.

"I'm pleasantly surprised that you have not brought along your smoking pipe," observes Noah. "Is it not addictive?"

"It is, no doubt," says Sir Walter as he gazes out at the passing countryside. "I'm trying to quit, however, as Her Majesty detests it, and refuses to allow it indoors, except in a few places she never visits. She's even gone so far as to decline permission for the grocer to supply it to me at the Tower." He turns to Noah. "Now, what's all this secrecy about?"

"I have been granted a commission by Her Majesty."

"Oh? I hope you're not investigating *me*!"

"Of course not!" says Noah, drawing the commission from his pocket, and handing it to Sir Walter for perusal.

As Raleigh reads it, the blood drains from his face. He hands it back to Noah, and turns to gaze at the passing landscape.

Noah is dismayed by his reaction. "It was not my intention to surprise you, Sir Walter. If you would prefer to collect your thoughts for a few days, it will not delay matters in the least…and I shall make no notation of it, I assure you." Concerned, he leans in to Sir Walter. "I hope you don't feel I have abused our friendship in any way."

"No, of course not," says Raleigh dismissively. "I must tell you frankly, Noah. I would not wish to be charged with such a commission."

Noah puts the commission back in his pocket. "It would be less than truthful if I were to say I have no misgivings of mine own."

"This commission charges you to interview me concerning Lord Essex's fitness for command?"

"In part."

"And, by implication, I am charged with telling you whatever I know that might reflect on his fitness?" As Noah nods in reply, Raleigh turns to face him. "And just suppose I were to tell you things that cause Her Majesty to conclude he is *unfit* for command. And suppose he were consequently left to rot at the Lord Keeper's house?"

Noah's at a loss to see where this is going. "I suppose that's possible, Sir Walter. But rest assured I'm not the judge in this affair. Her Majesty will form her own judgment, as will the court that eventually hears the matter."

"You sell yourself short, Serjeant Ames. If the Queen weren't confident in your thoroughness and judgment, she would *never* have granted you this commission. And you, of all people, know perfectly well that, what Her Majesty believes, the court will believe also."

Noah's own experience has taught him that, just as Sir Walter has suggested, in trials at special courts of irregular session, the Queen's influence can often be decisive. Yet, Noah believes Sir Walter has overstated his influence on the Queen's views. "You flatter me beyond reason, Sir Walter. But, pray, let us suppose, as you suggest, that you provide information adverse to Lord Essex's prospects for command, and suppose also that he remains under house arrest at the Lord Keeper's house." He waits expectantly.

Raleigh looks through the window once more. "And suppose Essex then becomes King of England."

Here it is again! The Succession must have leapt to the forefront of everyone's mind at the same moment.

"*King of—!*" Noah is flustered. "I'm no expert in primogeniture, Sir Walter, but I know Essex's genealogy. I cannot *imagine* by what right he could attain the Crown."

Sir Walter frowns. "Please, Noah. The Crown is not always attained by means of genealogy. Why, Henry Tudor became Henry the Seventh by descent from Henry the Sixth. Have you ever traced how those two were related?"

"I have," says Noah gravely, as such talk has caused many heads to roll. "They were quite distant relations."

Raleigh nods. "But, just for the sake of this conversation, assume Essex *were* to become king. He would know that he had been deprived of command for the remainder of Queen Elizabeth's reign in part because of what I may tell you today. What *then*?"

Noah scratches his head. "If he were to wish to take an evenhanded revenge, Sir Walter, he would have to treat with you the same as the Lord Admiral, and everyone else who'd have given adverse proof."

"Have you interviewed the Lord Admiral already?"

"No, but I know that, just as *you* will not lie in such a matter as this, *he* won't, either. So, I expect your two proofs to be consistent. Surely, you do not expect the Lord Admiral to *deceive* me to protect himself from Essex!"

Raleigh scoffs. "The Lord Admiral would sooner slap Essex in the face than lie to avoid his wrath. But he also has other reasons not to fret about Essex's revenge. Now that Drake is dead, the Lord Admiral is the greatest living hero of the Spanish Armada. He literally saved England! I can boast no such distinction."

"You would have earned many additional distinctions yourself by the time of any such frightful succession, Sir Walter." Noah's becoming exasperated. "Look, I will not proceed if I expect you'll tell me less than the truth. Nor will I allow this commission to be subverted into a cause for hounding *you*. If need be, I'll forego this interview entirely, and proceed on the basis of other witnesses' proof. *And there an end!*" He folds his arms and closes his eyes, as if to doze, yawning to emphasize his feigned unconcern.

"Wouldn't the Queen notice the absence of my proof?"

"I suppose," Noah mumbles. "And she would reprimand me for failing to insist upon your interview. But, what can I do?" He shrugs.

"She wouldn't be too happy with me, either, I suppose."

Noah opens his eyes, as though not quite sure why the topic has persisted. "To say the least. And, not that I am a person of any importance, but a wrathful Essex would have *me* at his disposal, too." He sits up, as though his interest has been piqued once more. "You and I simply cannot serve Her Majesty well if we're preoccupied with pleasing her as-yet unidentified successor."

There's a long silence, during which the only sounds are the clopping of hooves, and the clatter of wheels under the carriage.

At last, Sir Walter speaks. "You're right, of course. I just wanted to run that fox to ground, so to speak. So, how shall we proceed?"

Noah sits up attentively. "However you wish."

"Very well." Raleigh's eyes focus far away. "As my knowledge of Essex is derived from sea voyages, let me give you a little background. We need go back no further than Drake's expedition that has since become known as the 'Singeing of the King of Spain's Beard' in"—he searches his memory—"1587, so about twelve years ago. Drake was already commonly regarded by other seaman as a natural son of Neptune."

"Was he so known for his extraordinary good fortune at sea?" asks Noah.

Sir Walter looks at him askance. "I'll let that remark pass, Noah, but only because it was *you* who made it! *No one* could be lucky enough to accomplish what Drake did! His seamanship was unparalleled, as were his knowledge and understanding of winds and tides, and his uncanny understanding of naval weaponry and formation. Add the luck of the gods to that, and you've got Drake. I could barely believe it when he died returning from his New World expedition this year. Of *dysentery,* of all things! What an ignominious ending for a man of that stature and skill! But I digress. To return to the 'singeing.'

"The Queen had dubbed Drake a 'privateer,' which is nothing more than a pirate lawfully funded by 'private investors,' which included Her Majesty, a few of the adventurers, and some London merchants. Perhaps someday you'll enlighten me as to how the Queen of England can legally be considered a 'private investor,' especially when her contribution consists of warships of the Royal Navy.

"Drake took his fleet to Cadiz, Spain's biggest port city, and humiliated and sank a good portion of the Spanish fleet, which was no match for either Drake's seamanship or his armaments. He sank more than thirty warships, and cost the king a fortune, which set back the king's plans against England by many months. But *that's* not what fascinated all England, nor the Queen."

"No," confirms Noah. "It was the *booty*, as I recall."

"It was, indeed. But many people don't know the true story. You see, after blowing a gaping hole in the king's purse, Drake sailed off to the Azores, hundreds of miles offshore in the Atlantic. As another of Spain's possessions, those islands are used as a watering point for the king's ships returning from the New World with gold and silver. Drake literally struck gold that time. After a fight, he raided and boarded a ship...and brought it home with him. It was called the São Filipe, and was so laden with gold it nearly sank of its cargo's weight. Do you know that one ship and its cargo brought in well over *one hundred thousand pounds. One ship!* It not only paid the costs of the whole expedition, but made the investors rich. And who do you suppose was the largest investor?"

"The Queen?" ventures Noah.

Sir Walter nods. "She got back all her expenses, and she also received fully *half* the profits of the expedition, as well as kicking her adversary's bum. I suppose you can see why naval expeditions became the Queen's preferred method of warfare."

Noah whistles softly. "Yes, I see."

"Ever since Drake's expedition, every military officer in the realm has been promoting himself as the man to duplicate the accomplishment. *Especially* Essex! And Drake's renowned success in defeating the Spanish Armada the following year simply sealed his place in Essex's mind as the man to emulate. Of course, what Essex *really* admired was the great harm Drake had inflicted on the king's naval capabilities in battle, while suffering little loss of his own. Now Essex, being no fool, recognized that treasure was important to Her Majesty. Still, it held no fascination for him. For reasons I have never fathomed, achieving glory in battle seems to be his only reason for living. He cares not a whit for anything else."

Noah is enormously grateful that Sir Walter decided to tell the whole story. Not only does it mean that he still has Sir Walter's trust, but a thoroughgoing perspective such as this would have been impossible to extract by means of question-and-answer, which most laymen fail to realize is a deficient technique for seeing the overall picture.

Noah looks out of the window, and the miles seem to fly by. As Sir Walter seems to have reached a break in his narrative, Noah decides to probe. "So, Essex has no interest in enhancing his own wealth?"

Sir Walter shakes his head emphatically. "No. Though he never had much property, and what he did have he owed mainly to the Queen, he's always wagered everything *and more* on his military adventures, and has little to show for it but debts that the Queen helps him to pay—although he did marginally well on the Cadiz expedition. But we're getting ahead of ourselves, as we haven't discussed his forbidden participation in the disastrous *English* Armada expedition that took place in 1589, the year after the defeat of the Spanish Armada."

"Ah," says Noah. "I know something of this voyage, as my deceased former client Doctor Lopez helped to finance it, went along on the expedition, and lost everything he had. As I recall, the object of the expedition was to place Don Antonio on the Portuguese throne, to ensure that Portugal would remain independent of Spain."

Raleigh nods. "Then, perhaps you know that the Queen forbade Essex to go, but he went nevertheless? Even without more, insubordination of that kind would have cost you or me our very lives."

"No doubt," concurs Noah. "I also heard that Essex pounded on the gates of Lisbon, challenging all comers to individual combat in defense of the Queen's honor."

Raleigh drops into a dark reverie. "Can you imagine placing the lives of thousands of English military in the care of a man as *rash* as that?" He shakes his head mournfully, and shrugs. "And yet, that is what Her Majesty has done *time after time*! I have seen Essex personally lead movements so audacious that the enemy was too amazed to take full advantage. Well," he sighs, "one may not fault him for lack of courage. That's sure."

Noah says: "After that came the Cadiz expedition, which is commonly understood to be Essex's high-water mark. What may we learn from that?"

"That expedition was somewhat unusual in that, as far as I'm aware, it was the only instance in which Essex did not deliberately flout the Queen's instructions, which were to sack and capture coastal cities, sink Spanish naval ships wherever they might be found, and bring home as much Spanish booty as we could hold. Once again, Essex mortgaged his lands to the hilt to help finance the expedition. We were given about five thousand soldiers, and enough ships to transport them. Five thousand is not enough to invest a distant city against recapture, but it's enough to sack the city and steal everything in sight before the cavalry arrives.

"Most of our soldiers were sorely disappointed when Essex gave strict orders that nothing was to be stolen by the men. Everything *they* took was to be paid for. It was for officers *only* to decide what to sack and bring home. And English soldiers were forbidden to rape or murder indiscriminately. When we reached Cadiz, the Dutch who'd joined us turned out to be uncontrollable in that regard, their own country having been mercilessly marauded by the Spanish, you see. But Essex would have none of it, and put the Lord Admiral and me in charge of breaking up their revenge."

Noah finds this most curious. "He was a model of chivalry."

"Oh, yes. He even made a point of inviting some women of mean class to dine with the officers. They were treated like real English ladies, and were all smiles when they bade us farewell. But, as the Queen has reminded us all, she does not send us abroad to behave as gentlemen, but rather to vanquish her enemies. The chivalry was all Essex's idea.

"If you bear in mind that Drake was Essex's ideal, it will not surprise you that Essex bypassed Lisbon on the way south, which he should really not have done, as we had learned the city was ill-prepared for assault from the sea. But his decision to pass straight on to Cadiz turned out to be highly advantageous. If Lisbon was ill-prepared, Cadiz was *really* caught with its breeches down.

"When the Lord Admiral saw that the town's defenses were entirely unmanned, he told Essex we would be going in from the sea, and Essex interpreted this as permission to lead an immediate landing. I'll let the Lord Admiral tell you what happened then, but I can say this much. The landing point chosen by Essex without advice of his senior staff, including myself, was so exposed to hostile fire, it was *insane*. In addition, he exposed himself to great personal risk performing other heroic but needless deeds, such as planting the flag, which risks the Queen had expressly forbidden him to take. And she'd sworn to hold each member of the general staff responsible should any injury befall Essex, her dear favorite and near kinsman.

"We did enormous damage to Cadiz, and took a fair deal of bounty, but our damage to the king's navy was limited. Worse, we knew our bounty was insufficient to render the expedition profitable, so the consensus was to follow Drake's example and go to the Azores to try to catch some of the king's gold inadequately guarded and too far from Spain for the king to interfere. But Essex insisted that, if we were to do that, he would remain at Cadiz and take personal charge of holding the city against the Spanish. As our numbers were insufficient to hold the city against a determined onslaught by land, and we'd all been made to fear for Essex's safety, on my advice none of us would agree to his proposal. So, we came home instead, to the cheers of the crowd, and the outrage of the Queen.

"It was unfair of her, really, as we'd sought her permission to remain off the Spanish coast for the purpose of intercepting the king's West

Indies gold shipment, but she turned us down. We learned later that the gold ships arrived not two days after we left for home. We barely missed bringing her a king's ransom in gold."

Raleigh turns to Noah. "I understand the Queen has a soft spot for you, Noah, but I expect you've seen her vent her spleen on courtiers and officers."

Noah shivers dramatically, and looks heavenward.

Raleigh nods. "Then, you know."

"Tell me something, Sir Walter. Sir Robert Cecil mentioned during Lord Mountjoy's presentation that England was caught unawares by a second Spanish armada in 1596. How could that have happened?"

"In the summer of '95, the conquistadors had conducted a few raids on Cornwall, which had shaken us all rather badly. Then, in '96, Essex received intelligence through his spy network (which one and all believed had been secretly 'inherited' from his father-in-law, Secretary Walsingham) that another armada was being cobbled together. Although I doubted that such intelligence was more than a phantom ploy, and have always doubted that river defenses could hold off a determined invasion, I was put in charge of defenses all around the Thames, and placed lookouts everywhere. As you and everyone else know, the Thames never saw a Spanish vessel.

"It took months to confirm that there in fact *was* an armada. Although it was huge, it had been assembled in haste, comprised largely of merchantmen, and foundered off the English coast. It was a major disaster for Spain. Now you see why you and I can ride along England's southern coast without fear of attack."

There's a sudden shout from Lieutenant Carter, and their carriage picks up a determined speed. "Perhaps I spoke too soon," observes Raleigh.

Noah tries to put his head out of the window to see what's happening, but Raleigh pulls him back, and pushes his head down. The boom of a musket some distance behind is immediately followed by the thwack of a ball piercing the carriage just above Noah's head. Another musket fires, this time *ahead* of the carriage, followed by the sound of a ball striking something meaty nearby, and an oath from Lieutenant Carter. The coach stops and Bucklebury rears, unaccustomed to the sound of firearms.

"I'm hit, sir!" Carter shouts to Raleigh. "Better grab a pistol!" A moment later, Carter's own pistol discharges. He lets out another oath. Hindered by his wound, he's apparently missed, and will have to dismount to reload.

Raleigh reaches behind the seat and draws out two short pistols, offering one to Noah, who declines the offer with a shake of his head and draws a short pistol of his own. "Good for you," says Raleigh. He juts his head out of the window and risks a glance up ahead. "The enemy is reloading," he says, and shouts through the window: "Lieutenant, can you still ride? We *must* get off the road instantly!"

"I can, sir," replies Carter with a pained grunt. "I see a likely hiding spot." He shouts to the driver. "Harry, follow me!"

Noah can only guess at what's happening outside. The carriage suddenly jerks ahead, and veers off to the left at a dangerous angle, accelerating to breakneck speed and leaving the road. Its wheels strike ruts and ridges that toss its two passengers about like a pair of ragdolls. It's all Noah can do to hold onto his loaded pistol, and he fervently prays it will not discharge from some freakish impact against the firing mechanism.

Suddenly, the carriage pitches forward and there's silence, as though it's been driven off a cliff. A terrifying moment later, there comes a splashing sound, as of riding through a deep puddle, and then the wheels seem to grip firmly again as they turn up the side of a small ravine. After what seems like an interminable jostling, at last the carriage swings about and comes to a halt. Raleigh bursts out of the door.

"Out, Serjeant!" he commands. "And keep *down*!"

Noah tumbles out of the carriage onto a patch of dry grass, and crouches down as low as he can. Turning to his left, he finds himself face-to-face with the terrified driver, who's jumped down off his seat, drawn his dagger, and now wears the dismayed look of a man who realizes he's come ill-equipped for the fight of his life.

Raising his head only slightly, Noah sees that the road they've been traveling runs atop a man-made embankment apparently built to elevate it off a flood plain. Carter has brought them down off the road and across a small stream into a wood, and then turned the carriage about to face the road.

Still seated atop Bucklebury, the wounded lieutenant's face is ashen, and he writhes in pain. Before Raleigh can help him dismount, however, he must becalm Bucklebury, who's near panic. Making a grunting effort, Raleigh helps Carter down, and lays him face up on the ground to examine his wound.

To Noah's shock, Bucklebury takes this as his cue to bolt in terror back the way he came, galloping across the stream and up onto the roadway, heedless that the horsemen who've attacked them from both front and behind have now met and dismounted there. Bucklebury very nearly runs them both down but, as he hurtles toward them, they leap out of his way to avoid being crushed.

Much to Noah's dismay, Bucklebury disappears down the other side of the embankment and, just like that, his black beauty has vanished. His heart sinks.

Apparently confident they're out of musket range, the two gunmen stand on the elevated road in broad daylight, each holding his horse's reins, brazenly choosing the best route to cross the stream and resume their attack. One, a tall man in dark garb, peers into the woods where the carriage now sits, while the other, shorter and lighter in appearance, points out various routes by which they might overtake their quarry with least resistance.

"Cheeky, aren't they?" remarks Raleigh, frightening Noah out of his wits. Raleigh has sidled up silently, carrying the lieutenant's discharged pistol.

As soon as Noah's heart drops from his mouth back down to his chest, he replies. "Considering there are only two of them, they seem entirely overconfident." He glances over his shoulder at Carter, who lies squirming on the ground. "How is Carter faring?"

Raleigh's gaze remains focused on the assailants, but he answers the question. "The ball traveled clean through his shoulder. So long as we can get a surgeon to stitch him up, he'll be fine, if a bit lame for a while." He points with his chin at the two men on the road. "I think those blighters are alone. Have you seen sign of any more of them?"

"No," replies Noah. "Don't highwaymen often work in pairs?"

"Those are not highwaymen," says Raleigh, reloading Carter's pistol by touch, his eyes riveted on the man pointing out various means of approach.

"They're not?"

Raleigh smirks. "Has anybody demanded your money?"

"No," says Noah curiously.

Raleigh beckons the driver over, and hands him Carter's reloaded pistol. "Harry, I want you to stay over there by Lieutenant Carter, and guard us against anyone coming from *that* direction." He points left. As the driver scurries away, Raleigh whispers hoarsely after him: "Keep your eyes moving."

"Well, if they're not highwaymen," asks Noah, "what *are* they?"

"They're assassins," replies Raleigh matter-of-factly. Glancing at Noah's expression, he laughs quietly. "And remember to thank the lieutenant when this is all over, as he appears to have taken a bullet intended for *you*."

"But, why would anyone wish to assassinate *me*?"

"I told you," says Raleigh, deftly reloading another pistol. "You continually underestimate your importance. That's a serious mistake, and you really ought to stop it. Could cost you your life someday...like today."

The two assassins lead their mounts behind the embankment and disappear from view, having evidently selected their route of attack.

"Hadn't we better warn Harry they're coming toward his side?" asks Noah.

Sir Walter shakes his head. "Clever lads," he says, with a note of sarcasm. "If I'm not mistaken, they'll cross the road together in a crouch, right—" His gaze moves in the direction opposite that in which the assassins had been moving just before they disappeared, and, using one of the two loaded pistols he now holds, points to a break in the bushes on the opposite side of the road. "*There!*"

To Noah's surprise, a minute later the two men pop their heads up at the precise point Raleigh anticipated. Evidently, their mounts have been tied off out of sight, as they now steal across the road on foot, each carrying a pistol. Noah and Raleigh, concealed behind a row of thick bushes, watch them move toward the near side of the road, then begin to approach in search of the stream.

As the assassins take cover in the brush, there's unexpected movement on the road immediately behind them. It's Bucklebury, who has quietly returned and now stands on the roadway, merrily swishing his tail, as though he's once again found himself among friends. It occurs to Noah that there's something to be learned from this, but it's not coming to him right away.

Sir Walter obviously notices the horse's return, as well, but evidently thinks nothing of it. "Our killers are coming close," he whispers. "We'll have to move on them soon."

"Wait!" replies Noah hoarsely, his mind racing. "I think Bucklebury has brought us more company!"

Just as Raleigh turns to look at Noah as though he's lost his wits, Arthur Arden and Andres Salazar ride heedlessly up the far side of the embankment, apparently following Bucklebury's lead. Cheerful Killigrew trots up behind, engaging them in conversation.

"Who the devil are *they*?" demands Raleigh, obviously alarmed at this intrusion.

"They're my assistants," replies Noah.

"Barristers?"

Noah nods. "Two are."

"Oh, *blast*! There's a bog on the other side of these killers, and a stream *behind* them. The way your assistants are blundering along, they're inadvertently *trapping* them." He turns to Noah, exasperated. "Your friends are about to get themselves killed."

The assassins, almost as though overhearing Raleigh's remark, turn with alarm toward the noise coming from the road, obviously spotting the newcomers. Sir Walter peers hard at the assassins. "The one nearer the road just cocked his pistol. *Blast!* We have to bring this confrontation to a head *right now!*" Without so much as turning to glance at Noah, he whispers: "Cover me against the other one!"

With that, Raleigh performs an act of cold-blooded bravery Noah could not have conceived in his wildest imagination. While the attention of the crouching assassin is riveted on Noah's young friends, Sir Walter silently walks right behind him, takes aim with one of his pistols, and fires at the assassin's head from point-blank range. The effect is quite devastating, as the top of his head explodes like a melon into a mist of red, splashing blood, skull, and shredded brain matter across the surrounding vegetation. Birds shriek, and dart up out of the surrounding trees.

In a moment, the dead man's confederate rises from a crouch and stands upright, staring Raleigh in the face, eyes wide, lower lip quivering in terror. As he brings up his shaky pistol hand, Noah prepares to shoot, but before he can do so, Raleigh raises his second pistol and shoots the second killer through the heart, killing him instantly.

A bit further into the woods, a rabbit scurries from cover, abandoning its hutch to escape some threat. Noah turns toward it, and can barely believe his eyes, as a *third* assassin stealthily rises from a crouch and raises his musket toward Sir Walter, who's oblivious to the remaining killer and out of ammunition.

Noah takes as careful aim as he can from a squatting position with no time to spare, aiming straight at the man's chest. He fires, and the recoil knocks him back off his feet. Throwing his hands back to break his fall, he drops his pistol to the ground and leaps to his feet, ready to assist Sir Walter in any further fighting.

Sir Walter is plainly in no need of further assistance, however, for there he stands in precisely the same spot, unharmed and smiling abashedly.

"A *barrister,* you say?" he asks merrily, and laughs aloud. He scratches his head and shrugs. "I suppose these devils were a bit more clever than I gave them credit for!" He tramps through the underbrush toward the downed musketeer.

Noah runs to join him, his heart pounding, earnestly hoping the man will survive, as the thought of killing another man is alien to his very being.

As they come upon the wounded man, he's conscious, lying on his back in a spreading pool of blood, his breathing labored. Noah can see that his round has struck its victim in the gut, at least a foot below his intended target.

Noah has conversed with enough soldiers to know that a shot to the gut is almost always fatal. Even if the victim survives the loss of blood, death will surely claim him by infection. But this man will not survive to suffer infection, as blood leaks from him at an impossible rate.

Noah now realizes he will shortly have something far more serious than hurtful remarks for which to seek divine forgiveness, and he knows that this moment will haunt him to the end of his days.

The wounded man seems pleading and regretful, showing no sign of anger or hatred. He appears to recognize Sir Walter, and grunts a few words barely audible over his wheezing breath.

"Are you...Sir Walter...Raleigh?" he gasps.

Sir Walter kneels by the man's side.

"I am," he replies hesitantly. "Have you aught to say to me?"

His reply seems to put the man at ease. "At least, I die...in the arms of...one of Her Majesty's true knights." He smiles so pathetically, it nearly breaks Noah's heart.

Sir Walter looks at Noah, perplexed, and places his arm gently under the dying man, lifting his head and shoulders off the ground. "As you love your Queen—and for the love of *God*—tell us upon whose instructions you have attempted this dastardly deed! If you do so, Her Majesty...and I...will forgive you your final trespass."

The man nods emphatically, as though he'll try, but is uncertain whether his breath will give out first. He struggles for voice. "Frenchman," he whispers hoarsely. Then, struggling for his last breath, he gasps: "Wolf." As he opens his mouth to say another word, all movement of his face ceases at once, and Noah marvels how a living man can be transformed so quickly and so completely into an inanimate effigy of flesh and blood.

Sir Walter lays him back down. "On behalf of Her Majesty Queen

Elizabeth and myself, your final trespass against us is forgiven," he says, making good his word. "And may God have mercy on your soul." He closes the dead man's eyes.

Although, from the corner of his eye, Noah can see Sir Walter looking up at him, he finds himself unable to take his eyes off the dead man. He suffers a regret more profound than he has ever known, except that which he felt on the death of his beloved first wife Rachel. At least *that* was a death he struggled mightily to avoid. But not this one. This one he *brought about.* Just as Cain killed Abel, Noah Ames has now killed this nameless wretch.

From somewhere far away, he hears Raleigh's small voice gently saying his name. "Noah," it repeats. Then, with a note of quiet command: "Serjeant Ames!"

At last, Noah looks him in the face. "Yes, Sir Walter?"

"You did no wrong in shooting this man."

Noah nods skeptically. "Perhaps."

Raleigh sighs, and speaks as though from his very soul. "When I was a young officer and my family was reclaiming its ancient lands in Ireland, I was ordered to put a whole village to the sword." He looks aside. "I obeyed my orders, of course. One by one, I watched my command put them all to death. Men…women—" He brings his hands up over his eyes to hide his shame and a flood of tears, and his voice breaks. "Children!" He lowers his hand to his mouth and looks beseechingly up at the sky in grief, his voice trembling. "Oh, God. God forgive me!"

Noah is too numb to be horrified, and his heart goes out to this agonized soul. "Why do you tell me this now?" he whispers.

Raleigh wipes his eyes dry. "Because *that* was a sin!" He shakes his head and points to the dead musketeer. "*This* was not. And you'll see the difference in time. Meanwhile, I thank you for my very life." He raises one knee, preparing to stand. "And as the Good Lord instructed Job: 'Gird up thy loins now, like a man!'" He rises, and returns to the wounded lieutenant. Noah trudges a few steps behind, staring at the ground.

"Serjeant Ames!" comes a youthful voice from across the road. It sounds like Andres Salazar.

Noah looks to Sir Walter for permission to go to his friends.

"You may as well go." He points his chin to the wounded lieutenant. "I'm pleased to say this young fellow is not nearly as bad off as I expected. His bleeding is stopped, and I wonder whether he will even need a surgeon."

Noah breathes a sigh of relief. As he reaches the road and looks down the embankment on the other side, his first impression is of some kind of horse farm. Not only have Arthur, Andres, and Cheerful dismounted, but Bucklebury is still wandering about on his own, looking very regal in the Queen's livery, and three unfamiliar horses are tied off together to a nearby tree trunk. It occurs to Noah that those three will need to be brought to a nearby town or cut loose, as their owners are dead.

"What was all the gunfire?" Arthur asks.

As Noah has no desire to report this disturbing news more than once, he waits to reply until the other two young men have also gathered round. He sighs. "We ran into a few highwaymen, now deceased. Sir Walter believes they were, rather, assassins."

"Were they after Raleigh?" asks Arthur, wide-eyed.

Noah shakes his head sadly. "Lieutenant Carter is the only one wounded, and he was shot on sight, even before we left the road." He points to his horse. "He was riding Bucklebury when he was hit."

Cheerful is the first to reach the obvious conclusion. "So, they were after *you*!"

"So it appears."

"But why?" asks Cheerful. "Is this about the theft of Mountjoy's map? The murder at the Tower?"

Noah is amazed. He wonders how Cheerful knows about *either* of those things. "If it had been about the murder alone, I expect Sir Walter would have been first on their list, as he is chief investigator. What do you know of a *map*?"

Arthur chimes in. "Jonathan thinks he's found it!"

"*Found* it?" says Noah. "It may never have been stolen! When did you speak with Jonathan? Had he and Jessica already reached London before you followed after me?"

The three skulk about instead of answering, which Noah finds alarming. "Out with it!" he commands.

Arthur speaks up. "No, sir. We haven't spoken with Jonathan, as neither he nor her ladyship had returned by the time we left. In fact, they were not even *on their way* to London. Jonathan had sent you a note that reached Holborn just as we were leaving your home. Mistress Ames gave it to me, to bring to you. The decision to open it was mine alone." He draws Jonathan's note from his pocket, and hands it to Noah, looking as though he's prepared to be dressed down for his presumptuousness.

"We *all* decided," shout Andres and Cheerful.

"You did the right thing, of course," says Noah, and turns away to read it.

Over his shoulder, he hears the boys disputing amongst themselves. "You see? You big dolt!" mutters Andres. "I *told* you he wouldn't be angry."

"Oh, be quiet!" Arthur replies, with irritation.

Noah turns and snaps at them. "Yes. *All* of you be quiet! Need I remind you, you're not at *Eton*?" There's silence. Noah regrets his snappishness, but he's just killed a man, and has now learned that his daughter has not been returned safely to London, as expected. He feels entitled to the quiet of his own thoughts.

Dear Sjt. Ames:

I write to you from the earl's residence at Wells. Lady Jessica is in perfect condition, but for her mood, which I trust will improve by and by, as I am about to escort her from the earl's premises. We shall stay tonight at Burt's farm, which is a few miles east of Wells, adjacent to the Bunch of Grapes tavern (near the River Sheppey by Shepton Mallet), which is operated by the selfsame Burt. (It is Burt's daughter Bessie who faithfully attended upon her ladyship during her brief sojourn in the small manor house on the earl's grounds.)

Please forgive me for what I must write next. Although I had intended to escort Lady Jessica directly to London, a higher duty has required a change of plans. While I deeply regret this unexpected turn of events (and am painfully aware that my tardiness may cost me dearly), I trust that, in my position, you would do no less for Queen and country.

On my way here, I had occasion to stop at the Hind in Brakenhale, where I saw (but was unseen by) Robert Poley, whose name will be familiar to you. In assisting the innkeeper in carrying the drunk and unconscious Poley to his room, I spied among his luggage a long leather cylinder, of a type used to transport maps. Before retiring to my room, the innkeeper informed me that Poley would be having dinner there the following day with one Nicholas Skeres, of whom you also know. By chance, I overheard Skeres and Poley discuss a meeting they needed to attend on Tuesday night at the Rose & Crown in Bridgwater, only a few miles from here. Skeres also told Poley that he was carrying (please forgive the language, as it is Skeres', not mine own) "the private parts of every high ranking officer in England," and mentioned that their expenses were being borne by someone named "Jake," of whom I saw no sign and learned no more.

Being aware of the unsavory reputation of these two men, when I saw them in possession of this cylinder, it occurred to me that they might be transporting the purloined military map of which you told me prior to my regrettable fracas, of which no further mention need here be made. Now, please do not be angry with me, as I do recall you thought it entirely plausible that no map was ever purloined, but I also recall your telling me that, if it had been stolen, it would bear Lord M's watermark. I cannot but follow these men on their westward journey until I am satisfied that they are not transporting this map, confirmation of which will require only a glance (although how I shall get that, as yet I have no idea).

I had no choice but to inform Lady J of my dubious quest, and offered to install her comfortably at Burt's farm until such time as you could send an alternative escort. She has insisted, however, upon accompanying me to the inn at Bridgwater.

By the time you receive this note, I fully expect my suspicions to have been disproven. Once that has been done, I shall write you immediately to inform you that I am escorting Lady J home to London without further delay.

On the off-chance I find these men to have the very map of which you spoke, it is my intention to install Lady J at a safe and appropriate place of her choosing, and alone to follow the map to its intended place of departure from the realm, at which point I shall attempt to secure it, and bring to justice those guilty of the most heinous treason.

Your Obedient Servant,
Hawking

P.S. I write now in haste, as Lady J has left the room in the expectation that this note shall be sealed presently without emendation. I fear my intentions stated above may be frustrated by her ladyship, who is the strongest-willed woman I have ever encountered. If I am compelled to follow these men beyond Bridgwater, I doubt she shall consent to leave off, but shall do my best to see that she does so, and safely, and I shall write you as often as I may. Rest assured that, before so much as a scratch shall befall her ladyship, your obt svt shall be dead already.

Noah finds the mental image painted by Jonathan's concluding reassurance to be anything but comforting. Yet, he cannot afford to dwell on it long. He considers the new information provided by Jonathan's letter. As Essex's lackeys are evidently involved in a map-smuggling plot, Noah wonders whether their involvement has been authorized by Essex himself. Although he doubts it (Essex being so isolated), if so, he would have little choice but to investigate the object of the plot and report it to the Queen. This might provide the satisfaction of exacerbating Essex's dilemma greatly, but Noah has no desire to place himself and his family at the center of such a storm.

As Noah frets, he sees Sir Walter walking toward him from the road. Raleigh doffs his cap as he passes the boys, who snap to attention like soldiers caught off-guard. Raleigh still appears to be musing about their reaction when he reaches Noah.

"We're all packed up and ready to go," says Raleigh. "I've made Carter as comfortable as possible."

"How far is it from here to Bridgwater?"

"As the crow flies? Oh, about a hundred miles, I should say."

"And from Mountjoy's place in Dorset to Bridgwater?"

Raleigh shrugs. "Say, half that. And, unless you happen to *fly* like a crow, Dorset is *on the way* to Bridgwater. Good roads out here are few and far between, but the road from Dorset up toward Bridgwater is quite reliable."

"Very well, thank you. Would you have any objection to my friends accompanying us as far as Dorset?"

"They'd be welcome. Even *more* welcome if they can shoot!"

"They can."

"Good. But, are they armed?"

Noah shouts to the boys. "Gentlemen, Sir Walter wishes you to present arms."

Before Raleigh can protest being misquoted, the boys go to their saddlebags and draw out knives, pistols, muskets, in short, every kind of handheld arms known to man, until they fairly bristle with weaponry. A few items clank to the ground, as there are simply too many to hold.

With a barely suppressed smile, Raleigh walks sternly about them, as though inspecting them on parade. In Salazar's hand, in addition to a short sword, is a shiny scimitar-shaped blade with a jeweled handle. Raleigh stands before him, and mutters: "I'm not even going to *ask* you where you got that."

He steps back. "You!" he shouts, pointing to Arthur, and then to the failed assassins' horses, "fetch those horses and tie them to the rear of the coach." He looks at Andres and Cheerful, and shouts again. "You two bring your horses to the carriage, and stand ready to mount."

"Yes, sir!" they reply.

As they lead their mounts across the road at a good clip, Sir Walter turns to Noah. "Serjeant Ames, would you be so kind as to ride your own horse for a while? We seem to be running low on healthy lieutenants."

Noah nods, turns toward Bucklebury, and bows. Bucklebury snorts, and high-steps over to Noah, practically handing him the reins.

CHAPTER 10

DRAWN BY TWO aging horses, a closed carriage clops slowly westward along a road flanked by deep forest. On the driver's bench, the venerable old thespian Augustine Phillips and his young footman sit abreast in shared silence, their faces bathed in the warm golden light of the rapidly setting sun. Behind them, the moon rises, and the azure sky gradually deepens to an oceanic blue. So late in the year, no bird takes wing, nor cricket sings.

From behind comes the sound of several horses galloping together. All at once, the carriage is overtaken by three horsemen, led by the dark-suited Frenchman from the Rose & Crown. The other horsemen carry lit torches in anticipation of the oncoming darkness.

The Frenchman slows to a lope and keeps abreast of the driver's bench, while the other riders drop behind. Staring silently at the old thespian for a moment, he rubs the back of his head, wincing in evident pain. "You are on your way home to Cornwall, *Maître* Phillips?"

Phillips turns to the familiar voice, smiles at first, but then seems perplexed. "Why, you *know* that I am, monsieur!" he says kindly. "I had no idea you would be leaving Bridgwater so soon. Have the festivities come to an end?"

"Non, non," replies le Loup, "they are continuing."

"Ah, then they must have mounted an entertainment not to your liking. *Tsk, tsk.* Pity! I'm sure *something* will amuse you later on." He looks at the other two riders, who seem preoccupied with the contents of the carriage. "I see you and your companions have brought no bags. Are you out for a pleasure ride in the fresh air? You couldn't have chosen a more delightful autumn evening." He looks about with evident pleasure.

Le Loup clops along uncertainly, evidently unsure whether the old man is being friendly or playing him for a fool. "Tell me, *Maître* Phillips.

You have seen a young man and woman pass you on horseback tonight, *non*?"

Phillips looks to his footman, shakes his head, and shrugs. "No," he replies. "I don't think we've been passed by *anyone* this evening."

"Who is it that sits next to you?"

"This is Pedro, my footman. He's a Spaniard, and speaks little English, I'm afraid." The last rays of the sun disappear, and the road assumes that deathly silence that signals the onset of a clear autumn night.

"And, inside your carriage," demands le Loup, "who eez there?"

Phillips raises an eyebrow. "I'm not sure your tone is at all appropriate, monsieur. I feel as though I am being questioned by a parish constable."

Le Loup gives him an oily smile. "Do not be concerned. I am no constable, *maître*. But who is zees? Is she a woman?"

"She is my *mother*," says Phillips sternly. "See here, monsieur! You inquire into matters that are no concern of yours! Now, I will thank you to be on your way, and take your two friends with you. God give you good e'en!" He signals for Pedro to quicken their pace but, before Pedro can comply, le Loup whistles to his companions, and summons them to the front of the carriage, where they turn and stop. Alarmed, Pedro pulls the reins, bringing the horses to a halt before there can be a collision.

Le Loup smiles as though he's caught Phillips in a lie. "But your muzzer was not *wiss* you at zee inn, *maître*."

Phillips adopts a more conciliatory tone. "Ah, but she *was*, sir. We were only passing through and, during my brief performance, she remained in the carriage."

Le Loup regards him impatiently. "Alone?"

Phillips looks exasperated. "My mother is quite ill. She remained in the coach to avoid any possibility of contagion. That is why we had to leave immediately after my performance."

"I see. And what is her malady?"

"If you *must* know," he says in a hoarse whisper, "*leprosy*."

Le Loup looks to his two companions, who draw their horses a step back at the mere mention of the dread disease. He asks Phillips skeptically: "She is a *leper*?"

Phillips is obviously dismayed by the intrusiveness of this questioning. "Why do you think I ride out here in the open, sir? And, what is worse, she seems to have acquired another illness, as well."

Le Loup is incensed, and frowns at his worried companions, as though he finds them credulous fools. He dismounts impatiently, muttering to himself in French, strides back to the carriage, steps up on the running board, and juts his head inside, where an old woman in a shawl and gray cowl crouches over, her face down.

"Madame, may I see your face?"

"Aaaaaoooow!" says the woman in a loud, high-pitched voice that speaks of the lower orders of North London. "Augustine! Augustine!" she cries out shrilly. "There's an ugly Spaniard stickin' 'is 'ed in the coach!"

Losing all patience, le Loup steps down to the ground, swings open the door, and begins to tug the woman out by the hand.

"Augustine!" she cries, feebly resisting. "He's pullin' me outta the coach! Aaaaaaaooow! He's 'urtin' me! Git awwwiiy from me!"

With some effort, le Loup pulls her out onto the road. She crouches down, hiding her face, even in the near-darkness.

Le Loup is furious. "If you wish ziss ugly 'Spaniard' to go away, madam, you will have to *show him your face*!" He reaches down, and throws her cowl back over her shoulder. "Look at me, madam. *Look at me!*" He reaches for her hair, but she slaps his hand away.

"Don't *touch* me, you brute! Awwright! If you want to see me face so much, here it is, then. Have yer *fill*!"

The decayed harridan grimacing up at him is a hideous nightmare. Her teeth are rotten to black, small pieces of her face have sloughed off by disease, and the giant reddish bulb erupting on her forehead appears to be a bubo, the surest sign of deadly plague. The Frenchman recoils in horror, throwing his hands up and drawing away in alarm.

"Unclean!" his companions shout. "Unclean!" And before le Loup can gather his wits, they gallop off the way they came.

"Oh!" says le Loup contritely. "I am so sorry, madam!"

"Get awiiiiy!" she shrieks. She pulls the cowl back over her face, creeps pathetically back into the carriage, and pulls the door shut.

Le Loup slinks back to his horse. Before mounting, he bows to Phillips. "*Maître,* please accept…"

But Phillips clucks his tongue indignantly and points the way le Loup came. "I trust you will leave at once, and allow me to assuage some of the hurt you have needlessly inflicted *upon my mother,* sir!" Le Loup remounts, and is gone in an instant.

When he's disappeared from view, Phillips signals Pedro to move on. In another couple of miles, the carriage pulls far off the road behind a row of tall bushes, and comes to a halt.

A young man's voice comes from behind a nearby tree, imitating the old woman. "Aaaaaoooow! Augustine! Get this ugly Spaniard *awiiy* from me!" Jonathan emerges, carrying two pistols in one hand, leading two horses with the other. He deftly holsters the pistols and ties off the horses, then steps jauntily onto the carriage's running board and shouts through the open window. "Is *madame* prepared to meet her admiring public?"

He steps down onto the ground, opens the door, and bows low, making a sweeping gesture with his arm. Phillips and Pedro step down from their perch and look on, all smiles.

Having already removed the stage wig and makeup, as well as the ratty-looking cloak, Jessica steps down regally from the cab, curtsies, and smiles, revealing her own pearly white teeth. The men applaud heartily.

"Incomparable, madam!" says Jonathan. "May I have this dance?"

Pedro dons the pipe and tabor, and begins a merry tune to which Jonathan and Jessica spring into the most energetic dance they know. Phillips claps his hands in time.

After a few minutes, Pedro and Phillips fatigue, and the music ends. Pedro makes a small fire, and places across it four coneys pierced with sticks. As he boils some greens in a pot, a heavenly fragrance wafts about the campsite.

<hr>

EVEN AFTER THE music stops, Jonathan and Jessica continue to dance wildly to their own imaginary tune, laughing with abandon. There, in the firelight under the spreading maples, Jonathan is so happy he thinks his heart must burst, for surely no man can steal such rapture from the gods and yet be allowed to live.

When finally they can dance no more, he moves in to kiss her…and then remembers his place…and hers. But, to his surprise, as he holds her body to his, gazing deeply into her eyes, she makes no sign of protest. She seems rather to await his next move, perhaps as a test of his mettle. *Are you a gentleman, or no?* he imagines her asking. Though it's the hardest thing he's ever done, he withdraws a polite distance, smiles at her through his agonized longing, and bows his thanks for the dance, which she reciprocates with a most elegant curtsey.

At long last, they leave their imaginary dance floor of leaves and dirt, hand in hand, and assume their dinner seats, consisting of two logs. Pedro serves a modest meal on pewter plates that rest on their laps, with sweet red wine in pewter goblets that, for lack of a proper table, have to be set on the ground. Yet, to Jonathan it seems a feast, and he can tell from Jessica's expression that she feels the same way.

Once they've eaten sufficiently to feel no longer ravenous, Jonathan bows in place to Pedro and his host. *"Muchas gracias!"*

Pedro says something to Phillips in Spanish, who translates for Jonathan and Jessica. "Pedro says you are most welcome, and he wishes humbly to thank the lady for her magnificent performance."

Jessica's eyes light up. "Please extend my thanks to Pedro, Master Phillips. Given your own vast experience upon the public stage, I would be most interested to hear *your* thoughts on the matter."

Phillips hesitates, obviously unsure whether Jessica's seeking a compliment or wants his true opinion. Evidently, he decides it's the latter. "Well, I must give you high marks on the dramatic way in which you finally revealed your hideous mask. You set it up perfectly, and obviously it had the desired effect on le Loup. But I do have a few small notes."

"Pray, tell," says Jonathan, never wont to bypass an opportunity to tease Jessica.

"For one thing," says Phillips, "judging from the manner of *my* speech, would my mother really be expected to speak like a street vendor from North London?"

Jonathan snickers, and Jessica digs her elbow into his side. "What else?" he asks.

"Well, your insistence on wearing sloughing facial skin *together* with a bubo made it rather awkward for me to name the particular disease with which you were supposedly afflicted."

Jonathan nods. "Is it even *possible* to have both leprosy and plague at the same time?"

"I've no idea," replies Phillips. With a nod to Jessica, he adds, "But the important thing is, neither did le Loup."

Jessica offers Jonathan a self-satisfied smile. "Well," she says, "at least we shan't be seeing *him* any more."

"That's problematic," Phillips says thoughtfully, "as he evidently intends to travel the same road, and will be moving faster than we. I'd give odds we'll see him at least once more, when he passes us. And, who knows? He may even stay at the same inn as we do, once or twice."

Jonathan tenses when he considers that possibility. "That was something else I wanted to ask you," he says. "You said you had occasion to speak with one of the two men who arrived at the inn just before your performance."

"Yes, I did. I was enjoying an ale when the shorter of the two accosted me. Friendly chap. Seemed a bit shifty, though."

"That would have been Poley," says Jonathan. "When you and I spoke at the inn, you said he'd mentioned something about his destination."

"Only in general terms," replies Phillips. "I mentioned to him that I was headed to my family's home in Falmouth (which I have always thought of as the westernmost tip of Cornwall), and he replied that he too was going to Cornwall, but farther still." He looks into the little fire. "Yes, those were his exact words, 'farther still.' As there's not much beyond Falmouth but sand and sea, I'm sure I have no idea what destination he was talking about."

Jonathan looks to Jessica, whose refined features seem more prominent in the glow of the firelight, lending her face an air of serious contemplation. Though she says nothing, she looks back at him with obvious interest. He decides to prod a bit further.

"Tell me, Master Phillips, is it true that much smuggling is done out of Cornwall?"

Phillips nearly chokes on his wine, and his eyes dart about, as though to make sure there's no one in the forest to overhear. "I have no idea, of course. Why, that would be *unlawful*, wouldn't it?"

Jonathan shrugs. "I suppose so. Otherwise, it would be called 'import-export.'"

"Then you should *call* it 'import-export.' People on the seacoast are very tetchy when they hear that other word. In fact, we're very near Devon now, which has a lot of coastline. People 'round *here* would prefer not to hear that word, as well."

"I see. Well, I thank you for your admonition, and shall avoid the word altogether, where I can. But, suppose someone…someone *else*, of course…not *you or* I or anyone *we* know, were to wish to take some papers out of the country without being detected. Is there any point of departure west of Falmouth that comes to mind?"

"Headed *where*?"

"Not sure."

"Well, I don't suppose the direction really matters much, as the peninsula is so narrow at that point that traveling around it is usually fairly quick."

"Suppose the papers were going to Ireland," says Jonathan.

"I suppose one might consider any port town on the northern coast," says Phillips, and his aged brow creases in thought. "Perranporth is probably a bit too rocky, and St. Agnes has never been able to sustain a port…but St. Ives, perhaps." He shrugs. "In truth, Falmouth on the *south* would serve nearly as well."

"There seem to be towns with a lot of 'saint' names there. Was none of those ports established before the advent of Christianity?"

"Many were, I'm quite sure. Cornwall is one of the ancient kingdoms, of course, like Devon."

"Kingdoms?" says Jessica.

"Oh, yes, before England was unified. They even have their own languages. There have been ports in Cornwall and Devon since time out of mind...under different names than now, of course. Now, tell me something about yourselves. How do you come to know my cousin Anne?"

As Jessica appears confused, Jonathan explains. "Master Phillips and I discussed our mutual acquaintances from Cornwall. You and I know Anne Killigrew as 'Lady Anne Neville,' of course."

Jessica's eyebrows shoot up. "Of course, Auntie Anne! Oh, she's my *favorite*!"

It's Phillips' turn to be surprised. "Is she truly your aunt? For then you and I would be distantly related!"

"No," says Jessica, "Henry Neville—excuse me, *Sir* Henry now—was my father's best friend as I was growing up. I have always known him fondly as 'Uncle Henry,' and by extension, I suppose, his lovely wife as 'Auntie Anne.' I meant no disrespect."

"Of course not," says Phillips indulgently. "Who *is* your father, may I ask?"

Jessica looks to Jonathan for guidance, as she's unsure whether their true names have yet been revealed to the old thespian. When Jonathan nods encouragement, she replies: "My father is Serjeant Noah Ames, the Queen's own barrister."

Phillips seems surprised yet again. "Why, I have *met* the gentleman! He is a Hebrew, as I recall." He snaps his fingers. "Is your name Jessica?"

"It *is*, sir! Jessica, Lady Burlington," she says with her most winning smile. "Pleased to make your acquaintance. How did you come to meet Father?"

He laughs heartily. "Well, Sir Henry brought him to the theater one day, when we were playing *The Merchant of Venice*. Although your father enjoyed the play for the most part, he evidently detected some details in it that he believed had been stolen from his own life. The one that sticks in my mind was the name of the Jew's lovely daughter, Jessica. The Christian boy who won her away was named—"

"Lorenzo?" asks Jessica sternly. Evidently, she knew nothing of this coincidence before now.

"Lorenzo! Yes, that's it! How did you know? Have you seen the play?"

"No," she says solemnly. "Lorenzo was the name of my late husband, and he was Christian, of course."

Phillips evidently notices the change in Jessica's demeanor and is appalled to be the cause of it. "Oh, I am *so* sorry for your loss. Oh, my! I seem to have put my foot straight into things yet again! I *do* apologize."

Jessica's mood lightens. "Not at all," she assures him, "but I can see how Father might have detected the coincidence."

"Oh, he did much more than *detect* it. He came backstage after the performance and roundly berated Shakespeare, who was mortified, and denied any knowledge of your father's personal affairs. The two had apparently met a few times before, and your father felt betrayed. It took Sir Henry a bit of apologizing to calm him down."

Jessica's brow furrows. "Why would Uncle Henry be the one to apologize?"

Phillips becomes more circumspect. "Perhaps I've said too much." He seems lost in thought for a moment. "Sir Henry assured your father that he had discussed certain events with Shakespeare without mentioning that they were derived from your father's life."

"I see," she says. "Knowing Father's affection for Sir Henry, nothing like that could ever come between them for long."

"And it *didn't,*" says Phillips, clapping his thighs as though he's reached a happy ending. "I think we should retire, don't you? I assume your ladyship would wish to rest on a bench in the carriage."

———————⊰∘⊱————————

JESSICA HAS BEEN asleep only a few minutes when the sad dream of her deceased mother Rachel comes again. It's not so much a dream, really, as Jessica's sleepy re-imagining of an event first reported to her at the age of three by her mother's cousin Beth.

Jessica has no memories of her mother, who died when she was quite small. As any motherless child might have done, the young Jessica wove for herself an elaborate tapestry of her mother's life based upon a few snippets provided by relatives and friends. Father would rarely speak of Rachel, and Jessica avoided asking him anything about her, as whenever she put a direct question to him, he would drift off into a bottomless world of sadness from which no answers would ever emerge, and in which he might dwell inaccessible for hours, sometimes days.

The event giving form to Jessica's dream took place one fine day when Rachel was sixteen years old. She and Beth had been window-shopping together in one of London's finer districts, as both girls' families were still too poor to purchase any of the finery displayed in the windows.

A wedding among the higher nobility had just taken place at St. Paul's, and a formal horse-drawn procession of noble families was passing by. Rachel was enraptured by the beautiful raiments draped about the distinguished ladies in their lacquered carriages, drawn by the most beautifully groomed horses, each dressed in its owner's livery.

Rachel turned to Beth, and said, "How sad it is that we have only one life to live, and that all this splendor and respectability are foreclosed to us forever because we are Jews!" Aunt Beth reminded Rachel that she was the most beautiful woman in any dress, in any room, on any street, and that every man in a passing carriage could be seen to remark on her beauty, often tipping his hat or bowing in place. Still, Rachel took no comfort from Beth's reassurance, but rather sighed sadly, and turned away home.

In the retelling, Aunt Beth would ever be mindful to instruct Jessica on the principal moral of the story: *The woman who appreciates her God-given beauty requires little else for her satisfaction, while the woman who doesn't can never be satisfied.* Although Beth would also imply that Jessica, as heiress to her mother's beauty, could expect the same type of admiration and respect, she never stressed this subsidiary lesson, as she seemed to recognize it could dilute, or even drown out, the principal moral.

Jessica would naturally insist the story be repeated past the point of exhaustion, though the moral she privately drew from the tale was not the one that Beth provided, for Jessica sought not her *aunt's* advice, but any life-lessons she might glean from her *mother's* words and actions, however distorted they might have become in the retelling.

On this night, as on every night when the dream recurs, Jessica squirms and whimpers in her sleep.

Suddenly, she awakens to the sound of dried leaves crunching beneath boots, signifying approaching footsteps. Whoever it might be, he seems to be making no attempt to take her by surprise. Still, remembering where she is, her hand slowly closes around the handle of the unsheathed dagger under her pillow, and she opens one eye a slit.

Silhouetted in the moonlight just outside the carriage is Jonathan, who seems to be listening for something. She closes her eye once more. As she's just suffered through her recurring dream, she assumes he must have heard her weeping.

She's surprised, but hardly startled, when Jonathan opens the door and quietly takes a seat on the opposite bench. There's something so sweet and respectful about him. Still, she wonders why he hasn't simply returned to his own sleeping place, as there's no longer anything for him to hear.

In the peaceful night, she hears him whisper quietly, as though to himself. Although his words are spoken too softly to be heard, from their tone she guesses he's saying a prayer. Once it concludes, he rests quietly a few moments, then does something she would never have expected of him. He leans in, close enough for her to detect his sweet breath, and kisses her gently on the forehead. He turns and leaves, closing the door quietly behind.

This nocturnal visitation leaves her feeling most comforted. Though it made her tingle in a romantic way to feel his warm breath so near her in the night, his prayer for her tranquility and his kiss on the forehead made him seem rather...fatherlike.

She idly wonders what kind of father he would be to her children, and smiles to imagine him tumbling about with a little boy and girl who giggle as they climb all over him. But she puts the thought out of her mind as mere fantasy. That's not what she wants. No, not at all.

She slumbers, and dreams no more.

JONATHAN RETURNS TO his blanket and lies under the awning of susurrating leaves with his head raised high enough to watch the stars twinkling on the horizon. They seem to help him in musing whether he's better off in these woods than in London Town.

Ridiculous question, of course. How could he *possibly* be better off out here, where in town he has a good livelihood, even if it *is* presently imperiled?

Out here, not only is his very life in grave danger, but he truly has *nothing,* merely woods and sky, which, after all, belong to everyone alike...yet, he *does* have something here that he's never had in town, something that provides him with a feeling of true serenity.

He has *Jesse.* And, for this briefest of moments, she's his alone.

He knows in his heart that, without her, all the world's riches will be worthless. Yet, with her by his side, he would be rich beyond imagination, though he be a pauper.

He simply must find a way to win her. As he drifts off to sleep, he feels the strangest alternation between joy and despair. But somewhere in between lies…hope.

CHAPTER 11

THIS MORNING'S GLANCE at the map showed a tavern a few miles from Mountjoy's residence, but it's only as evening approaches that Noah catches sight of it in the distance. The sun has beaten down on the company all day, and his lips are parched. Even so, there'll be no stopping for ale now.

Keeping Bucklebury abreast of the carriage gives Noah an unobstructed view of its interior, where Sir Walter sits expressionless, and Lieutenant Carter lies asleep across the bench opposite. As of early afternoon, his two-day fever had not broken and, with the oncoming evening, it's expected to spike again, as it has the past two nights.

"How is he?" asks Noah through the window, stirring Sir Walter out of a dark reverie.

Sir Walter reaches across the coach and puts his hand on Carter's forehead. "About the same. Perhaps a *bit* cooler." He smiles wanly. "How much farther?" he asks Noah.

"Very near, indeed," replies Noah. "I'm sure a surgeon will be waiting."

Sir Walter searches his memory. "When did you send your young friend ahead to fetch the surgeon to Mountjoy's? Was it just this morning?"

Noah shakes his head. "*Yesterday* morning, Sir Walter. The days *do* run into one another out here, don't they?"

Sir Walter shakes his head. "These past few days have been infinitely varied by comparison to so many days at sea. At least *here* the shrubbery changes. On the high seas, every wave resembles every other...until they start to swell, which is downright dismaying, as it often signifies an oncoming storm."

Noah shields his eyes from the sun. Up ahead, he spots a hill that the map suggests will provide a view of Mountjoy's manor house. He's about to inform Sir Walter, when Cheerful appears on horseback atop the hill, his golden hair gleaming in the sun. Cheerful waves, and Andres and Arthur gallop ahead to meet him.

After a moment's conference on the hilltop, Andres trots back to the carriage to speak with Sir Walter and Noah. "The surgeon's been there since this morning. Cheerful's gone to tell him we've arrived."

A few minutes later, the carriage crests the hill, and Mountjoy's manor house comes into view. Although sizeable and well-maintained, its gardens are quite modest in size and design.

The driver must have spotted the surgeon waiting in the central doorway, for he picks up speed. He pulls up to the manor house, clambers down, and opens the carriage door for the surgeon.

The surgeon descends to the carriage and instructs the driver not to move the ailing lieutenant until he's been examined. Stepping up, he seems not the least bit fazed that his patient shares a carriage with the renowned Sir Walter Raleigh. Evidently, he's been advised. "Permit me to introduce myself, Sir Walter. I am Master Yatrow, Lord Mountjoy's surgeon. God give you good e'en."

"And you," says Sir Walter, who makes his report in crisp military fashion. "Lieutenant Carter was struck in the shoulder by a ball fired from a musket at some range, perhaps thirty yards. His bleeding stopped within twenty minutes, but he's had a moderate fever for two days now."

Yatrow places his hand on the patient's forehead and seems pleasantly surprised. "Well, he has none now."

Raleigh seems confused and places his hand on Carter's neck. "Indeed, he has *not!*" he confirms with relief.

The surgeon gently lifts Carter's wounded shoulder to examine the blanket behind it, which makes the patient wince and stir uneasily.

"No fresh blood there, thank heavens," says Yatrow, gently releasing the shoulder. "We *could* carry him in, but I think it less likely to aggravate the wound if he comes inside on his own two legs. We need support him only by his other shoulder."

"Allow me, Master Yatrow," says Raleigh. He helps Carter up off the bench and out the carriage door, assisting him up the stairs to the residence.

The surgeon steps out of the carriage and looks curiously at the three horses tied behind it. He bows to Noah, obviously spying the Queen's livery. "Pardon me, sir," he says. "I believe I have not had the pleasure. I am Master Yatrow, Lord Mountjoy's surgeon."

Noah bows wearily in the saddle. "And I am Serjeant Ames, Queen's barrister."

"May I ask, sir, do those three horses belong to other wounded men?"

Noah shakes his head gravely. "Those horses were recently in service of three highwaymen who confronted us along the way. Their owners are, I regret to inform you, beyond all aid."

"I hope we've not given up on them too soon," says the surgeon.

Noah smirks. "If you'd care to treat them, you'll have to move quickly for, by now, they're well above our heads…or, more likely, well below our feet."

Yatrow gasps. "Oh, dear!" he exclaims. "Dead!"

"Is his lordship in?" asks Noah.

"I believe he is expected, come morning," replies Yatrow, who bows and disappears through the front door.

Noah, Andres, and Arthur dismount, and hand off their horses to two young boys, who lead them off to the stables. Mountjoy's footman emerges from the front door. "Supper will be ready in a half-hour, gentlemen. Would you care to wait inside?"

Andres and Arthur defer to Noah for a reply. "No, thank you. If it's all right with you, we'll walk in the garden."

"As you wish," the footman says, and returns to the house.

Entering the garden, Noah scans the side of the manor house. The only open window looks out from a library that appears to be unoccupied. As he wishes to be certain not to be overheard, he finds a private spot near a few red roses that have managed to hold onto their petals well into October. Lush as they appear from a distance, however, the view from up close is disappointing, as the perimeter of each petal is withering to brown. Noah sniffs one. It seems to have retained its floral bouquet, but there's another scent mixed in, very faint, but distinctly unpleasant. He wrinkles his nose.

"Do you smell that?" he asks Andres and Arthur, who both sniff the air and shrug.

"Smells like every other stables to me," says Arthur.

"No, it's something else," says Noah. "In any event, Arthur, would you be so kind as to fetch Cheerful?" Arthur nods and disappears around front.

Noah turns to Andres. "Let me ask you for your candid view, Master Salazar."

"About what, sir?"

"Of the three of you, who is fastest and surest on horseback?"

Without hesitation, Andres replies. "Oh, that's easy, sir. David...er...*Cheerful,* by a long shot."

This is precisely what Noah expected. "And which of you is best with a firearm?"

This seems a bit more puzzling to Andres. "Hawking has become the best shot among us, sir. But, as he's not included in your question, I would have to guess it's likely *I* am best with a firearm."

Noah nods sagely as Arthur reappears, with Cheerful following him into the garden.

"Ah, there you are, boys! Come close, as I wish to speak with the three of you privately." He glances about furtively, and speaks in low tones. "Andres and Cheerful, I have an important job for you both." Their clear, youthful eyes regard him expectantly. "You must leave here early tomorrow morning on horseback, fully provisioned, and armed to the teeth. You must locate Jonathan and Lady Jessica, wherever they may be. Concerning their recent whereabouts, you know as much as I. To that, I may add only the name of the man who sent the highwaymen to assassinate me. He's a Frenchman going by the name of 'Wolf,' which in French would be 'Loup' or some such thing, of course."

"What should we do when we find them?" asks Andres.

Noah sighs. "There, I can give you only general guidance. First and foremost, you must tell them where I am, and then Cheerful must return here to tell me where *they* are, and where they're going. And in whose company, of course."

"Don't you wish David to escort Lady Jessica to you, sir?" asks Andres.

Noah rubs his chin contemplatively. "I don't know. That is, I don't know if she will leave Jonathan to complete his quest alone."

"We could *compel* her to accompany David, sir," offers Andres.

Arthur frowns. "Don't be an idiot, Andres! She's nobility. You two can't force her to do *anything!*"

"We can, at her father's *instruction!*" Andres shoots back.

"Wait, gentlemen!" says Noah. "Let's not quibble. First, although I am her father, she was married to a nobleman and is currently his widow, so I'm not legally privileged to compel her to do anything." He shakes his head. "Besides, Andres, as you'll realize when you're older, the problem is much more pervasive than you think. It's not *just* that she's a lady. It's that she's a *woman!* If you *once* invoke your authority, and try to compel her to do something against her will, she will disobey and resent you, then and ever after. She'll find some *infuriating* way of—Oh, never mind! I digress. Tell her that her father is in great fear for her safety, and that he wishes her to leave off this quest at the earliest possible moment, and to seek appropriate accommodation for a woman of her station and means. And, by all means, say I would prefer she come *here*."

"She'll do as her father wishes, I'm sure," says Arthur.

Noah scoffs. "She'll do precisely what she *would* have done, regardless. In any event, whether David returns here with Lady Jessica or merely with news, I'm afraid *Andres* must remain with Jonathan to the end." As Andres looks worried, Noah seeks to reassure him. "Look, there may be no map. Or, if there is one, it may be the *wrong* map. But even on the off-chance it's the *right* map, that is, the purloined map Jonathan suspects it to be, it's *imperative* that no attempt be made to obtain possession of it, for we already know the enemy would have knowledge of its contents, and our gaining possession would tell us nothing. If it's the purloined map, the important thing is to find out *where it's going,* which would enable me to confirm to Lord Mountjoy that the intelligence reflected on it has been compromised, and that he must make such military adjustments as he deems prudent. Finally, your purpose and your destination are to remain secret from *everyone.* Is that clear?"

"Even from Sir Walter and Lord Mountjoy?" whispers Arthur.

Noah nods. "It's to remain secret from everyone but the Ameses and the jesters...and Cheerful, of course, who I suppose is a jester now. Any questions?"

"I have one," says Cheerful. "Serjeant Ames, as Lady Jessica is no longer a child, why do you believe her to be as willful as you describe?"

Noah laughs darkly and opens his eyes wide.

"I knew her mother!"

AS THE BOYS have left to speak with Mountjoy's footman about provisions needed for the next day's journey, Noah walks about in the garden alone. He can't help but notice the stark difference between a bachelor's garden and a husband's.

Although there are numerous plants in Mountjoy's bachelor garden, few are purely decorative. Most are vegetables, and all but a few of those have been harvested for the year. Only a few hearty greens and squashes remain, as well as a lovingly tended pumpkin patch. As pumpkin is one of Noah's favorites, he hopes it will be part of this evening's supper.

"Noah!" shouts Sir Walter, rounding the corner from the front of the manor. "What are you doing out here alone? They're about to serve the soup."

"Oh! I expected someone would come fetch me," he says, striding toward Raleigh.

"Someone has!" says Raleigh, patting him on the back, and leaning into him. "We...or should I say Mountjoy...has an unexpected guest."

"Oh?"

"Admiral Howard."

"The Lord Admiral is here?"

Raleigh speaks jauntily as they walk up to the front steps. "No, no. This is *Thomas*, Lord Howard. He's a *Rear* Admiral. Before you ask, he's a cousin to the Lord Admiral, and served as a general officer on the Islands Voyage I was about to tell you about when we were...brutally interrupted. Good fellow! Saved me from the scaffold."

The scaffold? Well, there are no doubt many hazards in the adventurer's life about which Noah knows nothing. "And how is Lieutenant Carter?" Noah inquires.

"No sign of fever. He's sleeping so comfortably I didn't have the heart to drag him to supper. I'll have something sent up to his room later. Oh! Your young companions wanted me to tell you they're already at work preparing for an early departure. They'll sup informally in the servants' quarters, and retire to bed as soon as possible. So, they won't be joining us."

As they cross the threshold, the footman appears and leads them to the dining room, where several gentlemen stand behind their respective chairs, apparently awaiting their arrival. One wears a doublet of high quality, another ecclesiastical garb. The youngest is dressed in unsullied military fashion, much as Lieutenant Carter was before a ball drilled a hole through his shoulder.

"Lord Howard," says Raleigh, "may I present Serjeant Noah Ames, one of Her Majesty's barristers?"

A sandy-bearded man of about thirty-five says: "'Tis a pleasure to make your acquaintance, Serjeant. Sir Walter was telling me about your many accomplishments on Her Majesty's behalf. He informs me that you're a Hebrew."

This seems a bit early in the conversation for the topic of religion to arise, but Noah assumes Sir Walter had reason to get it out in the open as soon as possible, and has inadvertently piqued Lord Howard's interest. "I *am* a Hebrew, your lordship, though I do not regard it as an accomplishment, let alone one on Her Majesty's behalf." Howard laughs.

"If I may, lordship," says Sir Walter, turning to Noah. "Serjeant Ames, I mentioned your religion only to explain why I had instructed the staff to omit pork from this evening's fare."

Noah bows appreciatively at this extraordinary courtesy.

"Perhaps you will perform the Hebrew blessing over the wine and bread," suggests Lord Howard.

As Noah has always been careful to avoid the least appearance of proselytizing, he glances at the other two men.

"Oh, pardon me," says Lord Howard. "Serjeant, the distinguished gentleman to my right is Reverend Carswell, Church of England, while the young gentleman to my left is my adjutant and kinsman, Terence." He turns to them in sequence. "I trust neither of you gentlemen has any objection to such a demonstration by the good Serjeant?"

"Not in the least," says the Reverend. The adjutant merely shakes his head.

"Good," says Howard. "Please proceed."

Just then, two maids carry in a tureen of soup and a long loaf of bread on a silver tray. As they begin serving, Noah hesitates, his eyes on them. "Begging your lordship's pardon, I find that such demonstrations are sometimes resented by household staff."

"Don't be concerned," says Sir Walter reassuringly. "I can attest that Lord Mountjoy is careful to retain no bigots in his household." The serving maids curtsey appreciatively.

"Very well, then," says Noah, and proceeds to recite a brief prayer over the wine, and then over the bread, as he cuts it in two.

"Ah," says the Reverend, "and how would you translate those prayers for us English?"

Noah suppresses his displeasure at the implication that he is *not* English. "Well, over the wine, it's 'Blessed art Thou, O Lord Our God, King of the Universe, Creator of the fruit of the vine.'"

"And over the bread," interrupts the Reverend, exhibiting a pompous eagerness to demonstrate his own erudition, "it's 'Blessed art Thou, O Lord Our God, King of the Universe, Who brings forth bread from the earth.'" He smiles at Noah. "Are these not the same prayers Our Lord recited over wine and bread, whilst He lived?"

"Jesus was a rabbi of my tribe, Reverend, so they are the same *verbatim*. And they're even in the same language." As the kitchen door swings open and then closes, Noah catches a glimpse of a dark, weather-beaten manservant of about fifty looking at him askance. Apparently, not everyone on the staff is as ecumenically minded as the gentlemen at table.

Lord Howard sits and folds his hands reverentially, and the others do the same. Reverend Carswell recites the traditional Anglican prayer before the meal. "Bless, O Father, Thy gifts to our use and us to Thy service; for Christ's sake. Amen."

Lord Howard breaks the bread.

Noah ventures: "Permit me to thank you for your humane treatment, Lord Howard, for it is not everywhere in the realm that one of my faith is greeted so wholesomely."

Howard and Raleigh exchange a mirthful glance. "Serjeant Ames," says Howard, "aboard Her Majesty's naval vessels, one is tossed in among men from all corners of the globe. Some are papists, others Muhammadans. Still others perform rituals unknown to white men."

Carswell is appalled. "I do hope that none are worshippers of the Beast!"

Howard smiles. "Why, Reverend, I have already *told* you some are papists!" This results in general laughter, not shared by the Reverend. "Good Lord, some are *Dutch*!"

"But, surely," protests Reverend Carswell, "the officers do not permit the worship of gods other than the one true God!"

Howard turns to him with the weary cynicism of a battle-tested commander. "Reverend, we would recruit goblins from hell, if we could be certain they'd slaughter only Spanish!" He tears off a big piece of bread and sits back, self-satisfied.

So horrified is the Reverend that Raleigh hastens to put him at ease. "M'lord is being facetious, in part, Reverend. Although we cannot be choosy about the men who serve, they are certainly forbidden to engage in devil worship aboard Her Majesty's ships."

The Reverend relaxes, and smiles abashedly. "I see that I am but the latest victim of one of his lordship's renowned jests."

"Just so," says Howard indifferently. He turns to Raleigh. "I am told, Sir Walter, that you and Serjeant Ames have come all the way to Dorset to investigate a murder that took place at the Tower of London."

Raleigh speaks in hushed tones. "That is true, lordship, but it should not become a matter of general knowledge. As the investigation is at a particularly sensitive point, we are not at liberty to discuss it, I'm afraid."

Between bites, Howard glances toward the kitchen door and about the rest of the room with heightened awareness. "I see. Well, then we shall discuss it no further." He and Raleigh exchange a knowing look, which, if Noah reads it correctly, means that the two will discuss it privately later.

Raleigh changes the subject. "On the way here, Serjeant Ames was peppering me with questions about our Islands Voyage."

Howard's ears perk up. "Ah, I can help him there. I do wish they would stop calling it that, however. Makes it sound as though we were undertaking a casual frolic, rather than a serious military venture." The serving staff clears away the soup and brings in a hot, fragrant pie of pumpkin and venison.

"Serjeant Ames," says Lord Howard, "I expect you have not met a virtuous and brave knight by the name of Sir William Monson?"

Noah searches his memory. "Nay, m'lord. I do not recall meeting a gentleman of that name."

The serving maids cut a hefty piece of pie for each of them, put them on separate plates, and sprinkle each slice with extra cinnamon and sugar before serving it.

"Ah," says Lord Howard, "then Sir William has never entered a chamber in which you were already in attendance."

Raleigh snorts a laugh and covers his face, as though he knows what's coming.

Noah allows himself to be enlisted in the jest. "How can you be certain, m'lord?"

"Because, quite memorably, his testicles clack when he walks, as they're surely made of stone."

The serving maids' eyes go wide and they freeze, which Howard enjoys immensely. Reverend Carswell covers his reddened face with his napkin. The maids quickly finish up their serving and scurry off to the kitchen, closing the door quietly behind to a burst of laughter.

When at last it subsides, Noah says: "I take it the gentleman has demonstrated great courage."

"I should say so," confirms Howard, as he pours himself a full cup of red wine, and hands the bottle around. "It was on the very Islands Voyage about which you've inquired of Sir Walter. To begin with, Her Majesty had put Essex in charge of the expedition, but denied him the right to make any decision without the approval of a committee of six, which included Lord Mountjoy, Sir Walter, myself, and a few others."

"Is that common practice?" asks Noah.

Howard shoots Raleigh a glance, who replies for him. "No, it isn't. But Essex had been insubordinate to the Queen on numerous occasions, and she wished to be sure he would not expose himself to danger. As you can imagine," he says sardonically, "we very much appreciated being pressed into service as wet nurses. Only secondarily were we to help him avoid tactical blunders, and also avoid subjecting Her Majesty's ships to hazard. Lot of good it did."

Lord Howard takes a sip. "I believe his greatest blunder of the voyage was made before we even left Plymouth. At his request, we completely relinquished the contingent of land soldiers that was already aboard. That was Essex's idea, but, much to my regret, I went along, as did Sir Walter, however reluctantly."

"How was that a great blunder?"

"Without soldiers," replies Howard, "we were powerless to take our fight to shore. Anything to be accomplished would have to be done at sea, and an adversary who *knows* that has a huge advantage. Basically, all he has to do is get to land, and he's won. Of course, Sir Walter actually did take the port of Faial out in the Azores with sailors only, but that was done of necessity, and succeeded only because the enemy had failed to prepare for such a brazen eventuality."

Raleigh looks aside with a pained expression.

Howard changes the subject. "Essex made another great blunder after—based on bad intelligence—we abandoned our initial purpose of destroying Spanish vessels in port, and set out for the Azores. As you may know, the Azores are a band of islands in the Atlantic many hundreds of miles from shore, stretched out roughly east-west. Spanish vessels laden with gold and silver stop there for watering on their way to Spain. We searched for days on the high seas for treasure vessels. No luck. It's a big ocean out there, and the chances of finding a vessel far from port are quite slim, which is why it's generally a good idea for marauders like us to hover near port. Drake was a master of the tactic, may he rest in peace. Anyhow, after days of fruitless searching around the western ports, Essex decided to move the fleet by the northern route to the easternmost tip of the island chain."

"Why would he do that?" asks Noah. "Wouldn't that render it certain that any ship passing you would already be under full sail for Spain?"

"Just so. But none of us wished to take on Essex, as he'd already come very close to imposing severe discipline upon a subordinate for showing an excess of initiative. Anyway, to get back to the courageous Monson. He followed Essex's orders to come east, but on his own initiative came by the southern route, *below* the islands, on the off-chance he might spot something others might miss. Well, he *did*!"

"Did he *ever*!" says Raleigh.

Howard continues. "One dark night, Monson found his ship inadvertently sailing in the midst of a flotilla he was unable to identify. Unsure whether it was a detachment of our own fleet, he left his ship in control of his shipmaster, and put himself and a couple of men out in a small vessel, little more than a rowboat, to get a closer look." He pours himself another glass. "As it turned out, he was in the midst of a flotilla of Spanish treasure vessels, about twenty-five in all, two of which were sitting quite low in the water, which meant they were heavy with cargo. Well, of course, without help he couldn't really do anything against twenty-five vessels, however lightly armed. So, he thought to draw them toward us, many miles away."

"How could he accomplish that?" asks Noah.

Once again, Raleigh begins to laugh in anticipation. Howard continues. "He pulled alongside one of the vessels and began shouting at them in his execrable Spanish, making every obscene gesture he could think of. If his boatswain is to be believed, he went so far as to instruct his oarsman to drop his breeches and show the Spanish sailors an earthbound moon."

"Did the Spanish pursue him?"

"Lazy sots did nothing but reciprocate the obscenities in equally incomprehensible English. They fired a few pistols, but to no effect. So, Monson returned to his ship and did the next thing to occur to him."

"What was that?"

"He fired every cannon onboard simultaneously, which made a hell of a noise."

"But, could you hear it from so far away?"

"Oh, yes. You can't imagine how quiet it is out there on the ocean on a still night. We heard several loud explosions miles off to the south and saw some flashes, but Essex wasn't prepared to risk losing a vessel in the blackness, so he declined to send a detachment to find out what was happening. To be generous, it *could* have been distant thunder, I suppose. Even if it weren't, we'd no idea what it meant. After all, we weren't expecting any of our own vessels to approach from the *south*. By that time, the notion that anyone in the fleet would dare to exercise real initiative had been simply discounted."

"So, what happened to the treasure?"

Raleigh sighs wistfully, as Howard continues. "When we finally woke up to what was happening, we gave chase, but they made it to the shelter of port before we could catch them and, as we had *no soldiers,* we were powerless to do anything but watch them unload *unimaginable* treasure of gold and silver to land."

Raleigh interjects. "The best estimate is that two ships in the flotilla were carrying gold and silver worth ten million pesos in all, roughly *two million* English pounds, if you can imagine. Taking them would have paid the expenses of our voyage and numerous others to come. Indeed, the sum was so large, it is commonly believed that the King of Spain would have had no choice but to relinquish his long-held dream of reclaiming England for himself and the Pope. Even if we had merely *sunk* the vessels, it would have set the king back *years*. But, alas, it was not to be. And, worse, when we returned to England, we gradually realized that the king had learned of our trip to the Azores, and had seized upon our absence to launch a second armada against the English mainland, that being the failed one mentioned by Sir Robert that day in the map room at Westminster."

The rest of the meal is spent in small talk. When it concludes, Reverend Carswell takes his leave with many blessings, and an especial appeal to Noah to save his soul through membership in the Church of England. Noah politely replies that he will pray on the prospect in due course. Raleigh excuses himself to visit with Lieutenant Carter and retire to bed, and Howard dismisses his adjutant, leaving him alone with Noah and a bottle of red wine.

"So," says a slightly sodden Lord Howard, "you are a late-stayer, as am I."

"Sometimes I am, m'lord. Barristers keep strange hours. Your lordship, I would feel remiss if I were to neglect to tell you that Her Majesty has granted me a commission—"

"Yes, yes, I know. To investigate Essex. Raleigh told me when I first arrived."

"So, you understand that you are quite *outside* the group of named persons required to discuss such matters with me?"

"I didn't know it, but I thank you for your honesty. Would my uncle, the Lord Admiral, happen to be one such 'named person'?"

"He would, your lordship."

Howard pours himself another glass. "Well, you might as well ask *me,* as I doubt he would discuss such matters with anyone who's not Church of England. And he'd get away with it, too, as he's the Queen's near kin. Of course, you do have the advantage of not being a *papist,* but I doubt that would be enough. He might even refuse to sit with you. But never mind that, as he was not with us on the Islands Voyage. A bit too long in the tooth, you see. In any case, I have been happy to provide you with such assistance as I could."

"If you don't mind, m'lord, there are one or two additional questions I would like to ask."

154 | NEAL ROBERTS

"By all means," says Howard.

"You mentioned Essex punishing a subordinate on the Islands Voyage for showing initiative. Who was that?"

Howard chortles. "He didn't tell you?"

"M'lord?"

"It was *Raleigh*! Essex had left Raleigh hovering about the port of Faial without clear instructions, other than to remain there. The ships under his command had been there alone for many days without water, fresh provisions, or definite orders. The Spanish were harassing and taunting him. Morale was quite low, and Raleigh let it be known within the fleet that he was considering taking the port. Now, until that point, there had been not a single victorious day on the whole voyage (in fact, only one would follow), and it was understood that if there was any glory to be had, Essex wanted it all for himself.

"Essex had left one of his attendants aboard Raleigh's ship, and when he heard what was being considered, he harassed Raleigh incessantly, repeating at every opportunity that *under no circumstances* should he take the port, but after a few more days without instructions from Essex, Raleigh and his sailors took the port, watered and re-provisioned themselves, and sacked the city. Got away with some fair loot, too. That was the only victory of the whole expedition."

"So, Sir Walter stole Essex's thunder?"

"That's how Essex saw it, although he should have realized that, as commander, he would receive credit for it regardless. Instead, he was apoplectic, and threatened to court-martial Raleigh. Came damned near doing it, too. And he made it clear that, if found guilty, Raleigh would be hanged from his own yardarm. Well, knowing Raleigh as I did, I knew he would not be caught at unawares, and he was popular with his men. As soon as Essex let his intentions be known, everyone *but* Essex saw the real and immediate danger of mutiny, which would have ended in complete disaster. I personally told Essex that the committee would not support a call to court-martial, that Raleigh had not disobeyed a direct order—as a lackey's bleating does *not* an order make—and that Her Majesty would be quite cross if he were to execute his ancient foe. Only with a lot of hounding did Essex relent, and make amends. Raleigh knew it was only because of my intercession, yet he continued faithfully to execute Essex's orders to the end."

"*Was* Raleigh an ancient foe of Essex?" asks Noah.

"Not really," says Howard. "Essex's foes at court have always been mostly imagined. But, he *had* challenged Raleigh to a duel, and they *had* dueled." Noah's eyebrows shoot up. "And, if you're unaware, he'd done the same with Lord Mountjoy, years before. But neither of them *ever* held any ill will toward Essex. Their 'enmity' was the product of Essex's fevered imagination."

"Indeed?"

"Oh, certainly. And, just as his enemies are imagined, so are his friends. The whole world revolves about him, you see. Others are not real people to him, so they are good or bad only according to whether they suit his purposes at a given moment. I do not think the man has any genuine fellow feeling of his own. It's as though he's only pretending to." He takes a sip that must be bitter, as he sneers.

"I take it you deem Lord Essex unfit for command?"

Howard sighs. "Look, I'm no great seer into other men's souls, nor am I a perfect commander. Far from it. But, given a choice, I would never place Essex in command of a military venture of any importance." He leans in confidentially. "Incidentally, I would appreciate it if you would avoid putting my conclusion on paper. Although we are forbidden to discuss such matters, as a fellow subject you must know that one is never sure what use may be made of our statements by...a later monarch."

There it is, yet again! The Succession. Noah tries not to react visibly. "One last thing, m'lord, as you've been so kind. You mentioned a lackey who hounded Sir Walter not to take the Port of Faial. What was his name?"

Lord Howard nods, and finishes off his cup before replying. He sets it down on the table, and spits out the name.

"Gelly Meyrick."

———————— ⊸०⟨⟨⟨⟩⟩⟩०⊂ ————————

ON THE WAY to his room upstairs, Noah passes an open doorway and sees Raleigh seated on a chair, quietly watching Carter sleep in the candlelight.

Noah sticks his head in the doorway. "I trust this vigil betokens no misfortune."

Raleigh looks up. "Oh, not at all. His fever's gone for good. He'll be well enough to travel in a few days."

"That is good to hear. You don't suppose he'll be gun-shy now?"

"Unlikely. Like all men of war, he's had to come to terms with his own mortality quite young. Besides, each of us understands that dying in battle is hardly the worst way to go." Sir Walter gets up, shuts Carter's door behind him, and accompanies Noah down the hallway to their own rooms.

"I had no idea that soldiers have an order of preference in ways to die," says Noah.

"Some are worse than others, believe me. A man dying onboard of dysentery is far more miserable than one dying on the battlefield of a wound inflicted by the enemy."

"Why?"

"Because dysentery seems such a *meaningless* way to go. You haven't even begun the battle for which you were consciously prepared to risk your life."

"Is illness regarded as the worst way to die?" asks Noah.

Raleigh opens the door to his chamber, but stops in the hallway to respond. "No. I've spoken to many men who believed they were dying, only to be rescued at the last possible moment. Most believe the most terrible end is to drown after one's ship is wrecked in a storm."

"I'm no expert in such matters, but I should think drowning would be relatively *painless*."

"Yes, but it's not physical pain they fear. When they're down in the soup, treading water in the hope that some vessel will happen by and save them in the few moments remaining to their lives, they gaze up at that merciless black sky, and feel as though the face of heaven has turned away."

"So, it's a crisis of *faith* they fear most?" asks Noah.

"In a sense. I once spoke with a man who'd nearly drowned in a terrible tempest. After floundering in the water a few minutes, he saw a beacon stream through a break in the clouds, and it gave him hope that the eye of God would never turn away. From that moment, he refused to despair, and it gave him the courage to tread water until a ship came along and pulled him to safety.

"He said it was as though God had chosen to attenuate a single black cloud, and pierce it with heaven's blinding rays, all for the purpose of assuring him that there is *always* hope. I'll never forget what he called it." Noah waits expectantly. "He called it an 'impress of heaven.'"

CHAPTER 12

IT'S A DARK and chilly midday in Cornwall as Jonathan and Jessica ride up to an ancient, weather-beaten inn and strain to discern the writing on its faded sign. A storm is brewing and the salt in the air is palpable.

"'Davey Jones's Inn,' I think," says Jessica, squinting at the sign. "Yes, that's what it says. Looks rather forbidding. Do you suppose Davey Jones is the proprietor?"

Jonathan shakes his head, glancing at the map. "Launceston is only twenty miles from the ocean in either direction, so it's more likely an old seaman's jest. To sailors, 'Davey Jones's Locker' is the bottom of the sea, where a doomed sailor comes to his final rest."

Jessica seems perplexed. "Then, doesn't the name suggest that this inn is where a doomed *traveler* comes to his final rest? Why would anyone name an inn after such a horrid place?"

Jonathan shrugs. "Dark humor, I suppose. Let's go in."

Jessica balks and regards him apprehensively.

He sighs. "Jess, you shan't find a place to wash or a bed to sleep in, out here on the moors." He feels sure this will motivate her, as they haven't been indoors for several days, and Jessica passed last night without even the modest shelter of a closed carriage. "To say nothing of our dwindling rations," he adds.

"Oh, *why* did we have to go on ahead of Master Phillips and Pedro?" she laments.

"Because his relatives in Devon hadn't invited us to stop at their farm."

"But they probably *would* have," she insists, "if only we'd shown up there with Phillips!"

"Jess, we're not on holiday. Are we?"

"No, but we haven't caught sight of Essex's men or le Loup for days!

We may have missed them entirely, so what's the rush?"

At last, she relents, and they tie off their horses at the entrance. As this doesn't seem the kind of inn where one simply saunters into the salon uninvited, Jessica knocks at the door. When it swings open, it takes a moment for them to recognize what they're looking at. It's the figure of an enormous man, that's sure, but his neck is the highest part they can see.

The giant steps aside, and a huge head with a hairy face appears at an odd angle, observing them with interest through the doorway. His curly hair is nearly jet black, and his face a leathery brown, evidently wrinkled by habitual exposure to Cornish wind and sun. Jessica recoils, and takes an involuntary step backward, bumping into Jonathan's shoulder. Jonathan places his arm about her waist to steady her.

"What can I do for you weary travelers?" the giant inquires in a voice so deep it seems to rumble up from his belly, making him seem a character in a folk tale.

The effect upon Jessica is quite complete. "We are in need of rooms for the night, Master Giant," she replies, her voice suggestive of a young mother's bravado in reading the line aloud to her children.

Although Jonathan is concerned that the giant might be offended, he merely rumbles with laughter and steps back from the doorway to invite them in. "You may call me Joss. What're *your* names, may I ask?"

Having regained her composure, Jessica steps confidently inside, and looks up at his broad face. "I am Lady Patricia, and this is my footman Caius."

Joss bows low, as gracefully as a man of his enormous proportions can manage indoors. "And where d'ye come from, m'lady?" he asks.

"We are from London, Joss. It is a pleasure to make your acquaintance. Do you suppose you might have adjoining rooms for us, preferably upstairs?"

The giant scratches the top of his head. At least, that's what he *appears* to be doing. From Jonathan's more earthbound viewpoint, it's impossible to see up there.

"Yer in luck!" says the innkeeper. "In fact, that's *all* I got at the moment. There's two guestrooms together upstairs. They're not connected by a private door or nothin', though."

"No matter. But *are* you otherwise full up?" asks Jessica. "We passed your stables before coming in, and—"

"Oh, yah, the stable's nearly empty. Right now, there are only four guests stayin' here, all women. But I'm waitin' for some guests who've arranged their stay in advance. They're expected this evenin'."

"Very well, then," says Jessica. "If you will show us our rooms, we would much appreciate it."

Joss glances outside and closes the door. "Ye come by horseback, I see. So, ye'll have little baggage. Folla me." As he leads them to their rooms, the stairway creaks and groans under his weight, and he keeps his head down to avoid butting the ceiling. Though he's forced to contort himself in the strangest ways to get around the narrow angles and doorways of the old inn, he seems long accustomed to them, and does so with little effort or thought.

He leads them to the end of the hallway, and opens the doors to the only two guestrooms upstairs, which pleases Jonathan, as he wishes to avoid encounters with other guests. The further into Cornwall they advance, the more loudly Phillips' warning resounds in his mind about the possibility of running into le Loup.

Of the two rooms, the corner is the larger and better appointed, so Jonathan naturally assumes it will be hers. As Jessica makes polite conversation with the giant, Jonathan looks out his own window at the chipped and faded shutters between his room and Jessica's, swaying gently in the breeze. They appear quite substantial, as one would expect in a locale battered by frequent storms. He imagines, however, that during a high wind their bulk would slam against the inn repeatedly, disturbing everyone's repose all night. And they might even fly off their hinges and smash the windows.

Although Jessica's conversation seems to please the innkeeper immensely, Jonathan feels it important enough to interrupt. "Pardon me, m'lady. Joss, is there some of way of securing these shutters? A storm is coming, and they seem to be flapping freely in the wind. I'm concerned they might bang against the inn and keep m'lady awake, or even fly off."

The innkeeper gives him a patronizing smile, opens the window, and shows him a tortuous length of wire affixed to the inn by a nail, with the other end hanging free. He loops the loose end around a few slats of the shutter, pulls the shutter flat against the inn, and secures it in place by a simple twist of the wire. The shutter's swinging has been reduced to a barely visible flutter. "This is a thin wire," says the innkeeper, "but it'll hold. Here in Cornwall, y'see, shutters ain't fer decoration. When a big storm hits, we close 'em over the windows and use the same wire to fix 'em to these loops on the sill. In *really* bad weather, I go outside and nail 'em shut. Don't want no broken glass. Glass is hard to come by in these parts." He smiles at Jessica, and rumbles reassuringly. "But not as rare as beautiful guests. We couldn't allow such a lovely lady to be hurt by flyin' glass now, could we?"

The giant turns back to Jonathan. "Nah. These shutters are strong enough to hold *my* weight. I know because I put 'em on. As for them flyin' off the inn, well, if that 'appens, say yer prayers, because any storm strong enough to do that will soon blow the whole *inn* to pieces." He turns to Jessica again. "But ye needn't concern yerself about that, madam. This inn is a hundred years old, and has stood up to every gale that ever was."

Jessica curtsies her thanks for the assurance and arranges for a hot bath, something for which she's been longing for several days. As is the custom, she arranges for her servant to bathe in the same water after she's done. And she also arranges to have their clothing laundered, so they won't have to wear soiled clothing over their newly clean persons.

Finally, she pays Joss for his services in advance, and Jonathan marks how much the scene resembles an old children's illustration, as the giant eagerly counts the coins in his hand, his face aglow in light reflected off his lucre.

"When yer all done splashin' about," says Joss, "come down to the dinin' room. We'll have a staff o' three tonight, and I'll have the cook fix y'up some victuals."

AN HOUR LATER, Jonathan walks down the hall to the tub room that Jessica has just vacated. She shuffles past him going the other way, wearing a robe with a belt tied about her tiny waist, and a towel wrapped around her hair like a turban. Though the robe was thin enough to keep tucked away in her saddlebag, it reveals little of her figure, leaving it to Jonathan's imagination to conjure up what she must be like under there, all untrussed and powdered.

As she opens the door to her room, she looks back and favors him with a quick smile that seems to say she knows precisely what he's thinking, but that he'll just have to do without, same as every man. Well, he supposes, all men must act the same way whenever they're near her. *Don't touch, and better not be caught looking.*

As he opens the door to the tub room, he's greeted by a residual puff of her perfumed white powder that makes him cough. The water's still warm, and so clear that it's hard to believe anyone has bathed in it.

It's wonderful to smell real soap, and use it to remove the grime of the past few days' travels. It will be particularly good to feel clean hair on his head again, as he's come to think of his hair as so many bothersome strands of oily mane. He scrubs and scrubs, until every part of him is clean, and rinses off thoroughly.

Stepping out and drying himself with a towel, he spies a looking glass, and can't help but step over to see his reflection. To his amazement, he doesn't look the least bit shaggy. His beard is a bit uneven, true, but he still looks much as a respected young barrister should...perhaps a *bit* rougher. And, best of all, the swelling over his left eye has gone completely. The only remaining evidence of his altercation with Meyrick is a fading bluish stripe running horizontally along a small arc of the socket beneath the eye.

He returns to his room, puts on his last remaining items of clean clothing, and knocks on Jessica's door. She opens it fully dressed, and invites him inside.

He bites his tongue as he enters her room, and brushes lightly past her. Here she is, in the middle of nowhere, with no lady's maids in attendance, and none of her more elegant clothing, yet she looks like a dream come true. And there's something about her smile, something...different.

It takes a moment for him to figure out what has changed there, then he has it. Nothing is being...withheld. Gone are the suspicion and anger that hung about her like a black cloud when he first came up to the earl's house to fetch her. Gone the nightmares that haunted her sleep and made her weep every night, until that one little kiss in the woods. Now, she seems...happy.

And that makes *him* happy. He looks at her pretty face, and lips. God, those lips! There's something so alluring and exotic about them. Perhaps it's her Hebrew heritage. *Do all the women of Arabia have lips like this?* He supposes it could be a trick of the light, but, no, her lips look this way in *every* light. His gaze returns to her long brown eyes, and he realizes once again that he cannot let his true feelings show, for surely they'd frighten her away. God, he wants to kiss her! He wants to say "I love you."

Instead, he says, "Shall I sup with the servants?"

She smiles. "It *would* look a bit strange for us to sup together in the common room, wouldn't it?" She closes the distance between them, until he's looking down at the center part in her silky brown hair. Her clean scent hits him like ambrosia. In a moment, he's nearly drunk with it. She pokes his chest repeatedly with her index finger. "Why don't you tell the innkeeper that m'lady is feeling very fatigued from her long trip on horseback, and will be taking supper in her room this evening, *and* will require her footman to take his meal in the adjacent room?"

This is not an invitation he can or will decline. "They shall insist on serving her meal, I expect."

She smiles up at him. "Then *you* shall insist it be served only by her faithful footman."

"For Queen and country, then," he replies staunchly, bows, and leaves, thinking himself freakishly lucky to be supping alone with Lady Jessica in her room. His head is spinning and, on his way downstairs, he grips the railing firmly to avoid falling…or floating away.

JESSICA HASN'T NOTICED until quite recently just how charming Jonathan can be. There's no question his appearance is much improved since the swelling around his eye receded and that peculiar yellowish bruising began fading away. But his handsome appearance is not new to her. She's seen his face and form many times before this adventure.

Yet, somehow his charms largely escaped her before now. Perhaps she's noticing them now simply because she's alone with him for the first time. But no, that's not it, either, for she's been alone with him before this journey, though for only a few minutes at a time. A few times, she's conversed with him in Father's library, when she was staying with Father, and Jonathan had arrived early to see him. True, Jonathan was charming then, but she didn't take him all that seriously.

But now there's the gentle touching. She cannot remember his touching her before today, except for that fatherly kiss in the carriage. Yet, he's touched her *twice* today, if only incidentally; once when she backed away from the giant who runs the inn, on which occasion Jonathan steadied her on her feet, giving her the courage she needed to deal with the giant as a human being, rather than a monster of nature. And he also brushed past her just now as he entered her room, which made her body tingle all over. That's all. Probably, he hasn't even *noticed* the touching. She's learned that men are wont to disregard such things, deeming them mere trivialities. Perhaps he even found them embarrassing.

As she awaits his return, gazing through the window at an indistinct sky in which dark clouds fade to black, the daydream she had that night in the woods returns to her, with her imaginary children climbing all over Jonathan, laughing. She vaguely recalls dismissing the fantasy at that time, but can no longer remember why. This time, she giggles along with them all.

IN JESSICA'S ROOM, Jonathan and Jessica are sharing a second glass of wine after dinner when they hear the outer door slam downstairs. As Jonathan rises from his chair to look outside, thick globules of rain smack hard against the window panes, as though nature has suspended her rules and made the rain fall sideways.

From Jessica's upstairs window, he can see that a carriage drawn by two well-fitted warhorses has drawn up to the inn. Even in the dim light that escapes from the salon window downstairs, he can see that these are no ordinary carriage horses, but two full-size white chargers impressed into routine service on what is no doubt an extraordinary errand. They're outfitted in some livery he cannot discern through the rivulets of rain running down the window.

Jessica, who's been stacking their plates and putting them aside, looks at his face. "Trouble?" she asks.

"I'm not sure," replies Jonathan. "Well, he'll have to go back outside in a moment to tend to the horses and carriage. I assume a little light will be shed on the matter once he opens the door again."

Jessica picks up the two trays of dishes and opens the bedroom door. Jonathan expects her to leave them outside on the floor, as the cook requested. Somewhere far away, she says, "The cook did such a magnificent job on supper, perhaps I'll save her a few steps," but Jonathan is straining so hard to make out the horses' livery, he pays no heed.

A new blaze of torchlight escapes the doorway, illuminating the tangerine-and-cream livery of the Earl of Essex, which means trouble. Over the din of wind and rain, he hears the rumbling of men's voices outside, as a bulky figure goes out to the horses, his back to the inn. There's something familiar about his peculiar gait. When the figure turns toward the light for a moment to shout something toward the door, Jonathan's heart leaps into his mouth.

"Now that the dishes are downstairs, I'll just bring these cups down, too," he hears Jessica say.

"*What?*" Jonathan says in disbelief, and turns to her. But before he can stop her, Jessica is out of the door and halfway down the hall to the stairs. He catches her just as she reaches the landing, and prays no one is watching as he places his hand over her mouth, lifts her off her feet, and transports her backwards down the hallway to her room. He backs in, shuts the door, and puts her down.

"What the devil do you think you're doing?" she whispers hoarsely.

"What am *I* doing? You must be jesting! What were *you* doing?"

"I'd taken down the trays, and was about to bring down the cups—"

"You *what*?" says Jonathan, astonished. "You already took down the trays?" She nods. "Did he *see* you?"

"Did *who* see me?"

"The man who just arrived."

"I don't know *who* saw me," she says with irritation. "I was doing nothing improper. Why should I *care* who—"

"That's *Gelly Meyrick,* you dimwit!" It's out before he can stop himself.

"*Dimwit,* am I?" she says, her posture stiffening in the candlelight.

"No, I—I'm sorry, I meant—Do you know who Gelly Meyrick *is*?"

"Well, let's see if this *dimwit* can recall!" She places her right elbow in her left hand, and taps a forefinger on her cheek, as though searching her memory. "He's a long-time attendant upon the Earl of Essex, the man who wounded Father at the ferry, and was knighted by the earl for his service at Cadiz. Well? Did this *dimwit* pass your examination, Professor *Ninnyhammer*?" She turns her back to him in a huff.

"Jesse, I'm sorry, I—"

"Don't you 'Jesse' me! You wait till my father—" She stops in midsentence, as two pairs of footsteps start up the creaky stairs.

One set of footsteps is extremely heavy, and obviously belongs to the giant innkeeper. The other is somewhat less so, and has a hitch to it. Evidently, Meyrick has still not fully recovered from his flight through the tavern window. Jonathan's eyes dart about the room in a panic, as he realizes that, with one knock on Jessica's door, he'll be discovered. He's trapped!

"I don't think he's ever seen me," she whispers.

Jonathan searches his memory. "He *did* see you once, but from afar."

"How do you—?"

The footsteps reach the landing at the top of the stairs, and Jonathan puts his finger to his lips, wide-eyed.

"They cannot find you in my room!" whispers Jessica. "It would destroy my reputation!"

"Meyrick cannot find me *anywhere*!" he whispers excitedly in her ear. "He'll suspect I've seen the map, and kill us *both*!"

The footsteps stop at the tub room, followed by some quiet conversation.

"If ye just gimme yer wet things," says Joss, "I'll dry 'em out by the fire. The boy'll bring up the hot water soon now." There's a moment's silence, then a soft whistle. "That's some scratch on the back o' yer neck there, master! Well, I suppose the other feller got off worse'n you."

"Not yet," says Meyrick. "But he will, as soon as I get back to London. Gave him a pretty good black eye, though."

Jessica turns to Jonathan, and points inquiringly to his formerly black eye. Jonathan nods, shamefaced. Much to his irritation, Jessica laughs silently.

JOSS SAYS, "JUST wait here for the boy, master. I need to see to the young lady who's staying up here with her footman."

A moment passes. "Wait!" says Meyrick. "Did you say she's traveling with a footman?"

"Aye."

"Hand me that robe," says Meyrick. "I'll join you."

A minute later, the giant innkeeper knocks on the lady's door.

"Who is it?" comes a young woman's sleepy voice.

"Lady Patricia, it's me, *Joss*," he says, as though there might be *two* grumbling giants at the inn, and it's necessary for him to specify which is at her door. He places his hand on the knob.

"I'm in bed, Joss. Is there a problem?"

"No, m'lady, but…beggin' yer pardon…are you alone in there?"

A moment later, the lady responds. "Of course I'm alone, sir! What are you insinuating?"

Meyrick grabs the knob out of Joss's hand and pushes the door open. The young lady sits up with a start, guarding her eyes from the candlelight in the hallway, concealing her face. "Sir!" she says indignantly. "What is the meaning of this intrusion? Joss, who is this porcine man with you?"

Meyrick takes a long moment to glance around the room. He looks especially hard at the folds of the blanket, but there's obviously no one in the bed but the incensed young lady. "Beggin' yer pardon, m'lady," he says, "where's yer footman?"

"I don't *know*, you insolent swine! Perhaps in his own room. Joss, get this feral boar out of here at once, or I shall be forced to summon the constable."

A huge hand emerges through the doorway, lifts Meyrick up like an errant piglet, and pulls him out into the hall, smacking him roughly against the far wall.

Joss juts his large head through the doorway. "I'm very sorry, m'lady," he says contritely. "It won't happen again."

"See that it doesn't!" she says, pulls the covers up, and lies back down. Joss closes the door quietly, but firmly.

After a subdued, but intense, argument in the hallway over Meyrick's outrageous conduct, and several threats to eject him from the inn, "knight or no," Joss knocks on Jonathan's door. There's no answer. He tries the knob, but the door's locked. He pulls a keyring out of his pocket, finds the right key, and turns it. The knob turns readily.

The room is vacant. Joss thrusts his candle through the doorway, and invites Meyrick to peek inside. "But don't go in, and don't *ever* do that again, or I'll call the constable meself!"

Meyrick thrusts his head in, but there's obviously no one there. He steps back out, and Joss closes and locks the door.

"Then, where is he?" asks Meyrick impatiently.

"Don't know, and don't care. Man's entitled to some privacy, sir. He'll turn up in his own time. Now, why don't you just take your bath and get yourself settled? I'll have the boy bring some food up to the tub room, and you can eat there. Just make sure not to break any bottles on the floor. It cuts people's feet for months on end, no matter how much we sweep."

<hr/>

JESSICA WAITS FOR Joss's boy to begin pouring hot water into the tub in the nearby room, then tosses back her blankets. She quickly locks her door, lights a single taper, and races over to the window. It's still raining, and the wind is blowing very hard. She opens the window, reaches for the wire Joss pointed out earlier to Jonathan, and tugs on it, swinging the shutter towards her.

Fortunately, Jonathan has managed to find some footing on the lowest slat, as he still clings to the shutter, soaking wet and shivering. She assists him into the room. His clothes drip on the floor. She removes the saturated shirt from his muscular torso, and throws a blanket about his shoulders. As she has no hot water, she pours him a cup of wine, and his shivering soon becomes manageable.

"Th- that was close," he whispers.

"Very well," she whispers indignantly, "and now I would ask you to return to your room."

"Ret—How can I return to my *room*? I can't go out in the hallway! And I can't be found in my room! I'm telling you, they'll *kill* us! They won't look *here* again. And if they do, just send them away."

"Who's 'they'?" she demands equably.

"Meyrick and his friends," he replies. When she makes no reply, he adds: "Skeres and Poley."

"Oh? Did they arrive while I wasn't looking?"

"No, but it only stands to reason. They're working together—"

"Stands to *reason,* does it?"

"Look, m'lady...Jessica...Jess, or whatever you want to be called, who do you suppose are the other guests who'll be arriving tonight?"

"I suppose 'tis logical to expect 'tis they," she concedes. "Do you suppose le Loup will be with them?"

"I expect he'll either be with them, or *meeting* them here."

She pouts, and points to the window. "You can return to your room *that* way," she sniffs.

He gawps in disbelief. "For your information, my window is locked! I tried it while I was out there. Look here. Is this a question of modesty? Because I seem to have been companionable enough to sleep alone with you in the woods these past few nights!"

"It's not modesty. You have shown me *disrespect*!"

"I *respect* you," he insists, settling himself on the floor to sleep. "Now, would you be kind enough to hand me one of your several pillows?"

"No!"

"Why not?"

"Because you called me a *dimwit*!" she whispers sharply.

"I *apologized.* Didn't I?"

She blows out the taper, and gets under the covers in a huff, with her back towards him.

He laughs quietly in the dark.

"What's so funny?" she whispers.

"You're one of the most intelligent women I know. And how could you be a *dimwit,*" he asks, "when you're the daughter of...probably the smartest man in England?"

"'Probably?'"

"All right, *the* smartest!" he concedes.

"Are you just *saying* that?"

"No. I mean it."

He smiles when his head is struck by a thrown pillow. He rests his head on it, and dozes fitfully.

Jessica awakens for only a moment when the inn's other guests arrive, though she's vaguely aware that Jonathan has shifted on the floor, dragging himself closer to the door, presumably to hear better.

THERE'S NO TELLING how much time has passed since the other guests arrived, but the rain has stopped and it's still full dark when Jessica is disturbed by stealthy footsteps creeping up the stairs to her room. She lies alert, with her eyes closed. The footsteps pause before her doorway for what seems a long time.

Then comes a knock that's extremely quiet, almost beneath the threshold of hearing. When she doesn't respond, it comes again, this time with urgency. She wonders whether Jonathan has let himself out, and now wishes to gain reentry. For a moment, she considers getting up to answer the door, but now senses there's something sinister in the hallway.

She hears a pistol being cocked inside the room. Whoever that is in the hall, it certainly isn't Jonathan, for he's still in here with her.

The footsteps recede, and she falls back asleep.

JONATHAN AWAKENS TO a distant scream, sits bolt upright in alarm, and grabs the pistol by his side. Jessica sits up at the same instant.

"What is it?" she asks.

"I don't know," he replies. There's a gnawing feeling in the pit of his stomach.

"Are they still here?"

Jonathan shakes his head. "They left hours ago, shortly before daybreak. But it *was* them, and le Loup, too."

"Shall we see what happened?" she asks.

"I'll go," he says. "I would ask you to stay here with this." He hands her the pistol.

"Why, this pistol is *mine!*" she says with surprise.

"So it is. I couldn't get to *mine.* Remember?" He turns to her as he leaves. "Lock this door behind me." She nods.

As he descends the stairs, the cook runs past him down a hallway. Jonathan follows close behind, and it's a good thing, or he might have lost his way. The inn sprawls more than is apparent from the front, and has obviously been extended over many years, for each short corridor is of a different height, made of different wood, and painted a different color.

At the end of the last hallway stands the mournful giant, holding a woman's body across his arms. He paws at her face and listens for breath, evidently to no avail. The cook recoils, covers her face, and runs away toward the main part of the inn, weeping.

Jonathan walks up to the giant, and looks at the woman, or rather *corpse,* in his arms. Her face has been clubbed beyond recognition, possibly with a pistol butt, and her nightgown is bloodstained near the crotch. Apparently, whatever fiend committed her foul murder raped her, as well.

"Boy!" cries Joss. An errand boy runs in, sees the dead girl, and stops in the doorway. "Fetch the constable, but don't bother with the surgeon." He listens again for any sign of breath, but shakes his head. "She's dead. Dead." As he begins toward a neighboring room with the body in his arms, Jonathan steps out of his way into the open doorway of a vacant guestroom. As Joss passes by, Jonathan comes out to follow.

Once in the neighboring room, the innkeeper kneels, and places the body down tenderly on the couch. He smooths her gown, and looks at Jonathan, who stands beside him. The giant's size is such that, in his kneeling position, he looks Jonathan straight in the eye.

"Do you know who did this?" asks Jonathan, hoping he will not be accused. A fantasy rapidly plays itself out in his mind, where he's interrogated by the constable, who demands to know where he disappeared to the previous evening, as he'd been neither with his lady nor in his own room.

"I know it was *not* done by anyone hangin' on the shutters," says the innkeeper, "if that's what you mean."

Jonathan is both abashed and relieved.

Even in the face of tragedy, the innkeeper casts him a wry smile. "I'm a giant. Not a *fool,*" he says.

Jonathan nods. "Then, who did this?"

Joss sighs. "I shoulda known they'd be trouble as soon as that Frenchman told me some 'Jake' would be payin' for the whole lot of 'em. As for whodunit," he shrugs, "it was one of those what met the knight here. That crowd's been accused of this kind of thing before, but I never believed it, as I never saw sign of it in 'em. But one of them bastards is the devil himself, and that's sure. Perhaps I *have* been a fool. And now this poor girl has paid for my folly with her life."

"Was she a guest?" asks Jonathan.

Joss shakes his head. "A scullery maid. Barely made enough in wages to keep body and soul together."

"How many were here last night?"

"The knight, two other English, and a Frenchman."

"Was one of the other two English tall and cunning? And the other short, stocky, and probably drunk?"

"Surely drunk! You know who they are?"

"I've seen them all before. The one who called himself a knight in fact *is* a knight, by the name of Gelly Meyrick. He and the other two Englishmen attend upon the Earl of Essex. The Frenchman calls himself 'le Loup,' but I know little about him."

Jonathan looks at the innkeeper's huge ingenuous face, and decides he had no choice but to trust him. "Joss, I must confide something in you immediately, as m'lady and I are bound to follow those men without delay."

"You? Follow *them*? *With a lady*? Have ye lost yer wits?"

"Something like that. And to prove it, I shall tell you who I really am, and where you may find me, so that the constable does not take my absence as evidence of guilt."

"You sound like a barrister."

"I *am* a barrister! Of Gray's Inn, just outside London. My name is Jonathan Hawking. Will you remember that, and divulge it to no one other than the constable, and *that* in confidence?"

Joss nods. "And the lady?"

"I prefer not to tell you her name, but I *shall* tell you that her father is a barrister to Her Majesty Queen Elizabeth."

The giant's eyes flash. He puts his right hand over his heart as a sign of devotion. "God save her."

"God save us *all*," replies Jonathan darkly, nodding toward the murdered girl. "And now you know that my sleeping in m'lady's room was not for an unsavory dalliance, but to avoid being seen by those evil men. Please bear that in mind when you speak with the constable. And please instruct the staff not to allow my lady to be informed of this foul murder."

Joss nods. "Godspeed, then!" he says. "This won't keep quiet for long. Murder will out, they say. Your clean clothes are outside your room. Sir, do not go near those men without a lot of help. And keep them far away from the lady." He turns piously to the body, and begins to pray.

ALTHOUGH THE STORM has moved inland and left Cornwall sunny and cool, Jonathan and Jessica barely notice. The events of the previous evening have left them with little feeling but the grim determination to carry out their task. Neither labors any longer under the illusion that they will escape their quest unchanged, nor without grave risk.

Jonathan waits to be underway for several miles before lying to Jessica about the slaying, telling her that the scream came from a chambermaid who found a guest's strongbox pried open, its considerable contents stolen. He resolves to leave Jessica off in safe surroundings at the first opportunity, but wonders whether that opportunity might never present itself.

As the two ride abreast in mirthless silence, suddenly two horsemen appear on a hilltop in the distance ahead, looking off to the side of the road. Jonathan looks behind to see if he and Jessica are being surrounded, but there's no one there. No one *visible,* at least. Nevertheless, he nods to Jessica, and together they draw out their pistols and hold them uncocked at their sides. In this cautious manner, they proceed toward the horsemen as though they haven't noticed them.

One of the horsemen, tall and blonde, turns toward them as they approach, shielding his eyes from the sun. If he's a highwayman, he's an extraordinarily well-groomed and well-dressed specimen. And then he does something completely unexpected. He *waves* to them.

Jonathan's heart leaps into his mouth. "I think that's *Cheerful*!" he exclaims.

"*'Tis* David!" says Jessica, and tears well up in her eyes, reminding Jonathan just how burdensome it's been for her to travel into grave danger with no hope of aid or friend. And here they are, all unlooked for. *Friends, at last!* "The other one appears to be Andres Salazar, another barrister of Gray's Inn, and a friend of your father's," he says.

"What are they doing way out here?" she asks.

"Let's go and find out," he says, and they trot together to the hilltop. To the hilltop…and *friends*!

"David Killigrew!" shouts Jessica, as they drew near. "What are *you* doing out here?"

Cheerful smiles and shrugged. "Why, Lady Jessica! What a question! We're here to save *you,* of course!"

"Join the party!" she says. "So far, my catalog of protectors has only one entry, namely, Master Hawking!"

"It looks as though he's done all right, m'lady," says Cheerful. "After all, you're in one piece!"

"What news of the world, gentlemen?" Jonathan asks.

"What of my father in Holborn?" she adds.

"Well," says Cheerful, "your father is not presently *in* Holborn. He's fairly nearby, in Dorset."

"And what's he doing there, pray tell?" she asks.

"Investigating a murder that took place at the Tower of London about a week ago."

Jonathan says, "That would be soon after I left."

"The very next day," confirms Cheerful. "Serjeant Ames has accompanied Sir Walter Raleigh to Dorset to investigate."

"Why Dorset?" asks Jonathan. "A bit far from the Tower, I should think."

"Because Dorset is where Lord Mountjoy resides! And he is the gentleman who owns the map you were about to discover when last you wrote to Serjeant Ames. Have you in fact discovered it?"

"We *have*," says Jonathan with satisfaction, "thanks in no small part to Lady Jessica, and we have confirmed it to be the original bearing Lord Mountjoy's watermark!"

Cheerful and Andres tip their hats to Jessica, who smiles for the first time all day.

Jonathan looks about suspiciously. Even with good friends newfound, he feels uncomfortable remaining conspicuous on the road for more than a few moments. "Come, let's get off the road. There are some violent rascals about, and we've much to discuss." He leads the way with Andres beside him.

David drops behind and rides alongside Jessica.

"Your father is deeply concerned for your welfare," he says.

"Then perhaps he should have come to fetch me himself, instead of sending Master Hawking!"

"Well, Master Hawking was available at the time," says Cheerful, snickering.

"So I've been told," she says impatiently.

"Lady Jessica, Her Majesty relies quite heavily upon your father. But that makes him no less concerned about you. After all, he conscripted *us,* and sent us out here to see to your welfare. And, of course, it's taken us a while to find you."

"Oh, of course," she says apologetically. "I didn't mean to sound ungrateful."

"There's no way your father would have been able to get away this long himself. Not now, with an unsolved murder at the Tower. But he did send me to escort you back to him at Lord Mountjoy's at Dorset."

"You mean…now?" asks Jessica, her eyes shifting to Jonathan.

"Aye. Oh, you needn't worry about Jonathan. Andres shall remain with him until this business is quite finished. He's quite the marksman."

Jessica's heart sinks, and she pulls to a halt, her eyes fixed on Jonathan and Andres as they ride side by side, conversing gravely. From the corner of her eye, she sees Cheerful stop alongside her.

Is this how it's to be? she wonders. Is she to trot off to the safety of her father's care at Lord Mountjoy's manor house, while Andres takes her place beside Jonathan on this perilous journey? Somehow, the thought troubles her deeply.

Foolish, perhaps, but there it is.

CHAPTER 13

LORD MOUNTJOY FAILS to appear the next morning, and the next. At the end of breakfast the third day, his footman informs Lord Howard, Sir Walter, and Noah that, although his lordship has been unavoidably detained on military affairs, he will join them later that day.

"Well, that does it for me, I'm afraid," says Lord Howard. "Can't wait any longer. Too far behind in my own affairs. Sir Walter, please thank Mountjoy for his hospitality, and pass along my regret that I was unable to await his arrival."

"That's unfortunate," replies Sir Walter. "Will you be returning soon?"

"Quite possibly," says Howard. "I'll be nearby for a few days. Perhaps I'll call again." He rises to leave. "Serjeant Ames, it has been a distinct pleasure. I shall be certain to assure the Lord Admiral of your loyalty and discretion. Whether it will do any good, I'm afraid I can't say."

Noah rises. "You are too kind, Lord Howard. You've already been a great help to me in fulfillment of my commission. Your favorable mention to the Lord Admiral will be more than I could hope for." He bows respectfully.

Howard goes to the door, hands the footman a coin, and dispatches him to fetch his adjutant. As he waits, he silently beckons Raleigh to his side, and the two converse privately while Noah finishes his coffee, wondering whether Mountjoy's tardiness has anything to do with either the purloined map or the murder at the Tower.

As no one's paying him any heed, Noah decides to take a walk in the garden, and returns to his room for a jacket. On his way out, he notices a scuff mark on his boot. Bending over to rub it with his finger, he is again struck by the offensive odor he detected in the garden upon his arrival. He rises, and tries to sniff out which nearby room holds the source of the odor. To his left is the locked library door, and to his right are two doors to unoccupied bedrooms. He pokes his head into one of the bedrooms, and glances around, but there's no detectable odor, and nothing plainly amiss.

Stepping back into the hallway, he collides with a man standing directly behind him. It's the weathered manservant who scowled at him after he recited Hebrew prayers over the wine and bread.

"Pardon me!" says Noah suspiciously.

"Sorry, Master Jew," says the man through a set of blackened teeth. "Didn't mean to frighten ye. Name's Rafe."

"See here, sir!" Noah says sternly. "First off, I am 'Serjeant Ames' to you. Not 'Master Jew!' And what business have you with me?"

As Noah tenses for a verbal or physical assault, he's surprised to see the man recoil with a look of surprised innocence. "I—I'm sorry, sir," he says. "I don't see too well any longer, and overheard you sayin' prayers in the ancient tongue. Had to squint to see what was goin' on. I meant no disrespect. Didn't mean to frighten ye, neither."

"Very well," says Noah, relenting only slightly. "Did you wish to say something to me?"

"Wish to talk with ye private-like, if ye could spare a moment of yer valuable time. Not here," he says glancing about uncomfortably. "In the garden, where there's no one to hear us."

Noah decides he's probably prejudged the man unfairly. "Very well, Rafe. I'll meet you there in a few minutes."

Rafe nods agreeably, puts on his cap, and turns to the door. Noah returns to his room to strap on Uncle Avram's dagger, just to be sure, then goes out to the garden, where Rafe has begun whiling away the time, weeding the pumpkin patch.

"Oh, there y'are, sir. Sorry to startle ye like that. Stupid of me. Never feel comfortable indoors. It's always too cramped fer me. Too many delicate things to break with all my blunderin' about. I s'pose that's why they keep me out o' doors most the time now. Anyways, sir, ye struck as me as a very intelligent gentleman, and I was wonderin' if ye might 'elp an old clodpoll like me to solve a kinda mystery."

"Which mystery is that?"

"Well, sir, I 'eard about poor Lieutenant Trenowden—"

"What have you heard?" asks Noah, concerned that the matter has become public knowledge prematurely.

"Just that the poor lad was murdered at the Tower o' London, and you and Sir Walter come up 'ere to look into it." He smiles at Noah's surprise. "Can't keep somethin' like that quiet very long, sir. He was a member of the household, after all, and ye've been up here a few days already."

"I suppose not. But if *that's* the mystery you wish me to solve, I must confess its solution continues to elude me."

"No, sir. I was just wonderin' what 'appened to the *other* lieutenant who was 'ere before the murder. Lieutenant Braddock. The two of 'em was good friends, and disappeared the same time."

What's this? Why hasn't Raleigh been told? Or *has* he?

"Rafe, is there a map room in the manor house?"

"Nah. But I seen some maps in the library when I peeked in there once."

A repulsive thought bubbles to the surface of Noah's mind. "Was that the library across from the spot where you and I just bumped into one another?"

Rafe nods. Noah turns toward the library window he spotted open upon arriving at Mountjoy's. It has evidently remained open since then, despite the cold evenings. Dreading the worst, he walks to the window, and sniffs. The stench is strong enough to make his eyes tear. He returns to the gardener.

"I may have nosed your lieutenant, Rafe. Have you a key to the library?"

"No, sir. Nobody does, 'cept the two lieutenants, and possibly the baron."

Noah's head swims. "Rafe, please go and fetch Sir Walter to the library at once."

Rafe jogs off toward the servants' entrance. Noah dolefully goes to the front entrance, bracing himself for yet another awful discovery. By the time he reaches the library door, Raleigh has already arrived, and Rafe stands behind him, blinking nearsightedly. Noah twists the doorknob hard, but it will not budge.

"Any ideas for opening this door, Sir Walter?"

"One or two, but they'd infuriate Lord Mountjoy. Besides…are we even *permitted* to open it, under law?"

"Perhaps we'd need a magistrate if we were investigating his lordship," replies Noah. "But we're not. And this door is a possible impediment to the safety of Her Majesty, in any event. *I'll* take full responsibility." He places both his hands on the door at a point immediately above the knob, and shoves against it with all his strength. The door rattles open, shaking violently on its hinges. Small metal pieces of the lock and doorknob spring into the room, clattering to the floor.

The vile reek of putrefaction wafts over them. "Good Lord!" said Sir

Walter, removing a kerchief from his pocket and placing it over his nose and mouth. "Step aside!" he commands, and enters the library.

Noah was prepared to be hit with the stench, but the gardener was not, and can barely hold his gorge as he races for the nearest exit. Noah steps in behind Sir Walter, who's searching under the tables.

Noah crosses the library to the open window. Although it shows no sign of tampering or damage, there's a dusty bootprint on an adjacent ledge.

"I don't see anything," says Raleigh. "Do you suppose some beast came in through that open window and died in here?"

Noah turns back to Sir Walter, and sees that the bookshelf behind him nearly reaches the ceiling. The top shelf is taller than the rest, and deeply recessed. From it hangs a pallid, motionless human arm, its black-and-blue hand dangling inches above Sir Walter's head.

"A beast passed through this window all right," says Noah, "but I expect he was the human sort. And he was going *out,* not in." He rubs his eyes wearily. "Take a few steps toward me, Sir Walter, turn around and look up."

"Gawd!" Sir Walter exclaims. "Who is *that?*"

"If my guess is right, it's Lieutenant Braddock. The gardener Rafe just told me he disappeared about the same time as Trenowden. I wonder if this library is where the fateful note was torn."

"You surmise there was a struggle between Trenowden and Braddock?" asks Raleigh through the kerchief.

The reek is overpowering. "We should know shortly. If we can keep down breakfast."

Raleigh nods toward the corpse. "Shall we?"

Noah sighs. "Must we?"

Raleigh nods. "No one else here to do it, I'm afraid. Carter's up and around, but his shoulder will stay mangled for months. You gave Arden leave to exercise his horse this morning. And Mountjoy's servants must be regarded as suspects, so they can't be allowed to touch anything until the coroner comes."

Noah nods in resignation. "Besides, our lieutenants seem to be faring rather poorly of late. Let's get some chairs to step up on."

They stand on separate chairs, and together lift the rotting body down from the shelf. Although they were expecting the corpse to be rigid, the lieutenant has evidently been dead so long that *rigor mortis* has come and gone, leaving a corpse so flaccid that they nearly drop it as they step down.

A few disgusting moments later, the dead lieutenant lies on his back across a table in the center of the room. A dagger has obviously been plunged through his heart, as its handle still protrudes from his chest. As his short scabbard is empty, Noah surmises that, like Trenowden, this lieutenant was murdered with his own weapon.

The deceased evidently bled only a short while before dying, for a small brown splotch of congealed blood surrounds the wound. This time, the facial expression is not contorted, but peaceful.

Noah could kick himself. Another innocent young man dead, and here toil Her Majesty's best investigators, still blundering about a week or more behind the killer.

Raleigh goes through the corpse's pockets with one hand, holding his handkerchief over his nose with the other. "Pah!" he says, as he draws away in disgust. "Nothing! Who do you suppose killed him?"

"I don't know," replies Noah, "but I fear it was that blasted Frenchman."

There's movement in the hallway. A strangely accented voice says: "I trust it is not my whole *nation* being accused of this terrible act, monsieur, but rather a *particular* countryman." A middle-aged man stands in the doorway, wearing rich-looking French clothing, and a grave expression. "If so," he adds, arching an eyebrow, "perhaps I can…assist."

Although Raleigh's hand moved instinctively toward his dagger, he does not draw. "To whom do we owe the pleasure, sir?" he asks cautiously.

"I am the Comte de Tréville, monsieur, but my friends call me 'Jean.'" He pronounces "this" as "zees," and "Jean" as *"zhawn"* almost as a Frenchman might, but he inserts the slightest suggestion of an "s" before the "v" in Tréville, something no Frenchman would ever do. Certainly, his accent differs from any Noah ever heard in France.

Sir Walter and Noah bow respectfully. "But *are* you French, monsieur?" asks Noah. "Your accent is…complex."

"You have ze very good ear," says Monsieur de Tréville. "And, as I recognize this fine gentleman as being the famous Sir Walter Raleigh, I surmise that *you* are the Queen's advocate who calls himself 'Serjeant Ames'?" When Noah nods, he continues. "In fact, I am *Basque,* although my title is French, and I have the privilege of counting myself among the very good friends of His Royal Majesty Henri de Navarre."

"Ah, sir," says Noah, "now you mention an eminence whom it was my distinct privilege to meet on a European tour some years ago."

Although de Tréville obviously wishes to reply in equally courtly manner, Sir Walter turns the conversation back to the matter at hand. "Monsieur de Tréville, may I ask whether you are accompanied by Lord Mountjoy? For, as you see, a terrible crime has been committed in his lordship's house, and we need to speak with him at once."

De Tréville regards the corpse disdainfully and turns his nose up, as though detecting its offensive odor for the first time. "The Baron was some small distance behind me, as he planned to stop on the way. I trust we shall speak later, when I can share my information with all three of you." He bows and departs the doorway.

Raleigh turns to Noah. "Intriguing. In the meanwhile, we need to search the lieutenant's personal effects for the remainder of the note."

Rafe appears in the doorway, ashen and more than a little shaky. "I'm sorry I got sick to me stomach before. May I be of service to you gentlemen?"

"Yes," says Raleigh. "You can guide me to Lieutenant Braddock's quarters." Rafe leads Raleigh from the library.

Alone with the corpse, Noah holds his nose and studies the handle of the dagger protruding from its chest. As expected, the dagger is much the same as that used to kill Trenowden at the Tower.

There's something curious about the lieutenant's shirt, however. It's bunched about the lower ribs, as though the victim was tugging it closed when he was stabbed, which is most curious as, even now, it remains securely buttoned. As it seems most unlikely that the assailant would have buttoned up the victim's shirt after stabbing him through it, Noah wonders whether the victim was trying to protect something concealed in an inside pocket, perhaps something that remains there still.

Sir Walter reappears in the doorway. "Nothing," he says. "Searched his bureau, drawers, and so on." He shakes his head. "Spot anything here?"

"Possibly," replies Noah, "but to find out, we need to draw out the knife."

Sir Walter steps forward and draws the dagger out of the corpse's chest, briefly examines it, and offers it to Noah by the handle.

Noah waves it away. "It's not the knife we need to examine," he says contemplatively, "but the shirt." He unbuttons the dead man's shirt. Sure enough, there's a small pocket hidden inside. Unfortunately, it's a mere hair's breadth from the bloody wound, and has been drenched in blood. He holds his breath and reaches two fingers into the pocket, trying to ignore the tendrils of coagulate gore that crack apart as they're touched by his advancing fingers.

A small scrap of paper is stuck in there. He removes it as best he can. It's badly bloodstained, and no writing is visible from the outside. "Should I try to unfold it?"

"Might as well," replies Raleigh. "It's of no value unless we can read it."

Noah carefully unfolds it. To his surprise, it opens without ripping. Although its blotchy color suggests there was once writing on it, any writing has been obliterated by the blood.

He removes from his pocket the two scraps of the note found on Trenowden at the Tower, and is able to fit them all together perfectly. Disappointed, he looks up at Raleigh. "Well, all we can say is: This is the remaining scrap."

Raleigh shakes his head in disgust. "We came all this way and tarried several days for nothing."

"Not necessarily. We've confirmed we were right about the altercation, and that the killer knew nothing of the note. That suggests that Trenowden and Braddock struggled over the note. Perhaps they did not see eye to eye about what should be done with it. Also, we now know the killer was *here* and committed this murder before following Trenowden to the Tower of London."

"That's if there was only one killer. And it doesn't tell us how the bastard managed to get into the Tower."

"No, it doesn't. Let's see what Mountjoy's French guest has to say," suggests Noah.

LESS THAN AN hour later, the coroner has left with the body, the maidservants have opened all the library windows and scoured the room with vinegar water, and Mountjoy has arrived with two fresh lieutenants.

As Mountjoy's household prides itself on efficiency, despite all the tumult the company is served a late-morning meal of mutton and potatoes, a New World root vegetable that has gained popularity in recent years.

Noah picks at his food, as his stomach has not quite settled. Raleigh, he sees, has no such scruple.

As Mountjoy passes the roasted potatoes to Sir Walter, Noah turns to Monsieur de Tréville. "And how is your good friend and king, His Majesty *Henri*?" he asks.

"He eez as well as he can be, I suppose, with Spanish conquistadors walking freely across his northern possessions. He wishes ardently zat your Queen Elizabeth would contribute more freely to his fight against zese barbarians, who are as much a threat to ze English coast as to ours."

"Yes," says Mountjoy, "well, the Queen has already lent a good deal of money to the French king, and he has yet to agree to a schedule for repayment, so you can imagine how that goes. Serjeant Ames' dear friend has been sent to Paris to attempt to sort things out."

De Tréville seems intrigued. "What is your friend's name, Serjeant?"

Noah reluctantly admires how effortlessly Mountjoy deflected the Frenchman's attention to him. "Sir Henry Neville, monsieur."

"Ah, yes. I have met ze gentleman. He is very cordial and…how do you say? Expansive."

"Yes, monsieur," replies Noah. "He is truly expansive…in many ways, and in many directions." Noah's sly reference to Sir Henry's girth is met by general agreement and snickering, yet he feels no regret about it, as Sir Henry is always first to jest about his own heft.

"Still," says de Tréville, "it is very difficult for His Majesty to begin repaying such monies while he must pay his troops to fight the Spanish from day to day."

"So, monsieur," says Sir Walter, evidently eager to change the subject. "Have you any children?"

De Tréville's breast swells with pride. "My wife is with child. I have great hopes for him. I hope zat someday he will have ze privilege of being head of the King's *mousquetaires.*"

"Getting a bit ahead of ourselves, aren't we?" says Mountjoy, smiling. "Perhaps the baby will be a beautiful *mademoiselle.* That would not be all bad, would it?"

De Tréville's countenance softens as he contemplates the possibility of a baby girl. "Vraiment, pas de tout," he says. *Truly, not at all.* "In fact, in light of the tragedy of my wife's sister, it will be a blessing to see a healthy baby of either sex."

"Oh?" says Raleigh.

"Yes, in fact, it was this tragedy about which I wished to tell you, as it may help you to identify the Frenchman you suspect of murdering your young lieutenants."

Forks, spoons, and cups are put down, as though everyone has lost his appetite at once. All eyes go to Mountjoy who, since his arrival this morning, has been deeply disturbed over the loss of his second adjutant in as many weeks.

"Pray, continue, *monsieur,*" says Mountjoy.

"It is a very sad tale, gentlemen." He sighs. "Lady de Tréville had a younger sister, very *belle,* she had much *vivacité,* or, as you would say, she was very 'full of life.' Words cannot express how much my wife loved her—" His voice drifts off. As he seems overcome with grief, a maidservant comes to his aid, but he gently waves her off. "*Pardonnez-moi,* my friends, as this story is a difficult one for me to tell."

Mountjoy interrupts. "Would you prefer not to discuss it at present?"

De Tréville waves his hand indulgently. "*Non, non, mes amis.* I wish to finish saying it now, so that I may say it only one time. My wife's sister…her name was 'Aimée.' She had her choice of many suitors. For some reason, she fell in love with one, a nobleman of low rank (who can say why, in an affair of the heart?). He courted her ardently, a true *romantique,* one might say. All of her family told her she should forget this one, because he was…how do you say, he…had an insatiable appetite for women of low station. But she refused all advice. He was…truly hypocrite, you might say, for he was very jealous of her attention, especially to one man in particular, Guillaume, who was secretly…*homosexuel.*" He looks up at the company, and asks ingenuously, "You have such men in England?"

Were it not for the sadness of de Tréville's tale, the Englishmen at the table would have met this naive question with a burst of laughter, for each of them knows many such men. Mountjoy morosely glances at each of them in turn, ensuring there shall be no outburst. "We know one or two," he replies.

Mountjoy's absurdly understated concession strikes Noah as even more humorous than a false denial, but he suppresses his laugh and turns bright red instead, staring at his place-setting in the hope that no one notices.

"Ah, I see. So it is much the same with you," resumes de Tréville. "Aimée's beloved would become enraged when she would favor this Guillaume with a smile or some…*petit cadeau,* as you would say, 'little gift,' no—" He searches for the right English word.

"A trinket?" suggests Noah.

"*Exactement,* monsieur. A trinket, or…a 'burble'?"

"Bauble?" offers Noah.

"*Précis!* That is to say, something which has no value, except sentiment, you understand. One day, the beloved *monster* found an item of Guillaume's clothing in Aimée's sleeping chamber, and he—" He breaks off for a moment, tormented by the memory. "He…raped her, and he struck her *visage* many times, until it was crushed, and she could no longer be recognized, except by her clothing." He pauses without looking at his companions. "It did not suffice, you see, to kill her. He wished to obliterate her *identité*." He looks to Noah. "Is this well said, sir?"

Noah replies sadly. "It is translated perfectly, *monsieur,* but not 'well said,' for in England that is what we call something we are pleased to hear."

"I see," says Tréville. "Later, we found out he had done the same thing to several women of low station, and had escaped by threats, or bribery of public officials."

Mountjoy glowers. "And you think this could be the man who murdered my adjutants?"

"Perhaps, Baron. His custom is to kill *men* only at need, as he takes no pleasure in it, but he *is* fond of the dagger, and he is known to be in England. He has been seen as far west as Falmouth, and as far east as *Londres*…pardon me, 'London.'"

"And his name?" asks Noah.

"As he is a nobleman, he has a very long name, but here in England, he goes by 'le Loup.'"

Noah exchanges a knowing glance with Sir Walter.

The Frenchman sees the exchange. "You are familiar with zees man?"

Noah leaves it to Raleigh to decide how much to divulge.

"Assassins attempted to murder Serjeant Ames and myself on our way from London to Lord Mountjoy's manor. They wounded my lieutenant, who is still recovering. Before they could shoot any more of us, we shot them all. The last one died in my arms, and identified their master as a Frenchman known in England as 'Wolf.'"

Mountjoy turns to Raleigh. "You were in a coach bearing my livery, for heaven's sake! He might have been sent to kill *me!*"

De Tréville's eyes go wide. "But, *messieurs,* this is why I have been sent here by His Majesty, to apprehend this villain and bring him to prison, or, if that is not possible, to see him apprehended by Her Majesty's men and *killed,* if need be." He turns excitedly to Mountjoy. "My lord, upon my honor, you must accept my word that this man does not act on behalf of the King of France. He is a *criminal* in our country, and the king wishes him to be *executed!*"

"Becalm yourself, *monsieur,*" says Mountjoy equably. "I have every confidence that this man was not sent by King Henri to murder me."

Unbidden, Rafe bows his way into the dining room, and approaches the foot of the table, hat in hand, squinting to locate his master. "Beggin' your pardon, m'lord. I don't mean to meddle in the affairs of my betters, but I couldn't help but overhear you gentlemen talkin' about a Frenchman named 'Loo' what murdered your lordship's adjutants. I just had to tell ye I seen that very same Frenchman talkin' with both them adjutants."

Mountjoy seems amazed. "When, Rafe?"

"I seen him skulkin' about the garden *lotsa* times, m'lord, tryin' to catch their attention without catchin' anyone *else's*."

Noah can contain himself no longer. "M'lord, if I may put a question?" Mountjoy nods assent. "Rafe, as your vision is poor, how can you be sure *whom* you saw?"

Rafe smiles. "I'm nearly blind, Serjeant Ames, it's true, but I'm not deaf. As for the adjutants, they clanked when they walked, always carryin' a lot of metal, swords, keys, and so on. As for the Frenchman, I *heard* 'im talkin' to the young adjutants. His English was...very bad. Could barely understand it."

"Did he talk as I do?" asks de Tréville.

"No, sir. From yer accent, I woulda taken you for Spanish. And your English is much better. This fella spoke like a Frenchman who only left *Paree* the first time a week before."

Noah asks, "Did you ever learn what he was talking to the lieutenants about?"

"No, sir. But I kinda figgered he was a messenger-like. Always on the move, goin' hither and yon. Always had brambles stuck to his clothes and his hair, like a wild man, almost."

"Thank you, Rafe," says Mountjoy. "Ask Cook for a drink to calm your nerves, as I know how fond you were of my adjutants." Rafe bows sadly, and turns away. As he reaches the door, Mountjoy adds, "And Rafe?"

"M'lord?"

"No more eavesdropping."

Rafe shakes his head gravely and is about to reach for the knob, when the door swings wide open, nearly striking him. To the amazement of all, David Killigrew bursts in, exhausted, and looking every bit the stern young officer. Spying Mountjoy and his guests at table, he drops to one knee. "I beg your pardon, m'lord. I'd no *idea*—"

"Nonsense, man," says Mountjoy in a commanding voice. "Stand up and speak your piece!"

"M'lord, my message is principally for Serjeant Ames." He rubs his eyes with one hand. "I've been riding all day and night for two days, having left Master Salazar with Master Hawking, as you instructed. I also attempted to persuade Lady Jessica to accompany me here, but she'd have none of it."

"That would be my daughter," says Noah wearily, dread turning in the pit of his stomach. "But, David, why are you so alarmed?"

David's eyes dart around the table. "I fear they're bound for a confrontation, sir, with the Frenchman whose men attacked you and Sir Walter!"

Noah shoots to his feet. As his mind strives desperately for his next move, he barely notices the surrounding commotion. Mountjoy has already begun shouting commands.

"The Frenchman's name?" demands de Tréville.

"Le Loup, sir!"

CHAPTER 14

"HOW LONG HAS it been since we've seen them?" asks Andres, clopping alongside Jonathan and Jessica in the crisp autumn breeze.

"Well, let's see," says Jonathan. "We *saw* Meyrick and *heard* the rest of them at the Davey Jones the night before you found us." Chagrined, he turns toward Andres. "Not since then, obviously. What is that? Four days, or five? I've lost track."

"How shall we ever find them again?" asks Jessica.

Jonathan surveys the forbidding countryside around them. "There's no guaranty we'll ever do that, but we must keep trying. This flat terrain isn't making it any easier." He spies a tall hill up ahead, at last, and picks up the pace. "There's a bit of hope! Let's go up and look about."

As they climb the hill, they find the footing more treacherous than it appeared from low ground. "I hope it's worth the climb," says Andres.

Their ascent requires them to pass through three stone portals, each surrounded by nothing but ancient woods. "These ruins must be very old," says Jessica. "There's no sign of the structure to which they provided admittance."

"Or, rather, to which they barred the way," says Jonathan, calling to mind the original purpose of ancient hilltop battlements. "The irony is, it was most likely built by the Cornish to keep out us English."

"*You* English," says Salazar. "My people were still in Portugal until a couple of generations ago."

"Most of mine were in Spain," says Jessica. "The Cornish language is pretty, and sounds very old. *Gwennap, Feock, Penryn.* Every village's name makes it seem a setting for a folktale full of elves and goblins."

"The language is indeed ancient, and a source of local pride," explains Jonathan. "It's called 'Kernewek,' and they've fought the English more than once to hold onto it, most recently against Her Majesty's father, during the Prayer Book Rebellion."

"I learned of that from Father," says Jessica.

"Not I," says Jonathan, turning to her earnestly. "I learned of it from Serjeant Ames." They share a laugh.

Andres rolls his eyes. "Isn't that precious?" he says. But it only makes them laugh the harder.

Jessica continues. "Father says that Henry the Eighth commanded everyone in the realm to abandon the Latin Mass, and say their prayers in the English Language. He says that, if the point of the law was to cast off Latin and its connection to papistry, it could yet have permitted people to pray in their own local language, without mandating English."

Jonathan arches an eyebrow. "But, ever the fair-minded advocate, Serjeant Ames also pointed out that, as the Cornish hadn't understood the Mass in Latin, they were no worse off for failing to understand it in English. I'd imagine, however, that another object of the law was to unify the language spoken throughout Britain…which has its advantages."

"Especially to the English," mutters Andres.

At the top of the hill, scattered stones dot the perimeter of a substantial battlement that must once have occupied the whole hilltop. Jonathan looks out over the surrounding area, and feels the sudden urge to keep his head down. He's surprised to see they're all of one mind, as without a word they dismount and quietly tie off their horses amidst a small copse of trees.

At one end of the hilltop stands a mighty oak whose gnarled and massive branches make it seem the first ever to appear in the world. On its highest branch perches a golden eagle who eyes the three travelers suspiciously, jealously guarding its giant eyrie.

The opposite end of the hilltop, which looks out over a cliff, provides an unobstructed view of a vast area through which the rustic road wends its way west over the horizon, and out of sight. Though there seems no sign of any traveler, they crouch behind a small row of bushes near the hill's sheer edge to conceal themselves from anyone on the road.

"What's that?" asks Jessica, pointing some distance ahead of the spot where they left the road.

Jonathan shields his eyes in the cloudy glare, and squints. What at first appeared to be a brown smudge in the distance is in fact a group of four saddled horses tied off together by the edge of the road.

Jonathan looks at Jessica incredulously. "Good Lord, Jess, how did you see them? They must be half a mile away."

"That's odd," mutters Andres. "There's no one anywhere near them."

Mere yards from the distant horses, a man stumbles backward seemingly out of nowhere, his pack hurled after him, striking him in the chest, as though he's been ejected from some invisible bawdy house.

Instinctively, the hilltop spectators lower their heads further, and satisfy themselves with the view through the branches.

"That's le Loup!" says Jessica, with uncanny certainty.

The tiny figure immediately drops his pack and begins gesticulating, as though shouting at the top of his lungs, though he's much too far away to be heard. Oddly, he seems to be enraged at…no one…until his three companions walk toward him, themselves suddenly appearing out of nowhere.

"There must be a cave there," surmises Jonathan. "And we're just too far away to see its mouth."

"Very like," says Andres. "Are those your four varlets?"

Jonathan turns to him. "*Our* four, if you please. And, yes, 'tis they."

"What do you suppose they're arguing about?" asks Jessica.

"Could be anything, I suppose," Jonathan replies with a shrug. "Gaming…liquor…women. Who knows?"

Jessica shoots a sidelong glance at him. "I like *that*!" she says in a manner that means she most certainly does *not* like it.

"You like *what*?" Jonathan asks innocently.

"Tossing women into the same category as gaming and liquor. As though women are something to be taken up as long as they're amusing, and then tossed aside when you grow aweary of them."

"I? *I?* We're talking about *them,* Jessica!"

"Oh, you're all alike," she waves away his reply without so much as a glance, "and don't pretend otherwise."

"Now, I like *that*!" he fires back.

Andres throws his hands up. "Will you two—Oh, for heaven's sake, you're *insufferable*!" He points toward their quarry. "Look, *they're* fighting, too!"

One of the tall ones, probably Skeres, takes a swing at le Loup. A scuffle ensues, and the short, round Poley is thrown to the ground. It ends suddenly when le Loup draws his sword, and brandishes it at Skeres. For a tense moment, nothing happens, then Skeres turns his back contemptuously on le Loup and tramps over to the horses, followed by Poley, who's managed to get up, with some effort.

"Look," says Andres. "They're mounting, preparing to leave. *And,*" he intones, "it appears there's been a parting of the ways. Three are leaving. The other one's just…standing there, watching them turn onto the road south, through the woods."

"The one standing alone is le Loup," says Jessica, shivering. "That pig must have disgusted even *those three*!"

"Difficult to imagine how," says Jonathan.

As the three riders disappear from view, le Loup throws his hat to the ground, and kicks it repeatedly.

"A nice little tantrum," observes Jessica.

Le Loup sits down hard on the ground, apparently talking aloud in a soliloquy that goes on for several minutes. At last, he rises and unties his horse, evidently preparing to mount.

"He has the map," observes Jonathan. "Look! It's jutting out of his saddlebag."

The eagle in the ancient oak behind them suddenly takes flight and begins circling the hilltop, emitting a call culminating in several long, ear-splitting shrieks.

Le Loup stops and turns to peer up at the great bird. Although he's very far away, and the three travelers are concealed, there's something in his hesitation, perhaps a suspicious turn of the head, that makes Jonathan feel they've been discovered.

"Blast. He suspects we're here," says Jonathan dejectedly.

"Don't be foolish," says Jessica. "That's just a feeling. He can't see us."

Jonathan rubs the back of his neck. "Perhaps not, but right now he's wondering whether something up here startled that blasted bird."

Andres chimes in, eying the circling eagle as though he'd like to shoot it. "Well, let's not give him any confirmation."

"Agreed. We'll sit tight until he's truly gone," says Jonathan. "And then I'll be exploring that cave."

$$\Longrightarrow\circ C\!\!\!\!\!\mathscr{D}\!\!\circ\Longleftarrow$$

DESCENDING THE HILL proves to be trickier than riding up, but they make it down safely and return to the road.

"It was right around here, if I'm not mistaken," says Andres. "Look, I think I can see the hoofprints where their horses were tied off together." They draw up to the spot, which abuts a rocky cliff.

"This is it, all right," says Jonathan, surveying the embankment, "but I see no cave." He estimates the very spot where le Loup appeared, and slowly draws up to it. He looks at the cliffside again, and points to the approximate place where Meyrick, Skeres, and Poley emerged into the sunlight. "It would have to be right *there*." He dismounts, and walks toward the cliff until his boots graze the rough brush growing along its base. He picks up a branch the size of a walking-stick, pulls off the few remaining leaves, and uses it to probe the cliffside. His first few taps are met by solid rock. On his next tap, the stick thrusts so deep into nothingness that he nearly loses both his grip and his balance.

"Got it!" he shouts, only to find that Andres is already right behind him. "I need a lit candle." Andres hands him one. "How'd you do that so quickly?"

"Flint and gunpowder. How else?"

Jonathan shrugs. "I didn't hear you do it, that's all." As he parts the strands of ivy dangling over the mouth of the cave, he realizes that Andres intends to accompany him inside. "Andres, you'd best stay out here, and keep Jessica out of sight. It's unsafe with all these rascals on the road."

"What makes you think it's any safer in *there*?" asks Andres.

Jonathan lets the question pass. "Keep the rope handy, and I'll be fine. I just want to see if they left anything near the mouth of the cave." When Andres regards him skeptically, he says: "I seriously doubt they went exploring the spelunk, for heaven's sake!"

"If you see anything, just shout," Andres says, and hesitantly withdraws.

Jonathan draws a deep breath, and takes a few steps into the mouth of the cave. The vines rustle shut behind him. He gives his eyes a minute to adjust, and holds the candle aloft.

He stands in a chamber the size of a small salon. Although the light from his little taper cannot reach all its edges, he spies nothing discarded by a previous occupant. As the floor seems fairly even, and free of stray rocks, he walks toward each side of the chamber.

"You all right in there?" comes Andres' faint shout.

"Fine. Don't leave Jessica alone," he replies.

As he moves toward one end of the chamber, the candle illuminates a shapeless heap that casts a long shadow along the floor. At first blush, it appears to be an abandoned sack. He stoops beside it and brushes aside some folds in search of an opening.

Instead, he finds what appears to be…hair, a great deal of it. He's startled to find himself looking at the back of someone's head. As there's no sign of life, and no smell of putrefaction, he surmises that this is le Loup's latest kill. He forces himself to take hold of the hair and turn the head about to reveal the victim's identity, but there's no way of knowing who this woman was, as no discernible face remains. The poor girl's own mother could not identify her from her remains.

"Still all right?" comes Andres' voice from outside.

Jonathan returns the corpse's head to its former position, and wipes his hands together. "Be right there!" he says with quiet annoyance, not at Andres' persistence, but at his own compulsion to disturb this crypt.

As with the dead girl at the Davey Jones Inn, Jonathan decides to conceal knowledge of this latest horrific find from Jessica. Yet, he realizes at the same time that keeping her beside him without full knowledge of what she's facing is terribly unfair and dangerous. Indeed, it would be selfish and foolhardy for him to bring her any further along this treacherous path. He will have to dispatch her with Andres, south to Falmouth, where David's Killigrew relatives can lodge her safely, with no vicious Frenchman to threaten her.

But he cannot send her away right here at the cave. If he sends her away now, she'll be taking the same road south as Meyrick, Skeres, and Poley. Besides, she'll insist on seeing the cave herself before going. No, he must wait until the next crossroads, near Redruth, a few miles ahead.

He hesitates inside the mouth of the cave. He cannot allow his expression to betray this awful find. He sucks in a deep breath and forces a smile as he shoves aside the vines and emerges into the open air.

———————⇒∘◖∘⇐———————

"I'M NOT GOING, Jonathan!" shouts Jessica, guiding her horse to a stop. Jonathan stops beside her. Andres, who's clopped along behind them to avoid being burned in the coming conflagration, brings his mount to a halt, as well.

"M'lady," Jonathan replies deferentially. "Neither you nor I have any choice in the matter. Serjeant Ames was quite clear that you are to accompany me no further than Falmouth. And Falmouth is *that* way." To cover his bald-faced lie, he directs her attention to the southbound road.

"Don't you 'm'lady' *me,* after all this time, you impudent sod! My father has no power to control my actions." She pounds her chest. "I'm a baron's *widow,* and I answer to *no* man!"

"Perhaps *you* do not, madam, but I do! I am an officer of the Court of Queen's Bench, and have been ordered by a senior Serjeant—"

"— who happens to be my father!" she shouts.

"Be that as it may, I am lawfully forbidden to proceed any further with your ladyship in my charge. And I am impelled to place you in the charge of my associate Master Salazar, also of Queen's Bench," he glances at Andres, who's already cast his eyes down, "who shall accompany you to the Killigrew manor house in Falmouth, where you will be treated in the manner to which you are entitled and accustomed. There is nothing further to be said on the subject. Please accept my profoundest apologies."

"I'll accept your head on a platter, you ingrate!" she growls.

"Lady Burlington," he says humbly, "I am by no means *ungrateful* for all you have done for me on this unexpected journey. Why, had it not been for you, I would never have come this far! Quite apart from that, the pleasure of your company—"

"A pleasure with which you are now prepared to dispense! And rather summarily, I might add."

"Madam, please believe that your departure grieves me greatly. I shall now be entirely alone in my remaining task."

Tears come to Jessica's eyes. "Don't you realize you're likely to be killed in this affair, with no one to watch your back?"

"Never fear that, madam. Serjeant Ames has ordered me to keep my distance from these scoundrels. I am to gather only *intelligence* about the map, and am forbidden from interfering in its progress out of the realm."

"But your adversary is under no such constraint. He may feel he has business with *you*, even though you've none with *him*."

He nods. "And it's precisely that concern which impels me to commit you to the care of Master Salazar."

She regards him suspiciously. "You mean my father has left this decision to your discretion?"

"No, m'lady," he says, blushing.

"What did you find in that cave, Master Hawking? You haven't mentioned it."

"Nothing of consequence."

"Then, why the change of heart?" she asks, near tears.

He regards her with genuine anguish. "I could never have a change of heart about you, m'lady."

"I mean, why the change of heart about my accompanying you on the remainder of your quest?"

"This is not a change of *my* heart, madam. They are Serjeant Ames's instructions. I regret that I have kept them secret until now, but I had no choice."

"Did Master Salazar know of these instructions, as well?" Jessica looks to Andres, who slumps in the saddle, refusing to make eye contact.

Jonathan answers. "He's been given no choice, either."

Andres leads his horse around, to escort her southward.

"Very well, *Master Hawking!*" she shouts, quaking with fury. "But Falmouth is only a few miles away, and if I discover that you are lying to me about my father's instructions, *you can go and be hanged, for all I care!*"

Jonathan is struck to the quick, as though his heart might break. He solemnly brings himself up in the saddle, looks her in the eye, and speaks slowly and deliberately, fully aware that these might be the last words he will ever speak to her.

"And if I *am* to be hanged, m'lady, I shall at least have the satisfaction of peering down from the scaffold, and seeing your ladyship unharmed."

———————————∘∘⟨⟩∘∘———————————

THE SUN IS setting as Jessica and Andres approach the quaint Inn at Arwythel, which sits across the road from a little river.

"Shall we stop here for the night?" asks Andres. His voice croaks slightly, as he's spoken not a word since riding off south with the taciturn Lady Jessica.

His question rouses her from a long reverie. "Aren't you concerned we shall run into the other three blackguards?"

"I don't think that would present a problem any longer. After all, they've left the map with le Loup, so they'll see no hazard in running into you and me. They'd deem it mere coincidence that we're all arriving at Falmouth around the same time. Besides, as none of them has seen Jonathan on this journey, I shall play your footman, and they'll be none the wiser for the switch."

"Very well," she concedes. "I'm famished and tired." She looks wearily up at the inn. "Here's as good as anywhere, I suppose."

They resume their way, but Andres stops his mount some distance from the inn.

Jessica follows suit. "Why are we stopping here?" she asks.

Andres turns to her, flustered. After a moment's evident indecision, he says, "How can you *speak* to him that way?"

"I beg your pardon? To whom? Which way?"

"To Jonathan! Can't you see how he cares for you?"

She scoffs. "Well, if he does, he has an odd way of showing it."

"You mean, by risking his neck alone in the woods to ensure that *you're* safe and sound?"

She regards him skeptically. "Oh, is *that* why he's doing it?"

Andres says nothing, but regards her with a look of such impertinence that his meaning cannot be mistaken.

She realizes that Andres has inadvertently confirmed that the decision to send her away *was* up to Jonathan, which makes her smolder even more.

THE NEXT MORNING, Andres sleeps in, contemplating the events of the evening before. He and Jessica shared a nearly silent meal in a private room, during which he spied Meyrick, Skeres, and Poley enjoying a celebratory meal in the main dining room, jesting all the while that its considerable cost was being borne by "Jake." Though Andres kept a careful eye out for a fourth person who might have fit the bill as Jake, he spotted no one.

Before Andres and Jessica finished their meal, Meyrick and Skeres retired to their rooms, leaving Poley alone at the bar, drinking to his heart's content. Once Poley passed out and began snoring, Andres and Jessica crept up to their rooms and turned in.

Andres can see from the slant of light that it's now midmorning. He wonders how Jonathan is faring in the cold woods alone, and regrets being relegated to act as Jessica's escort. He washes perfunctorily and dresses quickly.

There's a quiet knock at the door. He opens it a crack. A pretty young chambermaid waits with fresh sheets. "Morning, sir. Would you be plannin' on stayin' an extra day?"

"No, we shan't, thank you. Miss, have the three men who were celebrating last night checked out of the inn?"

"They *did,* sir, quite early."

"Is the same stableman still on duty?"

She lets go a polite laugh. "If he's not, he's in trouble, sir, as we've only the one."

"I see," he replies. She seems about to say something, but rather than stay to hear it, he descends the stairs to the stables.

"Stableman!" he calls out.

The young stableman smiles broadly. "Would you be wantin' yer horse now?" Before the words are out, he's already begun to step away into the stables.

"Not yet, thank you," Andres calls after him. The stableman shrugs and returns. Andres hands him a shilling. "Did you see those three men leave this morning? Two tallish ones, the other small and—"

"And *drunk,* sir?"

"Aye, those are they. Which way did they head?"

"South, sir. Said they was goin' to Falmouth."

"How early did they go?"

"Well, wasn't still dark or nothin', but they weren't wastin' any daylight. Kinda surprisin', what with them drinkin' so much the night before. Especially the little fat one. Come to think of it, they left only a few minutes before yer lady. 'Course, she was headed the opposite way."

Andres' heart begins to pound. "But surely you're mistaken. My mistress is the pretty, slender young lady."

"Oh, I know that, sir. Not too many women in these parts can turn heads as fast as she can. Meanin' no disrespect."

"But she's asleep in her room upstairs!" Andres insists, with a pleading note in his voice.

The stableman's eyes widen. "Not unless she come back and left her horse elsewhere." He shakes his head sympathetically. "She's long gone, sir."

Andres races up the stairs to Jessica's room. The door's wide open, and the chambermaid is changing the sheets.

As he bounds down the steps two at a time, he mutters aloud: "Oh, my God. My God. *I've gone and lost her!*"

Though he reaches the stables in only a few seconds, the stableman already has his horse's reins in hand. Without another word, Andres leaps into the saddle and gallops north at breakneck speed, his eyes wide with panic.

CHAPTER 15

BEHIND THE SILHOUETTED towers of Pendennis Castle, a full moon glows deep red in the black October sky. Wispy sepia clouds trail swiftly inland after the departing storm. Midnight will soon usher in All Hallows' Eve, and mild autumn threatens to transform into dead winter overnight.

A warm glow in the windows of the Star and Garter invites the three weary travelers inside. Upon entering, two glance around cautiously, while the third, a roly-poly fellow, seems already enraptured by the yeasty scent.

The tavern is occupied by several small groups of men, some gathered in corners murmuring in conversation, others sitting around tables, sharing a pint, smoking, but engaging in little talk. Taking a table in a far corner, the three travelers order pints all around.

At the next table sits a lone man, his face concealed beneath the hood of a drab woolen cloak stained with years of travel. Before him sits a small plate of parsnips and a tankard of ale.

Skeres leans toward the stranger, and whispers. "Mind if my friends and I talk privately?"

No response.

"Are ye deaf?"

The hooded figure shakes his head slowly and silently.

"Ah, well. Mind if my friends and I talk privately?"

The hooded figure shakes his head once more.

Meyrick and Poley look at each other and snicker. "You'll have to come right out and tell him what you want, Nick," says Poley.

Skeres grimaces at Poley, contorting his scarred face into a sneer. He leans aggressively toward the stranger. "Look, goodman. I don't know if you think you're bein' funny or not, but you best move from this little table o' yours, if you know what's good for ye."

Still no reply. In a moment, the figure rises. But instead of moving away, he calmly draws the fourth chair out from under Skeres' own table and sits down, his face still concealed by his hood.

Skeres is visibly angry. "Look, mate. I don't know who you think you're dealin' with—"

"I know *precisely* whom I'm dealing with," says the faceless stranger in a hoarse, raspy voice. "You're Essex's men. And you shall do well to keep your voices down."

Meyrick and Skeres sit up in alarm.

Poley says, "And how would you know that?"

The hooded figure turns to him. "Quiet, you drunken sot. Keep out of the affairs of your betters. Do you not know there's a knight present? And I don't mean me." Poley seems cut by the remark, and drowns his sorrow in a deep swig of ale.

Meyrick, for his part, seems intrigued. "Why do you think one of us a knight?"

"Because I've spoken with you before, Sir Gelly. Several times," hisses the stranger, "far from here."

"Who the devil *are* you?" demands Skeres.

"Do you not know my voice, Goodman Skeres? For you and I have met before, as well, in a tavern much like this one."

"Where?" Skeres asks.

"In Eastcheap, years ago, though you did not see my face then, either."

Skeres turns his head suspiciously. "Are you the masked earl?"

The dark figure snickers in most sinister fashion. "I am no earl, and yet I know why you would think as much."

Skeres turns to Meyrick. "This blighter makes my skin crawl. Let's get out of here," he says.

The hooded figure shakes his head. "You'll never reach the door, and you'll squander an opportunity to save your life."

Skeres glances about the room, and sees that every eye is subtly focused upon him. "What the—"

The cowled figure turns to Skeres. "And now, permit me to turn your own request back upon you, albeit with greater courtesy than you used in posing it to me. Would you be so kind as to accompany your little drunken friend to another corner of the room, whilst I talk private business with Sir Gelly?"

Skeres shoots a glance at Meyrick, as though the stranger is mad to ask. But to his evident dismay, Meyrick simply nods sadly. "Take Bob to another table, Nick. I'll tell you when I'm done."

"But—" he sputters.

Meyrick looks at him reassuringly. "It's all right, Nick. I believe this gentleman means us no harm."

"I hope you're right," says Skeres indignantly. He rises, and drags Poley by the arm to a table across the room, never taking his eyes off the stranger.

"Have you guessed who I am, Sir Gelly?" asks the dark figure.

"I expect I have, but I dare not guess aloud, for fear of the consequences if I'm wrong."

"I understand," says the figure quietly, but in his natural voice. "Please do not let on, but I am the person you have occasionally addressed as 'Master Jew.'"

Meyrick nods. "I suspected as much. But I've to ask why you're here. If it's about your friend, I thought we had an arrangement."

"I'm not here about him, Sir Gelly. At least, not the way you mean. You see, I know precisely what you've been doing this past week. And that is why I have come."

Meyrick regards him askance. "How could you know that? Did you follow me here?"

"No."

Meyrick relaxes slightly. "Then, I don't suppose you could know much of what I've been doin'."

Noah shakes his head. "I know enough. I know that you're engaged in a conspiracy to smuggle a secret military map out of this country, and turn it over to a foreign power."

Meyrick's face goes white. "And how would you know that?" he croaks.

"That I shall not say. I came not to provide you with information, but to give you a choice."

Meyrick begins to look desperate. "What choice?"

"In a moment," says Noah. "But first I need a piece of information that will tell me whether I'm in a position to save your hide." He leans into Sir Gelly and studies his face for a reaction. "Does Lord Essex know what you've been doing, as regards this map?"

Meyrick looks him square in the eye. "No, suh. As I told ye that day at the Boar's Head, I've 'ad no contact with him since he's been holed up at the Lord Keeper's house. On me soul, suh."

Noah is satisfied that Sir Gelly is telling the truth, especially as his answer conforms to Noah's own expectation. For Essex to engage in such a plot under present circumstances would too likely have proven suicidal.

"Very well," says Noah quietly. "Let me explain my dilemma. "I have evidence enough to arrest you and your two friends on at least two counts of cold-blooded murder, and one of attempted murder, as well as of an even more serious crime."

"Murder?" says Meyrick, amazed.

"How do you think le Loup got the map?"

Meyrick is stunned by this mention of le Loup. "What crime's more serious than murder? And attempted murder of *who*?"

Noah laughs darkly. "Your obedient servant."

Meyrick is sweating now. "I'd no idea, suh. You must believe me."

"Oh, I believe you," says Noah. "And in return for your civility to me outside the Boar's Head, I have come to propose a course of action that would render it unnecessary for me to arrest you here and now on grounds of high treason against the Crown, a crime substantially more serious than the murder of an individual. You see, arresting you would require me to fetch the local magistrate, and he would make a permanent and public record of the arrest and the charge. After that, I'm afraid there'd be little for you and your friends to look forward to, but the scaffold."

"But you'll have to arrest me later, anyway, is what you're sayin'."

"Not necessarily," says Noah. "In fact, I'm giving you the only chance you have to escape a horrific death at Tyburn. I can't guarantee anything, mind you, but it's a shot."

"And what would I have to do?"

"You and your two friends would have to remain voluntarily in the custody of those men in the corner, until I can sort this thing out," says Noah, pointing with his chin at three men in military garb.

"And whose men are they?"

"His!" says Noah, pointing again with his chin.

Meyrick squints through the smoke. "Oh, Gawd! Is that Raleigh?"

"Aye, Sir Gelly. That's your old friend Sir Walter, and you'll be pleased to know he remembers you well from the Islands Voyage."

Sir Gelly turns his eyes heavenward. "You may as well just hang me now."

"If that's your choice." Noah turns to summon the soldiers.

"No, no, no!" says Sir Gelly. "We'll do it. That is, *I'll* do it. But I can't vouch for *those* two."

"Oh, but you must, Sir Gelly. Any deviation by *any* of you will result in the arrest of *all* of you, and there an end."

"Done," says Meyrick despairingly. "Is that all?"

"One more thing. You must tell me how to find le Loup at once."

Meyrick looks away in disgust. "That beast!" he says, nearly spitting. "Fact is, sir, I don't know where he is. Only that he's catchin' a boat somewhere west o' here. We, uh, parted ways a day or two back, and I've no idea where he's headed now."

Noah leans into him skeptically. "Between us, Sir Gelly, this involves the personal safety of my daughter. Have I your word as a gentleman that you do not know where to find le Loup?"

"Ye have, suh. Sorry. Only wish I knew."

Though Noah's sense is that Meyrick is telling the truth, he's worried about Jessica. "Very well," he says hesitantly. "But if I learn that you have withheld that information, I shall see you hanged, drawn, and quartered. Is that clear?"

"As *day,* suh. You shan't find any such thing. Of that much, I'm sure."

Noah rises to go.

"And for the record, suh—" says Meyrick.

Noah waits expectantly.

"That animal deserves no better than he gets, however bad it is."

⟶∘◦⟨⟩◦∘⟵

THE NEXT MORNING, Noah leaves the Killigrews' manor house with Sir Walter. As they walk to the harbormaster's vessel berthed along the wharf, the icy wind that's swept through Falmouth since last night makes them shiver in their light cloaks.

Crows called "choughs" circle overhead in large numbers, and cormorants squawk atop the masts of the dozen or so vessels in the harbor. Noah and Sir Walter draw their collars close.

"Was Old Killigrew any use to us last evening?" asks Noah.

"Believe it or not, Arthur Arden was very helpful in getting him to open up about his family's business," says Sir Walter. "But the old man was quite adamant that no Killigrew vessel is due to sail on the thirty-first, nor for several days thereafter. He told me we must have misread the note."

Noah reaches into his pocket, and draws out the note found on Trenowden's corpse.

Porth
Kil
Ch. Lev. 31   bre

"How's that possible?" asks Noah indignantly. "This last line simply *must* mean that the map is to meet a vessel on the thirty-first of October, as there is no thirty-first day of November. And December is too far in the future for those four miscreants to have brought it to Cornwall this early. If the second line isn't the beginning of the name 'Killigrew,' then I've no idea what it means."

"What about the rest of it?"

"If I'm wrong about it being a Killigrew vessel, then the date is all I've got from it, and, while we dither, the vessel could leave at any moment."

"But, from which port?" muses Raleigh.

"More like 'which Porth?' Unless that's just a spelling error."

"Why are we going to the harbormaster?"

"To check on Killigrew's 'memory.' Meaning no disrespect to Old Killigrew, but I'm sure there are one or two black sheep in the family."

"Smugglers, you mean?" asks Raleigh.

"What else would a black sheep do in Falmouth?"

As they walk the length of the wharf alongside the harbormaster's vessel, Raleigh points out the name painted on its side. 'Killigrew Falcon.'

"So much for asking an impartial third party," says Noah.

A blond boy appears on the deck and shouts down to them. "Are you the two gentlemen from London?"

Noah mutters to Raleigh. "Well, at least he speaks English!" He waves at the boy. "Yes. We're here to see the harbormaster!"

"Request permission to come aboard!" shouts Raleigh.

"Aye, sir," replies the boy, as he disappears amidships. In a moment, one end of a rope ladder falls to the wharf with a thud. "Permission granted!" the boy says, with evident glee.

Noah looks at the rope ladder as though it's a dead thing. "After you, Sir Walter."

"Certainly," says Sir Walter without comment, although he plainly knows that Noah needs his example to follow up onto the deck.

The wind on deck is even more biting and constant than on the wharf. It nips at Noah's face, and he wonders how the boy can stay up here hour after hour without ill effect.

"This way, gentlemen!" says the boy with irrepressible good cheer, making Noah wonder whether perhaps, like David, *all* the young men of Cornwall greet the day with unfettered joy. The boy knocks on a door leading below deck.

"Come!" says a voice through the door.

Instead of accompanying them down the inside steps, the boy holds the door for them and closes it securely behind them.

It feels good to be out of the cold. A few steps down, they enter a small cabin. At one end is a desk filled with nautical charts, and straightedges notched to various lengths.

A middle-aged man wearing a skeptical expression stands next to it, watching them enter. At the other end of the room, by a window and an active wood stove, sits an old man of similar appearance with a cup of steaming coffee in his hand, favoring them with a black-toothed grin.

"Good morning, gentlemen," says Sir Walter. "I am Sir Walter Raleigh, and this is my colleague, Serjeant Noah Ames."

Wonderment registers on the old man's face. He places his coffee mug on the table before him and comes over to grasp Sir Walter's hands. "It's a pleasure to meet you, Sir Walter!" he shouts with that strange mumble and ensuing whistle that sometimes emanates from people with few teeth.

The younger man steps forward. "Hold on now, gaffer!" He puts his face next to the old man's ear, and shouts. "You're shouting! Sir Walter can hear you!"

The old man smiles and nods. "If he can't hear me, I'll talk louder!"

"No, Dad. He *can* hear you!"

The old man seems puzzled. "Is he deaf?" he asks.

Exasperated, the young man escorts the elder back to his chair. "Stay here, Dad. I'll take care of this."

"Ask him what he wants!"

"Yes, Dad. I shall."

"And give him some coffee!"

The younger man turns to Sir Walter and Noah. "I'll be happy to answer all your questions, gentlemen. Meanwhile, would you care for some coffee?"

"He's a good lad, Sir Walter," shouts the old man. "You ask him your questions!"

The young man rolls his eyes, and turns back toward the old man, placing his finger vertically across his lips. "Shush, Dad! I'll deal with this!"

The old man grunts a few times, and picks up his mug, smiling from ear to ear.

"My name is Oscar, gentlemen," says the young man. "Please forgive my old dad. He was harbormaster here long before I was born. till the deafness creeped up on 'im, and I'd no choice but to take over. Would you care for coffee?"

"No, thank you," says Sir Walter. "We have only a couple of questions." He turns to Noah. "Serjeant, would you care to do the honors?"

Noah silently rereads his copy of the note and asks, "Are there any Killigrew vessels leaving port today?"

Oscar becomes openly skeptical. "I thought you two gentlemen were lodged with Old Killigrew!"

Noah's abashed. "We are, sir, and spoke with him about it, but we're here on Queen's business, and need to ask everyone separately."

"I see," says Oscar. "Well, off the top of my head, the answer's 'no,' but let me check the schedule." He picks up a few handwritten papers off his desk. "Nothing today. Nor tomorrow." He flips the pages. "Nor the following days, until the Cormorant leaves five days from this morning. That's a Killigrew vessel. Why?" He looks at them askance. "Did Old Killigrew say otherwise?"

Noah shakes his head reassuringly. "No, of course not. We're obliged to check with everyone having knowledge of such things, you see."

"'Cause y'know," says Oscar defensively, "we don't expect people to be questionin' the Old Killigrew's word about nothin' round here."

Noah nods. "We're well aware of the Killigrews' impeccable reputation and the family's importance in these parts, I assure you."

"'Important' don't cover the half of it, gentlemen. If there's no Killigrews, there's no Port of Falmouth. And that's the truth!"

"I see," says Noah. "Well, my next question has something to do with the Kernewek language."

"Oh? Well, we hear some of *every* language comin' through the port, gentlemen. French, Spanish, and so on. Kernewek is mostly spoken *inland* now. Some of us younger folks never had reason to speak it."

"Perhaps you'll know Kernewek words pertaining to ports, and sailing," suggests Noah hopefully.

"Well, you can try me," says the harbormaster dubiously. "I'll help if I can."

"Very well," says Noah, clearing his throat. "If I mispronounce anything, which I'm sure to do, please forgive me. Are you familiar with a town called 'Perranporth'?"

The harbormaster regards Noah skeptically. "Aye, sir. It's on the north shore, not twenty miles from here. I'd be some harbor master never hearin' of Perranporth, wouldn't I? Is that yer question?"

"Not the only one," says Noah. "Another of my questions is: Does the town's name have some meaning in Kernewek?"

Oscar shrugs contemplatively. "Well, I suppose 'porth' means 'port.' In fact, I'm sure of it. When I was a lad, Dad also used it to mean a gate or doorway, even. 'Perran' prob'ly means *Saint* Piran. He's patron saint in these parts. So, the name means 'the Port of Saint Piran.'" He arches an incredulous eyebrow. "Did you gentlemen come all the way from London to ask me that?"

"We're not through yet," says Noah. "Do you know of a town in these parts whose name *begins* with 'Porth'?"

"They don't want no coffee?" shouts the old man.

The harbormaster turns to his father and shakes his head. "No, Dad. No coffee!"

"Eh?"

"No *coffee*, Dad!"

"Gotta do everythin' meself!" complains the old man, as he gets up and walks to a squat cabinet, opens a door, and points to a half-full sack. "We got plenty more down here!"

Oscar offers Noah and Sir Walter an apologetic smile, and ushers the old man back to his chair. "We *have* coffee, Dad," he shouts. "They don't *want* coffee!" He turns to Noah, flustered. "The answer is: I don't know of a town whose name starts with 'porth.' Why?"

Noah is at wit's end. They're losing a desperate race in which his own daughter is at risk, and all because he's failed to find anyone who can help him to interpret the note. Out of sheer desperation, he asks: "How about your dad? From what you just said, *he* knows some Kernewek. Does *he* know of any such town?"

The harbormaster shrugs, and leans into his father's ear. "Dad, is there a town in these parts whose name starts with 'porth'?"

The old man's brow creases in thought. "Perranporth?" he ventures.

Raleigh laughs quietly. Noah shoots him a dark glance.

"No, Dad," says the harbor master. "The name must *begin* with 'porth'!"

The old man searches his memory and shakes his head several times, as he appears to consider and dispense with each new possible solution.

"Nope, gents," says the harbormaster. "Sorry. Can't help ye."

As Noah and Sir Walter bow and prepare to leave disappointed, the old man mutters something to himself. It's the first time in the brief interview that he hasn't *shouted* his thoughts.

"What did your old dad say?" asks Noah.

Oscar shouts to his father. "What did you say, Dad?"

"I said, not for years!"

Oscar shrugs. "Sorry, gents."

"Wait!" says Noah, speaking directly to the old man. "Is there a town whose name *formerly* started with 'porth'?"

"Just one. Porth Ia! Hasn't been called that for ages, though!"

"Is the port gone now?" Noah asks the old man.

"Aye," the old man replies.

Noah's crestfallen again.

"Well, never was much of a port," the old man adds. "*A few boats use it still. Smugglers, mostly!*"

Noah's heart pounds. "What's the town called now?"

"Saint Ives!" says the old man.

Excitedly, Noah turns to the young harbormaster and grabs him by the jacket. "Where *is* it, man? How far from here?"

The harbor master is wide-eyed with surprise at Noah's newfound vigor. "It's less than thirty miles, sir, but you'll have to go through Redruth. The other roads are no good."

Noah hugs the harbormaster, kisses the old gaffer on the forehead, and leaves an angel spinning on the plotting desk.

Within a half-hour, a party of fifteen men led by David Killigrew have taken to horse, and race off toward Saint Ives.

CHAPTER 16

JONATHAN AWAKENS SHIVERING in the cold woods outside the cozy inn where le Loup spent the night, and breakfasts on day-old bread and icy spring water, wondering which kinds of hot food his quarry has enjoyed.

It's late morning by the time le Loup appears at the inn's door, carefully peering in every direction before stepping out into the sunlight, carrying his pack and the map cylinder. He goes to the stables and emerges on horseback, the cylinder jutting out of his saddlebag.

As there's some horse and foot traffic on the road, Jonathan easily follows undetected, a short distance behind. They reach the outskirts of the little port village of Saint Ives around noon, and le Loup turns down the main street toward the village center.

Jonathan is not as surprised by this move as he might have been, even though this will be the first time le Loup has left the road since his confederates abandoned him at the mouth of the cave. For, though le Loup has formerly steered clear of populated areas, last evening he lowered his guard enough to take a room at an inn, whereas earlier he slept outdoors. Jonathan vaguely recalls the old thespian mentioning Saint Ives, and he begins to feel fairly certain that Saint Ives will be the stolen map's point of departure from England.

Le Loup stops at an inn on the village's main street, evidently for an early dinner. The sign swinging outside says "George & Dragon," and bears a colorful, if weather-beaten, image of Saint George in full armor, slaying the dragon of legend.

As le Loup has time for dinner, Jonathan imagines he'll be meeting a vessel at an appointed hour that has not yet come. He decides that the respite will be put to best use snooping about the port, and so continues on his way, being careful not to glance aside at the inn, in case he's being watched through a window.

At the wharf, he dismounts and walks his horse down a sandy slope to the beach. From here, he can see there's no activity on the wharf, and little on the water. Only two small boats are tied off at the dock, one a fishing vessel, its elaborate netting folded neatly on deck, and the other an unrecognizable derelict in such poor repair as to place its seaworthiness in grave doubt.

He shields his eyes and peers out to sea. At first the horizon appears entirely clear of vessels traveling in either direction. But as his eyes adjust to the glare, he spots the stern of a small two-mast vessel leaving port.

In the same line of sight, approaching the port, he spots the bow of a single-mast boat, of a type his old master Graves called a "packet boat." For no reason other than the absence of another suitable vessel, Jonathan surmises this will be the one to transport the map to its illicit destination.

Imagining himself in the place of the boat's skipper, he scans the coastline for a sheltered cove where he'd have the best chance of avoiding detection and arrest. And there it is, a cove not a quarter mile back the way he came, visible only because the beach there curves northward, affording him an unimpeded view.

The cove's only drawback as a landing point is that it's flanked by a pair of thirty-foot headlands, each of whose sheer, stony sides has been worn away by the incessant action of the sea, leaving a rocky beach at its base. From land, Jonathan imagines, access to any vessel in the cove would be severely restricted, making it an inappropriate point for taking on or discharging bulky cargo. But, for a cylinder of illicitly obtained documents, and possibly its bearer…it would be just right.

Gazing at the twin promontories and the cove between, he notices that a short distance behind them is the very George & Dragon where le Loup stopped to dine. He shifts his gaze back over the water again, and realizes that the incoming packet has made considerable progress. It's now much closer than he would have expected. He's misjudged either its original distance or the time he's spent lost in thought. He leads his horse back to the road, remounts, and canters back toward the inn.

JESSICA COULD KICK herself for her own impetuosity. Here she sits for yet a *third* hour at the George & Dragon, at a complete loss as to how to locate either Jonathan or Andres.

Until now, she'd felt certain that Andres would learn of the note she left at the front desk apologizing for leaving his care, and telling him she'd be searching for Jonathan at Saint Ives. After all, this is obviously the next town in their westward journey along the northern coast.

But now her confidence is waning. Andres knows that she paid for their rooms the previous evening, so he need not pay the innkeeper. What if, when he discovers her gone, he bolts off in a panic without speaking to the innkeeper (which, now that she thinks of it, is more than likely)? Then, he would have no idea *where* to find her, and she would simply have been wasting time sitting here.

Even if she had an escort, which way would she go? Where *could* she go *without* an escort? Her anxiety overwhelms her. She feels a fool. *What is she doing here, all alone in the middle of nowhere?*

Struggling to regain her composure, she gazes through the window from the upholstered chair in her private room. In the distance is a small copse of trees. Beyond it, two headlands jut out over the water. It's a beautiful spot, true, but perilous for a woman alone.

Suddenly, a man enters the room uninvited, blocking her view, standing too close for her to see his face. He pauses a moment, and insinuates himself in the chair across from her. It's le Loup, wearing an infuriatingly smug expression.

"Although I would love to have our assignation at this little inn now, mademoiselle—or should I say 'your ladyship'?—there is a small errand I must take care of. You shall accompany me, *non*?"

"No!" says Jessica.

Le Loup regards her with a sneer of contempt. He rises, grabs her arm, and twists it. "Get up," he says with false bonhomie. "Don't worry, I will take you along on my little boat ride, and we will become…good friends. Eh?" He deftly thrusts her out in front of him, picks up the cylinder in his left hand, and jabs her in the back with his right. She feels the pinprick of a sharp blade. He kisses her earlobe gently. She turns to him with a bitter smile, and spits in his face.

With no change in expression, he lifts a corner of the kerchief she wears knotted around her neck, wipes his face with it, and lets it drop back into place. He sneers. "You will pay for that, *ma cherie.* Now, go! And, if you disobey me, I will cut out your heart, and leave it for your…footman."

AS ANDRES REACHES the crossroads at Redruth, he can no longer avoid making the inevitable choice: *East or West?* What makes it worse is that he can't make his decision based upon what he expects *le Loup* to do, nor even upon what he thinks *Jonathan* expects le Loup to do.

No! Andres will have to make his choice based upon what he expects *Lady Jessica* expects Jonathan to do, which in turn depends upon what she expects *le Loup* to do, and that's something about which he's sure she has not the slightest clue.

Lost in his own thoughts and the unfathomable muddle of everyone else's conjectured thoughts, he's rudely reminded by the chill wind that in his rush he left his heavy coat at the inn. So, he cannot stay outdoors indefinitely, nor sleep outdoors for even one night. On top of that, he'll be blamed for Lady Jessica's fate, and, if he guesses wrong now about which way to go, he'll be absolutely unable to help her.

Blast! He gazes up at the sky, where a few rays of sun pierce the rapidly advancing clouds. *God help me,* he thinks. *I doubt I've ever done anything wicked enough to deserve this!* His self-pity is interrupted by a galloping thunder in the south. He turns about.

A phalanx of horses is headed straight for him at full gallop. Though they're nearly a mile away, he can already feel the rumble in his gut. He squints. At the very fore of the squadron is the unmistakable blond mane of David Killigrew, his black cape flapping behind him in the breeze. There are more than a dozen horsemen to his rear, and for one terrifying moment, it seems David is being pursued by hostile riders. But as they approach, he recognizes Arthur Arden, then Noah Ames, then Sir Walter Raleigh.

Though it strikes Andres as horribly selfish, his most immediate hope is that, when they overtake him, they won't ask him which way to turn. Rapidly closing the distance, David points at him with a devilish smile, then wildly and repeatedly points left. *So, it's west!*

"Go, go, go!" David shouts, his voice barely overcoming the thunder of the hoofs. "Go ahead! We'll catch up!"

Andres jerks the reins west, and instantly spurs his horse to a gallop. Though in a moment he hurtles down the road, it's no more than a few seconds before David pulls alongside him, shouting at the top of his lungs to *keep up*! From the corner of his eye, Andres sees Noah Ames pull next to them at the head of the squadron to hear what he has to say. So great is Andres' shame at losing Jessica that his heart leaps into his mouth.

"Where did you leave them?" shouts David.

"I was bringing Jessica to Falmouth," shouts Andres, unsure he's being heard above the rush of wind and pounding of hoofs. "She gave me the slip this morning. I have *no idea* where she is!" With a glance, he can see the dismay on Noah's face. His heart sinks. He simply *has* to make amends.

"We know where the map is going," shouts David. "We have to assume *they're* going there, too."

"Where?" shouts Andres.

"Saint Ives!"

"Let's stop at the edge of town!" shouts Andres.

"What?" shouts David. "Can't hear you!"

"Stop at the edge of town!" repeats Andres, a bit louder. "We can't ride in like Her Majesty's cavalry! We don't know where they are, or where le Loup is! We could be placing them in *danger*!"

David appears to ponder his point, and then nods in reluctant agreement, even though, Andres knows, every fiber of his being wants to rush in on horseback.

"Let me make the first pass alone!" Andres shouts. "I'll come fetch you!"

Again, David nods.

"Don't botch it this time!" comes Arthur's ever-helpful voice behind him.

<hr />

JONATHAN HAS RETURNED to the George & Dragon and slipped well into the woods across the road when he sees Jessica emerge through the inn's front door, wearing a forced smile. He can barely believe his eyes. *What's she doing here, so far from Falmouth?*

When le Loup follows immediately behind her with the cylinder, his right hand pressed hard to her back (and following much closer than is proper), Jonathan realizes he's holding a knife to her. Apparently, le Loup has caught her at unawares, and has decided to take advantage of her propitious appearance to enlist her as a human shield in completing delivery of the map. Perhaps he might even intend to spirit her away with him. A cold fury seeps into Jonathan's heart.

Andres is nowhere to be seen. If he were anywhere in the area, this would not be happening, for Andres had been informed of le Loup's grisly murders of young women and would never have allowed Jessica to appear unprotected in so public a place. Could le Loup have murdered Andres? He's certainly capable of it. Far more likely, though, Jessica gave Andres the slip.

Jonathan now bitterly regrets his own decision not to tell Jessica about the murders for, if she'd known of the extreme danger, surely she would not have traveled alone to so obvious a place. She's headstrong, but far from stupid.

As the mismatched pair cross the road, Jessica stumbles on a rock. Le Loup keeps her from falling but shoves her all the harder when she recovers. They'll have to pass Jonathan to reach the end of the promontory, but not close enough for him to overtake them unseen. At the nearest point, he estimates, they'll pass about thirty feet from where he now stands. To reach them, he'd have to leave the cover of the woods, giving le Loup plenty of time to cut her throat or do her other grievous harm.

Jonathan has nearly despaired of catching le Loup unawares, when he spots a stairway of chiseled stone leading up from the cove along the near side of the promontory. If he takes a flying leap, he could come down on the small landing, then race up the remaining steps and emerge at the promontory's edge. But he can't manage it if le Loup is facing the sea, which he now is. Jonathan desperately needs some type of diversion.

⫘∘⫘∘⫘

ANDRES CLOPS ALONG as nonchalantly as he can, knowing there are fifteen armed horsemen awaiting his signal to invade the town like so many cossacks. He's passed the George & Dragon on his way into the village, and is now about to pass it again going the other way. If he finds nothing, he'll trot about a quarter mile and give the cavalry the signal to invade the town. On his left is a hedge. Once he passes it, his view will open out onto a pair of grassy promontories.

He hears a sharp whizzing sound, and something small and hard strikes his left shoulder so hard it makes his eyes tear. He stops his mount, and rubs the sting with his right hand, checking for blood to see if he's been shot from afar. But there's none.

He looks to his left to locate whatever unruly brat threw the missile, and is shocked to see Jonathan gesticulating wildly at the edge of the woods. Before Andres can grow angry at this childish prank, Jonathan holds his finger to his lips, signaling *quiet,* and points to a young couple who have already passed Jonathan on their way up the promontory. The man is carrying a long cylinder. Is that le Loup? *With Jessica?*

Andres's eyes go wide. Jonathan's somewhat ambiguous hand signals seem to be imploring him to chat with le Loup from the road, in order to provide Jonathan with an opportunity to assail him from behind. Andres nods, and Jonathan disappears into the woods.

JONATHAN SPRINTS THROUGH the woods toward the cliff. Preparing to take a running jump onto the small landing, he tightens his holster straps, and shoves his dagger securely down into its sheath. He tries not to look down or think about what will happen if he fails to reach his target or, worse, overshoots. From the corner of his eye, he sees Andres waving an unfolded map around like an idiot…but le Loup is looking at his map, which is all Jonathan needs.

He flings himself off the cliff, and spends what seems an inordinate time aloft. As he comes down, he sees that he's failed to account for a thin coating of slippery moss on the landing, which upsets his footing. He skids, nearly flying off the cliff into the cove. Instinctively, he grabs onto a handful of bushy grass, which slows his progress enough for him to clamber back onto the landing, his heart thudding in his chest.

For a split second before recovering his footing, he saw the packet moored in the cove below. He peers over the cliff and sees that, had he continued his slide, he would likely have impaled himself on the mast. The alternative landing point would have been little better, as he would have wound up splayed on the hard deck after a fall of a good thirty feet.

A young man sits alone on the packet's deck, looking remarkably like David Killigrew, albeit with a reddish tinge to his hair. He's quietly reading a nautical chart, evidently heedless of the small racket Jonathan made above him.

As Jonathan peers down into the cove, his pistol falls from of its holster and over the cliff. He draws back from the edge and grits his teeth, hoping the pistol will hit the water, as a hit on the deck will result in one very curious smuggler.

Ploop! So, it has dropped into the water. As he hears the rustling of the smuggler's nautical chart, he prays that the gun's wooden stock won't bring it to the surface. Apparently, it does not, at least not right away, as there's no commotion on deck. Jonathan rises gingerly, and climbs the steps to the promontory on all fours.

ANDRES DECIDES HE has two advantages in distracting le Loup: first, le Loup has never laid eyes on him; second, Andres looks quite Spanish. Before bringing his horse up into the clearing, he cocks the pistol in his saddle holster, and draws out his map, unfolding it and holding it up in a deliberately awkward configuration.

"Essscuse me! Señor!" he shouts after le Loup, looking as helpless as possible. "Esscuse me! Can you helb me?" He nearly laughs at the sound of his own voice, as he's imitating the most execrable English he's ever heard, namely, that issuing from his deceased great aunt. He'd always found it remarkable that he could follow her Spanish or Portuguese without error, but would immediately be confused by her mangling of English consonants. To his great relief, le Loup turns (albeit reluctantly, and with a great deal of suspicion), keeping Jessica in front of him.

It's a good thing for Jessica that she has her back to le Loup, for her eyes go momentarily agog as she recognizes it's Andres. She quickly suppresses any sign of recognition.

"Wait, señor! I ride up to you!" Andres says, as though riding his horse over to them will make him as small a nuisance as possible.

"No, no, señor!" shouts le Loup. "Por favor, do not ride to us! Leave your horse, and walk!"

"Si, señor," replies Andres, as he slowly dismounts, concealing his disappointment. Approaching the "couple" on foot will require him to leave his pistol behind in its saddle holster. It's prudent for le Loup to insist on it, for Andres has every intention of blowing his head off, as soon as he can do so without harm to Jessica.

As Andres traipses slowly up to them with his big smile and his map flapping in the breeze, from the corner of his eye he sees Jonathan hurl himself off the cliff. He prays there'll be a safe landing on some unseen platform. Andres turns the map this way and that, as though at a complete loss.

"Zat ees close enough, señor," says le Loup, and Andres stops. "What are you seeking?"

"You talk like me, no? You are from Lisbon, also?" He follows this with a string of Portuguese that obviously escapes the Frenchman entirely.

"No, I am not from Lisbon, señor. I am from Paree!"

"Oh," says Andres rhapsodically, "that is a city muy linda, señor!" *Most beautiful!*

"You were looking for…?"

"Oh, yes, I look for de Green —" he searches one of the quadrants of his map. "Green Dragon? Is Green Dragon. A place for dormiendo." *For sleeping.* Andres is running out of conversation for stalling, and he wonders what's taking Jonathan so long.

"Well," says le Loup pointing at the inn, "zat is the George & Dragon!"

Andres glances behind him, and regards le Loup as though he's a bit dimwitted. "Ees not *green,* senor! I look for *Green* Dragon."

"What town is it in?" asks le Loup.

"Town? Oh, *villa?*" says Andres, carefully translating le Loup's broken French-English into broken Spanish-Portuguese English. At last, Jonathan's head pops up over the cliff directly behind le Loup, and Andres is relieved to see him take a surefooted step up onto the promontory.

"It is in—" Andres searches his memory. "Redroof!"

"Red*root!*" exclaims le Loup, pointing east. "That is—"

"No, no, sir. Red*roof!*"

Andres is never sure thereafter whether it was the deteriorating quality of his performance, or le Loup had heard Jonathan's rapid approach from behind, but the realization suddenly spreads over the Frenchman's face that he's been *had.*

But his realization has come too late.

JONATHAN RACES UP behind le Loup, and reaches in front of him, pulling his dagger hard backward, plunging it into the Frenchman's chest with full force.

Le Loup gasps in horror and tries to inhale deeply, as though suddenly suffocating. In his alarm, his hand goes instinctively to his pistol, which is already cocked. He withdraws it wildly from its holster, and the pistol-stock strikes Jessica hard in the back of the head. She staggers a few feet, and falls to her knees.

Jonathan reaches for the gun, but le Loup grasps it with surprising tenacity. From the corner of his eye, Jonathan sees Andres scoop the dazed Jessica into his arms and race down the promontory, heedlessly kicking the cylinder aside.

Le Loup's pistol hand flails wildly in the air as Jonathan tugs it toward himself, and le Loup struggles to wrest it free the opposite way.

Boom! The pistol discharges in the general direction of the inn. Though Jonathan prays the ball has not struck Jessica or Andres, he can't spare a moment to look. He abandons his attempt to seize the now-discharged pistol, and does precisely what he's wished to do since discovering le Loup's first grisly murder. He strikes him in the face with all his might, so hard he wonders whether he hasn't broken his own fist.

Until now, le Loup has shown surprising strength for a man with a knife in his chest. But Jonathan's blow staggers him, at last. Jonathan strikes him in the face again, and again, just as the scoundrel did to the defenseless young women who fell prey to his twisted desires.

As the Frenchman bleeds profusely from his nose, and teeters near the cliff's edge, Jonathan glances toward the inn, spotting several horsemen in the distance riding cautiously toward the promontory, and a crowd of people gathering before the inn, pointing at him excitedly.

Taking advantage of Jonathan's momentary distraction, Le Loup hurls himself upon him, clearly aware now that he's losing the fight of his life and needs to escape Jonathan's wrath if he's to have any hope of being taken alive.

Le Loup's nose is shattered beyond recognition, and his eyes are blinded by the blood that runs down into them from his battered scalp. Jonathan strikes what remains of his face repeatedly.

Le Loup's mouth now gapes in agony and horror but, to Jonathan's consternation, no realization of defeat yet appears on his face.

Jonathan jeers at him. "How does it feel when it's done to *you,* you miscreant *filth*?"

The blood-blinded Frenchman teeters on the cliff, his back to the cove. But Jonathan's taunt has betrayed his own position, and, with lightning speed, le Loup draws out an unseen dagger and stabs him in the chest. Jonathan looks down in disbelief at the handle protruding from his chest. He staggers. The crowd gasps.

Determined to ignore the pain, Jonathan draws himself up and delivers a blow to le Loup's face that proves powerful enough to fling the Frenchman over the cliff. Jonathan holds his breath until, out of the cove below, comes the loud boom of a body striking a wooden deck with full force.

Jessica screams, appearing out of nowhere, racing through the crowd past the amazed soldiers. "Jonathan, you're hurt!" she cries, helping him to a kneeling position. He's still conscious, but fading fast.

———————— ⊸०⊂⊅०⊂⊸ ————————

AS ANDRES REACHES the road with Jessica in his arms, a pistol shot cracks behind him. Where the ball flew he has no idea, but it's struck neither Jessica nor him.

Reaching the inn with both hands occupied, he kicks the door open and places Jessica on an upholstered chair just inside. The diners gawp and the innkeeper shouts *hey*! as he runs back out of the door to help his friend, only to be nearly knocked down by the oncoming horsemen who could no longer await his signal once they heard the boom of a gun. Behind him, diners emerge to see what's going on across the way.

Andres is horrified by the scene at the far end of the promontory, where Jonathan now stands alone at the edge of the cliff with a dagger's handle jutting from of his chest. The horsemen evidently halted their progress halfway to the cliff, as the two combatants were locked in mortal combat so near to the edge that their mounted approach might inadvertently have sent them over the side together.

As Andres stands there gawping, Jessica races past him and through the amazed horsemen. Andres follows, and catches up with her just as Jonathan collapses into her arms.

Mountjoy's surgeon, Master Yatrow, dismounts, and runs to Jonathan, as well, feeling his neck for a heartbeat. Without removing the dagger from Jonathan's chest, Yatrow orders two horsemen to carry him to a ground-floor bedroom at the inn and place him carefully on the bed. Jessica follows, weeping, as Andres follows anxiously behind.

<hr />

BEFORE FOLLOWING HIS patient to the inn, Yatrow wipes the blood off his hands with a white cloth, and casts Raleigh a grave glance. Raleigh sees it, and nods solemnly. Noah sees it, too, and buries his face in his hands.

Sir Walter goes to the edge of the cliff and looks down into the cove. "Arrest the master of that boat!" he commands two lieutenants. Scooping the cylinder up from the grass, Noah hears Sir Walter's order, and takes him aside to speak with him urgently.

"Belay that order!" shouts Sir Walter, after speaking with Noah. "Lower the anchor, and padlock the wheel! Take the captain to the inn, and detain him under armed guard. No arrests yet!"

The plump innkeeper walks stoutly up to Sir Walter. "Pardon me, sir!" he says, "But that's *my* inn yer talkin' about!"

Raleigh replies impatiently. "It *was,* sir, and it *shall* be again. For the moment, however, it belongs to the Queen of England." When the innkeeper stands defiant, Sir Walter looks him straight in the eye. "Is that clear?"

"Now, you look here!" says the innkeeper, raising a finger as though in debate.

Raleigh summons two adjutants. "If this man says another word to me unbidden, chain him in his own cellar." He pats the innkeeper's ample belly. "And put him on short rations until further notice."

The innkeeper turns and storms away, still talking...but only to himself.

Noah peers down at the vessel in the cove. "We should take a look at that boat at once." Raleigh nods, and together they carefully descend the stone steps chiseled out of the cliffside. As they tread over the highest landing, Noah notices a smear in the green moss that seems of quite recent origin. "There'll be some of that moss on the bottom of Jonathan's boot, I surmise." Raleigh grunts.

They alight from the bottom step onto a sandy beach dotted with chalky rocks. Raleigh's lieutenants have manacled the boat's young skipper and are leading him to the steps when Raleigh stops them, looking hard at the skipper. "You look familiar," says Sir Walter uncertainly. "Wait here a moment."

As Noah has already noted the young skipper's close resemblance to David Killigrew, he ignores him for the moment, and crouches down to inspect the bow. The little boat's name has been covered with a tape of fabric, and painted over. Noah surmises it was done quite recently, as the glossy paint still shines. He draws a handkerchief from his pocket, and tugs the tape away with a single deft motion. The chipped and faded lettering says: "Killigrew Puffin." He points it out to Raleigh, who nods.

Noah walks up to the handcuffed skipper, and deliberately stands very close, eyes wide, nostrils flaring. "How *dare* you shame your family's name with such an errand as this!"

Tears form in the young man's eyes. "I wouldn't have done it, sir, but for the best o' reasons!"

"Best of—?"

"I was told I'd be transportin' important papers, sir. And that it was for the good of England...and Cornwall." He casts his eyes down.

"Where were you transporting these 'papers,' as you call them? To Ireland?"

"No, sir," replies the young man tearfully. "I would *never* do that! The Irish can hang, for all I care, together with their Spanish masters." He looks at the corpse strewn across his deck. Its battered head, having broken loose as it struck the boom, now rolls about with the gentle motion

218 | NEAL ROBERTS

of the deck. "I was told the Frenchman would be tellin' me where to take them."

"Well, he shan't be doing that now," says Noah. He shouts in the young man's face. "Who was *paying* for this excursion?"

The young man clearly wishes to tell, but appears to be restrained by some notion of…what can only be called "honor," even in the disgraceful context of smuggling.

As Noah needs more information quickly, he tempers his voice. "Was it…'*Jake*?'"

The young skipper nods, puffing up his chest in defense of his challenged principles. "Aye. But I cannot tell you who 'Jake' is, sir. I have sworn it, and shall not break my oath." He looks disdainfully down at his feet. "But 'Jake' is a term of disrespect, sir, and I would *never* use it to—!" He stops as though he was about to give something important away, and balks at completing his thought.

But he doesn't need to. Because the pieces of the puzzle now fall together in Noah's mind, and everything comes clear to him. Absolutely everything. "Good God!" he mutters to himself. He turns to the lieutenants. "Take this man to the inn. *No one* is to question him. Do you hear me? *No one!*"

The lieutenants bow smartly and somberly escort their prisoner up the stairs, leaving Noah alone in the sandy cove with the empty packet boat, le Loup's headless corpse…and Sir Walter Raleigh. As the footsteps fade, there's a thoughtful pause, during which nothing is heard but the sizzle of white caps breaking against the cliffside, the occasional bang of the light hull against the restless water, and the cries of a few distant gulls. At long last, Noah looks up at Raleigh, who avoids his gaze.

"You knew," Noah says, in quiet amazement at first. And, then, in an accusatory tone, "You *knew!*" Raleigh hangs his head in shame, and says nothing.

Noah turns on his heels, and storms up the stairs alone, clutching the cylinder tightly to his side.

CHAPTER 17

FOR A LONG time, images and sounds swirl around him. Flocks of birds winging high over Cornwall, sometimes soaring, sometimes swooping, always in formation, always in motion. His feet sliding over the slippery green grass of the promontory. Andres mumbling strange words in an unknown language. Then, the pain comes once more, squeezing his chest, always squeezing, and the Frenchman's bloody face appears before him, white matter oozing from vacant eye sockets. Then the pain passes, and, after a merciful respite, Jessica appears, her perfect face shadowed with worry.

Suddenly, there's the smell of ammonia. He's being stirred. Someone's giving him a drink of water. So cold. But good.

"Jonathan, open your eyes." It's Noah Ames's voice. Calm, but very near.

My eyes are open, he thinks. *Why can't I see you?* Then, he realizes that, *no,* his eyes are still closed, and he's on the edge of waking. With great effort of will, he overcomes the weight of his heavy lids, and forces his eyes open. With a vengeance, the sharp pain returns to his chest and he squirms.

He's in bed. The room is very warm, and the light on the ceiling flickers orange. He can smell the smoke of a wood fire. The windows are dark. It's night. Noah looks anxious.

"Jonathan," says Noah, "don't try to speak. Just nod. Can you hear me?"

Jonathan tries to speak nevertheless, and is punished with a stabbing pain in his chest that takes some time to subside.

An older man's voice comes, but Jonathan has neither the desire nor the strength to seek out his face. "As I told you, Serjeant," says the voice, "he has just overcome the fever, and cannot be expected to think straight."

"Doctor, please leave the room and tell my daughter to await my summons."

"But, Serjeant—"

"At once!" says Noah, in that subdued, somehow commanding, voice he affects when someone doesn't do precisely as instructed.

The door opens and closes. Jonathan wants nothing more than to close his eyes, but Noah will not leave him alone.

"Can you hear me, Jonathan?" asks Noah again.

Jonathan nods weakly.

"And see me?"

He nods again. Questions, questions. *Let me sleep.*

"Jonathan, the doctor says the stabbing was a near thing, but that you will recover, so long as you take his instructions."

Jonathan licks his parched lips, and shapes them into something that can form words. "How long?" he croaks.

"You've been out for three days and nights. And it will be several weeks before you're feeling quite yourself."

The pain is incessant, but Jonathan forces himself to speak again. "Jesse?"

Noah half-smiles, which is a welcome change from his earlier scowl. "Jessica is well. She hasn't left your side since the incident. She's waiting outside this room as we speak. I had to exclude her to tell you something secret. Jon, this is very important. Will you remember what I tell you now?"

Jonathan nods.

"Very well," says Noah. "But first, I must know something. Have you told anyone of the pouch of letters that was in the tube along with the map?"

That's right. I was chasing a map, thinks Jonathan. *A tube. There were letters in a pouch. I didn't see the writing.* He ponders a moment whether he's told anyone of the letters. "No one," he murmurs. "Perhaps Jessica saw. Can't remember."

"But you never mentioned them to anyone else, such as Andres or Arthur? Perhaps David?"

Jonathan smiles to think of young David's apt nickname. "Cheerful," he mumbles fondly. "No, I told no one."

"Then promise never to mention the letters again as long as you live which, by the grace of God, will be a good long time."

"Never," promises Jonathan.

There's a light knock, and Noah glances at the door. "That will be my daughter. She'll be furious with me if I don't let her in before you sleep again. May I?" This is a rare stupid question from Noah Ames. Jonathan nods.

"Remember," cautions Noah, "never mention the letters again."

Jonathan shakes his head. He hears the door open. There's a brief whispering, followed by a rustle of fabrics as Jessica rushes in. Her angelic face appears before him, and she strokes his hair, ever so gently.

"My poor savior," she says in a whisper. "You have paid such a price for my worthless life!" She brings more water to his lips, and he drinks. "I shall stay with you, and nurse you until you are well."

He nods, and smiles through the pain, which is somehow less, knowing she'll remain with him.

"Jessica," says Noah, gently placing his hands on his daughter's shoulders, "the doctor said we must let Jonathan sleep. Now that you have seen him awake, you must come your ways, dear. Come."

Reluctantly, Jessica allows herself to be escorted from the room.

Noah appears again. "Jon, I want to thank you for my daughter's life. I no longer see you as an inexperienced young man, but rather as an accomplished and dedicated fellow."

Jonathan's eyes are closing involuntarily, but he feels impelled to say something before he sleeps. It's a rare opportunity to toss Noah's words back at him.

Noah leans in to hear.

Jonathan mutters: "The most sought-after barrister in all England." He hears a soft, chesty laugh.

"Indeed," says Noah. "And soon to be more. Sleep now."

IN THE DYING wintry light, Mountjoy's garden is bleak, nothing more than a manicured field dotted by brown masses of indeterminate shape and size. Now that the frosts have begun each night, what were once fruitful vines and lively shrubs now offer neither bounty nor beauty, nor the promise of either.

Bucklebury chuffs to see the now-familiar stable. Noah strokes his mane down to the withers, and mutters comforting sounds. Alongside the manor sits the resplendent coach of the Lord Admiral, evidently too large for the stable to hold.

Noah draws up to the manor's front door. Behind him, several mounted lieutenants and two carriages pull to a halt. Sir Walter has ridden with the convalescent Lieutenant Carter in Mountjoy's borrowed coach, after conscripting Cheerful, Arthur, and Andres to assist his healthy lieutenants in guarding Essex's three attendants, Meyrick, Skeres, and Poley. Of the three, the one who seems to suffer most by his detention is Poley. While a single tankard of ale each day suffices for Meyrick and Skeres, such a limited ration of spirits leaves Poley in a state of unremitting gloom.

As several stablemen approach the company, Mountjoy's footman descends the steps and takes Bucklebury's reins. "Lord Mountjoy bade me inform you that he and his guests look forward to hearing of your crime-solving exploits these past weeks."

Noah nods, wondering whether that could possibly be true and whether Mountjoy truly wishes such matters to be discussed before the famously hidebound Lord Admiral. "Yes, well, you shall need to convert an unoccupied portion of his lordship's cellar into a guardhouse, I'm afraid. We have several guests who need to be kept under guard, all in one place."

"For detention, sir?" asks the footman.

"Well, yes, in a sense."

"Very well, sir," says the footman. "I'll instruct the stablemen to see to it."

As Noah dismounts, Raleigh approaches. "Prepared to meet the Lord Admiral?" he asks.

"Under these circumstances?" says Noah. "No."

"Oh, he's not so bad. Just keep reminding him you're not a papist, and you'll be fine."

Ignoring Sir Walter's jest, Noah enters the house first.

Mountjoy's cheery voice emerges from the salon. "Oh, there they are! Sir Walter! Serjeant Ames! Won't you come in? I believe you are already well known to Lord Howard and Monsieur de Tréville. I should like to introduce you to my esteemed cousin, the Lord Admiral."

Noah and Sir Walter exchange a trepidatious glance, and proceed into the salon. There's a bright blaze in the fireplace.

"We were just about to have wine before supper, hoping you'd be in time to share the feast," says Mountjoy, arranging wine glasses on the tabletop. He turns to a very distinguished older gentleman whose present costume, Noah expects, cost more than a busy barrister can earn in a year. "Lord Admiral, please allow me to introduce Sir Walter Raleigh and Serjeant Noah Ames."

Noah and Sir Walter bow low and long.

"M'lord," says Sir Walter, rising, "I believe it has been my distinct pleasure to meet you once before."

"I know it," says the Lord Admiral dourly. "In any event, I am pleased to see you were not hanged by Essex. My cousin tells me it was a near thing."

The respectful smile drops from Sir Walter's face. "Thank you, m'lord" is apparently all he can think to say.

The Lord Admiral continues. "And this fellow...*Ames,* isn't it? My cousin Lord Howard informs me that you are the personal barrister for my *royal* cousin." Noah nods respectfully. "Tell me," says the Lord Admiral with a look of mild distaste. "How is it that a *Hebrew* comes to be so trusted by Her Majesty?"

"When I was a lad," begins Noah, who's been forewarned of the Lord Admiral's staunch religious views, "Her Majesty thought me worthy of an education. Since that time, I have practiced before Queen's Bench in the defense against accusations of high crimes. I came to Her Majesty's attention again as an adult when she commissioned me to defend Doctor Lopez in the Court of Oyer and Terminer. As your lordship served as a Commissioner in that case, you may recollect my argument seeking its transfer to Queen's Bench."

"Hah! I could hardly forget it," says the Lord Admiral with grudging admiration. "Essex nearly had a stroke. I have never seen an angrier human being in my life."

"Actually, I tried to *avoid* angering his lordship."

The Lord Admiral regards Noah skeptically. "Didn't seem that way to me. Or anyone else, for that matter. I understand your client Lopez was put to death later on."

"Indeed, m'lord. There was a clemency hearing pending before Her Majesty arising out of his conviction in the Court of Oyer and Terminer, when the Lord Chief Justice (who'd also served as a Commissioner at the earlier trial) suddenly re-tried him at Queen's Bench, convicted him, and sent him to an excruciating death at Tyburn."

"Another Jew, wasn't he?"

"He'd been born a Jew, your lordship, but had since become Church of England."

"Like you?"

"No, lordship. I am not Church of England." He offers the Lord Admiral an ingratiating smile. "But neither am I a papist."

"No. You're not even a *Christian!*" comes the retort.

So much for Raleigh's advice about how to placate the Lord Admiral.

Mountjoy gracefully interrupts. "Serjeant, my footman and menservants shall see to your adjutants, and…your reluctant guests."

"May I ask," says de Tréville impatiently, "whether you gentlemen were able to arrest le Loup?"

Sir Walter replies wryly. "I'm afraid he eluded capture by the clever ruse of being beaten to death."

De Tréville seems offended. "Surely, Sir Walter, you cannot jest about a matter so serious!"

"No jest, monsieur, in all faith! He succumbed to a thrashing by one of Serjeant Ames's young colleagues, namely, Master Hawking. In fact, we have le Loup's head in a sack, for you…to bring back to your lovely wife, or King Henri, at your discretion. Shall I have it brought in?"

De Tréville is momentarily speechless, and his face goes white. When he recovers his composure, he says, "No, Sir Walter, thank you. I shall go outside to see it. Gentlemen," he says, bowing to the three lords, "you will please excuse me, as I am overcome by this news, and wish to ponder it alone. I shall join you during supper, if that would be acceptable."

"Very much so, monsieur," says Mountjoy, bowing in return. "And please accept my congratulations on the success of your trip to England." De Tréville leaves in a daze.

Lord Howard turns to Noah. "So, Serjeant Ames. Tell us how you solved the crime!"

Noah hesitates before answering. "We have solved *all* the crimes, lordship."

Mountjoy looks confused. "Did you say *all* the crimes?"

Noah nods respectfully.

"Which crimes?"

Noah exchanges a glance with Raleigh. "Perhaps, m'lord, we'd best discuss these matters when we are alone," says Noah, glancing at the Lord Admiral, who continues to regard him skeptically.

"Nonsense!" says Mountjoy. "Anything you have to say to me can be discussed in the presence of the Lord Admiral and Lord Howard."

"Well, m'lord," says Noah. "How shall I begin?"

A servant appears and pours everyone a glass of wine, and Mountjoy waits for him to leave. "Begin at the beginning, which, I suppose would be the discovery of the murder at the Tower."

"Actually," says Noah, "it began the previous day, in the map room at Westminster, when your lordship exhibited certain military maps to the Secretary of State, Sir Walter, Sir Francis Bacon, and myself. While you were explaining one map showing certain military positions in Cornwall and Ireland, as you will recall, I noticed that it was lacking the watermark of your family's crest that had appeared at the center of all your other maps."

"I recall," says Mountjoy.

"I was concerned that it may have been an illicit copy of the original bearing the watermark, and that perhaps the original had fallen into the wrong hands. Walking home from Westminster with my trusted young colleague, Jonathan Hawking, the very one who has now bested le Loup in mortal combat, it occurred to me that I was probably mistaken; that any thief copying the map would have returned the original to your lordship's library and removed only the copy. I mentioned my initial error to Master Hawking, offering no detail about the contents of the map, of course, other than that it showed sensitive information about troop positions in Ireland and Cornwall. That evening, I happened to receive a letter from my only daughter, Lady Jessica—"

The Lord Admiral interrupts. "Your daughter is a noblewoman?"

Noah bows. "She is, Lord Admiral. *She* is Church of England."

The Lord Admiral grunts skeptically.

"My daughter's note asked me to fetch her at once from the home of the Earl of Somerset in Wellston."

"Why?" asks Lord Howard.

Noah shrugs abashedly. "Who can tell, m'lord, with affairs of the heart?"

This is met by a vague shrug.

"Continue," says Mountjoy.

"Well, as I was scheduled to appear before Her Majesty in two days' time, I found myself unable to go. So, I dispatched Master Hawking to fetch her in my stead." To Noah's great relief, no one asks why a young barrister would be available to perform such a time-consuming errand at the start of a new court term. Evidently, this is a question that would occur only to another lawyer.

"What has any of this to do with solving the crime?" asks Mountjoy.

"Please bear with me, m'lord," says Noah. "I shall have all this tied together before supper. Anyway, the next day, as you know, Sir Walter and I discovered your adjutant brutally murdered at the Tower with his own dagger. You will recall, Lord Mountjoy, that your lordship informed us that the lieutenant's name was 'Trenowden,' which you identified as a Cornish name, though you told us that the lieutenant himself was from West Devonshire, which abuts Cornwall."

"You have a good memory," says Lord Mountjoy.

Noah bows appreciatively. "It was a ghastly scene, as you will recall, yet we managed to recover two torn pieces of a bloody note. One was found in the adjutant's closed fist. The other, which had some writing on it, was found under the table where the victim had fallen. I brought it with me to aid in the investigation." He searches his pockets. "Ah, here it is," he says, and lays it on the table.

> Porth
> Kil
> Ch. Lev. 31   bre

The Lord Admiral shows especial interest in the note, and studies it for a few moments, as though there's something familiar about it.

After waiting a respectful time for the Lord Admiral's attention to return to him, Noah resumes. "As the murderer had not removed the note from the murder scene, we wondered whether perhaps Lieutenant Trenowden had been involved in a prior altercation, during which the paper was torn. As you will recall, lordship, though Sir Walter and his men searched every inch of the Tower that day and the following day, no other piece of the note was recovered. One other possible clue *was* discovered, however. The chain to Traitor's Gate had been sawn through, a curious choice, as the Tower locksmith said it would have taken only a fraction of the time to saw through the lock, instead. When your lordship discovered that Francis, a Yeoman Warder, had both escorted Lieutenant Trenowden to the chamber where he was murdered, and discovered the sawn chain, you ordered his arrest.

"Now, as Lieutenant Trenowden had come to the Tower that morning to advise the Secretary of State and Sir Walter concerning the means used to secure your lordship's maps, we naturally surmised that the murder had something to do with the question I'd raised the previous day, about the map which lacked your lordship's watermark.

"As your lordship was unable to identify any of the keys found on the victim as fitting the door to your map room, Sir Walter asked if your lordship had such a key on your person, and you were unable to answer with any degree of certainty, as such maps were routinely handled by your adjutants, rather than your lordship personally. Since a thorough search of the Tower provided no additional clues, we had no choice but to travel to the storage place of your lordship's maps, to wit, this magnificent manor house in Dorset.

"On the way here from London, our small company was ambushed by three men I took to be highwaymen, until Sir Walter pointed out that they never demanded our money. They simply started shooting. They shot Lieutenant Carter as he was riding my horse bearing the Queen's livery. This led us to suspect that I may have been the assassins' intended target. Thanks to Sir Walter's courage and marksmanship, and more than our share of luck, we shot and killed them all. Before the last one died, he identified the man who hired them as a Frenchman named 'Wolf.' Lieutenant Carter is recovering from his wound. He is asleep upstairs as we speak.

"As we were about to resume our progress to Dorset, my assistants found me on the road, and handed me a letter that Master Hawking had written me from the earl's residence in Somerset."

"What did it say?" asks Lord Howard.

"In the letter, Master Hawking advised me that he had just arrived in Somerset to fetch my daughter. On his way there, however, he had evidently stopped at an inn, where he came across someone unexpected."

"Whom?" asks Lord Howard.

"Robert Poley, one of Lord Essex's least important attendants, a notorious drunkard. Goodman Poley is presently...a guest...downstairs in your lordship's guardhouse."

"What has this Poley person to do with your investigation?" asks Mountjoy.

Noah studies Mountjoy's face as he replies. "Poley had in his possession...a leather cylinder, which Master Hawking suspected might contain the possibly purloined map that I had mentioned to him."

Mountjoy's color drains, but as yet he retains his composure. "And?" he says.

"Master Hawking learned that Poley would be met at the inn the following day by another of Lord Essex's attendants, named 'Skeres,' who is known to me to be a very dangerous man. He also is staying in your lordship's guardhouse this evening."

"Getting pretty crowded down there!" says Lord Howard, already a bit in his cups.

"Indeed, your lordship. To continue. Now, Master Hawking—"

"*He's* not down there, too, is he?" asks Lord Howard merrily.

"Thomas!" warns the Lord Admiral, apparently not given to jest.

Noah bows to Lord Howard. "Nay, m'lord. Master Hawking is in Falmouth, recovering from a serious stab wound to the chest."

"So sorry," says Lord Howard contritely. "Please forgive my

flippancy. Pray, continue."

"In the letter, Master Hawking informed me that, though he'd found my daughter ready to depart the earl's residence, on the off-chance there might be a military map about to be smuggled out of the country to Her Majesty's enemies, he had no choice but to try to stop it."

"So, what did he do?" asks the Lord Admiral.

"He offered to escort my daughter to a reputable neighboring family, and to lodge her at their home until a suitable escort could arrive and return her to London."

"Good lad," says the Lord Admiral. "And what did *she* do?"

Noah sighs. "I'm afraid she foolishly insisted upon accompanying Master Hawking in pursuit of the map."

Lord Howard stands erect with pride. "Good English lass, by God!"

The Lord Admiral looks askance at his young cousin. "Hardly, Thomas. As her father is a Hebrew, so must *she* be, as well."

This observation places Noah in a difficult position. There are many ways to handle it, but any one might go ill. "Perhaps we flatter ourselves to think ourselves English, Lord Admiral," he ventures.

Fortunately, the Lord Admiral seems mollified. "I see. Go on."

"In his letter from the earl's residence, Master Hawking also mentioned that Skeres had said aloud that the expenses of their expedition were being borne by someone named 'Jake.'"

Mountjoy is growing increasingly uneasy.

"When we arrived here in Dorset," continues Noah, "we had the privilege of enjoying Lord Mountjoy's hospitality for several days more than expected, as m'Lord Mountjoy had not yet arrived, and there was no one on the premises having a key to the map room. Indeed, it was not until the morning of m'lord's arrival that we discovered that the maps were kept, not in a dedicated map room, but rather in the library.

"When one of the servants informed us that another of m'lord's adjutants, a Lieutenant Braddock, had disappeared around the same time as Trenowden, I recalled detecting a foul odor outside an open library window upon the day of my arrival. As the matter was most urgent and involved the safety of Her Majesty, I took it upon myself to break into the library, where we discovered Lieutenant Braddock's body. According to the coroner, Braddock had been murdered many days earlier, well prior to the murder of Lieutenant Trenowden at the Tower.

"In a concealed pocket of Lieutenant Braddock's shirt, we discovered another scrap of paper, which fit perfectly with the pieces of the note recovered from the body of Lieutenant Trenowden. Alas, the writing on this new scrap had been obliterated by blood from the victim's fatal wound."

Lord Howard speculates aloud. "It seems as though the two adjutants tore the note as they quarreled over it. Is it possible Trenowden murdered Braddock, and ran off to the Tower with the written portion?"

Mountjoy shakes his head dismissively. "Don't be ridiculous. Trenowden was not a murderer, and certainly would never have murdered his *friend*!"

"Well," says Lord Howard, "it sounds as though you were stuck!"

Noah nods sagely. "Yes, m'lord, and we could not discount the possibility that events had transpired exactly as you have just suggested. Of course, a note precipitating such a deadly quarrel between two close friends would have had to contain some desperately important information. Unfortunately, however, we had no idea what the legible portion of the note signified.

"Shortly after Sir Walter and I brought Lieutenant Braddock's body down from its place of concealment in the library, Monsieur de Tréville introduced himself to us. Later that morning, he informed us that his wife's sister, as well as several other Frenchwomen, had been brutally murdered by a Frenchman named 'le Loup,' which is, of course, French for 'wolf,' and that the French king had dispatched Monsieur de Tréville to apprehend this criminal in England, where he had been spotted at various points from Falmouth to London. Lord Mountjoy's gardener, who had overheard our conversation, pointed out that a man calling himself 'Loup' had been seen secretly conversing with the adjutants who were later found murdered.

"Suspicion now shifted to le Loup for the murders of both Trenowden and Braddock. It now appeared likely that, immediately following the altercation between Trenowden and Braddock, le Loup had come to Braddock, expecting to receive the map. Upon learning that the map was on its way to the Tower of London, le Loup apparently killed Braddock, and then followed Trenowden to the Tower, where he murdered *him* and took the map."

Lord Howard scratches his head. "What sort of disagreement about the map would give rise to such an altercation between the two lieutenants?"

"I believe that they disagreed about whether it was fit to obey an order they'd been given," replies Noah. "If you will hear out my tale, I believe the answer will become clear.

"Within minutes of learning about le Loup from Monsieur de Tréville, one of my young associates returned from Master Hawking with further news that this same le Loup was one of the men being tracked into Cornwall by Master Hawking and my daughter. A short time later, this same young associate informed us that Skeres, Poley, and le Loup had been joined by Sir Gelly Meyrick, yet a third of Lord Essex's attendants (one known to all of you gentlemen, other than possibly the Lord Admiral), and that they were headed to an unknown port at the western end of Cornwall, from which the map would surely be dispatched to an unknown point outside the country. Incidentally, Lord Howard, this evening Sir Gelly also is enjoying the hospitality of Lord Mountjoy's crowded guardhouse."

"So, how did you proceed?" asks the Lord Admiral impatiently.

"We rushed to Falmouth, as it was the westernmost port in Cornwall that seemed of any importance. We thought that perhaps there we could solve the puzzle of the writing on the torn note. Lord Mountjoy was kind enough to lend us several of his lieutenants, as well as his surgeon, together with horses and a carriage, which eased our travel greatly. Thank you heartily, Lord Mountjoy."

"Most welcome," mutters Mountjoy, whose spirit seems to have flagged.

"We stayed with the family of one of my young associates, the Killigrews."

"Fine family," says Lord Howard.

"Indeed, it is, m'lord," says Noah. "Well, for some time, it had been my suspicion that the torn note had been written to indicate the map's intended embarkation point from England. I had surmised that the letters 'kil' on the second line of the torn note indicated that it was to leave on a Killigrew vessel (perhaps unbeknownst to the vessel's owner). It also appeared to me that the writing on the third line indicated the vessel would depart on the thirty-first of a month ending in 'bre.' As we knew the map had already made its way to Cornwall, it took no great leap of imagination to realize it would be departing on October thirty-first, which was the day after we arrived at Falmouth.

"As we were now in Falmouth, it occurred to us on the morning of the thirty-first that we ought to ask the young harbormaster whether he knew of a Cornish port whose name begins with 'porth,' as such a port would fit the first line of the note. Although he knew of none, his father, who was his predecessor in office, recalled a port formerly known as 'Porth Ia,' which is now known as 'Saint Ives.'

"As the very day of the map's departure was fast passing, we left immediately for Saint Ives. By the time we arrived, Master Hawking had freed my daughter from le Loup's clutches, and was engaged in mortal combat with him on a promontory jutting out over a cove in which a small packet boat was moored. Master Hawking bested le Loup, but not before he himself was stabbed in the chest. Doctor Yatrow told us Jonathan was fortunate that le Loup had been off balance when he struck, or the blow would likely have been fatal. With his final blow, Master Hawking knocked le Loup off the cliff. Le Loup's head struck the boom as he tumbled down to the little boat, which decapitated him before he landed on the deck in two pieces. I add this only to explain that we did nothing so bloodthirsty as to remove his head for a trophy. As it turns out, the vessel was the 'Killigrew Puffin.' Baron Mountjoy, we've gone through a great deal of danger to retrieve your map. If I may, I'd like to return it to you now."

Noah withdraws the cylinder from an outsized bag he's brought with him. "Would you mind telling me, your lordship, whether this cylinder is familiar to you?"

"It is not," replies Mountjoy.

"As I expected," says Noah, handing it to Mountjoy, who seems less than thrilled to accept it.

"Thank you," says Mountjoy listlessly.

Lord Howard seems shocked by Mountjoy's ingratitude. "That's it? *'Thank you?'* Aren't you even going to open it?"

Mountjoy regards him with irritation. "It's not a Christmas gift, Thomas! I know what's inside, and have already expressed my gratitude for its return."

Mountjoy locks eyes with Noah, who sternly returns his gaze.

"Yes, your lordship," says Noah. "Please open it. I really must insist."

"You?" replies Mountjoy indignantly. "Who are *you* to insist?"

"Open it!" commands the Lord Admiral, obviously suspicious of the grounds for his cousin's reticence.

Mountjoy removes the cap from the cylinder and perfunctorily glances inside. "Yes, that is the map," he says. "Thank you."

"Don't you wish to confirm it bears your watermark?" asks Noah.

"Very well," says Mountjoy peevishly. He tilts the cylinder, draws out the map, and holds it up to the fading sunlight at the window. And *there* is the impress that denotes the map as the original. "Yes, Serjeant Ames. Sir Walter. It is the original. I thank you heartily for its return." There's something in his voice that clearly indicates he's neither relieved nor grateful.

"What's the problem, Charles?" demands the Lord Admiral.

Mountjoy chuffs, and glares at Noah. "Why don't *you* tell them?" he asks. "That's what you want, isn't it?"

"No, your lordship," Noah says wistfully. "It has been my fondest wish that, during my absence, *you* would tell them."

Lord Howard says, "Is this about the other 'crimes' you and Sir Walter mentioned when you entered?"

"It is, m'lord," says Noah.

"What other *crimes,* Serjeant Ames?" shouts Mountjoy.

"As you insist, your lordship, I shall say in a moment. Permit me to put one additional question to you first, however. When your lordship left for London to inform the Queen of your plans for defending Ireland, did you leave the watermarked map in the care of Lieutenant Braddock?"

"Yes," replies Mountjoy sulkily.

Noah nods. "As I expected." He turns to the others. "Gentlemen, you see the crime we thought was taking place was not taking place at all. Our natural assumption was that the map was heading for Ireland or Spain, or some other place controlled by the enemies of England."

"It *wasn't?*" asks the Lord Admiral.

"No, Lord Admiral. It never was. If you will take a close look at the note, you will see the name of the month, as written, ends in 'bre.' Although our English spelling is not completely standardized, 'bre' is not the way an Englishman would end a spelling of 'October.' Also, the numerical date *precedes* the name of the month. We English do not use that style. As you will also note, on the third line, where one might expect to find the map's destination, appears the French abbreviation for the word 'chateau.' An Englishman would say 'castle,' and would not have used a French abbreviation. So, as you see, the entire note appears to have been written by someone speaking *French* as his native tongue."

"But what does *that* prove?" asks Lord Howard. "It may have been written by le Loup!"

Noah shakes his head. "No, it can't have been. He was the only Frenchman known to be involved in this whole map business. It would have made no sense for him to leave a note in his own handwriting on the corpse. That would have been as suicidal as leaving his calling card. Besides, le Loup was the *messenger,* so that the note would more likely have been written to him.

"Though it is written in a French hand, it is not likely to have been written in France, as the French on the continent have changed their dating system to the Gregorian calendar, which is ten days ahead of the English Old Style. A Frenchman on the Continent advising someone of a vessel's departure date from England would need to specify whether he was using New Style or Old Style. As well-traveled men of the world, you all know that Englishmen writing from the Continent will customarily write "O.S." to the right of the date. Absent this specification, the messenger could miss the vessel by ten days.

"Nor have we yet fully addressed the significance of 'Ch. Levan,' which designates Levan Castle as the map's destination. Lord Admiral, I expect you know where that castle is located."

The Lord Admiral nods grimly. "I do, having sailed past it several times. It is a small castle located at the mouth of the port of Glasgow, in Scotland."

Noah nods. "And that port is barely fifty miles from the Scots capital city of Edinburgh." He glares at Mountjoy. "Now that the Frenchwoman known as 'Mary Queen of Scots' is dead, what surviving person located in Edinburgh, writing in the French Language, using the Cornish, pre-English, name of the port, being derisively nicknamed by underlings as 'Jake,' would insist upon receiving an *original* map, as a demonstration of authenticity and a show of his correspondent's anticipated fealty?"

"The answer is obvious," says the Lord Admiral. "It's the son of Mary Queen of Scots, namely, King James the Sixth of Scotland, likeliest heir to the English throne." The Lord Admiral thunders at Mountjoy. "Charles, did you dispatch this map to King James?"

"*Please do not answer, m'lord!*" shouts Noah, then bows to the Lord Admiral. "Lord Admiral, I pray your forgiveness. Once I hear the answer to that question, however, I expect I will have no choice but to arrest Lord Mountjoy and several other of Her Majesty's officers on charges of high treason by espionage, as well as several violations of the Succession Act, which seems to have been at the forefront of everyone's mind since the Queen took sick. Permit me to reply to Lord Howard's earlier question."

He turns to Lord Howard. "The two adjutants had been ordered to dispatch this map to King James, and a dispute arose between them over whether to obey an order which, on its face, seemed treasonous against the Crown. As near as I can tell from the evidence as we found it and a conversation with Sir Gelly Meyrick about his discussions with le Loup whilst he lived, the two adjutants disagreed about whether to obey the order. Braddock apparently showed the note to his fellow Trenowden to demonstrate the lawfulness of turning over the map pursuant to the order of Lord Mountjoy, but Trenowden thought the order unlawful.

"Trenowden insisted he be allowed to take the map to Lord Mountjoy and that he be given the note to use as evidence for his own protection in

234 | NEAL ROBERTS

case he were accused of purloining or transporting the map against orders. Braddock protested that *he* would need the note for his own defense, as it was he to whom Lord Mountjoy entrusted the note. The two scuffled, and Trenowden forcibly took the map from Braddock, knocking him cold.

"As the note had been torn during the fracas, Trenowden took with him the part he'd wrested away, and left the rest with his unconscious friend, presumably in the hope that having even a piece of the note would suffice to protect each of them. Trenowden then took a fast horse and, consistently with his orders, left for London to confer with m'lord at the Tower. Contrary to orders, however, he carried the map and half the note.

"After that, le Loup returned here to Lord Mountjoy's manor house, after having been put off by the lieutenants, and found Lieutenant Braddock alone in the library. A footprint found on the library's window ledge suggests that he entered that way. He demanded the map. Braddock told him that the plan had changed and, under duress, confessed that Trenowden had left for the Tower the previous night, with the map. The furious le Loup blurted out that he would follow Trenowden and take the map from him. When Braddock protested that Trenowden would not give it up, le Loup told him that he would kill Trenowden, if necessary.

"Braddock tried to stop le Loup from following Trenowden, and the two grappled. But, before Braddock could draw a weapon, le Loup stabbed him to death. Le Loup then put Braddock's corpse on a high shelf out of sight, hastily cleaned up, and climbed back out of the library window to attempt to overtake Trenowden in transit, which he was unable to do."

Lord Mountjoy looks askance at Noah. "But how did he get into the Tower to kill Trenowden?"

"Well, I can say with relative certainty that the sawn chain played no part in this affair."

"None at all?" asks Mountjoy skeptically.

Noah shakes his head. "Surely, there is any number of plots to gain entry onto the Tower grounds unfolding at any given moment. The sawn chain was likely part of another. Sawing through the chain would need to be done over a very long time, weeks or months, perhaps. Fortunately, it was discovered quite by accident in time to foil whatever plot was afoot. For our purposes, what's important is that le Loup *did* get in and viciously killed Lieutenant Trenowden. Although the rest of the chronology is mostly guesswork, I expect I have deduced what happened afterwards, both from the evidence I have just expounded and from my conversations with those currently in your lordship's cellar. As they're liars, of course, their words must be sifted."

The Lord Admiral nods sagely. "And what do you guess?"

Noah continues, a bit hesitantly now. "Le Loup, who could not afford to be seen in London, discreetly located Nicholas Skeres, of long acquaintance. When le Loup said he needed Skeres to transport the map, Skeres gave him the empty cylinder. Le Loup accepted it, rolled up the map and deposited it into the cylinder. When Skeres wasn't looking, le Loup slipped in something else, which we'll get to shortly. Le Loup forbade Skeres to open the cylinder thereafter, on pain of death. As Skeres knew that le Loup was perfectly capable of carrying out such a threat, neither he nor his henchmen ever opened the cylinder.

"Le Loup then handed Skeres the cylinder containing the map and the other item, and asked him to transport it to points west, giving him some money and the promise of much more, and telling him of the map's importance. Le Loup obtained Skeres' promise to meet him with the map at the inn at Bridgwater at an appointed date and time, which would allow them sufficient time to meet the departing skiff.

"Before leaving London, Skeres told Gelly Meyrick about the plan. Meyrick told Skeres that he would meet him and Poley at Davey Jones' Inn in Cornwall on an appointed day. Skeres then entrusted the map to his friend Robert Poley, who took it as far as the Hind of Brakenhale, where Skeres was to meet him. Before Skeres arrived there, however, Master Hawking had arrived and seen the cylinder, which he suspected might contain the missing map."

Noah turns now to Mountjoy. "Lieutenant Trenowden did not have the cylinder with him when he was murdered at the Tower. He must have had the map concealed upon his person. In case your lordship is curious why I asked whether this cylinder is familiar to you, it was to determine to a certainty whether Skeres was being truthful in telling me that the cylinder had been supplied by him only after the map was stolen at the Tower."

Lord Mountjoy seizes upon the occasion to justify his actions to the Lord Admiral. "Lord Admiral, Her Majesty's officers regard themselves as being free to correspond with His Majesty King James."

The Lord Admiral seethes. "I cannot fathom why they should feel free to do so! One Sovereign at a time, Charles! One cannot fulfill his oath of undivided fealty while currying favor with the king of a foreign country."

"M'lord," pleads Mountjoy, "Essex is known to have been corresponding with King James for a long time!"

The Lord Admiral turns to Noah. "Is this true, Serjeant Ames?"

"It *is,* m'lord. Her Majesty has known it since Lord Burghley told her of it ten years ago. Needless to say, it has not helped to earn Lord Essex any preferment. Far from it. It has done him a great deal of damage at court, although I doubt he knows it."

"Still," says the Lord Admiral, turning to Mountjoy, "it is infinitely worse to send a map bearing military secrets to a foreign Sovereign! What if the king were to send it to England's enemies, to curry favor of his own?"

"But, Lord Admiral!" pleads Mountjoy. "King James has much reason *never* to do so! He expects to succeed Her Majesty! Why, he would be damaging his own inheritance!"

"It's not his inheritance *yet,* Charles, and may never be! Besides, some disloyal *minister* of King James' might put it to ill use. Who knows how many hands such an item would pass through before the king even learned it had arrived? Worse still, how many *messengers* could turn such a map to ill use? As such messengers operate outside approved channels, they obviously come with no *bona fides*!"

Mountjoy is clearly dismayed.

Noah seeks to bring the discussion to a close. "I also have in my possession," he says, "a set of items that neither Master Hawking nor myself has ever read, or even fully identified. It constitutes, I expect, the only written evidence in existence whose discovery would render it *impossible* for me to avoid making the arrests I have mentioned." He produces the leather pouch. "This pouch was found inside the cylinder, having evidently been secretly slipped in by le Loup. It contains as-yet unidentified letters. My suspicion is that these letters were written by high-standing officers of Her Majesty to a foreign potentate, namely, King James of Scotland. At this moment, it is a suspicion only." Noah turns to Mountjoy. "M'lord, I offer you the opportunity to throw these letters in that fire, and burn them."

Mountjoy regards him suspiciously. "And why would you do this?"

Noah shakes his head. "It is my object to obtain your lordship's compliance with a law designed to protect Her Majesty, not to deny Her Majesty the services of her most competent subjects."

"What do you demand in return?"

Noah takes umbrage. "I am no extortionist, m'lord. I demand nothing in return, except your solemn promise as an Englishman, a gentleman, and a God-fearing Christian that you will never violate the Succession Act from this day forward, nor reveal state or military secrets to anyone other than Her Majesty and Her Majesty's officers similarly sworn to secrecy."

"Is that all?"

"I have a few other minor requests, your lordship, which I expect you will freely grant after burning the letters. But that is my only *condition.* If you accept it, I shall never mention this incident again. Indeed," Noah laughs darkly, "it would likely cost me my head to do so."

Mountjoy takes the letters from Noah's hand, and tosses them into the hottest part of the fire. The company watches silently as they burn to a cinder.

"Now," says Mountjoy, much more calmly, "what are your 'requests,' as you call them?"

"The first is that your lordship instruct Sir Walter to release the Yeoman Warder Francis from prison, as there is no evidence whatever linking him to any of these crimes, and that you authorize Sir Walter to reinstate him to his former position without reservation of any kind."

"Sir Walter, please do so. Your next 'request,' Serjeant Ames?"

"I request that I be permitted to transport Sir Gelly, Skeres, and Poley to London, and release them without prosecution. Although they clearly know of the map, I believe they do not know of the letters. I have asked each of them sidelong questions that would surely have caused them to betray such knowledge to me, which they did not do. In any event, they are no threat to us, as they have no evidence. Further, for them to admit knowledge of such a thing would quickly dispatch them to the gallows."

"Granted. What else?"

"I request your permission to release the young man who captained the 'Killigrew Puffin' to his grandfather, without prosecution. He never had it in his mind to transport the map to England's enemies. And he has been sworn to secrecy, for whatever that's worth."

"Very well. What else?"

"I have one final request. Before making it, however, permit me to point out that your lordship's clandestine correspondence with King James has resulted in the murders of two of your own adjutants, the shooting of one of Sir Walter's lieutenants, and the near-fatal stabbing of Master Jonathan Hawking of Gray's Inn. In addition, during le Loup's rampage, he cruelly raped and murdered at least two additional young women, and seized my daughter with the intention of doing the same to her."

"Your request?" demands Mountjoy indignantly.

"I ask you to encourage Her Majesty to grant preferment for Master Hawking. He nearly gave his life in the belief that risking it would save the lives of many of your lordship's own soldiers. Her Majesty already knows of him, as he has appeared before her several times. And she has spoken to me glowingly of his skills and loyalty."

Mountjoy looks to the Lord Admiral for guidance.

The Lord Admiral nods and says: "I shall add my own voice to this chorus, Serjeant Ames."

"My profoundest thanks, Lord Admiral."

The Lord Admiral turns to Mountjoy, Lord Howard, and Sir Walter, who has stood silent throughout. "Gentlemen, please go ahead to supper. I wish to speak with Serjeant Ames privately." They file out and close the door behind them.

Noah notices that snow has begun to fall outside the warm salon. A light coating already covers the branches in view.

The Lord Admiral gently breaks the silence, his tone now sympathetic. "In your position, Serjeant, I suppose you cannot but be furious with Sir Walter. No doubt, you realized only too late that he *knew* the map was not on its way to the Irish rebels, and that all the pain and peril endured by your daughter and Master Hawking might have been avoided, had he simply disclosed to you the map's true destination."

Noah sighs and shakes his head indulgently. "Sir Walter was bound by his oath of secrecy to Lord Mountjoy, m'lord. Until quite late in this affair, neither Sir Walter nor I had any inkling that my daughter and Master Hawking were engaged in an effort to retrieve the map. Indeed, Sir Walter learned of their involvement…and their peril…no earlier than I did. By that time, it would have made no difference to our actions if he'd told me of the map's true destination. I am satisfied that he did everything in his power to speedily remove them from harm's way."

The Lord Admiral nods admiringly. "My cousin made a worthwhile investment in your education, Serjeant."

Noah bows appreciatively. "So now," he says, returning his contemplative gaze to the snowcapped trees outside, "it will be put abroad that Jonathan Hawking saved thousands of English soldiers by preventing a secret military map from being smuggled out of the country to Her Majesty's enemies, in the course of which effort he slew the foreigner who'd stolen the map and thereby avenged the foul murders of Lord Mountjoy's young adjutants…and nothing else will be known."

"Makes for a good story," observes the Lord Admiral, unperturbed.

Noah sighs. "I wonder how much of our storied English history has been tinkered with in this fashion."

For a moment, the Lord Admiral seems lost in thought. "You cannot possibly imagine," he says. "At least, in this case, the story's protagonist *believed* that's what he was doing, and *did* risk his life for England. In many cases, it's not so. In some cases, the real protagonist and villain have exchanged places in the popular story." He turns to Noah thoughtfully. "May I call you 'Noah?'"

"Aye, m'lord. I would welcome it."

"Her Majesty cannot live forever, Noah," says the Lord Admiral wistfully. "No matter how much one wishes it."

"I know it in theory, Lord Admiral," says Noah, trying to hide the ache in his voice, "but I cannot accept it in my heart. I wish to serve no other mistress...nor master."

"We grow old," says the old Lord Admiral, almost to himself. "We die. It is not for us to choose how long we live, or whom we serve. These things are fixed in the stars, Noah. Besides," he gibes, "who ever heard of the hard-hearted Jew being so soft? Are we not taught that they turned their faces away from Our Lord?"

Noah cringes at the Lord Admiral's light-hearted allusion to this ancient libel, and tosses it back at him in the same spirit. "The Sanhedrin may have condemned Him as a false prophet, m'lord, but it took the crown's officers to crucify Him."

The Lord Admiral snorts softly at this humorous retort.

Noah turns to him. "Words cannot express who Her Majesty is to me, m'lord. I know she is your lordship's near cousin. But I was reared without a mother, and Her Majesty has been nothing less than the finest mother one could hope for. I hope to make her remaining years as safe and pleasant for her as I may."

"The universal prayer of the good son," says the Lord Admiral. He looks at the torn and bloody note that still lies face-up on the table. "What shall be done with this?"

Noah shrugs, having little remaining interest in it. "I leave that to your lordship's discretion."

The Lord Admiral picks up the note, takes a long look at it, and tosses it into the fire. Thin billows of smoke lick at its sides, and hungry flames devour it from the center. "Here I am, an old man who's spent much of his life at court," he mutters, "yet that's the first time I've burned something written in a king's own hand. Well," he shrugs, "I expect we'll be reading much more from him in years to come." He escorts Noah toward the dining room. "Come. Let us eat. And then you can pose your questions to me about Lord Essex's military exploits."

CHAPTER 18

IN HIS FIRELIT bedchamber at the George & Dragon, Jonathan sits propped up against the pillows, his shirt open, his inflamed wound exposed to Jessica's gentle ministrations. He glances out of the window at the moonlit silhouette of the twin promontories against the shining water. Jessica breaks the comfortable silence.

"Why didn't you tell me le Loup had murdered those women?" she asks, wringing reddish water out of the cloth into a little pewter bowl.

Jonathan has pondered that question quite a bit lately, and hoped to have a satisfactory answer by the time Jessica posed it. But somehow he persuaded himself she'd let it rest until he was up and about. "Do you suppose that question can wait till morning?"

She arches an eyebrow as she blots the circumference of his wound. "Oh?" She looks him up and down in his weakened condition, his lower body wrapped in warm blankets. "Are you planning on trotting off to rejoin the regiment just now?"

"No, but I'm afraid I'm getting a bit sleepy."

She eyes him skeptically. "I'd no idea! I'll leave you to your repose." She begins to rise, calling his bluff.

He places his hand on hers. "Sit, Jess, please. I wish you'd never leave." Hoping for some reciprocity of affection, he detects only amusement.

"Well," she says, resuming her seat, "I shall have to leave eventually, but I *would* care to hear your explanation this evening, if that would not impose *too* great a burden upon your convalescence."

For a brief moment, he looks straight into her eyes. She seems to take pleasure in this little cat-and-mouse game. His chest wound twinges. "If you must know, I didn't wish to worry you."

"Oh, I see," she says skeptically. "And you blithely disregarded the possibility that I might encounter that monster alone, out in the wild?"

"You never *would* have," he replies, "if you'd remained with Andres all the way to Falmouth, as I'd asked you."

"As *you'd* asked me? Why, Jonathan, you made it eminently clear that those were my *father's* instructions, not yours."

He studies her face for some hint that her father has denied giving such instructions. "Spoken to Serjeant Ames about it, have we?"

She gets up, empties the contents of her little pewter bowl into a large bedpan, and pours fresh water into her bowl from a terra cotta pitcher. "I asked him about it, yes," she replies, and sits back down with the fresh bowl in her lap.

"I'm sorry I had to fib to you, Jess, but—"

"Ah," she says, her eyes wide. "So, that *was* a fib!"

"I thought you said you spoke with your father about it."

"I *did*!" she says. "But he wouldn't answer. Hah! I felt sure that an experienced examiner such as yourself would never fall for such an ancient trick."

She's caught him out...again. "Clever girl! I didn't tell you about le Loup's murders because I didn't wish to upset you. Things were frightening enough out there on the cold, hard road."

"Is that the *only* reason?"

He looks into himself, as only she seems able to make him do. "No," he admits. "There was an additional reason."

"And that was...?"

"Shame," he says.

"I don't see how that monster's actions reflect shame upon *you*," she replies.

"No. Shame for my whole sex, which seems bent upon dominating yours."

She looks confused. "How is *murder* domination?"

"Destruction is domination in its most absolute and infantile form," he muses. "If you consider how some children treat small animals, you'll see what I mean."

"And you believe *all* men wish to dominate women?" She pats his wound with a dry cloth, using her lightest touch. "Let that dry a while before closing your shirt."

"Thank you, nurse," he says, pondering her question. "I think men *generally* wish to dominate women...perhaps all but the few men who truly love them."

"Not just madmen, such as le Loup?"

He shakes his head. "Not just madmen. Your viscount, for example."

She furrows her brow. "Whatever do you mean?"

"Well…has he been writing to you?" Though he's wanted to ask for several days, he hasn't found an opening until now.

She picks up the bedpan, bowl, and cloth, and stands at the foot of his bed, obviously contemplating how much to reveal about the viscount. "I received a packet of letters from him yesterday. It took until then for his messenger to locate me here in Saint Ives. I haven't finished reading them through yet, but, so far, I haven't come to a point where he seeks to *dominate* me."

Jonathan smirks. "That's what *you* think." He regards her skeptically. "What did he say?"

She shrugs. "Pretty much what any man would say to a woman he loved."

"Not loved. *Desired.* There's a difference, y'know."

"Oh," she says haughtily, "and I presume the sage Jon Hawking shall now teach me the difference between desire and love."

He's pleased to see he has her a bit flustered now. "Tell me an example of what he wrote," he says, pressing his advantage.

"Oh," she says dismissively, "silly things."

Jonathan raises an eyebrow expectantly.

"One that comes to mind," she says at last, "is that, if I were to be threatened by a demon from hell, he would go there and slay him, so long as he could return to my side." She smugly awaits his reply.

Because she's about to leave for the evening, all comfort abandons him, replaced by the empty feeling in the pit of his stomach that seems to dwell there whenever she's away. He studies her face, so its memory can keep him company after she's left. "And *there's* the difference between desire and love, Jess. For, if you were threatened by a demon from hell, I would go to hell and slay him…though there be no *hope* of return."

She becomes suddenly serious, and opens the door to go. Before closing it behind her, she regards him skeptically once again, and closes it without the blithe "good night" she's offered him every previous night after tending his wound.

As the door clicks shut, he nestles his head in a pillow, and smiles.

⊸∘⧷∘⊶

JONATHAN HAS PASSED a difficult night. Though he found the distant thunder strangely comforting, he was awakened several times by an unrelenting cramp in his chest, as though his muscles had just awakened to the injury they'd suffered the previous week and had decided it was high time to protest. He supposes he overdid things the previous day, cooperating with the maidservants' thorough bathing of his body, and a long-overdue change of sheets and blankets. At least he smells better.

It's very early morning when Jessica creeps into his room, sporting a dress that looks no less beautiful on her for its simplicity. She carries a bowl of thin breakfast porridge and places it on the night stand beside him.

"Good morning," she whispers, and glances at the fire. "*Tsk.* See the fire dwindle, and today's to be so cold and damp! Well," she says, brushing her hands against each other, "we'll soon see to that." She tosses a few more fagots on the fire that quickly ignite. She turns to him and shrugs. "Hotter than it looked," she says, with a big smile that soon dissipates. "Jonathan, you look quite wretched!"

"*Thank* you, Lady Burlington," he replies sardonically. "Yet, you yourself look as delightful as ever."

"Seriously, Jon," she says.

"Well, I was awakened a few times by this blasted—"

"No, it's not that. You're wasting away. Why, you look as though I've been *starving* you to death! Come, eat," she says handing him the bowl. "There's a good lad."

He can't help but smile at her patronizing manner, treating him as though he were a boy of ten years. He eats hesitantly, being careful to avoid inducing any further muscle spasms. "Your manner reminds me of Goodwife Graves," he says, wiping his chin with a small cloth that Jessica brought for that purpose.

"Not of your mother?" she asks.

He sadly places the spoon back in the bowl, and returns it to the night stand.

"Oh, I'm so sorry, Jon," she says. "I should have been more mindful."

"No, no, Jess. You've been a godsend. I…suppose I've never told you. I have no recollection of my *real* mother, or what one might *call* my real mother. I've always thought of Goodwife Graves as my real mother, in any event." He stares through the window. The rain's coming down hard now, and the wet wind makes a *whooshing* sound as it shoves its way forcibly down the chimney flue.

"How old were you when she and Goodman Graves took you in?" she asks.

244 | NEAL ROBERTS

He searches his memory. "I suppose I couldn't have been much older than three years, as I can barely remember the day." He looks up at Jessica, who sits down in a chair close to him.

She hands him a cup of water and encourages him to drink. "You're still parched. I can hear it in your voice. Tell me more of Goodwife Graves."

Jonathan can't help but smile at the thought. "She was a wonderful woman in her own way. No great beauty, you understand, to anyone but Graves and myself. But she had her charms."

"Do tell."

"She made a warm and inviting home for us both. She could take the mundane ingredients of a stew and fashion it into the most delicious meal. One time, she went to visit her sister out of town. She almost never traveled, so you can imagine how upsetting it was for Graves and me. I must have been no more than ten or so. Anyway, she left us the recipe for her coney stew scribbled in her rudimentary hand, and lined up all the ingredients on the table, so that we could manage on our own for a day or two. Well, that evening, Graves and I struggled to duplicate her stew precisely. We had the recipe right in front of us, for heaven's sake, so it should have been a simple matter." He covers his eyes, trying to suppress a laugh he can barely contain, lest his wound rebel.

Jessica smiles. "I take it things did not go well."

He breathes deeply before trying to speak. "Well, we put out dishes of the stew for ourselves, and sat down. Graves recited the Anglican prayer." He laughs. "I can clearly recall his look of utter dismay as he took his first bite. Then, I took a bite. It tasted like…pig's guts! We laughed ourselves silly. It was bad enough to be tossed away in good times, but that was one of those lean years when one wastes naught. So, we suffered through two full meals of it, and swore we'd never again allow Goodwife Graves to leave us for more than a few hours." He lets out a hearty laugh, despite the pain. "We decided that only some form of witchcraft could enable her to cook so much better than we'd done. From then on, if her sister wanted a visit, well, we'd just go *fetch* her sister, willy-nilly."

"It sounds like a happy home. Oh, say more of her!"

"Well, we had her for only a few more years after that. Then she was taken by the plague."

Jessica's smile drops away. "The poor thing. Good heavens! How did you and Goodman Graves manage to escape infection?"

Jonathan sighs in sad recollection. "I *didn't*. I came down with it. But Graves never did, and somehow he managed to nurse me back to health.

God knows how."

"Surely, you must have other happy tales of her," says Jessica, obviously trying to brighten his mood.

"Oh, many. Of all the things she would do, my favorite was the way she'd light the tallows every Friday night." He gazes out of the window, as though the rain somehow aids his recollection. "Every time, before she lit them, she'd tell me she'd been taught to do this by a very *special* person. Although Graves was often there with us, she'd always look at *me* when she said that word 'special,' as though this person had something to do with me, personally." He laughs softly. "In my childish mind, I imagined her as a young girl learning a magical incantation at the foot of some old gypsy, although why she'd make it part of her weekly habit, I knew not, and *still* know not." As Jessica seems rapt with the tale, he continues.

"She'd light the candles, and waft the light toward her face...three times. Always three. I know that sounds absurd, as one cannot waft light, but that seemed to be what she was doing. And doing anything *three* times, of course, reminds one of every magical folk tale. But then, the strangest effect would occur. You'll think me mad, but it seemed as though the light emanated less from the candles than from her *face*...and she would cover her eyes, and recite a half-remembered incantation in some gypsy language. Let's see. It started with something like," he strains to recall, "'baraka tada nyhellum...'" His voice trails off. "I can never recall the rest, but it was brief. I once made the mistake of asking someone what 'baraka' meant, and he said it was Spanish for 'witch,' so I never spoke of it outside the home again, lest someone arrest her and we'd be forever stuck with our terrible coney stew.

"One time when Graves and I were carting some food for a sick friend, I mentioned to him that, whenever Goodwife Graves said the prayer, it seemed as though the light was coming *through* her face, as though, in some magical way, her face had thinned out, and the light of heaven shone through. As though her countenance itself were a watermark...you know, like the one pressed into Mountjoy's maps to show their authenticity...an 'impress of heaven,' so to speak.

"Well, he stopped the cart...I remember this clearly...and he said he thought *he* was the only one who'd been mad enough to think that...*he'd* seen it, too, you see...and that we'd best never speak of it, lest he and I be taken to Bedlam Asylum." He turns to Jessica.

She's speechless, and has the most heartbreaking, beseeching look in her eyes. Tears run down her cheeks, and she brings her hands up over her face. Although Jonathan wishes to raise her spirits, on second thought, he says nothing. Still weeping, she stands, unsteady on her feet, and ambles blindly out of the room with her shoulders bowed forward, like someone who's been struck hard in the back.

While he wonders why she took the story so personally, he decides not to mention it when she returns, for fear of making her feel even worse.

⟶∘◁⧂∘⟶

AN HOUR LATER, the inn has returned to life. Through his closed door, Jonathan can hear boots clomping down the hall. Refined voices give commands that coarser ones obey. But no one having any say in the matter will be going abroad today, as the rain is coming hard and steady enough to flood the roads.

Although he's longed to rejoin the bustling world each of the past few mornings, he's just as pleased to spend this inclement day indoors in the shelter of his room, especially with Jessica here, when it's truly paradise.

Jessica re-enters sheepishly. "I'm sorry for that dramatic exit," she says, her eyes still red-rimmed. "Here I try to bring you good cheer, and instead start bawling like a schoolgirl."

He sits up. "You need never hide your tears from *me,* Jess. I'm just sorry I said something that upset you. I *would* care to know what it was, though…if only so I can avoid it in future."

She silently fusses with the fire for what seems a long time, apparently gathering her thoughts. At last, she returns to her chair by the bed. What little daylight remains in the room is now overwhelmed by the firelight that plays upon her face, warmly illuminating every curve and detail.

Her face is almost too beautiful for him to look at, and he tries without success to avoid staring. Fortunately, her eyes remain fixed on the flickering flame.

"Like you," she says, at long last, "I have no memory of my mother. I know almost nothing of her."

Jonathan's heart goes out to her. "Your father told me that she was sweet and intelligent, profoundly beautiful, and that she had a natural elegance."

"Indeed, that's what he told *me,* too," she says almost to herself. She smirks darkly. "In fact, it's nearly *all* he told me about her. And, like the child of some historical personage, I have spent my whole life trying to live up to the few reports of those who survived her. It was as though I'd been instructed: Be sweet and bright. Be beautiful. Be elegant." She looks up at him with bitterness. "Who knows if my mother really had *any* of those qualities?" She gazes listlessly into the fire.

Jonathan reaches his hand to hers, which causes a jab of pain that he refuses to show. "*I* know, Jesse," he says, stroking her hand. "She was *all* of those things."

Jessica frowns. "How could you possibly know?"

"She *must* have had all those qualities, Jesse, for she passed down every one of them to you intact. You're simply the most beautiful, intelligent, good-hearted woman I've ever come across. Obstinate and heedless as you may be concerning your own safety, I would lay down my life for you."

Her eyes wander to his wound. "Indeed, Jon. You nearly did, so you'd better mind your oaths. I'm endlessly grateful to you for it. In any event, no further proof is required of you." She looks back to the fire. "To answer your question, your fond reminiscences of Goodwife Graves brought to mind imagined memories of my own mother." She turns to him. "I was told that my mother longed for all the accouterments of nobility: security, splendor, respectability, and that she deeply regretted that these things were out of her reach, as she and my father were both Hebrews."

Jonathan nods. "Perhaps if she'd lived till now, she would have been satisfied. Your father is advisor to the Queen, after all, and his colleagues are the most powerful men in the land."

Jessica shakes her head. "He's still an outsider. I'm sure you've seen him treated thus by many."

Jonathan nods equivocally. "But I've seen him *win over* nearly as many."

"Perhaps," she replies. "But he's known as the Queen's pet. If it were not for *her* protection, who *knows* what position he would occupy? As a Hebrew, he can have no title in his own right."

"But you are *already* titled. There's no further need to fulfill your *mother's* dreams. You've already done that. Isn't it time for you to live your own life? To be true to *yourself?* If I may be so bold, can I ask why you persist in wishing to marry upwardly?"

She regards him with genuine surprise. "Why?" she parrots defensively. "Why, Jonathan? Because it's the only path available for a titled woman to advance herself! What would you have me do? Shall I take up residence at Gray's Inn, and put my name to the roll of barristers?" she asks. "To be sure, there are not many Jessicas and Janes on *that*, for a woman is *forbidden* to practice law." She puts her hand to her cheek, miming contemplation. "Perhaps I should take up one of the trades, paint a bootmaker's mark on a sign, and set it swinging over the entrance to my parlor."

Jonathan frowns. "Things are not so black-and-white any longer, Jess. Look at your stepmother, Marie. She has continued to conduct the affairs of her deceased husband, and smartly so, if I may believe what I'm told. And there are men who'd gladly marry *you,* and provide for you very comfortably—even one or two at the very Gray's Inn to which you've alluded." He hopes she'll see that his allusion to his residence is really to himself. But no luck.

"I suppose," Jessica admits wistfully. "Indeed, I was so advised by a dear, dear friend, years ago."

"Was it…Her Majesty?" asks Jonathan. Jessica's eyebrows shoot up, which makes him laugh. "You are not so opaque as you think, Jess. You obliquely referred to your conversation with the Queen as you roundly trounced the viscount's advances."

"Her Majesty *may* have suggested that I not entirely discount the prospect of marrying a man in the professions, or the merchant class."

"Well, Jess. Since the Queen of England thinks you ought to consider it, then what's the remaining source of your fascination with someone like the viscount, who does *not* truly love you?"

Her eyes flash. "And how do you *know* he doesn't truly love me, Master Hawking? For your information, he writes me. Sheets and sheets."

"Is love now purchased by the *sheet*, Lady Burlington? Tell me. When the viscount failed to obtain his parents' consent to marry you, did he not propose to make you his concubine?"

She stiffens, extends her graceful neck, and stares proudly at the fire. "That is no concern of yours."

Jonathan persists. "Didn't he say he'd go to hell to slay a demon for your sake, Jess? Why, he wouldn't even *argue with his parents* for your sake."

She stands and turns defiant. "*He* chooses his fights carefully, Jonathan." Her color's up. "He's not the type of man to get a black eye in an alehouse brawl!"

"Oh, and I *am,* I suppose?"

"Evidently," she says, patiently resuming her seat now that she's stood her ground.

"Well, for your information, my sweet, even in that, I was defending *your* honor!"

"*What?*"

"Oh, yes," he assures her. "I'd suffered through insult after insult from that fat knight, Sir Gelly. He threw piss on everything he knows me to hold dear. My dead parents, my *adoptive* parents, my membership in the bar. Yea, even my association with your father—"

"My *father!*" she says with outrage, humorously unaware of the insults she's ignored.

"Yes, and even *that* I sat through with equanimity. But when he started on *you,* I snapped."

"What did he say about me?" she demands.

"I don't know what he was *about* to say, but it would have been part of a long string of derision, I can tell you. As I recall, all he got out was 'that Serjeant's daughter,' and I let him have it." Remembering how he caught Meyrick unawares, he could not help but laugh. "I flung him through the tavern window with all my might. And when your father showed up a moment later, I could see from his face that he thought I'd killed him."

Jessica's face is a picture of delight, as she playfully punches the air before her.

He tries to change the mood. "Jesse, tell me you'll consider what I've said."

But her eyes still shift around excitedly, as she continues to imagine his fisticuffs with Meyrick. She rises absentmindedly, and kisses his forehead. "I'll go fetch us a bite." Still in a trance, she walks out, leaving him in doubt she's heard a blessed thing he said.

⇒∘⊙∘⇐

IT'S TEN DAYS since Jonathan was stabbed, and he's feeling much better, but for the occasional twinge that reminds him how seriously he was wounded. Yesterday, after a thorough examination, the surgeon pronounced him out of danger and free of infection, and said he'd be encouraged to walk a bit on his own in another day or two.

As soon as Jessica left for the local dressmaker late this morning, Jonathan began preparing for her return. Several additional chambermaids who'd arrived at the inn to work the weekend crush "oohed" and "aahed" as they bathed him thoroughly, each one remarking how nicely his frame had filled out. They even washed his hair, and combed it out neatly, dressing him in the clothes he'd been wearing during the fight, which had been thoroughly laundered, of course. Only the shirt was new, as the old one had been too badly torn and bloodstained to be salvaged. Finally, he scrubbed his own teeth with salt and mint powder.

250 | NEAL ROBERTS

Now, as the Late-November sun casts its dying rays through his window, he can hear wagon wheels approach, crunching through the fallen leaves. A glimpse outside reveals it to be Jessica's carriage, returning from the day's excursion. Though his own door is closed, he hears the inn's front door open and shut several times. Evidently, Jessica has acquired a few packages. Disappointed when she does not appear presently, Jonathan drifts off, exhausted by the formerly simple act of washing.

It's nearly full dark by the time her distinctive steps arrive outside his door, but the fire burns bright. He hears her stop in the anteroom to place something heavy down on the floor. She knocks.

"Come," he says, sitting up.

She enters smiling, wearing a new dress, simple in form, made of cloth subtly woven in autumn colors. Before even looking his way, she twirls as widely as she can in the little room. "Well?" she asks, then gasps as she catches sight of him fully dressed, lying atop the blankets. "Why, Jonathan, you look wonderful!" she says with evident delight.

He smiles broadly. "I was just about to say the same of you, Jess." He rubs his eyes. "Of course, you never don an article of clothing without exalting it quite."

"I received a letter from Father today," she says, "and stopped to read it in my room. Otherwise, I would have come here straightaway from my little trip."

"What had he to say?"

"He said that, so long as your wound has closed up satisfactorily, I ought to allow myself to be escorted to London by two of Sir Walter's lieutenants, as I'm much in demand there this time of year."

"Do you truly *wish* to go?" asks Jonathan, hoping she doesn't.

She sits on the edge of the bed, and strokes his hand comfortingly. "Would it be such an imposition upon you, my leaving? After all, you'll be only a week or two behind." She arches an eyebrow. "I was supposed to be home more than a *month* ago. And *would* have been, if it hadn't been for a wayfaring young hero who spirited me—"

"Spirited you?" he exclaims. "I could hardly be *rid* of you!"

She appeases him with a smile. "I'm jesting, of course. But, you'll have Lieutenant Carter to accompany you. And, you know, my station does bring with it certain obligations. I *am* supposed to be in town this time of year."

He shrugs. "I know nothing of social seasons, but I *was* supposed to participate in Michaelmas Term at Queen's Bench. At this rate, I'll barely make it in time for *Hilary* Term, and heaven knows what's become of my practice during my absence." He sighs. "Oh, I don't mind your going on ahead…though, now that I think of it, I suppose I shall miss you."

"And I you," she assures him, though he's far from assured. "But you shall be home for the Christmas Season, and we shall all feast upon a big fat turkey with all the trimmings. Won't that be wonderful?"

"So long as we're all there together," he admits begrudgingly.

"I, for one, certainly *shall* be there," she says, gently touching his nose with her fingertip.

He wishes he were truly certain she'd be there for him. But the viscount has recently intensified his courting-by-correspondence. "What of the viscount? Will *he* be in attendance?" he asks, hoping she'll scoff at any mention of him.

"No," she assures him. "This Christmas is reserved for my hero and savior, Jonathan Hawking!"

"Oh. Has the viscount suddenly disappeared from the scene?" he asks hopefully.

"Far from it," she says, as she rises and paces about the room. "I suppose it's no secret that Lord Essex's public revelation of Father's religion transformed me from 'belle of the ball' into something of an exotic. Oh," she laughs darkly, "men still wanted me, of course, but not in the marrying way, which is why I set myself apart from the social scene for so long. Well, it's taken some time, but the viscount has evidently persuaded his father that I am a worthy match. We shall see what happens with him." She turns to Jonathan. "But rest assured that neither he nor any man will ever interfere with my high regard for *you,* Jonathan."

That would be fine, he thinks, *if all I desired were your high regard.*

"Oh, wait," she says. "I brought a surprise for you! Close your eyes, and don't *peek.*"

He closes his eyes and hears her bring in the heavy item she put down in the anteroom. A few times, he hears her open and close what sound like little boxes. "Just another minute," she says. "Don't peek!" He hears her fussing about the fireplace, and closing his door. "You may open your eyes now!"

There she stands at the foot of the bed, beaming at him behind a small candelabra that holds three unlit candles. She's dressed just as before, but has donned a modest bonnet. The straps hang down, hiding themselves in her flowing brown hair. In her hand is a reed of tinder, its tip aglow.

"As you know," she says, "it's Friday evening, which is the beginning of the Hebrew Sabbath. You see, I believe Goodwife Graves was performing the Hebrew candle-lighting ceremony to be performed by the lady of the house. My mother performed this ritual in Father's house many times, or so I'm told."

She smiles as she lights the candles for him, and Jonathan's heart wells up with love, joy, pride, hope, loss, so many feelings he could not name them. She wafts the light to her face three times, covers her eyes, and intones the prayer in proper Hebrew, which he's never heard before. It begins: "Baruch Ata Adonay Eloheinu..." As she finishes reciting the prayer and drops her hands to her side, her face glows with that familiar unearthly fire.

Unable to restrain himself, he rises from the bed for the first time since being wounded.

"Jonathan, don't get up!" she protests.

Though his legs are unaccustomed to supporting his weight and nearly buckle under him, he forces his will upon them, and staunchly takes the few steps over to her. Pausing a mere moment to look down upon her amazed expression, he takes her in his arms, draws her against his pained chest, and kisses her squarely on the mouth with all the passion he can convey.

After a moment's hesitation, to his amazement, she reciprocates his passion utterly, surrendering herself to his embrace, succumbing to the ardency of his kiss. Placing her hands on the back of his head, she kisses his face.

"Oh, Jonathan!" she says in a quavering voice.

He draws his face away slightly, and gazes deeply into her eyes. "Jessica, I love you. I love you with more passion than I thought remained in this feeble body you've restored to me, and for which I thank you."

To his amazement, his legs begin to give out, and he leans into her involuntarily. Realizing she'll be unable to support his whole weight, he quickly turns, and staggers the few steps back to the edge of the bed, where he sits down and emits a long strangled gasp of pain. As he regains his wind, Jessica leans into him, and opens his shirt to check his wound.

"It's still red," she says, "but shows no sign of reopening."

Jonathan reaches for her, draws her face toward his, and kisses her again. This time, she surrenders instantly, and kisses him a long time. But when she draws away, she seems truly upset.

"Let's not make a *habit* of this, Jon," she says, red-faced, "for I don't know what's got into me. You make me feel so confused, I don't know *what* I should be doing." She sits on the nearby chair, her face a mixture of puzzlement and amazement. "You must forgive me for reciprocating your kiss," she says, flustered. "I'm not…quite myself."

"Ah, but there you're wrong, Jess," he says in a husky voice. "For the first time in your life, you're *becoming* quite yourself."

CHAPTER 19

FRESHLY FALLEN SNOW has whipped about Bucklebury's hooves all through this dark morning. By the time he bears Noah to the Lord Keeper's house, he's tramping through drifts that reach nearly to his knees.

Though winter is still a few days off, late autumn has turned bitter, and for none more so than Essex. Closing ceremonies for Michaelmas Term at Star Chamber were a veritable parade of the Queen's favorites, each publicly condemning the rampant libels against the Queen perpetrated by Essex's vocal supporters, who've had the temerity to demand his immediate release and reinstatement. Noah's continuing obligation to complete his investigation into Essex's military exploits provided him with the perfect excuse to skip the ceremonies altogether.

As Noah draws up to the Lord Keeper's house, he envisions the crowds that formerly gathered here during good weather to cheer Essex on in his quest for reinstatement. There's not the least sign of them now, which brings to mind all the cynical conclusions to be drawn from their absence in bad weather. The stableman accepts Bucklebury's reins and leads him off to shelter.

Noah is once again led by the Lord Keeper's footman through the labyrinth of hallways into the wing reserved for Lord Essex. A somber and humble air has entirely supplanted the proud defiance that prevailed when he last visited. The footman halts before a bedroom door, and knocks.

There's a cough inside. "Come," says Essex's hoarse voice. The footman steps in gravely, followed by Noah, who bows low. Essex sits up in his bed, propped up against the pillows.

"Thank you, Samuel," says the earl. "You may go." He turns to Noah. "To what do I owe this visit by the Queen's favorite?"

"I promised to come see you upon my return to London, lordship. Perhaps you'll recall."

At first Essex's memory seems clouded, but recognition soon registers on his face. "Yes, of course. That silly business with Meyrick and...Hawking. Correct?" Noah nods. "So much has happened since then—so many *awful* things—I barely remembered. Well," he asks, "what of it?"

"The whole matter is resolved, m'lord, and there is no need to trouble your lordship further. I thank you most humbly for your forbearance in this matter."

Essex raises an eyebrow, which accentuates the heavy black circles around his eyes. "Made amends, have they?"

Noah nods. "After a fashion, m'lord. Master Hawking prevented one of Lord Mountjoy's maps from being smuggled out of the country, after which Sir Gelly...saw fit to forgive him his trespasses."

Even in his fatigue, Essex smirks at Noah's politic description. "From what port was this map to leave England?"

"Master Hawking traced it all the way to Saint Ives, in Cornwall, m'lord."

"Where was it headed?"

Noah hesitates, wondering how much is safe to tell. "Ireland was its presumed destination, m'lord."

"Was the thief caught?"

"Aye, m'lord, and killed by Master Hawking."

"*Killed!* Who was it?"

"A Frenchman by the name of 'le Loup,'" Noah replies.

A flash of recognition passes over Essex's ashen visage. "Good for Hawking," he says with mild admiration. He regards Noah skeptically. "And Meyrick just...*forgave* him because of that?"

Noah takes a moment to decide that he can answer affirmatively without lying. "Just so, m'lord," he says reassuringly.

Essex laughs aloud, bringing on a coughing fit that takes a moment to subside. "Most *diplomatic*, Serjeant Ames." He strokes his beard contemplatively. "Serjeant," he says, "I find myself in need of good counsel."

"Medical counsel, m'lord?" asks Noah hopefully.

Essex shakes his head. "Legal. I need your help. Will you offer your services freely?"

"Lordship, I am bound by the Crown to refrain from offering my services to *anyone*," Noah replies. "Besides, I have been away from private practice for a very long time. Surely your lordship has any *number* of able barristers prepared to advise."

"But none of them knows the Queen's mind as you do," says Essex.

"Which is why Her Majesty would *never* grant me permission to—"

"She already has," says Essex, interrupting him matter-of-factly.

Could this really be happening? This case would be a *nightmare* of conscience for Noah. And could Marie ever forgive him for advising the man she believes responsible for the murder of her first husband?

"M'lord, I have not yet provided my report to Her Majesty concerning—"

"My fitness for command. Yes, I know."

"But...*how*?"

"Her Majesty told me indirectly through the Lord Keeper. Apparently, I have become an object of her pity. She sent the information to me together with a pot of broth, if you can believe it. She also informed me that she is prepared to dispense with your report, relying instead upon her customary hatchet men to gather evidence, notably Coke."

"But, even so, m'lord, I could not share with you the grievances of men who've entrusted me—"

Essex waves his hand dismissively. "I am prepared to forego any such knowledge. I *know* what they're going to say. I need to know what I should *do* about it."

Noah had spotted a cushioned chair just behind him as he entered. He turns and looks at it longingly. "May I?" he asks.

Essex laughs at his stunned reaction, and nods. "By all means. Be seated." He rings for the footman, who appears promptly. "Please pour Serjeant Ames a cup of wine."

The footman takes a flask of red wine from the desktop and pours a cup for Noah, who drinks it down in a single motion. Taking a moment to settle his thoughts, Noah hands the empty cup back to the footman, who carries it away to the kitchen.

"Feel better?" asks Essex, who seems perversely to be enjoying Noah's qualms.

"Somewhat, m'lord. Thank you. May I ask what your lordship has heard about any legal proceedings to be commenced against you?"

Essex nods. "Well, Her Majesty *had* planned to convene Star Chamber to hear the matter."

Despite the warmth provided by the wine, Noah shivers at the mention of Star Chamber. "Do I correctly detect by your lordship's choice of words that Her Majesty is equivocating about this?"

Essex gazes out of the window. "The ever-suspect Secretary Cecil has informed me that she is prepared to dispense with such a proceeding, should I plead abjectly for her to do so. She has even let on that I might be granted the liberty of mine own house, though without the privilege of visitors." He turns to Noah. "My most faithful friends advise me to avail myself of this opportunity."

Noah thinks for a moment, and nods sagely. "Your lordship's friends are quite right."

Essex seems surprised. "Why? Do you believe yourself incapable of mounting a defense on my behalf? My record is not so terrible—"

"No, no! If you were someone other than you are, I should mount quite a respectable defense. I *know* your record, m'lord. As your lordship's courage and chivalry are universally recognized, it is very unlikely they will even be placed in issue. *No,* I expect your accusers to attempt to make their case with two types of proof: first, a criticism of your lordship's military judgment in placing yourself and your men needlessly in harm's way, and, second, proof that your lordship has been insubordinate to Her Majesty's edicts. The first I could deal with roundly, as truly objective criticism of a military commander is nearly impossible, and can readily be made to smack of ignorance, envy, and insubordination. However, accusations that your lordship has been insubordinate to Her Majesty would be far more difficult to gainsay. But, I daresay a respectable defense *could* be mounted, if..." His voice trails off.

"If I were someone else," says Essex, dubiously completing the thought.

"Yes," says Noah, "your case is made much more difficult by your lordship's high estate. Star Chamber's specialty is the trial of Peers of the Crown. There are few assurances of anything approaching true justice there. The general public has no right to observe the proceedings. There is no jury. On the positive side, the Chamber lacks power to impose the punishment of death."

Essex is incredulous. "Do you mean to say that the days are past when an Englishman could be assured a fair trial?"

"There is far more justice and mercy in England's hearts than in her courts, lordship. I doubt there ever was a halcyon day when every Englishman could be assured a fair trial. It would be more accurate to say that *some* Englishmen can receive a fair trial in *some* courts *some* of the time. For example, nowadays a simple baker accused of murder will generally receive a fair trial at Queen's Bench."

"But not an earl?"

Noah considers how to emphasize his answer without offending. "The smart money would be on the *baker*, m'lord, as the court has no institutional interest in convicting him, unless he's guilty. An innocent baker is no threat to anyone, least of all the state. Ironically, it is your lordship's importance to the state, and your knowledge of the state's secrets, that render it unlikely your lordship would be tried publicly." He shrugs. "Except perhaps in a court of *irregular* session, such as Oyer and Terminer, where Lopez was initially convicted. In fact, the Queen is not even bound to use a court that's already established. She could constitute a special body for trial of your lordship."

"Can the Queen really do this?" asks Essex incredulously.

"The only limit imposed upon Her Majesty's authority in this respect is your right to be tried by other Peers of the Crown. So long as they sit on your jury, Her Majesty can pretty much assure herself of the desired result, by selecting as jurors those Peers who are most beholden to her."

Essex frowns. Evidently, this is news his other counselors have not provided him. "So you think a victory for us is far from assured?"

Noah pauses, wondering whether he's been truly understood. As the earl has doubtless consulted him based upon his reputation for outspokenness, he feels impelled to say what he truly thinks. "M'lord, I shall tell you the same thing I told Doctor Lopez. In such a court, you *cannot* win. You shall be convicted."

Essex is crestfallen. "Are you saying there is nothing I can do to change the outcome?"

"I do *not* say that, m'lord. Although you cannot change the outcome of the *trial*, you have it within your power to improve the outcome of the whole affair, as *that* will not be decided by a court. As happens so often, the real fight lies elsewhere."

"Where?"

"M'lord, yours is a fight for the affections of a woman, namely, Her Majesty Queen Elizabeth. When have a woman's affections ever been swayed by proof at trial? While I profess no expertise in women's affections—"

"Something only a fool would profess!"

"Just so, m'lord. I *have* learned a few things by courting, and being married twice. A woman is more likely to be swayed by contrition and constancy than by either military valor or lawyers' wiles. As Her Majesty feels you have disregarded her wishes, you must persuade her that you have changed."

There's a long silence, broken by Essex. "Do you think this can be done?"

Noah sighs. "M'lord, I have no *doubt* that it can be done, if you set your heart to it, but you must hereafter manifest two virtues which…if I may speak freely, m'lord?"

"Of course, of course," says Essex impatiently.

"You must manifest two virtues which have not been evident in your lordship's character. *Humility* and *patience*. Lacking either of these in abundance, I fear your lordship will never again achieve preferment commensurate with your station. You must accept in your heart both that she is *right* about this, and that it will take substantial time for you to persuade her that you have changed."

"How *much* time, do you suppose?"

"I counsel *patience*, m'lord. That means not expecting the process to occur on a schedule. And do not believe for one moment, m'lord, that the outcome of any trial will deviate one iota from what I have said. Mounting a defense against the formal charges will have precisely the *wrong* effect. Instead, you must *embrace* the trial as a forum to demonstrate your contrition and humility. Though the jurors will not vote to acquit, do not doubt they *will* report your new attitude to Her Majesty, which is all you really need them to do."

"Do you think it might take *years* to change her mind?"

Though Noah doubts that Essex has within him either the necessary humility or patience, he owes him the lawyer's duty of honesty. "I have little doubt it will, m'lord. But you are a young man yet, and closely related to Her Majesty. She *wants* to believe you have changed. My advice is to give her every reason to believe that you have."

Essex nods. "And suppose my other advisors are of the view that I should prepare to mount a vigorous defense?"

"The only harm in preparing a battle plan, m'lord, is that, come the event, one may be tempted to put it into effect against all odds." Noah leans forward for emphasis. "So much as a *feint* in that direction will set back your cause immeasurably." A stray thought occurs to him. "And, in the event there ever should be a trial, permit me to forewarn your lordship of your accusers, *especially Coke.* He will *goad* you with false or grossly exaggerated tales of your disloyalty, relying upon your lordship's reputed pride and choler to prompt you to speak intemperately, which he will then gleefully report to the Queen to perpetuate your current situation. Your lordship *can* defeat him, but only by suffering his slings and arrows with holy patience and serenity, like Job of the Bible."

Essex wipes his nose with a handkerchief. "Like Job," he parrots grimly, and turns to Noah with forced equanimity. "May I call upon you again for your advice?"

"So long as Her Majesty does not forbid it, m'lord, please call upon me as you like. I will be pleased to repeat my advice, and elaborate upon it. But I doubt it will change."

"And shall you enter your appearance on my behalf if there is to be a trial?"

Noah sighs, anticipating Marie's furious reaction. "Should Her Majesty permit, lordship, it would be my privilege to do so."

"Thank you, Serjeant Ames. You may go."

Noah bows and turns. Although he feels he's been given a fair hearing, he despairs utterly that Essex will ever be able to change his ways. He tries to fight the thought, but knows in his heart that this will all end very, very badly.

<hr>

MARIE GLOWERS AT Noah in the entryway to her home in Holborn. In one hand, she holds a single sheet of paper, together with the slit envelope in which it arrived. In her other hand is a letter opener which, Noah cannot help but observe, seems unnecessarily long and sharp.

"He *declined*?" Noah asks, being careful not to ruffle her feathers further.

"Quite," she says petulantly. "And is it any wonder, with all this talk abroad of your daughter's upcoming betrothal to the viscount? I'm not surprised Jonathan wishes to have nothing to do with her."

"He *declined*?" Noah repeats incredulously. "Is he canceling *Christmas dinner*? I mean, this betrothal business is mere rumor, is it not?"

"Christmas dinner will still be served," she assures him impatiently, "but Master Hawking will not attend." Marie puts down the blade, and shoves the letter back into its envelope, shaking her head all the while. "And how is Jonathan to know of her reservations about the viscount, if she refuses to admit them even to herself? Serjeant Ames, you are hopeless in these matters. I'm of a mind to have a long talk with Jessica myself, as you appear unwilling to do."

"Marie," he says, placing his arm around her shoulders, "I encourage you to speak with her as though she were your own daughter. You know this. But Jessica has never been known to take advice in such matters."

"Whenever she comes here, do you *see* how she mopes about all day? She dreads the very *prospect* of this betrothal. She doesn't *love* the viscount. She loves *Jonathan,* and yet she persists in this public courtship, no doubt hoping that love will arrive later, which it never does. This public farce is killing any *hope* of true love."

"I suppose it's not a farce, if she and the viscount in fact wed."

She turns on him. "No, it's not. Then it becomes *tragedy*! Oh, can't you see we must do something to help her get out of this? Or she shall regret it to the end of her days."

"Very well, Marie," he says. "But what can *we* do?"

Marie seems downcast. Then, her face brightens a little.

<hr/>

AS JESSICA'S CARRIAGE rounds the corner onto High Holborn, she glances out at Marie's house, and is surprised to spy a tall man on the steps wearing Queen's livery, holding a letter in his hand. He turns toward the sound of her approaching carriage.

The carriage draws to a halt in front of Marie's house, and Jessica steps down to the street. As the carriage clops away, to her further amazement, the man walks straight up to her and bows low.

She protests before he can open his mouth. "There must be some mistake, sir," she says. "This is not my residence. I have come merely for a brief visit."

"Good afternoon, madam," says the man. "I am Francis of the Tower Guard, and have been instructed to deliver this letter to"—he peeks at the envelope—"Jessica, Lady Burlington. That's your ladyship, is it not?"

Surprised yet again, Jessica replies. "It *is,* Francis. Is this about my father?" She adds with concern, "Is he all right?"

Francis nods. "I saw the gentleman just this morning, madam, and he looked sound to me." He hands her the envelope. It's engraved with a golden ER, which means the letter inside was written on Her Majesty's personal stationery. "I was told to advise you to open it immediately, ma'am."

Jessica glances around skeptically. "What?" she asks incredulously. "Here on the street?"

"Immediately, your ladyship. Those were Her Majesty's instructions to me."

She turns away, unseals the envelope, and draws out the letter. In an elegant feminine hand is written:

262 | NEAL ROBERTS

It would please us very much to speak with you tomorrow, four of the clock, at the Tower residence. Bring no one. *Tell no one.*

E.R.

Jessica's heart pounds, and her mind races. Why would the Queen be contacting her after all these years? And why the secrecy? She wonders whether this has something to do with Jonathan's exploits in Devon and Cornwall. Or perhaps with the viscount.

Francis, who has patiently waited until now with a bemused expression, bows again and speaks. "Would your ladyship like me to bring a reply back to…the Tower?"

Jessica is disoriented. "I…uh…haven't any writing paper here on the street, Francis."

"No, madam. But, I can remember a few words, if you'll tell them to me."

"Oh, of course. Please tell…" she swallows hard, and can scarcely believe she's about to utter her next words, "…Her Majesty that I am most grateful for the invitation, and shall be delighted to attend."

Francis smiles. "Very well, madam." He bows smartly, mounts his steed, and trots back toward London, leaving Jessica thunderstruck on the street.

Partly regaining her senses, she glances up at Marie's house. From the corner of her eye she spies some small movement at one of the curtains, but thinks no more of it. She walks up the steps. Still in a trance, she knocks and waits, wondering how she can make it through coffee without telling Marie what just happened.

CHAPTER 20

"HER MAJESTY IS already arrived," says Sir Walter, as he and Noah chafe their hands before the fire alone in the Yeoman Warder's mess. "And there was not a blessed thing I could do to dissuade her from the place for another moment. Until quite recently, this was her family's principal residence. It's been so since the Norman Conquest. I suppose she feels safe here."

As Raleigh lights another bowlful of the pipe weed he keeps in a small leather pouch on his person, Noah escapes the worst of the smoke by stepping over to the window and gazing out onto the wintry Tower grounds. There across the yard, behind a double-gated portcullis, stands the main gate through which he and Uncle Avram passed to make their most important grocery delivery many years before.

"It seems not to trouble Her Majesty," says Noah, "that we have still not eliminated the possibility that the killer had a confederate who remains at the Tower to this day." For all their success in solving the case of the purloined map, they're no closer to discovering how the killer got into the Tower to murder Lieutenant Trenowden and then left the Tower, all while avoiding detection. As he gazes outside, he cannot help but remark to himself how little has changed here over the course of his life. He asks wistfully: "Are groceries for the royal residence still delivered by a little oxcart?"

"They are," replies Raleigh.

"How often?"

"Well, I expect there's a schedule at the guardhouse, but I can't tell without seeing it. Wait! As I recall, today being Wednesday and as it's nearly three o'clock, there should be one coming through presently." Noah wonders vaguely why Raleigh would know nothing about deliveries, except those made on Wednesdays.

264 | NEAL ROBERTS

"If you ask me," says Sir Walter, blowing smoke rings that hover a surprisingly long time in the stillness of the mess hall, "the killer had a confederate on the grounds."

Noah shakes his head. "Now you sound like Lord Mountjoy. Perhaps we should re-arrest poor Francis." A smoke ring rolls past his face, and dissipates into a pungent gray cloud. "It just seems unlikely to me, but if it's true, he could still be here, in which case *we* would be to blame if Her Majesty were to be harmed in any way." He coughs, and waves the smoke away from his face. "Good heavens, Sir Walter! That is a *disgusting* habit, and should not be allowed indoors. Didn't you say Her Majesty *declined* your request to have pipe weed delivered by the grocer?"

Sir Raleigh takes a heavy draw from the tip of the long stem. "Indeed, she did!" he says, smiling. "And she has prohibited its use indoors...everywhere but here in the Yeoman Warder's mess hall." He winks. "She never comes in here, you see."

"Lucky me," says Noah, his eyes burning from the haze. "Well, if you can't get it delivered by the grocer, where do you get it?"

Sir Walter's smile drops away just long enough for Noah to realize he's about to evade the question, probably with a fib. "Oh, here and there," he says. "Out and about."

Noah raises a skeptical eyebrow. "Hither and yon?"

"Well, *yes,*" says Sir Walter, clamping the stem between his teeth. "All *about* London, y'know."

The door opens, and a cold breeze enters that blows Sir Walter's smoke rings apart. Francis enters, shivers, and walks over to the fire, removing his gloves and rubbing his hands. He turns to Noah. "Getting bitter out there. Incidentally, Serjeant Ames, your Master Hawking is expected any minute now."

"Good," says Noah. He's very much looking forward to seeing his young colleague again. Jonathan was sorely missed at Christmas dinner, which was unspeakably solemn in his absence.

Raleigh finishes his latest bowl of weed and extinguishes the few remaining embers using the head of a small nail. He empties the pipe onto the floor near the fireplace by tapping it on his boot, and sweeps the charred weed into the fire using the little fireside broom.

"So, then how did le Loup gain entry to the Tower?" muses Noah, staring through the window at the portcullis across the yard.

"Confederate," Raleigh intones wearily, as though the matter has been effectively decided, and the others are a bit too slow-witted to draw the inevitable conclusion.

Raleigh's smugness on this simple point begins to chafe at Noah, and he's reminded that Raleigh failed to inform him that Mountjoy's map, rather than being stolen and bound for England's enemies, was in fact dispatched by Mountjoy himself to the King of Scotland, Her Majesty's likeliest heir. Surely Raleigh was *ordered* to withhold the information from Noah, but still it rankles that his failure to provide it wound up exposing Jessica and Jonathan to unnecessary mortal hazard. "*No,* a confederate inside the Tower is not how he got in...or out." In the distance, the inner gate opens, and a grocer's oxcart slowly emerges.

"Then, how?" asks Sir Walter, stuffing the bowl of his pipe with weed.

Jonathan Hawking enters wearing a heavy black cloak.

"Jonathan," says Noah warmly. "So good to see you!"

"And you, sir," Jonathan says cheerily. He nods to the two Warders, who reciprocate. "Sir Walter. Francis."

Noah dons his cloak. "You're just in time. Keep your cloak on. Everyone else, put on a warm cloak and follow me." Without waiting another moment, he flings open the door, and a cold gust blows in.

"But I just got here!" complains Jonathan.

"Never mind that," replies Noah jauntily. "I'll make it worth your while."

As Sir Walter, Jonathan, and Francis trail behind, Noah strides across the yard toward the front gate, where the grocer's oxcart makes its way slowly from the inner gate of the portcullis. Its driver is a mature man of slight build. Perched on the seat next to him sits a boy of perhaps eleven years.

Jonathan catches up to Noah. "Noah, I wish to tell you why I've come to the Tower today."

"Your news will have to keep just a few minutes more, Jon. Let's see if we can't get the grocer's attention." He waves broadly as he walks, and the others join in. For a moment, the grocer appears not to see them at all. When he spots them at last, he seems unsure whom they're waving to, and looks behind to see who else is there. When he sees no one behind him, he returns their waves, and steers the oxcart toward them.

As Noah approaches the cart, he smiles. "Good Lord!" he mutters. "That could be the very oxcart that belonged to Uncle Avram."

"Wouldn't that make it *extremely old*?" suggests Jonathan, tongue in cheek.

Noah glances at him sidelong. "Best secure that rattle, Master Hawking," retorting with a jest that both exaggerates Jonathan's youth and tells him to hush. He signals the cart to halt, and walks up to it. While it does indeed closely resemble the cart formerly used by Uncle Avram, it differs in one or two features. He walks up to the grocer's young assistant, who regards him sheepishly.

"Hail, young grocer's boy!" Noah says loudly, in good humor. "I was once a grocer's boy, as you are now!"

The boy glances sheepishly at the grocer sitting beside him and says nothing, but smiles in return.

"There's a good lad," says Noah. "Tell me, my young lad, where is Sir Walter's tobacco?"

"Noah!" exclaims Sir Walter.

"Beggin' yer pardon, suh," says the grocer to Noah, "but I'd appreciate your puttin' any questions to me, 'stead o' the boy."

"Very well," replies Noah cheerfully. "Where is Sir Walter's tobacco?"

The grocer rubs his nose with the back of his hand. "Don't rightly know what you mean, sir."

"*Don't* you?"

The grocer glances at Sir Walter and offers no reply.

"Come here, Goodman Grocer," says Noah. The grocer steps down and follows him, glancing apprehensively back at his cart. "Don't worry, sir. No one but you shall touch your wares." As Noah leads him for a short stroll, Raleigh, Hawking, and Francis follow close behind. "Look here, good fellow. Look at my face. Do I appear to be a fellow who would seek to punish you on grounds that you smuggled into the Tower something so trivial as Sir Walter's pipe weed?"

The grocer regards him skeptically. "Well, no, sir," he admits. "But this is the Tower o' London," he gulps, "where anything can happen."

Noah tries to put himself in the grocer's place, and glances about the yard and up at the prison cells. Truly, he hasn't seen the Tower through such eyes as these for a very long time. It is indeed a place of great risk. Only in rare cases is there a corresponding prospect of great reward. He decides to cut short his jest.

"Yes, I see. Anything *can* happen here. I'll tell you what. You dig out Sir Walter's tobacco, and he'll pay you *twice* what it's worth. What do you say to that?"

The grocer's eyes light up. "Twice, sir? Why, it would be my pleasure!" He glances back at his cart, which is very publicly exposed in the bright winter afternoon. "Right here, sir?"

Noah looks from the cart to the windows of the royal residence. "Oh, I think you'll be fine, so long as you're quick about it."

The grocer has a word with his boy, and together they unload every crate from the cart, placing it carefully on the ground. At last, the cart's empty.

No tobacco.

Noah beckons the other three to the side of the cart, so they can watch what happens next. The grocer places a sharp blade between two slats of the cart bed, and pries off a sizeable hatch that conceals a compartment containing a few articles of contraband, including Sir Walter's tobacco.

"Pay the man," Noah says to Sir Walter.

"Long way to go for a jest!" Sir Walter grumbles. "Doubled the price of my weed, too." He digs into his pocket, counts out the proper coins, and glares at Noah as he *doubles* them and hands them to the grocer, accepting the pipe weed in exchange.

The grocer and his boy are about to close the hatch and begin reloading, when Noah raises his hand. "Stop! Sir Walter, please examine that compartment, and tell me if it's large enough...to hold a Frenchman."

The grocer's eyes go wide. "I don't know nothin' 'bout no Frenchman, suh!"

"Silence!" says Noah sternly, as he waits for Sir Walter to climb into the cart, look about the compartment, and clamber back down.

Sir Walter regards Noah seriously, and nods. "Damned if it isn't."

The grocer can hold his tongue no longer. "I got no idea what you're talkin' about! On me mother's soul, suh!" He's near tears.

Noah takes Sir Walter and Jonathan aside. "I remember such a compartment from the single time I saw my uncle pack it with articles I didn't recognize. This man is likely telling the truth. There must be at least four or five other vendors admitted to the Tower every week. I'll warrant every *one* of them has a compartment such as this, and fills it with contraband." He sighs. "Well, one of them filled it with a homicidal Frenchman. My guess is...*that* one's *dead*." He turns to Sir Walter. "Has any of them stopped coming since Trenowden's murder?"

Sir Walter ponders a moment. His eyes widen, and he nods. "One only."

"Find his corpse and examine his cart." He taps Sir Walter's chest with his finger. "I told you. *No confederate!* You may as well let this man go about his business. The Queen's in no danger. In future, you'd best require the carts to be completely unloaded and searched before passing through the second gate of the portcullis. That's what the tunnel's for, isn't it? Now, let's go have some ale." He muses, "The more I think of it, the greater the public service appears to have been performed by our Master Hawking here."

Jonathan makes a sweeping bow.

Sir Walter reassures the grocer that he's in no trouble of any kind, and sends him on his way.

"Now," says Noah, placing his arm about Jonathan's shoulders, "you have news?"

Francis interrupts, taking Jonathan by the crook of his arm. "Sorry, Serjeant, but Master Hawking's been summoned to the royal residence. He must accompany me right away."

Noah's eyebrows shoot up. "Very well, then," he says. "Best of good fortune to you, my young friend."

⊰•◦⫷⁂⫸◦•⊱

AS JESSICA'S CARRIAGE enters the Tower stables, she sees Francis guiding her driver toward a small door cut into a stone wall. She steps down.

"Follow me, madam," says Francis, and sweeps her through the little door and up a flight of stairs so narrow they're compelled to walk single file. To Jessica this hardly seems a proper way to escort an invited guest into the royal residence of the Tower of London.

Francis tramps up the stairs in front of her. "It's a back door few people know about, madam," he says. "Been here for centuries, used mostly by knights and other horsemen. Rumor has it our blessed King Henry the Eighth used it often in his wild youth. When we're a bit nervous about Her Majesty's safety, we sometimes ask even *her* to use it." He opens a door onto a beautiful well-lit hallway, and invites her through it. "When we *do*," he whispers, "she always looks as unhappy about it as you do right now." He assists Jessica in removing her cloak. "Madam, please come this way down the hall."

As they pass several closed doors to their left, Jessica notices that the many windows to her right look down onto the Tower yard. Francis stops before a beautiful wooden door.

Jessica turns to look at something curious in the yard. As the glass is wavy, her view is distorted. But there appears to be a group of four men jesting with a man driving an oxcart. There's a boy seated next to the driver. As three of the men on foot have their backs to her, she's unable to see their faces. But the one facing her looks familiar. "Is that...Father?"

she asks.

The door behind her opens noiselessly.

"Your father's duties at the Tower are many and varied," says an older woman's voice. "But they do not include the inspection of grocer's carts."

Jessica gasps, turns, and curtsies low, averting her gaze to the floor. "Pardon me, Your Majesty. Since receiving this invitation, I have been concerned for Father's welfare." The Queen reaches down and lifts Jessica's face by the chin.

Looking back at Jessica is the famous face she has seen only once, years before. The Queen's hair is still red, her skin still pale and clear, but she now smiles with her mouth firmly closed. Jessica recalls Father telling her that the Queen has become embarrassed by the poor condition of her teeth. Her eyes, formerly bright and clear, have fogged visibly, and her brow is now more wrinkled, affording her a dignified, but careworn appearance. But still, there's something undeniably warm and feminine about her.

The Queen has been observing Jessica's face just as closely. "Charming," she observes. "Dear, you have become lovelier with the years, a rare gift of the gods. But do not take it for granted for, like every other gift the gods afford to womankind, it will abandon you at a time of its own choosing, for some other sweet young thing who can make better use of it in *her* time."

"Madam?" says Francis softly. She nods and waves him away. His boots clop away down the hall.

"Come in, dear," says the Queen, drawing Jessica up to full height, and leading her into the small, beautifully appointed room. "I have had coffee brought up."

Jessica glances about the room. There's no one else there but a pair of the Queen's female attendants, who quickly and quietly scurry out, leaving her alone with the Queen of England. The moment Jessica realizes this will be a private audience, a thrill shoots up her spine, and she momentarily stands on tiptoe as she was wont to do as a child. She's relieved to see that the Queen was turned away for that brief moment.

"Sit," says the Queen, assuming a gilded chair on which the Tudor crest had been colorfully woven into the upholstery. Jessica insinuates herself into the sumptuously upholstered chair across from her. "Lady Somerset recently came to see me. As she is inordinately proud of her son—heaven knows why—she told me that the viscount was expecting a lovely young lady to accept his proposal of marriage. When I asked for the name of the young lady, I was dismayed to hear it was *you,* my dear."

270 | NEAL ROBERTS

A maidservant appears, and hands the Queen and Jessica each a cup of coffee on a saucer. "Sugar, Lady Burlington?" asks the Queen.

"No, madam. Thank you very much."

Another maidservant appears with numerous fresh pastries on a silver tray. The Queen takes two: a creamy one, and another covered in baker's sugar. She nods for Jessica to partake. Jessica chooses a small plain shortbread, which has always been her favorite.

The Queen mutters enviously. "And now we see how to keep one's waist as thin as a wasp's."

Jessica smiles and nods. "Thank you, madam." She responds to the Queen's earlier remark. "While Lady Somerset has been most kind and hospitable to me, I do not know why she would assume that I shall accept her son's proposal of marriage, as I have given him no such assurance."

"Well," asks the Queen, "how long have you been seeing each other?"

"I first met him when I visited the earl's manor in Wells. That would be perhaps three months ago. That visit did not end particularly well between the viscount and myself."

The Queen purses her lips indignantly. "So I have heard...in *disgusting* detail, albeit not from her ladyship. And, since your return from your patriotic adventure with Master Hawking, for how long have you been seeing the viscount socially?"

"Since my return? I suppose I've seen him for perhaps...two months."

The Queen raises an eyebrow. "And you wonder why her ladyship would expect you to be soon wedded to her son?"

"I have been forthright with the viscount, madam. I hope that I have not transgressed. I remember, however, that Your Majesty once advised me it might be a good idea to marry outside the nobility."

The Queen cocks her head. "That is a peculiarly slanted reminiscence of our earlier encounter, dear, and I see that perhaps you missed my principal point."

Jessica courteously protests. "I have forgotten *nothing* of our conversation, madam, which I shall ever hold dear to my heart."

The Queen smirks. "Then, perhaps you would be so kind as to refresh *my* recollection of how I advised you at that time."

"Your Majesty advised me, first and foremost, to marry for true love *only*. And, that I should not restrict my suitors to noblemen, as there are many 'rotten apples' in the nobility, and many men of good character and secure means in the professions and in trade."

The Queen nods. "It's good to see you have inherited your father's long and precise memory for words. But, tell me, are you hesitant to marry with the viscount merely because I advised you not to restrict your courtship to the nobility?"

Jessica shifts, and tries with little success to hide her discomfort. "No, madam."

"Indeed, that is good to know. Can you tell me why you would see the viscount even *once* more, after he made his ignoble proposition to you?"

Jessica shrugs. "He is a man, madam. I have been told that *all* men want what they want, and one must therefore draw distinctions between them on other grounds."

"Well, as the daughter of Henry the Eighth and Anne Boleyn, I am in a poor position to gainsay your notion that men want what they want. I will tell you something I have learned, however; that, even in *this,* men are not alike. There are men, such are your father, who behave very kindly toward women, and respect them with all their hearts. Are there not?"

Jessica sighs. "I have begun to despair of finding a man such as my father who, for most of my youth, pined for my lost mother, and had little use for women otherwise."

"Until at last he found another worthy woman, to whom he remains unquestionably devoted," adds the Queen, who then looks indignant. "I must say that I was *appalled* to hear that you entertained the viscount's overtures for even a moment after his indecent proposal." She pauses in thought. "Well, if your hesitation to marry him arises not from a faulty interpretation of my earlier advice, then what *is* the source of your hesitation?"

Jessica can feel her face redden. As she carefully places her cup and saucer down on the table, she's dismayed to see that her hand is shaking. She turns to the Queen, and tries to steel herself against the wave of emotion that threatens to engulf her. *Oh, God! Don't weep now. Not in the Queen's presence.* Her feelings are nearly contained, but when she sees the Queen's face set in the most sympathetic expression imaginable, she begins weeping, and continues doing so until her breath comes in great sobs. She takes a handkerchief from her sleeve and blows her nose. As she collects herself at last, she wipes her eyes and glances up at the Queen, who has also returned her cup and saucer to the table and now peers at the floor with a sad, faraway look, as though remembering similar feelings from her own youth.

"Please forgive my outburst, Your Majesty." Jessica breathes deeply several times before continuing. "I have hesitated to be wed to the viscount because...I love *another.*" There, she's said it, and feels much better for it.

"Oh?" says the Queen, tilting her head curiously. "Whom do you love?"

"That same Jon Hawking whom Your Majesty mentioned earlier."

"Oh," she says with concern. "I do hope he did not take advantage of you while you were alone in the woods together."

"No, no, no, madam," protests Jessica. "He was a gentleman to me, always. He guarded me at night from those who might do me harm. He placed my welfare ahead of his own at all times. And he was companionable and loving to me without fail. In fact, he was badly hurt while saving me from death, or worse, and, as I nursed him back to health, he even taught me a thing or two about myself that I could never have realized alone."

"And you left his side to rejoin courtly society?" The Queen regards her skeptically. "And *the viscount*?"

Jessica can merely nod, feeling foolish and ungrateful.

"Well," resumes the Queen, "now that you've learned that men are *not* all alike where women are concerned, I shall tell you that the way a man treats his woman is the most reliable bellwether of *her* future happiness, as well as his. In any event, your young barrister Hawking is not the *only* marriageable man of virtue. As you now acknowledge that I did not advise you to disregard *all* noblemen, there is a young baron I would like you to meet. He is here at the Tower." The Queen smiles.

"Oh, but madam, I could not," says Jessica. "Now that Your Majesty has lifted the veil from my eyes, I realize that Master Hawking is the only man I truly love. I should not wish to lead anyone to believe that I shall consider another."

"Has Master Hawking proposed to you by way of marriage?"

Jessica is horrified to realize that he has not, and berates herself silently for keeping him at such a distance that he'd feel it hopeless to do so.

"I see from your face, Lady Jessica, that he has not done so. We must always pay heed to the possibility that he may *never* do so. In any event, I don't suppose there could be any harm in simply *meeting* a young nobleman. Could there?" Jessica's expression must be pathetic indeed, as the Queen nearly laughs aloud. "Look here, Lady Jessica. I may lack the power to tell you whom to marry, but I have all the authority I need to tell you whom you may *not* marry. Though I am loath to exercise such authority, if you decline to meet this young baron, who, I must tell you has a very good carriage, a strong leg, a nice cheek, then I may be inclined to stand in your way of marrying Master Hawking, should he someday propose marriage to you."

Jessica stifles her horror. "Surely, Your Majesty would never—"

"Never is a long time, m'lady. And princes have long memories." The Queen's momentary sternness soon gives way to her former kindly demeanor. "Will you not make this trifling effort for your Queen?"

Jessica relents. "As Your Majesty advises. But I doubt the beauty of any man could draw my eye from the image of Master Hawking that is forever engraved upon my heart."

"Spoken like a worthy subject, and a virtuous woman." The Queen rises from her seat and Warder Francis appears, as if by magic. "Francis, please escort Lady Burlington to the library." She turns to Jessica. "If I do not see you again before you leave the residence, my dear, allow me to take this opportunity to wish you the best of good fortune. I look forward to hearing from you whenever you can spare time to write."

"Thank you, Majesty," says Jessica, curtseying low. "I shall always have time to write Your Majesty. Indeed, I shall need to take care not to burden my letters with trivialities."

The Queen smiles, and nods to Francis.

Francis leads Jessica down the hall to the open door of the library, which contains a magnificent assemblage of books, such as she has never seen. The bookshelves are comprised of several levels, some so high off the floor that a foot stool has been left in each corner to enable a browser to reach any book without hazard.

On the other side of the room, a man stands on one of the stools, reaching for a book. From the back, he appears to be dressed very solemnly, wearing a handsome dark-colored doublet with an unfamiliar coat of arms.

Francis clears his throat, so as not to alarm the gentleman by a sudden announcement of Jessica's entry. "Baron Saint Ives, permit me to introduce Lady Burlington." He bows and disappears down the hall.

As the baron turns about with a book in his hand, Jessica's stunned to see it's Jonathan Hawking! He seems as surprised to see her as she is to see him.

"Why—why—" he stammers, putting the book down. "Jess—Lady Burlington. I did not expect to see *you* here."

"N—Nor I you...Baron. Permit me to congratulate you upon your creation as a baron."

He regards her apprehensively. "Have you come to seek Her Majesty's consent to your marriage to the viscount?"

"No, Jonathan...Baron," she says, struggling to find her footing in this most awkward conversation. "I have no intention of marrying the viscount."

"Indeed," he says. A momentary gleam of hope gives way to sadness. "Someone else, then?"

She grows indignant. "You seem in a rush to marry me off, your lordship. Do you think me the type of flighty woman whose affections can change so rapidly?"

Jonathan shakes his head sadly. "Alas, Lady Burlington, I no longer trust my judgment where your affections are concerned." He smiles at her wanly. "I thought at one time that I knew them well. But you surprised me."

"What is it that you thought you knew concerning my affections?"

He sighs. "I once foolishly thought you loved me."

"And when was that?" she asks.

"When you lovingly tended my wounds, in Saint Ives."

"And now you're quite certain you were wrong?"

He regards her with confusion. "I'm quite certain I don't know *what* to think. If you *did* love me then, you chose a strange way of showing it, running off to London to rejoin the viscount, whom I'd heard you swear would never again gain admittance to the town, let alone to your company."

"And did you love *me* at that time?" she asks, girding herself for the worst.

He draws himself up proudly, as though to make the most tragic confession. "Madam, as I told you then, I did love you. I loved you *before* then. And it hurts me to the quick to admit that I am doomed to love you *always*." He smiles bitterly, and awaits her reply.

"And yet you never proposed marriage."

His eyes flash. "You had never given me the least inkling that you would be favorably disposed toward such a proposal. To the contrary, you led me to believe that, notwithstanding Her Majesty's advice, you would never marry outside the nobility. And I was most assuredly not a nobleman."

She regards him wistfully. "And now you *are*," she says. "And now you would *not* propose marriage to me, as you believe I deemed you unworthy while you were just yourself, and not a nobleman." She turns away from him. "And who could blame you? You would think yourself a fool to seek my hand now. For, why should you take the risk that I would reject you? And why would you *want* someone whose affections are so conditional as mine appear to have been?" She turns to him with tears in her eyes. "Jon, I've been such a fool…and so unspeakably cruel to you. Could you ever forgive me? I feel as though I've been living someone else's dream, and have awakened only now, to find I've left it too late."

Jonathan draws himself up manfully, steps around the side of the little table, drops to his knees, and places his hands together imploringly. Jessica's heart nearly leaps out of her chest.

"Lady Burlington," he says solemnly, "would you do me the eternal honor of becoming my wife?"

Tears run down Jessica's cheeks. She puts her hand to her mouth, slowly withdraws it, and speaks in a shaky voice. "Baron, I accept your proposal with all my heart."

They hold each other so tightly they can barely kiss. But they manage to, and for a long time.

⇒∘☾⋙∘∘⇐

NOAH AND MARIE dine at home by themselves in the evening. At a lull in the conversation, Noah broaches a sore topic.

"Marie," he says, "what I'm about to tell you must remain between us. If it's repeated, it could cost me my position and leave us both in disgrace."

Marie perks up expectantly. "I'm duly forewarned, Serjeant Ames."

"Lord Essex has decided to refrain from defending himself against the charges of insubordination leveled against him."

"Oh?" she says, a bit suspiciously.

Try though he might, he cannot look her in the eye. "Yes. He has been persuaded by…friends…that things will go much better for him if he appeals rather to Her Majesty's mercy."

Marie nods dispassionately. "And will it?" she asks.

"It may."

She raises an eyebrow. "And are you one his lordship's 'friends' who has so advised him?"

"He asked me if his friends were correct in their advice. I told him they were." He turns to her. "But he is well aware that I am *not* his friend, Marie."

"Why inform me of this now?" she inquires. "No doubt it will be all the talk, the day after his trial."

He refolds his napkin on his lap. "The Queen has asked me," he says, "to enter my formal appearance on behalf of Lord Essex at his upcoming trial." He awaits an explosion.

To his great relief, Marie remains composed. "Tell me," she says, "if he were to change his mind at the last moment, would you actively defend him?"

"No." He shakes his head emphatically. "In that unlikely event, I have arranged for Arthur Arden to handle all witnesses and make all arguments on Lord Essex's behalf. I've informed both Essex and Her Majesty that I would be too deeply conflicted to do so, and would defer in all respects to Master Arden."

She seems surprised. "And they were in accord with that?"

He sighs. "I didn't leave it up to them. I let each of them know that this a matter of personal conscience with me, and that I would simply refuse to defend him, though I be led away in shackles."

She furrows her brow. "Do you think it might come to that?"

He shakes his head. "No. I've earned at least that much respect at court."

"Then, why do they wish you to enter an appearance on his behalf?" she asks.

He shrugs and looks her in the eye, at last. "I have asked myself the same question a hundred times, Marie. I can only conjecture that my appearance on his behalf at the Queen's request is regarded by both of them as a token of her continuing regard for him."

"Do you think it will help return him to Her Majesty's good graces?"

He considers this through a long draught of wine. "If Essex were not himself, such a token of hope might help him to mend his ways. As he *is* himself, however, I think he simply *cannot* comport himself in a manner that might result in his return to her good graces." He regards her gravely. "I expect he shall doom himself."

"Very well," she says, and stands to clear away the dishes.

To her surprise, Noah rises, embraces her, and gazes admiringly into her soft brown eyes. "I cannot tell you, Marie, how exalted I am by your infinite trust. I want you to know that I shall never let you down. Never."

They kiss ardently, content with each other in a way they never expected.

———————————⊷∘⟨⟩∘⊶———————————

WHEN THE JUDGES of Star Chamber convene court on the opening day of Hilary Term, they expect the Earl of Essex to appear for trial. Instead, in the privacy of their chambers, an emissary of the Queen reads aloud a letter from Her Majesty. In light of the earl's newfound contrition, she has dispensed with the need for his prosecution in their court. As she gives no indication that the earl will be released (and as each new day brings public demonstrations demanding just that), the judges are left wondering which court will be selected for the earl's prosecution.

It's not until early June that an extraordinary court of inquiry convenes for the earl's trial in the house of the Lord Keeper of the Great Seal, the resplendent site of the earl's earlier confinement.

Noah and his long-time associate Arthur Arden assume the seats reserved for them in the front row. They are both surprised to see a large number of merchants sitting side-by-side with high nobility, for the room is too small to accommodate the customary space between the two classes.

Noah is about to turn to admonish an old woman and her husband for their bigoted remarks, when he rises instead to answer the Secretary of State's call for a formal appearance by Essex's counsel.

"Serjeant Noah Ames, for the prisoner," he says, his clear voice ringing through the chamber.

A murmur arises from the spectators behind him, followed by howls of protest against the "Jew lawyer." Evidently, the spectators have been given no foreknowledge that the barrister who'll be defending the earl is the very man most commonly believed to *despise* him. Amidst the tumult, Noah silently recites a Hebrew prayer asking God's forgiveness, though almost nothing will be required of him in the day's proceedings.

"Very well," says the diminutive Secretary of State, Robert Cecil. "The prosecution may open."

That simple opening is followed by a cascade of prolix accusations by the most renowned barristers in the land, each excoriating the earl for his unforgivable ingratitude and his willful disobedience to the Queen's commands. Throughout, Essex kneels with his head down, silently enduring the scorn heaped upon him, which works well until Coke closes by characterizing the earl's "willful and malicious contempts" as "disloyalty."

Despite Noah's warning to Essex that Coke would inflate the charges to include disloyalty, and despite his advice to avoid snapping at the bait, the earl rises in protest.

"M'lords," says Essex. "I have prayed on the accusations which have been so eloquently made against me, and believe they have sufficient merit to require my admission of their essential truth. I shall therefore say not a word to justify my actions, which, with the guidance and persuasion of good friends and counselors, I hereby acknowledge to have been taken in grave error. I do protest, however, the insinuation that my actions betokened any *disloyalty.*" He sneers at Coke. "And now that my *honor* and *loyalty* have been called into question, I have no choice but to justify myself an honest man!" He raises his right hand, and pats his chest with his left. "This hand shall pull out this heart, should any disloyal thought ever enter into it." He resumes his posture of pious humility. "All other matters, I freely admit, and, with submissiveness, I beseech the mercy of Her Most Sacred Majesty."

In light of the earl's admission in open court of the truth of the charges, no witnesses are called by either side. Rather, after a few lords rise to attest to the earl's loyalty, the lords unanimously dismiss Coke's rash charge of disloyalty, but convict Essex on all other counts. The Lord Keeper sentences him "to forbear doing anything as a Privy Councillor, Earl Marshal, or Master of Ordnance, and to return to the place whence he came, under such restraint as before, until Her Majesty's pleasure should be further known."

Noah and Arthur follow as Essex is escorted by two guards down a long hallway to a small chamber, where Essex and one of the guards enter and shut the door behind. The remaining guard holds up a restraining hand to Noah and Arthur.

A moment later, the guard emerges from the chamber, and addresses Noah. "His lordship will admit only Serjeant Ames, with no assistants." He turns to Arthur. "Sorry, sir. You'll have to wait out here." Arthur nods and takes a seat on a bench across the hall.

Taking a deep breath, Noah proceeds into the chamber, and shuts the door behind him, each guard taking up a post outside.

The earl sits alone on a simple bench, the only item of furniture in the small room, and glowers at Noah.

"I do not know why I took your advice," he says with undisguised contempt, "nor that of my other 'good counselors.'"

"This unfortunate occasion is merely the first step on the path to your lordship's restoration," says Noah as encouragingly as possible.

Essex appears not to hear. "I've never asked you, Serjeant, whether you would have advised Her Majesty to do anything differently than she has done."

"Lordship, Her Majesty has never asked my advice on the subject. So, I have never come to a hard and fast view."

"Please," says Essex caustically, "do not insult my intelligence, but rather *answer my question!*" His face reddens.

"In broad strokes, m'lord, I would not have advised Her Majesty to do otherwise, except that I would have advised against putting your lordship though the public humiliation you have just endured."

"*You think me unfit for command?*" Essex demands, amazed.

"At the time of your arrest, lordship, you *were* unfit for command, and I would have said as much to Her Majesty, if I had been asked. I would have advised her to wait to see whether time and experience might tame your lordship's youthful exuberance."

"Youthful—!" Essex seethes with anger. "Look at you, you simpering Jew, toadying up to whoever tosses you the few crumbs you're allotted, parading about in the somber robes of an English barrister, hiding behind the Queen's livery that, for some reason known only to God and Her Majesty, you are authorized to wear." He raises his voice and cries out. "Oh, why did I *listen* to you, and choose to remain in this servile position for an indefinite term?"

Noah was prepared for Essex's bigoted onslaught, but still it's hard to bear. "I see that I have displeased your lordship. May I be dismissed?"

"No!" Essex spits out. "I'm not through with you."

Noah sighs. "We have no choice, you and I, but to remain subjects and therefore 'servile' all our lives, if you would so call it."

Essex seethes. "*You* must remain so," he says, excluding himself.

"As must *you,* m'lord, though you need obey only *one* mistress, where I must obey *many* mistresses *and* masters. Our sentence of servility ends only with our earthly lives." He shrugs. "Still, it is better to serve in heaven than rule in hell."

Essex grumbles. "*Do* we serve in heaven?" He laughs bitterly, looking about the room. "And here I thought this was *England.* Perhaps it *seems* like heaven to a heathen such as yourself, as it's no doubt vastly better than the scalding hell you're bound for." He turns to the wall, chafing under his humiliation. "Well, England is hell to me. And it would be a damn sight better for me to *rule* in hell than *serve* in hell." He turns to Noah and mutters. "Perhaps it's time the bitch shoved over."

Though Essex's remark is treasonous, Noah does not wish to force the matter while the earl is so obviously overcome. "Your lordship is incensed," he says graciously, "and knows not what he does."

"I know *precisely* what I do…*toady.*"

Noah turns an insolent eye to him. "I can hardly believe that, lordship, as you know not what you *say.*"

The earl rises and approaches Noah like a lion about to pounce, until there's not a hand's width between them, his face fixed hard in defiance and contempt. "I know *precisely* what I say," he says.

Noah leans into him, closing the narrow gap between their faces even further, his face as hardened as the earl's, speaking slowly, barely above a whisper. "If you ever say anything like that in my presence again, so help me God, earl or no, I shall see you carted off to Tyburn, though *I* be in the next cart." He turns to go without awaiting dismissal. At the door, he turns back to Essex, who looks as though he's been unexpectedly slapped in the face. "And I am not incensed, and I know what I say, as well."

As Noah emerges from the chamber and slams the door behind him, Arthur approaches, wide-eyed at his sudden and angry appearance.

"You have not been dismissed!" comes Essex's furious voice through the door, and then it cries out much louder. "*I'll see you in hell!*"

Aghast, Arthur goggles at Noah, who shakes his head, and mutters as though Essex were there to hear. "If *you're* there, then I'll know it is *indeed* hell."

It strikes him as the epitome of irony that the prosecution's accusations of disloyalty, so often lodged without grounds, have been erroneously dismissed in this case because of his own strategy. He wonders whether he's sacrificed the credibility he will sorely need to persuade the Queen to protect herself against Essex, who is far and away her most dangerous and disloyal subject.

He turns on his heel and storms away, robes flying, with Arthur following nervously behind.

ACKNOWLEDGMENTS

First and foremost, to my good friend and correspondent Brenda James, who alone deciphered the code in the dedication to Shakespeare's sonnets and who, together with William Rubinstein, began the long and arduous—but fascinating—task of introducing the true bard to the world.

To the several members of the Long Island Romance Writers who helped to instruct me in what women regard as romantic, even though I'm "such a guy!" They are innocent of the many imperfections in my learning on the topic.

I'd also like to extend my heartfelt thanks to my treasured wife Myra, to Gigi, to the ever supportive and lovely Jennifer Nagler, Joanna Volpe, Uncle Jack, the Donovans, Good Cousin Barbara (think screenplay), Nadine Rabinowitz (who first brought Mrs. James's work to my attention), Mom, George, my wife's mother Lily (who was first to request a book featuring the beautiful Jessica), and all the other relatives and friends who've lent their time, and their moral and literary advice and support to this project.

To my editor, Martin Jones, I extend my sincerest thanks, especially for ensuring that Noah fully explicated the intentions and actions of the nefarious plotters. To my ever-faithful reader and proofreader Laurel Busch, and the world's best (and most patient) cover designer Greg Simanson. To my book manager Samantha Williams, for her continuing Herculean efforts in dragging the recalcitrant niche of historical fiction into the 21st century.

Finally, many thanks to my good friend, the talented photographer Jeffrey Loeser, who took my author photo, and in so doing accomplished the   extraordinary   task   of   making   me   look   presentable.

Sneak Peek at Book 3 of
In the Den of the English Lion

A DRAGON IN THE ASHES

Prologue

Town Square
Krakow, Poland
April 19, 1539

AS NAOMI THE milkmaid finishes her morning delivery to the queen's town home and turns to go, she finds her way blocked by a platoon of soldiers carrying a terrified old woman securely bound to a makeshift ladder of twine and kindling. The woman is so near to her that Naomi can see she's praying intensely, despite the jostling.

The soldiers reach the woodpile assembled in the town square and clumsily insert the ladder's feet into two post holes, bringing the ladder and the old woman erect with a jolt. An eager crowd gathers under the lowering sky, evidently enthralled by the prospect of watching this old woman shriek, die, and burn to ash.

Naomi fervently hopes that this does not mark a resumption of the burning of Jews, that barbaric practice long prohibited by Good King Sigismund the Old. She shudders to contemplate the possibility that, unbeknownst to her, the king may have died, leaving her and all the other Jews of her village unshielded from the Inquisition. She takes a cautious step toward the woman to discern whether she's praying in Latin or Hebrew, but cannot hear her words.

Naomi turns around and spies Queen Bona standing on her ceremonial balcony, wringing her hands. Beside her stands a man cloaked in official-looking robes, his complexion dark like a Spaniard's. By his serene expression, he is accustomed to such horrid "acts of faith," as the Christians call them.

She curtsies, catching the queen's eye, but instead of her customary reward of a reginal smile, she receives a glimpse into the soul of a woman consumed by remorse for an atrocity about to be committed in her name.

The pretty milkmaid is horrified to see that she has also caught the unwelcome eye of someone else on the balcony: the queen's youngest attendant, a tall, swarthy, sharp-eyed youth about her own age. He gazes at her, evidently oblivious to the queen and the Spanish ambassador beside him, and uncaring of the atrocity taking place in the square. Although he cannot help but realize that Naomi has caught him looking, the lout lacks the grace to turn away. Instead, his gaze becomes a leer, a sickening mixture of desire and contempt that makes Naomi's skin crawl. She shivers and turns away.

A handsome young Jew approaches her from a distance. Although it takes her an extra moment, as his expression is unusually grave, she recognizes him as David from the village.

He sidles up to her. "You appear to have caught the eye of the queen's boy." He's chosen to speak in English, evidently to avoid being understood by the surrounding rabble. As David's family, like Naomi's, was deported from England, their families continue to speak English in their homes.

"What do you know of the queen's boy?" Naomi asks.

"He's a sly little shit, from what I've heard." David points with his chin to the woman about to die. "Do you know this poor soul, my beauty?"

"No," she replies, ignoring his ill-timed flirtation.

"Her name is Katarzyna Weiglowa."

"A Jew?" she asks.

He shrugs. "It depends upon whom you ask. She was born a papist, and professes to be one still. But, if you'd ever spoken with her, as I have, you'd know that her beliefs are quite the same as ours. She denies the papist doctrines of the trinity of God and the divinity of Jesus."

"But she's never converted?"

"No. Instead, she's foolishly insisted on promoting her beliefs to other papists, a crime known as 'Judaizing.'" David shakes his head. "Our rabbi would never help her to convert. You know what rabbis do when a gentile asks to convert, don't you?"

"No."

"They slam the door, literally. Makes sense, too. We Jews are left alone only because we don't try to persuade others of our faith. If we were seen to proselytize as gentiles do, we'd be wiped out without a second thought."

Naomi shivers to think how susceptible her people are to the vagaries of public sentiment.

The crowd murmurs louder as a long, somber train of chanting priests emerges from the church and begins its doleful, inexorable procession toward its victim. The priest at the forefront is dark and unfamiliar, vaguely resembling the man on the queen's balcony.

"I don't believe I've seen that priest before," says Naomi.

"And let's hope we never see him again," David replies. "He's an Inquisitor...from Spain. Here to purify the faith."

She frowns. "I've never taken Queen Bona for a religious fanatic."

David shakes his head. "She has no say in the matter. This poor wretch has been condemned as an apostate by the Archbishop of Krakow."

The Inquisitor stops the train near enough to be heard by the victim and the crowd, but far enough to avoid being scorched by the coming pyre. "Do you, Katarzyna Weiglowa," he shouts, "believe in God's only son, our Lord Jesus Christ?"

The old woman stops her praying long enough to respond. "God had neither wife nor son, nor does He need this, for only mortals need sons. We are His children...and all who walk in His ways are His children."

The Inquisitor ignores the reply, and demands again, "Do you, Katarzyna Weiglowa believe in God's only son, our Lord Jesus Christ?"

A bolt of lightning splits the sky, and thunder rumbles across the square. Naomi expects that the threat of a dousing rain will cause the Inquisitor to hasten completion of his heavenly task, dependent as it is upon the earthly expedient of a dry woodpile.

Naomi is unnerved to find that she's now become the object of the serene gaze of the old woman about to die. "God had neither wife nor son..." pronounces the old woman, repeating her previous response.

But Naomi finds she can no longer hear the woman's words. Instead, she hears her thoughts, as though the woman has taken up residence inside her head.

"Leave this kingdom with your husband and never return, or he will kill you," pleads the old woman urgently. "Keep your child safe, my beauty! Go now!"

He? Jolted by the old woman's incursion into the innermost precincts of her mind, Naomi assures herself that she has nothing to fear. She must have imagined the old woman's voice. At the very least, she must have misunderstood it. Naomi is but eleven years old, after all, and unwed. Although she's daydreamed about marrying David (and has caught him secretly admiring her more than once), they're little more than children. And at present she has no child to keep safe.

She recalls her mother saying that those about to die are given the gift of prophesy, and her eyes go wide. She recoils, and steps back hard into David.

"What's wrong?" he asks, lifting her weight off his toes.

"She...she spoke to me," Naomi replies fearfully.

David regards her skeptically. "She was speaking to everyone, Naomi. She was just looking at you."

"No, David. She spoke to me...in...in my mind." She's flustered by David's incomprehension. "Oh, let's get away from here!" She turns on her heel and flees the impending horror, plowing her way through the crowd just as the first twigs burst into flames behind her. She shoves her way past a rowdy group of young men, and drops her milk pail. Though it clatters to the ground, she fails to notice.

So many urgent questions race through her mind! But one thing she feels no doubt about is just whom the old woman meant by "he," the one who would kill her and her future husband. She glances up at the balcony where the hideous queen's boy continues to leer at her, and lunges away in a stumbling run.

David picks up the pail and runs after her, amazed.

<hr />

THOUGH THE RAINS of heaven arrive too late to save the old woman from immolation, they rapidly disperse the crowd. The blackened corpse hisses and steams in the sudden downpour.

As Queen Bona's attention is too fixed on the horror to notice the rain, the Spaniard unctuously interrupts her dark reverie. "Shall we leave the balcony and go inside, Your Highness?"

She allows the boy attendant to lead her by the hand to the parlor, where she assumes the seat that customarily serves as a substitute for her throne. She whispers something in his ear. He nods respectfully, disappears from view, and soon returns with a scroll bound by a simple blue ribbon. She accepts it and places it on a table beside her. The Spaniard bows respectfully.

After a thoughtful silence, the queen addresses him with conviction. "That is the last barbarous act of faith that will take place in this realm, Master Ambassador, unless His Holiness himself comes from Rome to officiate. Upon your return to Spain, please advise King Charles that no Inquisitors, Spanish or otherwise, will again be permitted to perform such acts in Poland."

"I am your obedient servant, madam, and shall pass your wishes along to His Highness."

The queen nods. "Now that this...business is out of the way, we can address the Spanish Crown's request that I lend the money needed to purchase a parcel of my local property."

The ambassador bows and draws a sealed scroll in a red ribbon from his robe. "I thank you for broaching the subject, madam. King Charles has instructed me to assure you that I am his plenipotentiary for purposes of negotiating and sealing the bargain." He hands her the scroll, which she opens and reads. "As you can see," he says before she's finished, "I've been given final say in negotiating terms on His Highness's behalf."

She nods. "The paper is in order, Master Ambassador." She hands him back the scroll, and opens the one brought to her by the boy. "But I doubt there will be further negotiation." She points to some writing on the paper. "As you can see, King Charles and I have already agreed upon the size and location of the property, as well as its price."

The ambassador reads the writing indicated by Queen Bona, and nods in agreement. She returns the scroll to the boy, who rolls it up and ties the blue ribbon around it.

"Your Highness," says the ambassador, "I am led to understand that the property is presently occupied by a village of..." his mouth purses in genteel disgust "... Jews. Is this so, madam?"

Queen Bona sighs. "King Charles and I have already agreed that management of the property will remain subject to my sole discretion." She sees that her answer has not satisfied the ambassador. "The Jews are tenants only," she assures him. "They pay their way, and I have no intention of evicting them so long as they continue to do so."

The ambassador smiles unctuously. "Then I assume Your Highness will have the necessary deed drawn up?"

She raises an eyebrow. "The deed and mortgage, you mean."

"Mortgage, madam? Surely the Holy Roman Emperor is as good as his word?"

She smiles. "Of course he is. Yet, it never hurts to have these things in writing."

"His Highness has forbidden me," says the ambassador, "to execute any loan document that will be recorded in a public place." As the queen regards him askance, he buttresses his point. "It would be imprudent to inform all the world of business affairs between crowned heads. I hope you will agree."

She weighs his words. "I will keep the mortgage in my personal possession, and produce it only if Spain defaults in payment, or His Highness passes away. Please advise His Highness that, although I trust him implicitly to refrain from trying to sell the property unburdened by my mortgage, I have no such assurance that his eventual successor will feel so bound."

The ambassador persists. "But King Charles's heir apparent is Prince Philip! Although Philip is yet but a boy, his cleverness and handsome figure are already renowned throughout Europe. And, of course, he has very great expectations, madam, ample for this purpose. I expect Your Highness will have no problem in obtaining repayment should King Charles...no longer rule. Please, madam, let us dispense with this commoner's notion of a...mortgage." He pronounces this last word with practiced contempt.

She equivocates, then decides on a middle ground. "I will produce the mortgage only if Spain defaults in payment, or if both His Highness and Prince Philip have passed away. Would that be satisfactory?"

The ambassador makes a show of equivocating.

She frowns. "Take it or leave it," she says in a grave monotone.

The ambassador bows again. "Very well, madam. You drive a hard bargain. But, we shall take it."

She finds something about the ambassador's concern to be unsettling. Why should King Charles care if the mortgage is publicly recorded and available for public perusal? It occurs to her only in passing that, according to the bargain she has just struck, the king and his successor are assured that there will be only one record of the mortgage's existence...and it will be stowed in her closet.

"Very well," says the queen, "I shall have the papers drawn." She turns to the swarthy boy. "Show the ambassador to the door."

The ambassador bows, and follows the boy through several hallways and down a staircase to the street level. Before the boy opens the door, the ambassador glances about. When he's confirmed they are alone, he hands the boy a bag of gold coins and addresses him in quiet, familiar fashion.

"The Holy Roman Emperor, King Charles, instructs you, once the mortgage is signed, to report its location to me, and only me. Each time it is moved, you are to tell me precisely where it is located."

The boy bows silently and remains in that position until the ambassador places his hands on his shoulders and recites the expected blessing.

The ambassador brings the boy's chin up and looks him straight in the eye. "You are truly one of the faithful. And, as I've promised you," he says, "His Holiness of Rome shall surely learn of your good works, and you shall have his blessings, as well."

The boy nods and, without a word or change of expression, lets the ambassador out, discreetly pockets the pouch, and returns to his duties.

ABOUT THE AUTHOR

Neal Roberts and his wife live on Long Island, New York, where they have two grown children. Neal is a practicing attorney and adjunct law professor, and spends as much time as possible researching his next novel while enhancing his lawyer's pallor. When he's not writing Elizabethan politico-legal novels, practicing law, or teaching, he's an editor of an international peer-reviewed publication in the field of intellectual property law. Neal is also an avid student of Elizabethan literature and politics, which subjects form the basis of his first novel, *A Second Daniel*. His analysis of Shakespeare's Sonnet 121 has been extensively cited by some of the most important authorities seeking to identify the true author of the poems and plays attributed to William Shakespeare. Connect with Neal at his website or on Facebook and join his mailing list to know when upcoming books release.

Made in United States
North Haven, CT
02 February 2024

48249447R00174